"WHAT DID YOU DO WITH MY CLOTHES?"

No storm could be as fierce as the one that raged in Alexandria's flashing eyes as she faced Drake across the cabin. "I demand that you return my things at once!"

His brows went up. "You demand? Careful, princess, your snobbish airs are showing. Remember, on this ship the only one who *demands* is me." He crossed the room, ignoring her as if she were no more than an annoying child that he had dismissed.

He took off his shirt, then tossed it carelessly onto the chair. Alex gasped and turned her back. Tossing his breeches next to his shirt, Drake climbed into his berth.

"May I douse the light?" she asked.

He gave his permission and in the dark she undressed and put on one of his shirts. Her bare feet padded across the room. Then, a thud and a cry of pain.

"Alexandria? What is it? Are you badly hurt?"

When he heard her soft sobs, Drake reacted instantly, pulling her into his arms.

They became aware of each other at the same moment. He was totally naked. She was clad only in a thin white shirt.

She needed comfort. He needed more . . .

Books by Andrea Kane

My Heart's Desire
Dream Castle
Masque of Betrayal
Echoes in the Mist
Samantha

Published by POCKET BOOKS

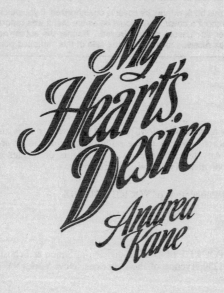

My Heart's Desire

Andrea Kane

POCKET BOOKS

New York   London   Toronto   Sydney   Tokyo   Singapore

An *Original* Publication of POCKET BOOKS

POCKET BOOKS, a division of Simon & Schuster Inc.
1230 Avenue of the Americas, New York, NY 10020

ISBN: 0-671-73584-5

First Pocket Books printing October 1991

10 9 8 7 6 5 4 3 2

POCKET and colophon are registered trademarks of
Simon & Schuster Inc.

Printed in the U.S.A.

MY HEART'S DESIRE is dedicated, with immeasurable love and thanks, to my four best friends, who I am also fortunate enough to call my family:

Brad, my partner, my anchor and my eternal champion; we did it, love!

Wendi, my little daughter with the BIG heart and the wisdom and maturity far beyond her tender years.

And Mom & Dad, who have shared the dream all my life and never stopped believing, even when I did.

Acknowledgments

To my three K's, who saw me through:

   Kathryn Falk, who opened the door and told me I could;

   Kathe Robin, who gave me the chance and told me I would;

   and Karen Plunkett-Powell, whose unsurpassable commitment and friendship ensured that I did!

Chapter 1

She was free.

The irony of the thought made Alexandria smile. Here she stood, in the unprotected shadows of night, amid the deserted warehouses of London's unsavory docks. She was totally alone but for a relentless dream and a well thought out plan to guide her. Yet she felt no fear, only exhilaration. She had waited long enough. It was time.

She inched her way through the narrow path between the buildings and paused to listen. Instinct told her it was safe. Cautiously she stepped out into the inky blackness. The March night was cold and gloomier than usual due to the heavy fog that clung to the wharf and hid the Thames from view. But Alexandria could feel the river's presence. She had a sixth sense for the water; a born sailor, her father had once grudgingly admitted. Of course, sailing in a sheltered cove off the English Channel was quite different from sailing the ocean in a storm. But then, the weather was the captain's concern, not hers. All she had to worry about was getting to the ship. The ship that, according to the answers to her discreet questions, would be departing at daybreak.

Alexandria stretched her cramped limbs. She had stood pressed against that blasted brick warehouse wall since four o'clock when the gatekeeper officially closed the docks for the day. Hardly daring to breathe, she had heard the sounds of the busy wharf subside—the hoists and winches ceasing to unload cargo, the workers filing out, jovial at day's end. At last all had grown quiet. But still she'd dared not move; not until she could be concealed by darkness. Until now. It had seemed an eternity.

The pungent smell of beer accosted her, together with a burst of raucous laughter that caused Alexandria to start. But it was only the sailors who frequented the numerous alehouses along the docks, celebrating their last night of freedom before taking to the sea. Soon the intoxicated revelers began to sing a cheerful bawdy tune in exuberant though slightly off-key voices. Alexandria grinned. There was no danger here. The men were too deep in their cups to notice her. Unless, of course, they mistook her for one of their doxies, she thought with a troubled frown.

Another howl of laughter sent her scurrying along. The blood pulsed through her veins faster and faster. A delicate apparition in the night, Alexandria looked anything but a doxy. Her muslin gown was of a rich Devonshire brown, its simple skirts rustling about her ankles with each rapid step of her slippered feet. To avoid tripping, she stilled the movement by clutching the soft folds between her nervous fingers. Although she possessed an innate regal carriage and grace that bespoke noble birth, Alexandria was aware that soon she would be transformed from a well-bred miss to an outcast of the *haut ton*.

Pushing these thoughts aside, she moved silently over the wooden boards of the dock.

She could make out the dim outlines of the ships now, their wooden hulls bobbing and tugging to be set free. But the powerful hawsers that bound them securely to the dock were stubborn and would not relent. The tall masts, bare and waiting for their sails to be hoisted, towered above the decks and were but vague shadows in the murky sky. Waves lapped gently at the shoreline, their caressing motion causing the ships to sway slowly from side to side.

Alexandria slowed, caught her breath, and paused before each ship. She squinted, studying the carefully lettered names one by one. It was difficult to make out the words, so dense was the fog. Thus far it had served in her favor. Now she found herself fervently hoping it would lift by morning, else she'd be going nowhere and all her scheming would have been for naught.

At the end of the dock she found her mark and caught

her breath in wonder. The ship was more splendid than she had ever imagined, sleek and powerful, the words *La Belle Illusion* boldly printed on its impressive bow. Compared to Alexandria's small skiff, *The Sea Spray*, on which she did her own covert exploring, *La Belle Illusion* was positively grand.

Tearing her gaze from the vessel, she glanced furtively left, then right. The night was still but for an occasional shout of laughter from far away. Triumphant, the taste of victory on her tongue, she hurried up the ramp and onto the ship.

She was just releasing her breath when she saw the man. He sat on the deck, directly in her path. Obviously he was here to guard the ship against trespassers. Her heart sank to her feet. How could she have been so stupid?

She was trapped. *Trapped.* Frantically her eyes searched for safety. Any place where she could hide. But there was no escape. Her plan had failed.

Tears wet her lashes as she imagined what fate would await her at home. Her mother would suffer an immediate attack of the vapors. Upon recovering, she would deliver lectures and accusations, resulting in more stringent chaperoning and a more structured life.

Worst of all, it would mean a Season of introductions aimed toward a loveless, empty marriage to a cold, uncaring nobleman. Life was already intolerable. Alexandria couldn't bear for it to be more so.

She stepped forward, prepared to beg. Perhaps the man would take pity on her, allow her to escape and find other means of arriving at her destination.

"Sir . . ." The word was barely a whisper. The man gave no response. "Sir?" she murmured, a bit more audibly. He responded with a loud snore.

Alexandria couldn't help herself; she began to giggle. It was all so preposterous, and her nerves were taut to the breaking point. The poor man was out cold, his head sagging on his shoulder, an empty bottle lying beside him. Hardly a fearsome adversary. She said a silent prayer. The fates continued to smile down upon her.

Sweeping past the ineffective sentry, Alexandria hurried to the stern of the ship, then down the cramped stairway. Here she hesitated. Which door to try? She put her ear to the widest one, listening intently. No sound came from within. She reached out hesitantly, pressed the handle, and pushed the door open.

In the darkness she could barely make out the outline of a desk and a trunk in one corner and a narrow bed in another. The bed caught her eye. Perfect! Quietly closing the door behind her, Alexandria hastened across the room and slid beneath the neatly made berth. She offered herself hearty congratulations on the excellent choice of a hiding place.

Judging from the sparse contents of the room, she hoped this cabin would be unoccupied during the voyage. It would serve her well.

As she settled herself on the hard floor, prepared for a long and uncomfortable night, Alexandria smiled.

Her new life had begun.

She was free at last.

"Off on another adventure, are we?" The caustic words received no immediate reaction from the powerful, virile man who strode down the seemingly endless marble hallway of the mansion. Ignoring the butler's attempt to assist him, he flung open the heavy door and glanced toward the waiting carriage. Assured that all was ready for his departure, Drake Barrett turned cold green eyes to address his younger brother's mocking comment.

"You were well aware of my intention to sail today, Sebastian," was the icy reply.

The slighter, thinner man considered his brother's response. "I suppose I should be used to your comings and goings by now, Drake. Tell me, does Father know you are leaving today?"

Drake leaned against the open doorway, a humorless smile on his face. "Of course."

"Then I need not ask what sort of mood I will find him in. We both know how he feels about his beloved elder son, Marquis of Cairnham and heir apparent, pursuing his less than acceptable activities, now, don't we?''

Drake folded his arms across his broad chest. "I'm sure you will do your best to comfort him, Sebastian. You always do."

Sebastian gave him an innocent look. "Well, someone has to be here to look after him. After all, his health is not what it used to be."

"Yes, I know. So try to remember that and spend less time gambling at White's and more time at home."

"Is this touching concern all for Father, or is it for Samantha?" Sebastian asked shrewdly, his cool blue eyes watching Drake's face.

Drake frowned at the mention of his sister's name. "Sebastian, she's just a child. Yes, I worry about her. When I'm away, you are the only one here to look after her."

Sebastian gave a derisive laugh, turning away. "We both know how little comfort she takes in *my* presence, Drake. As far as our little sister is concerned, the sun rises and sets on *you*."

Before Drake could respond, a tall, slender young girl flew into the room and flung her arms about his waist.

"Drake! Were you planning to leave without saying good-bye?" she asked, her voice quavering, her soft green eyes brimming with tears.

Drake's hard expression softened as he stroked the sable hair back from her lovely, anxious face.

"Of course not, Sammy," he soothed gently. "I was planning to go to the stables and search for you. I have never left without seeing you first, have I?"

She shook her head, a worried pucker forming between her brows. "You will be careful? You will come home safely?"

"Yes and yes." He laughed, giving her a hard hug. "And I expect you to behave yourself while I am away. Is that understood?"

She nodded, wiping her eyes. "Just come home soon . . . please?"

"As soon as I can," he promised, squeezing her hands. He glanced over her head and met his brother's cold stare. "I need to talk to Sebastian before I leave, little one. Why don't you go for your ride now? I'll be home before you have time to miss me."

With a pang of guilt he watched Samantha go, then turned toward Sebastian. "As soon as I reach Canada, deliver the supplies to York, and load the timber for our shipbuilding company, I will return."

"That will take months. Aren't you concerned about the fate of Allonshire during your absence?" Sebastian's voice was laced with sarcasm.

"Allonshire is quiet during the Season. If Father were concerned he would not have come to London with you and Samantha. He has managed quite well without me until now. I have no reason to doubt that he will continue to do so."

"But he would prefer you to remain in England and help him run all the estates, not to mention his business holdings," Sebastian baited him. "Instead of disappearing every few months to—"

"Enough!" Drake's eyes were chips of green ice, his tone tense with anger. "I have no time for verbal warfare, Sebastian. My coach awaits." He strode out of the town house, his buff pantaloons hugging his muscular legs, his brown wool coat fitted snugly across his broad shoulders. The footmen beside the gleaming coach snapped to attention as Drake approached, for the future Duke of Allonshire did not like to be kept waiting.

Drake paused, one foot in the carriage, then turned back toward the doorway where Sebastian stood impassively watching his departure. "Good-bye, Sebastian. I am certain we will continue this discussion upon my return. We always do."

Sebastian did not reply, watching as the team of grays moved off, carrying Drake toward his destination.

On its heels a second carriage appeared, halting before the great house. Sebastian remained where he stood, his face expressionless, as an expensively clothed gentleman alighted from the carriage. Nodding to his coachman, the silver-haired man glanced nervously about before hurrying up to the entranceway where Sebastian waited.

"Has he departed?" the older man asked, his features taut, his hands clenching and unclenching at his sides.

Sebastian smiled slowly. "Mere moments ago, Reginald, my friend," he replied. "Your timing is impeccable."

The visitor nodded, shifting from one foot to the other. "Please . . . let us be done with it."

Sebastian shrugged. "As you wish." He stepped aside, allowing the man to precede him into the hallway. "Come." He gestured toward the library. "We can speak privately in here."

Once the door had closed behind them, the two men stood facing each other, neither bothering to sit down.

"Well?" Sebastian demanded.

"I did what you asked. It has been delivered." The words were wrenched from his mouth, casting his soul into a hell of its own creation.

Relief was evident on Sebastian's sharp features. "And without a moment to spare," he muttered, half to himself.

"My debt has been repaid," the elegant gentleman reminded him in an anguished voice.

Sebastian chuckled, the icy sound echoing throughout the room. "So it has," he agreed. Turning, he strode over to the desk, reaching into the drawer that held the promissory note. He placed it in the man's trembling hand. "Here is the document you are so impatient to receive." His eyes were cold, his smile tight-lipped. "It has been a pleasure doing business with you."

The other man did not smile, nor did he reply. As soon as the hated paper was in his possession he turned and fled, desperate to escape his torment.

"God, forgive me," Reginald whispered as he hurried to his waiting carriage.

But he knew there could be no forgiveness, nor was there any escape. Men could die, and he was responsible.

The guilt would be with him forever.

Chapter 2

"Not t' worry; here's the cap'n now, Smitty." Thomas Greer, the youngest sailor on *La Belle Illusion*, stepped back from loading cargo into the hold of the ship and gestured toward the dock. In response, his portly companion pushed a thick shock of white hair off his face, his weathered features relaxing.

"Thank goodness," Smitty muttered, half to himself, as the tall, raven-haired captain loped down the wharf and swung himself effortlessly onto the bustling ship.

Drake's emerald eyes missed nothing as he quickly scrutinized the activity around him, then turned to the older man who now regarded him with a mixture of concern and annoyance. "Is everything under control, Smitty?" He didn't wait for a reply. He already knew what the answer would be. Whether at home as Drake's valet or at sea as his first mate, Smitty was the epitome of organization and capability. Drake cast an eye to the river. "Fortunately the fog lifted early this morning," he continued, ignoring Smitty's expectant stare. "Otherwise, we would never be able to sail."

"I was beginning to wonder if we were going to sail." There was no missing the meaning of Smitty's pointed comment.

Drake grinned. "I apologize for being so late. I had no idea that the meeting with the War Department would take this long. It turned out to be rather important."

Smitty's expression changed. "Is there some problem, my lord?"

"I have a message to deliver to Major General Brock

when we arrive in York." Drake frowned. "At least I am not the only one who believes that a war with the Americans is imminent and that another war could cripple England. Regrettably, many of our politicians ignore these truths. I do not."

"But it appears that others share your view," Smitty put in.

Drake leaned back against the railing of the ship. "Yes, but not enough to form a majority. I fear it will be too late before enough people realize what a war in North America would mean for England. Napoleon is isolating us from our resources in Europe; therefore we badly need Canada's timber. If, for any reason, we lose access to that as well, things will become quite bleak."

"And your message to General Brock?"

Drake shrugged. "I, of course, am not privy to the contents. My guess would be that he is being urged to prepare the defense of Upper Canada in the event of an American attack."

"And will he?"

Drake gave an emphatic nod. "Brock is quite astute. I believe he is taking the situation seriously. We will soon find out." He stood abruptly, six feet one inch of commanding power. "Are we prepared to sail?"

Smitty felt the change immediately and snapped to attention. "At once, my lord."

"We're at sea now, Smitty," Drake put in mildly. "Please cease to address me as 'my lord.'"

Smitty chuckled. "A small slip, Captain. I'll see that it doesn't happen again."

"See that you do." Drake's tone was severe, but Smitty recognized the spark of mischief in his eyes. "Else I'll be forced to address you as Smithers. Imagine the reaction of the crew to that tidbit of information."

"You've made your point, Captain," was the dry response.

Drake's grin widened. "I believe I have, Smitty."

A short time later the hawsers were unbound and the large brig was maneuvered from the dock. Though the fog had lifted, the day was gray, with a brisk wind that would

9

easily carry *La Belle* into open waters. The men moved quickly, each one knowing his job and doing it without question. Drake hand-picked only the finest, hardest working sailors to compose the crew of *La Belle Illusion*. He was a demanding yet unconventional captain who chose not to limit himself to barking orders and administering discipline. Instead, while accepting nothing short of perfection from his men, he worked equally as hard as each and every one of them. He offered excellent pay, fair treatment and, as a result, received the crew's absolute loyalty and undying respect.

Drake watched from the quarterdeck as the mainsail was hoisted, listening to the men's banter as they readied the ship for its long journey. He was not fooled by the calm onset of the voyage. There would be many weeks fraught with tension and impending danger before they reached their destination. Times were turbulent, the world situation grim, the odds for survival less than good. He would have to proceed with caution. His life and the lives of twenty other men were at stake.

Nevertheless, exhilaration surged through Drake's blood. These moments were his happiest. His anticipation was heightened, his senses keen and alert. Here on his beloved *La Belle Illusion,* with its spotless decks, its immaculately cared for wood, he was home. At sea his purpose was clear, his challenges real. He belonged here far more than he belonged at Allonshire amid the life of shallow indulgence typical of the nobility. Indeed, it was not nobility that resulted in one's inheriting great wealth and position, but luck. He thought of his father's vast wealth, his enormous fleet of ships. The war could annihilate all of that in an instant, for what fate would await these grand vessels without the wood needed to build them? The timber that was so rich and plentiful in Canada's woodlands was the very backbone of the great British navy. Without it, they would crumble.

A triumphant cheer interrupted Drake's thoughts, and he looked up to see the billowing sails catch hold of the steady wind, propelling the ship down the Thames. He felt a renewed surge of purpose. *La Belle* was on her way.

Drake stretched, allowing the cold air to work its magic. His other life would disappear along with the receding shoreline. Lord Cairnham would, for the duration of the voyage, cease to exist.

As if reading Drake's thoughts, Smitty looked up from the helm.

"Captain?" The sharp black eyes took in Drake's stance, recognized his mental and emotional transition. The fact that Drake had relinquished control of the helm to him meant that his captain was satisfied with their position and speed. Not until they were cruising down the Thames at a brisk clip, did Drake relax and allow his rapt attention to wander.

"Yes, Smitty?"

"The waters are choppy, but not so that young Thomas couldn't manage," Smitty suggested.

Drake smiled. Diligent as always, his Smitty. "I agree."

"Then perhaps you might want to change your clothes now?"

Drake glanced down at himself in surprise. He had completely forgotten his formal coat and pantaloons. Such elegant attire was most inappropriate for grueling weeks at sea, he thought with a grin.

In truth he looked forward to donning his proper sailing attire, for it completed his transition to this other, happier life. To the crew it mattered not how their captain was dressed. His identity was no secret to them. And it made no difference. For though their captain was a born nobleman whose family built and owned the very ship on which they sailed, he was, first and foremost, the proven and undisputed commander of the brig.

With a chuckle Drake agreed. "I believe you are right, my friend. I was in such a hurry to get here from my meeting that changing clothes was out of the question." He strode across the deck. "I'll see to it now." He felt no need to ask if his trunks had been loaded. No doubt Smitty had overseen the task himself. Like his captain, Smitty considered no job on *La Belle* too menial. He relished the challenge offered by his diverse roles at sea, which were in sharp contrast to his rigid duties at Allonshire.

As Drake headed below, Smitty commanded Thomas to take the helm. Seconds later his heavy steps sounded close behind Drake's as he followed him to the captain's cabin. Drake smiled inwardly. A lifelong friend, a superb sailor, and first mate, Smitty would never cease to perform his duties as Drake's valet. To allow his master to dress himself would be blasphemous in Smitty's eyes. Though time and again Drake reminded him that this was not Allonshire, it was all for naught. Well, it would give them a chance to talk about the journey ahead.

Alexandria was distinctly unhappy. Her muscles ached, her extremities were numb, and she was convinced that her body would be forever frozen in a contorted position beneath the bed.

The earlier hours of the night had been part of the exciting adventure that awaited her. Alone in the deserted cabin, she had allowed her mind to drift, thinking of her mother's face when she had come to Alex's room that evening to collect her for the ball at Almack's. Instead of her radiant daughter, prepared to meet the potential suitors of a first London Season, she had no doubt found a hysterical Lucy, Alexandria's lady's maid, and the note Alex had left. She would be furious but unsurprised. After all, Alex had pleaded for months to be allowed to join her father in Canada, but to no avail. As usual her parents were close-minded and rigid, cold and emotionless, as they had been all her life.

Alex could not change her past, but she intended to change her future. She was certain that this journey represented the opportunity to take matters into her own hands.

Certainty had become indecisiveness just after midnight and had deteriorated into doubt before dawn. When the huge trunks had been brought in and placed in the center of the cabin, doubt had exploded into panic. And as she had listened to the ship come to life, felt it move gracefully from the dock and down the river, she was forced to accept the fact that these quarters were not to remain exclusively hers. Then whose?

Masculine voices just outside the closed door alerted Alex to the fact that her answer was forthcoming. A surge of fear pulsed through her veins, and instinctively she moved farther beneath the bed, closer to the bulkhead, and waited.

The heavy door swung open, and two pairs of male legs entered the room. No doubt there were bodies atop the legs, but from Alex's vantage point she could not see them.

"I wonder if this journey will be uneventful." Smitty spoke while locating a pair of black breeches and a white shirt for his captain to wear.

Drake shrugged. "Soon enough we will see if Napoleon has any surprises in store for us. As long as his reign continues, anything is possible." He sat down heavily on the bed, contemplating the situation. Unfortunately there was no way to know; he could only prepare for the worst.

Smitty tugged off Drake's boots and placed them beside the bed. "Once we have loaded our timber, we ought to hasten our departure from Canada, should your suspicions of impending war be correct."

Drake stood, tossing his coat and shirt aside and carelessly dropping his pantaloons. "I agree," he replied, stretching.

Smitty was unbothered by Drake's nakedness.

Alexandria was not.

Flat on her stomach, she had frozen at the sound of the bed slats as they groaned beneath Drake's weight. Once she realized that she was not to be crushed, she remained still, listening to the conversation of the two men above her.

Smitty's comments were lost to her. All she could focus on was the deep baritone that belonged to the other man. His voice was like rough silk—deep and shivery, yet so pleasing that she strained to hear more, happy to remain there forever.

Until he began to undress.

Although not overly modest, Alex had never seen a man clad in anything less than neck-to-foot attire. Oh, she had wondered from time to time what her reaction would be to an unclothed man. But never in her wildest dreams had she imagined the reaction she was having now, when confronted with the strong, hair-covered legs just inches away from her nose.

Taut muscles defined the well-shaped calves, tapering down to narrow ankles and large feet. He *looked* like rough silk. A blush suffused Alex's body as she realized that, instead of closing her eyes and turning away from this forbidden sight, she had a dreadful urge to poke her head out and see just where the powerful hair-roughened limbs would lead. Or worse, to reach out and touch them, to see if they *felt* like rough silk as well.

And all the while that incredible voice continued to speak, commanding and sure. How could such a devastating voice and such an overpowering body belong to one man?

Alex's mouth went dry.

Unaware of the emotional turmoil transpiring beneath his bed, Drake finished dressing, waving away Smitty's efforts. "Please, Smitty, I do believe I am capable of buttoning a shirt." He grinned. But when it came to his boots, Smitty's grumbling grew so loud that Drake relented, allowing his friend to help.

Moments later they exited the cabin, leaving a trembling Alex bewildered and alone.

Alex waited many minutes after their footsteps had faded. When she could bear the discomfort no longer, she wriggled out from her hiding place, whimpering as she flexed her cramped limbs. She was still shaking from the intensity of her physical reaction to the bare-legged stranger. Taking a deep breath, she tried to calm her raw nerves. Sanity returned, slowly. *It's just fatigue,* she assured herself. *Fatigue and tension are causing me to panic.*

At last she felt her heart rate slow. Whoever the mysterious occupant of the cabin was, he was merely a man.

* * *

At five bells an exhausted Drake, satisfied with the ship's progress, informed Smitty of his intention to go below to dine in his cabin. Upon opening his door, he expected to find one of cook's fine meals and a hearty drink. What he found instead was a beautiful but disheveled woman clad in a somewhat dusty muslin gown, whose golden brown hair was tousled about her exquisite, delicate features and whose fathomless gray eyes gazed up at him with a mixture of apprehension and candor.

But the haughty words uttered by the unbearably sensual mouth were anything but meek.

"I'm quite hungry, sir. When will luncheon be served?"

Chapter 3

"Who the hell are you?" Even as Drake's furious voice boomed out, he realized that his first impression had been accurate. The fairy-tale creature sitting stiffly at his desk was terrified, the vein in her slender neck pulsing rapidly despite her bravado. At his angry words she swallowed and clutched her hands more tightly together, but she did not flinch or drop her wide gray gaze from his shocked, burning one.

She replied in a voice that rang with confidence, "Who am I? I am Lady Alexandria, daughter of Geoffrey Cassel, the Earl of Sudsbury and the newly appointed governor of York."

"I don't give a damn if you're the queen," Drake fired back, striding toward her. "What the hell are you doing on my ship?"

Alex blinked but held her ground. "There is no need for profanity, sir, nor is there cause for you to bellow like a wounded animal. If you will address me properly I shall be more than happy to answer your questions."

Drake almost laughed out loud. Here she was, blatantly trespassing on his beloved ship, yet gazing up at him through those damned spellbinding eyes as though she expected an apology. And, worse, he felt like offering one. He shook his head in amazement.

"All right, Miss . . . excuse me, *Lady* Alexandria." He spoke in a mocking voice that was deadly quiet. "Now that we have established who you are, may I repeat my second question?" He paused. "What are you doing aboard my ship?"

"Traveling to York and to my father, of course," she answered primly.

"Of course," Drake muttered through clenched teeth. "And how, may I ask, did you gain access not only to my ship but to my cabin?"

Alex gave him a bright smile. "I stole in during the night and hid beneath your berth. I had no idea this particular cabin would be occupied."

Drake counted slowly to ten, then took a deep breath. "Am I to understand that you stowed away aboard my ship without the knowledge of or permission from anyone, including your father?"

A veil of uncertainty momentarily clouded Alex's clear eyes. "More or less," she admitted in a small voice. "However," she continued, regaining her composure, "I am quite certain that Father will welcome the visit."

"Then why did he not provide you with proper passage and an appropriate chaperon?"

Alex was silent at Drake's probing question.

He was not surprised.

An image of Geoffrey Cassel appeared in Drake's mind. He did not know the cold, rigid man well—just well enough to know that the Earl would not care at all for this sort of disruption.

The realization suddenly struck Drake that Alexandria Cassel had no idea of his identity. Further, even if she did, his name would probably be meaningless to her, as it was highly unlikely that her father would discuss business in her presence. Therefore, as far as the nobly bred Lady Alexandria was concerned, Drake was merely a common sailor.

Drake studied the beauty before him, careful to keep his face impassive. So this was Lord Sudsbury's daughter, this fiery, arrogant creature. She was not what Drake would have expected. Actually he gave her high marks for honesty and for audacity. She really expected him to take her to Canada. Obviously the spoiled little thing was used to getting everything she wanted. That would account for her colossal nerve and bold tongue.

Alexandria felt anything but bold. Her knees were knocking, and her hands felt like ice. Nothing had prepared her for this man who stood before her now, rage contorting his chiseled features. He looked like an avenging Greek god, bronzed and beautiful, with thick black hair and eyes like jade fire, eyes that burned straight into hers, turning her body to a quivering mass. Rather than succumb to her powerful reaction to him, Alex was trying to appear cool and unruffled. But it appeared that she was failing miserably. This sea captain was not impressed with her father's title or position, and she had an uncomfortable feeling that her next plan, to offer him money, would be no more successful in persuading him to take her to York.

Panic seized her. If she could not persuade him to allow her passage on his ship, it was quite possible that he would dock at the nearest port and demand that she leave. She couldn't have that. She had come too far to fail.

Moistening her lips, she stood, hoping to minimize the difference in their height, thus giving herself more confidence. Her ploy failed. Even standing tall, her shoulders back, he dwarfed her by more than a foot.

It was time to change tactics. Alex looked up at him pleadingly. "Please, sir," she began, "I must get to Canada. I would be happy to pay my way."

"This is not a passenger ship, my lady," was the cool reply.

"I am aware of that. And therefore I would expect to

pay considerably more for my passage. Also"—Alex smiled winningly—"I am an excellent sailor. I could help relieve your men."

"The kind of relief you would provide would not be at the helm, princess." The way his eyes raked her slender form left no doubt as to his meaning.

Alex blushed and lowered her lashes.

A nice touch, Drake thought to himself bitterly. *The innocent maiden. She really belongs on the stage.* Yet a vague feeling of guilt tugged at him. And when a tear slid down her cheek, that feeling intensified.

"Why is it so important for you to travel to York?" he asked in an even tone. "Are you running to something or from it?"

"Neither," she told him truthfully. "I am just seeking something that I have yet to find."

"Which is?"

"I cannot tell you until I have found it."

Drake ran his fingers through his hair in exasperation. He would be crazy even to consider allowing her passage. She was a woman and that meant trouble anywhere, but especially at sea, among men who would be without a woman for months. This exquisite little thing would be too tempting a morsel for any man to resist.

"The sea is no place for a woman." He was stunned to hear his own voice, which sounded as if he was actually contemplating the idea of taking her to Canada.

Alex heard it, too. "I promise to stay out of everyone's way," she said eagerly. "I'll do anything you ask, Captain. Please." Once again the soft voice and the fathomless gray eyes beseeched him, and Drake felt himself weakening. The weakness infuriated him, and he tensed, staring down at her, wondering at the effect she had on him.

Alex saw him stiffen. *I am not reaching him at all,* she realized sadly. *He must be made of stone.*

Until that moment, Alex would have been correct. But she could not know of the war that now raged inside Drake. While his heart was indeed encased in stone, he could not resist the enchanting vision she made, so small and yet so determined, pleading for passage to York. A faint flicker of warmth sparked inside him. *What choice was there really?* a small voice in his head whispered. To leave her at some strange port would be barbaric; to turn back to London would be to lose precious time. *Besides,* he thought, a challenging light intensifying his emerald eyes, *the little wench said she could hold her own. Let's see her do so.*

Drake folded his arms across his chest and stared down at her. "Your clothes will have to go."

"Pardon me?" Alex's fingers flew instinctively to the front of her gown.

"I said your clothes have to go. I can't have you walking around the ship dressed so . . . er, provocatively. Instead of working, my men would be . . . attempting to enjoy your charms, shall we say?"

Alex's blush told Drake she understood his meaning.

"I have no other clothes with me," she protested weakly. "I left in rather a hurry."

That much was true. Unwilling to risk discovery, Alex had decided against taking a traveling bag with her, for fear that it might hinder her undetected departure.

For the third time his gaze moved over her, slowly this time, taking in every detail of her modestly clad body.

"You are tiny," he commented, almost to himself. "But I'm sure that young Thomas is not much bigger than you." He nodded decisively. "I'll arrange to have some clothes brought in at once."

"You expect me to wear *men's* clothes?" Alex asked in amazement.

"Any objections?" he drawled. "Because if there are, I have more than enough time to stop at the next port and—"

"No! I have no objections," Alex jumped in.

He grinned. "Good. Now you just stay right here like a good girl, and I'll go and see about your attire."

"Fine," she snapped back. Another thought occurred to her. "Do you have a name?"

He gave her a smile that nearly melted her bones. "Captain Drake Barrett at your service, *princess,*" he said with a bow. "But you may call me Drake. After all, we are going to be spending quite a lot of time together over the next weeks, aren't we?"

Alex wasn't sure why, but something about his tone made her distinctly uneasy. She drew herself up to her full height, just over five feet. "Thank you very much, *Captain*," she said. "I appreciate your hospitality."

Drake chuckled at the obvious formality, thinking that she much resembled a tiny and adorable kitten that had been playing in a dusty corner. A kitten with claws, he reminded himself. "I will return shortly, my lady. Remain within my quarters. If you choose to disobey me," he added, seeing the mutinous spark rekindle in her eyes, "I will not be responsible should my men decide to ravish you. Do I make myself clear?"

Alexandria swallowed, recognizing the truth of his words. Adventurous she might be; foolhardy she was not. "Yes, Captain Barrett, perfectly clear."

"Good. I will be but a moment. And to answer your first question, luncheon should arrive shortly. Feel free to partake."

With that he was gone.

Alexandria sank into the desk chair, trembling. Captain Drake Barrett was the most overwhelming man she had ever met. It was not merely his magnificent good looks or even that deep, commanding voice. There was an aura of raw sexuality about him that awakened every untried nerve in her young body. His blatant virility excited her, made her blood pound and her heart beat faster.

She had not counted on this complication. She had won; she was going to York. Now the trick would be to avoid Drake Barrett at all costs.

"Did you say a woman?" Smitty asked in a stunned voice.

Drake nodded. "Yes, Smitty, a woman. And not just any woman, mind you, but *Lady* Alexandria Cassel."

"The Earl of Sudsbury's young daughter?" Smitty was amazed.

"That's right. It seems the little chit has a thirst for adventure. She wants to travel to York with us, actually begged me to take her there."

"And you agreed?" Smitty gave Drake a suspicious look. "That doesn't sound at all like you, Captain."

"You're right, it doesn't," Drake agreed. "But she insists that she can withstand the voyage. She even claims to be quite a sailor and has offered to relieve the men. I, of course, clarified that point with her." He gave Smitty a bland look.

Smitty looked mortified. "Captain! The earl's daughter is little more than a child!"

"Oh, she's more than a child, Smitty," Drake assured him cheerfully. "Much more than a child, I'd say." He grinned.

Smitty did not smile back. He knew only too well what Drake's opinion of women was. He also knew why. "She must be hungry," he replied instead.

"Yes, hungry and arrogant. I wouldn't be surprised if she expected a footman to wait on her. It is what she is used to." Drake's voice was bitter. "But *you* are going to tend to her, Smitty, because you are the only crewman who is trustworthy enough to exercise self-restraint, should her *ladyship* be *en dishabille*."

"I will take some food and clothing to her." Smitty moved toward the stern of the ship.

"Just take the food. I'll tend to the clothing," Drake put in.

Smitty turned in surprise. "Very well, Captain," he said slowly, studying Drake. "I'll see to the food at once."

Alexandria jumped when she heard the door open. A moment later an elderly man with a kindly face and a wonderful-smelling tray of meat and biscuits appeared in the cabin. He stopped when he saw her, staring in utter astonishment, then crossed the room and placed the tray on the desk before her.

"Hello, my lady," he said in a warm voice. "I thought you might like something to eat."

Alex gave him a smile that could have melted a heart of

ice. "Thank you, sir," she replied. "I hope it wasn't too much trouble."

Was this beautiful angel with the soft voice the overindulged, willful brat that the captain had just described?

"It was no trouble, my lady. I hope it is to your liking."

"It looks heavenly!" Alex's mouth watered as she realized she hadn't eaten in nearly a day.

Smitty grinned at her open enthusiasm. "Is there anything else I can bring to make you more comfortable?"

She turned wide gray eyes up to him. "Oh, no. I have no intention of getting underfoot, really. But I do thank you. Captain Barrett is most fortunate to have such a fine man as you working for him."

Smitty beamed, captivated by the delightful and unspoiled young woman before him. She was too guileless to harm anyone, too special to leave anyone unaffected, even his captain. Feeling suddenly quite jovial, Smitty added, "My name is Smitty, my lady, and should you think of anything—"

"Lady Alexandria has everything she needs, thank you, Smitty." Drake's cold voice came from the open doorway. He wasn't sure why, but it infuriated him to see this beautiful and undoubtedly lethal young woman completely spellbind Smitty. He strode across the room, a small bundle of clothes beneath his arm. "You may go, Smitty," he stated flatly.

Smitty looked up in surprise. "Very good, Captain." He gave Alex a supportive smile and headed toward the door.

"Thank you again, Smitty," she called after him. "You've been very kind."

"My pleasure, my lady." And he was gone.

"Have you finished charming my crew, princess?" There was an angry gleam in Drake's eyes as he stood before her, formidable and strong.

Alex looked puzzled. "I don't know what you mean, Captain Barrett."

Drake snorted. "Let me make one thing perfectly clear, Lady Alexandria. You may have fooled Smitty, as you probably have the rest of the world, but I am not so easily deceived. Therefore, kindly save your coyness and your shy smiles, for they would be wasted on me. And never let me see you use your charms on my men, or you will be off this ship before you can catch your breath. Understood?"

Alex studied his blazing eyes in total bewilderment. "I don't know why you dislike me so," she said at last. "I have no intention of seducing your crew, Captain." She gave him a frosty look. "So you can rest easy. All I want is to reach York as soon as possible. Then you and I will be rid of each other forever. You see, I don't particularly like you either."

An explosive silence filled the room. Finally Drake tossed her the parcel of clothes. "Change. Now."

"I don't take orders, Captain." She lifted her chin defiantly.

"On my ship you do."

Alex took a deep breath and swallowed her pride. "Very well, Captain Barrett. If you will be so kind as to leave the room I shall be happy to comply with your *request*."

Drake cocked his head. "Leave the room? Princess, I have no intention of leaving the room. This cabin is mine."

"Very well, then. If you will show me to my quarters I shall be happy to be out of your way."

"You are looking at them."

"Pardon me?"

"I said you are looking at your quarters."

"Here?" Her tone was incredulous.

"Here."

"But you said—"

"I know what I said."

"That is impossible." Alex's hold on her temper snapped. "If you think I would share a room with you, then you are sadly mistaken."

"Am I? Then suppose you tell me just where you are going to sleep. There is not one empty cabin on this ship." Triumph gleamed in his eyes.

"But I can't . . . I never—"

"Oh, I'm sure you can, and I doubt you've 'never.' But fear not. I have no intention of sharing my bed with you."

"But you said—"

"I said that these are your . . . *our* quarters. I will arrange for a cot to be brought in here for you."

"Surely the cot could be placed elsewhere?" she tried in a small voice.

"Certainly. Which crewman would you like to sleep with?" Drake inquired smoothly.

Alex shuddered.

"Exactly," Drake replied. "So, if there is no further discussion, change your clothes."

Alex looked at the breeches and shirt she now held in her hands. "Turn your back," she demanded.

Drake grinned, leaning against the wall. "I see that you insist on continuing this virginal pretense with me. Princess, I know what your world is like and how little importance is placed on virginity—except by vehement fathers and ignorant bridegrooms, that is."

Alex stared at him for one last moment and realized that she would never win. Slowly she reached behind her for the buttons of her gown, opening them all the way down the back. With shaking hands, she pulled her arms out of the sleeves until the dusty gown dropped to the floor. The petticoat followed shortly thereafter. In her lacy chemise and pantalets, she stared at the floor, praying for courage.

Drake watched her disrobe, his reaction mixed. On the one hand he felt the need to break her, to force her to admit to what she was. He had learned very young, and firsthand, just how hypocritical most noblewomen actually were, beginning with the deceitful bitch who had borne him. And this one could be no different.

On the other hand she looked so very fragile, trembling as she undressed, that he almost believed she was just what she seemed to be—innocent, untouched, and terribly frightened.

In short he felt like a bastard.

Now, as she stood before him, head bowed, so very vulnerable, a third reaction set in. Desire. It exploded through his loins like wildfire, igniting everything in its path. So intense and sudden was this physical craving that it took every ounce of self-control for Drake to remain where he stood and not go to her.

But he found that control.

Cursing himself and the whole situation, he spun around and strode to the door. "I'm needed on deck."

He slammed the door behind him, leaving a shocked and dazed Alexandria standing in the middle of the cabin.

Chapter 4

"These blasted sleeves are endless!" Alex swore under her breath. Impatiently she cuffed them for the fifth time, at last revealing her hands and wrists. Fortified by her excellent meal, she was itching to explore the ship. But her borrowed clothing, it seemed, had other ideas. Putting on the damned shirt had taken forever, and she had yet to attack the problem of the breeches.

At that thought she glared over at the crumpled garment in question. The breeches lay in a disheveled heap on the floor, where she had thrown them moments ago in a fit of rage. Never again would she complain about the layers of feminine attire that Lucy assisted her with each day! They had never given her as much trouble as these simple men's clothes had.

Well, her initial optimism had been squelched, but grim determination remained in its stead. Alex strode across the room and lifted Thomas's breeches from the cabin floor. Come hell or high water, these were going on . . . now. With one purposeful tug the breeches were up. And just as quickly they were down, landing in a black pool on the floor.

So much for the pleasures of a tiny waist. Alex frowned,

considering her options. At last a solution occurred to her. With lightning speed she pulled the pins and ribbons out of her once carefully curled hair, which badly needed to be combed out anyway. Then she tied the ribbons together into a crude but serviceable belt.

Now for the breeches. Holding them up to her waist, she looped the makeshift belt around and bound it securely in front. Then with a disgusted sigh she leaned over and rolled the bottoms up again and again until she could walk without tripping.

Boots would be an impossibility, she decided. No man, no matter how young, would have such diminutive feet. Shrugging, Alex slid her bare feet back into her slippers. If she followed form she would be barefoot shortly anyway. She always was when she sailed. It was one of the freedoms she allowed herself when she was alone on her beloved skiff, unchaperoned and unhindered by convention.

Her hair. She needed no one to tell her of its appearance. A quick appraisal of the cabin revealed no comb. Ah, well. There was a solution to everything. Her fingers were the closest thing she had to a comb. Using them, she carefully untangled the thick waves until they cascaded in moderate disarray and total freedom to her waist. She longed for a mirror to tell her the results of her handiwork. There was none. Actually, she amended with a wry grin, that was probably a blessing, considering her state of dress.

Well, for good or for ill, she was ready. Alex moved along the deserted passageway leading to the stairs. She could hear voices coming from the deck above, as the men engaged in cheerful banter with one another. The ship's movement was brisk and steady as it cut cleanly through the slapping waters of the river.

Alex felt relief wash through her. *The crewmen are too busy to notice me*, she told herself as she climbed the steps. *My presence won't affect them in the least*, she assured herself, strolling onto the deck.

You could have heard a pin drop on the main deck.

Twenty pairs of male eyes stared, unblinking and unbelieving, as the shockingly dressed young woman walked calmly to the railing to inhale deeply of the cold air.

They are appalled by my atrocious attire.

They were stunned by her unconcealable beauty.

No amount of effort could diminish Alexandria's regal presence. The ill-fitting garments she wore hid some of her feminine curves, but they did little to detract from her fine-boned, delicate features or from the graceful sway of her hips, emphasized by the breeches that clung to them.

Embarrassed by what she construed as disapproval, Alex tried to ignore the men's stares. She gazed around her with genuine pleasure, noting every detail of the magnificent ship. Although still not allowed full freedom, the sails snapped proudly in the crisp wind, the heavy masts gleamed in the thin sunlight, and the decks shone, polished and clean. Alex ran her hand appreciatively over the timbers. She had never seen a ship of this size up close and had only dreamed of sailing on one. Like a child opening her Christmas presents, she wanted to take it all in at once—the smells, the sounds, the very essence of the three-hundred-ton merchant brig. The enthrallment of discovery glowed in her eyes and spoke volumes to the two men who watched from their lofty positions on the quarterdeck.

"That child is a rare treasure," Smitty commented. "I cannot blame the men for staring."

Drake gave the wheel a vicious turn. "That is shock you are seeing, Smitty. Total, utter disbelief. I should never have agreed to this insanity."

Smitty fought back his smile and his taunting retort as well. "Not merely shock, Captain," he disagreed mildly. "Admiration. Lady Alexandria is a beauty."

Drake's jaw tightened. "That's lust, Smitty, not admiration. Most people are ruled by lust—unless, of course, they are ruled by greed or power. In this case, it is lust." He gave a snort of disgust. "The fools cannot take their eyes off her. Do they realize how ridiculous they look?"

"I suppose not, Captain." Smitty again refrained from mentioning that, whatever the men's affliction, Drake seemed also to be suffering from it.

Drake could not tear his gaze from her. Damn it, he had thought the clothes would do a better job of disguising her charms. Instead, they clung in all the right places and made her look even smaller and more vulnerable, dwarfed within them. He wanted to wring her neck.

He hadn't noticed the color of her hair before; the cabin had been too dimly lit. It was like honey, rich and golden brown with droplets of sunlight drizzling through it. Loose and unbound, it was thick and silky, and Drake had an uncontrollable urge to wrap handfuls of it around his fingers, to feel its texture against his mouth. God damn her. She had to be doing this on purpose; no woman could be as oblivious as she to the impact her presence made. Yet she hadn't even looked at him—or at any of his men, for that matter. She couldn't seem to stop admiring the ship.

He watched her stroke the polished wood of the hull in a sensual caress that Drake could almost feel. His loins tightened so painfully that he nearly groaned aloud. He closed his eyes, struggling for control.

"You have an exquisite ship, Captain."

Drake's eyes flew open as Alexandria addressed him. He looked down to where she stood on the main deck, her clear gray eyes regarding him without a trace of guile.

Damn her.

"And you have excellent taste, my lady." His aloof tone gave no indication of the internal struggle that raged within him. "She is indeed a beauty."

"And she has a great deal of spirit," Alex noted.

Drake relaxed a bit. "Yes, she does."

"Of course, she should be allowed more freedom."

"Pardon me?" His brows rose in disbelief.

"We will soon be in open waters," Alex explained calmly. "Can you not feel the increase in motion? There is a fine breeze from the northeast, so it is unnecessary to keep her so tightly in check. She should be allowed to pick up speed, to move more rapidly with the wind."

Drake's eyes had darkened to a forest green, a warning light flaring within them. How dare she criticize the way he ran his ship. Not even Smitty, who knew as much about sailing as Drake did, would be so bold.

"Before long it will be night," she continued, oblivious to the tempest brewing before her. "You will be reducing sail by taking in the staysails, royals, and flying jib. Why not gain as much distance as possible prior to darkness? Then we can pick up speed when we set the canvas again at daybreak. That way—"

"Enough!" The eruption was expected—in fact, considered long overdue—by all those cringing sailors within earshot. But Alexandria looked stunned by the outburst.

Drake was blazing with rage. Hastily Smitty hurried to the helm, anticipating the confrontation that was about to occur. Drake swung his long body down to the main deck, taking slow, threatening steps toward a startled Alexandria.

"You neglected to include one small detail in your eloquent discourse." His tone was scathing as he stopped, his eyes burning down into hers. "And that is that the fair wind of which you speak will become a foul one when we reach the Strait of Dover, in which case we would have to wait in the Downs until nature chooses to reverse the winds and allow us access to the Channel. Should this be necessary, it would increase our risk in the Goodwins, the treacherous sandbanks that could mean our destruction. Therefore it is infinitely more prudent to move at a more cautious pace, hoping that the wind will change as we reach the strait and thus ensure our swift journey down the Channel." He drew in a slow breath, striving for control.

"Further," he continued, towering over her, "it will be a cold day in hell before I begin taking orders from a woman on how to sail my ship."

"I was not issuing an order, Captain." Realizing her error, Alex wanted desperately to back away from this fearsome man whose cutting words and piercing gaze were like daggers to her very soul. But his damned arrogance made her stubbornly refuse to give in to her urge to back down. "And," she added, raising her chin a defiant inch, "although I have not your experience on the Thames, I was merely offering you a qualified opinion." She placed her hands on slim hips, meeting his glare with a challenging look.

"Qualified opinion? And just where did you acquire your knowledge, my lady?" he sneered.

"Through my own sailing, through reading, and through asking frequent intelligent questions."

They faced each other in white-hot anger, oblivious to everyone else around them.

"Does that reply satisfy you, Captain?" Alex taunted.

Smitty glanced from one to the other, amazement and amusement on his face. Below him, twenty gaping mouths and twenty pairs of disbelieving eyes watched the scene unfolding. Never had they seen their captain lose control like this. And never had they heard a woman speak so knowledgeably about sailing. They were still reeling from the shock of seeing Alexandria on board. And now this. They froze, waiting to see who would react next.

They did not have long to wait.

"Right now we are discussing my ship," Drake replied in a deceptively silky voice. His fists were clenched so tightly at his sides that his knuckles were white. "We will discuss what will satisfy me later this evening in my cabin, my lady."

Alex's shocked gasp could be heard as clearly as Drake's crude words. Color flooded her cheeks, as she glared at Drake's mocking face.

"You are disgusting and rude, Captain. Were it not that I needed safe passage, I would—"

"But you do," he reminded her.

"Yes, I do."

"Then you will do as I say . . . *whatever* I say."

Alex bit back her reply. She became aware for the first time of the wide-eyed stares around her. Smitty, standing just beyond Drake, was frowning disapprovingly at his captain's back. Drake could feel Smitty's unspoken censure and his crew's shock, but he ignored them all, his jaw set, his gaze locked with Alex's.

She lowered her long lashes to her cheeks, feeling helpless. He was purposely goading her. She was at his mercy and he knew it. And if he wanted to demean her in front of his men, he had the power to do so.

"I recognize your superior knowledge of sailing, sir, and so I defer to you. However"—she raised her mutinous storm-gray eyes to his—"my concessions apply only on deck, not in your cabin."

She turned and strode away, pleased to have salvaged some of her pride.

The blood was pounding in Drake's head. And hearing Smitty's barely concealed chuckle did not help to calm him.

"Smitty, I'm warning you . . ." he ground out, returning to the helm. "As for the rest of you," he barked at the gaping crew members, "what the hell are you staring at? You're not being paid to ogle! Now get back to work!"

The deck was cleared in seconds.

Smitty patted Drake's shoulder. "There, there, Captain," he said blandly. "I think you handled yourself remarkably well."

Drake shot him a look. "The little twit does know something of sailing," he conceded, but only for Smitty's ears.

"So it would seem," Smitty agreed.

Drake's piercing eyes followed her to the ship's bow, where she leaned forward to view the world moving by her. She tossed back her hair, letting the wind blow in her face, unconcerned that the elements could mar her perfect complexion. She looked utterly free and abandoned.

He wondered if she was as abandoned in bed. He could imagine her—passionate, wild as a tigress, demanding as much as she gave. Ah, what a challenge she would be to tame. . .

Drake brought himself up with a start. What the hell was he thinking about?

Thoroughly disgusted with himself, he turned his attention back to the helm. Smitty had gone below, leaving Drake alone. Engrossed in his thoughts, Drake barely noticed his absence.

Their lovely passenger was right about one thing, he acknowledged: they were nearing open waters. He could feel it, and so could his ship. Like an eager child, her sails tugged at their restraints, longing to be free. Soon she would get her wish. They would not need to coast gently much longer, for the wind was already beginning to change. He had timed it perfectly. The ship would gracefully sail into the Channel, needing little time to pause in the Strait of Dover.

Triumph danced through Drake's blood. As always, he and *La Belle Illusion* made an incomparable team—he in planning the strategy and issuing the commands, she in sleekly and unconditionally carrying them out. She followed his orders without question, responded to his every touch, shared his thirst for freedom and adventure, and asked no more of him than he was willing to give. The perfect woman.

The sun began its descent, vibrant shades of lemon and orange streaking the western sky. Drake flexed his muscles, enjoying the beauty of the late afternoon.

"Congratulations, Captain. It seems you were correct, after all." At the grudging admission, Drake glanced down in surprise to see Lady Alexandria standing beside him, gazing out to sea. None of his men ventured onto the quarterdeck without permission. Yet there she stood, uninvited, as if it were her right to do so. The woman was maddening.

"I usually am." Taunting her gave him pleasure.

Alex knew he was not going to make this voyage an easy one for her. "Usually? But not always." She gave him a sideways look. "If you are fallible, Captain, surely you can accept my noble acquiescence in good faith and end this unnecessary bickering."

His anger faded into amusement. Acquiescence would hardly be the word he would have used to describe her reluctant admission. "Can I? Well, since you have admitted your inferiority, I suppose that it is the least I can do."

Alex swallowed, then gave him a practiced smile. "I might just succeed in taking you down a notch or two before we reach our destination, Captain."

"I look forward to the experience, princess." His husky

voice made her shiver, and she gazed out to sea, ignoring his comment.

Drake chuckled at her reaction. She really was a little spitfire. "Where did you learn to sail?" he asked curiously.

"At Sudsbury."

"And where, pray tell, is Sudsbury?" Drake almost laughed aloud at his own feigned ignorance. After all, he was supposed to be a mere ship's captain.

She did turn to look at him now, explaining as one would to a small child. "Sudsbury is my home. It is a large estate on the coast of Kent. Kent is along the English Channel, and its distance from London—"

"I know where Kent is," he interrupted, unable to endure her ridiculously patronizing explanation any longer.

Alex looked surprised, then nodded. "Of course. You must dock there on occasion."

"Of course." He could barely conceal the sarcasm from his tone.

"Do you stay in one place for any length of time?" It was her turn to be curious.

"That depends."

"On what?"

"On how potent the charms are in that port."

Alex flushed. "Do you never speak of anything but your animal needs?"

Drake gave her an innocent look. "I was speaking of the land, princess." He shook his head in mock dismay. "Careful, my lady; your true colors are showing. It does not befit your station in life. Remember, you live in a world far above us mere mortals. It would not do for your mind to be in the gutter."

Alex looked as though she had been slapped. Never had she been spoken to with such cruel disrespect. Certain that the hurt she felt was reflected on her face, she turned away, unwilling to let him witness her vulnerability.

She did not turn soon enough. Drake saw her reaction immediately and acted instantly.

"I apologize, princess," he said softly, touching her arm.

"You did not deserve that." It did not occur to him at that moment that he had never apologized to a woman before.

Alexandria turned back, her expression now curious. "Why do you assume that I feel superior to you?" she asked.

"It is part of your aristocratic education," he responded, wondering how she could change from a willful child to an arrogant "lady" to a beautiful and vulnerable woman in rapid succession. "I don't believe that you are even aware of it. But trust me, princess; I know of what I speak."

"You seem to know a great deal—about sailing, about women, about the nobility. Is there nothing left for you to learn, Captain?" She searched his face.

"Perhaps not, my lady. Perhaps I have seen it all."

"Then I envy you." There was no anger in her pearl gray eyes now, only sadness.

"You envy me?" He was shocked by her statement and amused by the irony of it. He, too, envied the man she believed him to be. Captain Drake Barrett, unencumbered and free. But he wondered at her reasoning. "Why?"

"Because you know who you are. Because you have everything you want. But most of all, because you have lived all the adventures of which I can only dream."

"What could I possibly have that you, in your fairy-tale world, would envy?"

She stared off into space, the sounds of the crew and the motion of the sea fading away. At his question her eyes became vague and dreamy. "Freedom, the ability to decide your own future, a place where you belong."

"You want those things?" He was dumbfounded.

Her gaze returned to his. "I don't expect you to understand, Captain." The softness was gone; the arrogance was back. She turned to leave the quarterdeck.

"You never answered my question," he reminded her. She paused. "Which one?"

"Where did you learn so much about sailing?"

"I told you. At home."

"Firsthand?"

"Yes. I have a small skiff. *The Sea Spray* is nothing

compared to *La Belle Illusion*, but she means a great deal to me."

That he understood. "There is a tremendous difference between steering a small skiff and maneuvering a large vessel like this one," he pointed out.

"I guessed as much."

Silence.

"Would you like to try your hand at the helm?" Drake had no idea what possessed him to ask the question.

Alex looked as amazed as Drake felt. Her shock quickly faded into little-girl eagerness. "May I?" Her whole face lit up.

Drake grinned, unable to resist the enchanting picture she made. Quite a contrast: a desirable woman with the enthusiasm of a child and the tongue of an outspoken shrew, dressed comically in the attire of a man.

"Man the helm, princess, before I regain my senses and change my mind." With an exaggerated gesture, he motioned for her to take the wheel.

She needed no second invitation but fairly flew to the helm. It felt glorious, the surge of power beneath her hands, the clean cut of the ship through the water. The proud snap of the British flag waving from the mast heralded her arrival and welcomed her. All around, the boisterous sounds of the sailors at work and the shrill of the boatswain's pipes filled the air. In those first seconds at the helm the world was hers.

Drake watched the elation on her face and felt an answering echo inside him. "The wheel is larger than you are," he chuckled, as she struggled to keep it steady. He placed his large tapered hands over hers, preparing to instruct her.

Her hands felt cold and small beneath his.

He might have been able to resist the protective and primitive instincts she aroused in him had it not been for the motion of the ship, which chose that moment to sway slightly, pressing Alexandria back against Drake's chest.

They both froze at the contact.

He was aware of her all at once—the scent of her hair, the fragile feel of her fine-boned body against his, the shivering warmth and softness of her body. Unleashed hunger pumped through his veins, and he gritted his teeth, striving for a control that appeared out of his reach.

Alex felt him tense, but all of her energy was being channeled into finding her own self-control. He was so overpowering, everything about him dominating and strong. His well-muscled body, parts of which she remembered only too vividly from her view beneath the bed, his masculine scent, his towering height, the sheer magnetism that radiated from his very presence. Alex closed her eyes, her heart threatening to beat its way right out of her chest.

His arms tightened around her and she allowed herself, for just a few seconds, to relax in his embrace, to forget the rest of the world.

Drake nuzzled her hair, his own breathing unsteady. "You have an incredible effect on me, princess," he muttered, his voice husky, his lips buried in her hair. He lifted one hand from hers, wrapped it around her waist, and pulled her more firmly against his throbbing body. "Incredible," he repeated, marveling at how good she felt.

Alexandria tensed. Inexperienced as she was, she knew what the hardened contours of his body meant. "Don't," she whispered in a small, frightened voice. "Please."

Drake drew back, surprised as much as frustrated. There was no mistaking the genuine panic in her voice. Had he heard disdain, he would have assumed she felt it beneath her to want a lowly ship's captain. But what he heard was not haughtiness; it was fear. He glanced down at her as she struggled to stand on her own.

"Let me go," she demanded.

"I thought you wanted to learn something?" He grinned.

"Not what you have in mind to teach!" she shot back.

He chuckled, moving to put a respectable distance between their bodies. "You win, princess," he conceded. "I promise to limit your education to sailing."

She eyed him suspiciously, then nodded. "All right. As long as I have your word."

"And do you trust my word?" Laughter lurked in the brilliant green eyes.

"I suppose I must."

"Thank you for your faith, grudging though it may be," he laughed. "Very well, let us begin your first lesson."

Alex took to the helm like a fish to water. Even Drake had to admit that she was a natural sailor. She hung on to his every word, asking frequent questions, then experimenting with the explanations. Despite her diminutive size, she was tireless, refusing to give in to hunger or fatigue.

Drake could have ended the lesson at any time, but the thought seemed not to occur to him. Long past the dinner hour they labored on the quarterdeck, sharing their great love of the sea. It seemed they had finally established peace between them, and the newfound companionship was sustained.

Until it came time for bed.

Chapter 5

"What did you do with my clothes?"

No storm could be as fierce as the one that raged in Alexandria's flashing eyes as she faced Drake across the cabin. Her expression was murderous, her small hands clenched at her sides, her tone lethal.

Drake closed the door behind him with a firm click. "By 'your clothes' I presume you mean that dusty gown and shredded chemise you discarded on my cabin floor?" He leaned nonchalantly against the wall, regarding her with amusement.

Alex was too angry to be shocked at his casual mention of her undergarment. "You know damned well what clothes I mean!"

"Now, now . . . such language, my lady. I am truly shocked."

She looked as though she might strike him.

"I demand that you return my things at once!"

His brows went up. "You demand? Careful, princess, your snobbish airs are showing. Remember, on this ship the only one who *demands* is me." He crossed the room, ignoring her as if she were no more than an annoying child.

She stepped in front of him, blocking his way.

"Did you want something, my lady?" He paused, studying her livid expression. She was as transparent as glass, her anger and exasperation clearly evident on her beautiful face. Drake grinned. "Your clothes are no longer with us."

The color in her face deepened. *"What?"*

"They were torn from your adventure."

"Liar!" she shot back. "There was no reason for you to discard them . . . at least not for the reason you just gave."

Her accusing tone made him chuckle. "You are quite correct, princess. The real reason is that I cannot have you parading around in your finery. My men are already lusting after you quite openly. We wouldn't want to further intoxicate their senses, now would we?"

"The only one on this ship who has treated me with any disrespect is you!" she retorted.

He folded his arms across his broad chest. "Then be grateful that I have limited you to men's attire. Perhaps you will be safe from my lecherous advances."

He moved away again, took off his shirt, then tossed it carelessly onto the chair.

Alex gasped and turned her back. She should have known he would be no gentleman. He had probably undressed in front of countless women and was quite used to it by now . . . maybe even enjoyed it.

She bit her lip in frustration. The evening had lulled her into a false sense of security. Drake had been hospitable . . . no, downright charming as he had instructed her at the helm. And Alex had been so enthused that she had almost forgotten the sleeping arrangements that awaited her. She had planned to wait until Drake was in bed, slip back into her modestly cut chemise, then climb into the cot. Now that was impossible.

Alex glanced down at her men's clothes. The breeches were fine for daytime, but far too uncomfortable to sleep in. But, she could remove them and remain in just the shirt, which would easily reach her knees.

Studying the shirt, she shuddered, seeing the black stains acquired during her stint at the helm. The thought of sleeping in a filthy men's shirt was distinctly unappealing. However, she had no choice.

With a resigned sigh, she listened as Drake prepared for bed. When she was certain he was safely beneath the bedcovers, she would attempt to ready herself for sleep.

Drake couldn't stop grinning as he watched Alex's rigid back, every muscle tense with discomfort. He had shocked her; of that much he was certain. But he was not certain why. Surely the sight of a naked man was no novelty to her, unless she was one of those prim types who insisted on making love only in the dark. Somehow he doubted it. She was too outspoken and exuberant to be prudish in bed.

Drake sat down on the bed to remove his boots. It was a good thing he had discouraged Smitty from performing his usual valet duties. Imagine Alexandria's horror if *two* men had been present to witness her supposed fall from grace.

Actually Drake had never seen Smitty display such blatant disapproval before. When Drake had suggested that he temporarily relinquish his valet role, Smitty had replied with a curt nod. Drake did not need to ask why he was angry or at whom the anger was directed. In Smitty's eyes Drake was taking unfair advantage of an innocent young woman from a noble family.

An image of the austere Geoffrey Cassel flashed through Drake's mind. With a twinge of guilt Drake admitted to himself that Smitty's opinion had merit. In the earl's eyes Alexandria would indeed be ruined. In fact, the discovery that his *untouched* daughter had been forced to share a cabin with Drake would probably cause him to call Drake out.

Drake weighed that possibility as he tugged off his first boot. Obviously the young and impetuous beauty who stood so nervously across the room had not considered that prospect. Actually she had not considered any of the repercussions of her rash act. Was it innocence and naive faith that drove her or willful and self-centered impulsiveness?

Drake frowned, seeing Alexandria wince as his boots hit the floor. Despite his firm resolve, he felt a wave of sympathy for her. No matter how arrogant and hypocritical she might be, she was still very obviously unnerved by the sleeping arrangements. Even with her back to him, Drake could tell, by the way she was looking down at herself, that she was considering her options for the most appropriate nighttime attire. Certainly none of the choices could compare with the sheer silk nightrails she was undoubtedly used to wearing to bed.

Tossing his breeches next to his shirt, Drake put an end to her torment by climbing into his berth.

"You can turn around now, princess. I am respectably covered," he assured her.

She turned slowly, her chin held high. But Drake could see her lips tremble.

"May I douse the light?" she asked in a small voice. "Or am I to be denied even a shred of privacy?"

The urge to hold her was so strong at that moment that Drake couldn't speak. He merely nodded, wrestling with the conflicting emotions that plagued him.

"Thank you." Alex turned down the lamp, plunging the room into utter darkness.

Drake listened to the rustling sounds that told him she was undressing. He visualized her gradually exposed beauty, as each article of clothing was discarded, revealing the naked splendor beneath. His heart quickened; his loins tightened painfully. Desperately he tried to focus on something else, but his brain stubbornly insisted on conjuring up images of Alexandria. Naked. Alone with him in his cabin. At his mercy . . . in his arms . . . beneath his body.

He shifted, groaning inwardly. His craving for her was astounding. Having spent his entire adult life being sought after by women, Drake regarded sex as an easily acquired, easily forgotten commodity. It was a sport that was thoroughly enjoyed by his body, rarely involving his mind and never touching his heart, for he knew firsthand how little the act of love actually meant. Once passion was spent, it was gone, as was the bed partner. For that reason Drake kept himself always, *always* in control.

But suddenly he knew that control was waning, that he would not be able to restrain himself during the months to come.

Drake made a decision. The moment Alexandria was safely tucked beneath the bedcovers, he would go to Smitty's cabin and bunk with him for the duration of the voyage. For despite his own physical need and the great satisfaction he would derive from their coupling, the last thing Drake wanted was to become involved with Lady Alexandria Cassel. The price was simply too high.

The cabin was silent. Drake could sense Alex's presence nearby, and he knew instinctively that she was not in bed.

"Princess?"

He heard her jump. "What is it?"

He cleared his throat. "Is there some problem?"

"No . . . yes . . ." She paused. "May I use your basin and some water to wash the dirt from my face?"

Drake smiled in the darkness. "Go right ahead. And, princess . . . if you can find your way around in the dark, help yourself to one of my shirts. They are clean and more than large enough to protect your modesty."

Again, silence. Then, "Thank you, Captain."

Her bare feet padded across the room. Drake listened to her opening the heavy chest, taking out one of his shirts, and slipping it on. Splashing sounds told him she was washing, followed by her soft footsteps as she returned to her cot. Then a thud and a cry of pain.

Drake was out of bed in an instant, moving toward the sound of her choked cry.

"Alexandria? What is it?"

"I walked into the cot," she whimpered.

"Are you badly hurt?"

In truth she was not. It had been a sudden painful blow, yet already the pain was subsiding to a dull throb. But it was more than she could withstand after her emotionally taxing day. Hot tears filled her eyes, spilled down her cheeks. Try though she would, she could not control the sobs that shook her.

"I'm sorry," she gasped. "I never cry . . . and it is not that bad a bruise . . . I just can't . . ." She shook her head helplessly, covering her eyes with trembling hands.

There was no forethought. Drake reacted instantly, pulling her into his arms.

"Shhh," he soothed, pressing her head against his chest. He felt her tears drenching his bare skin, her narrow shoulders shaking. "It's all right, sweetheart . . . don't cry," he murmured, raising her chin with his forefinger, wishing he could see her face. He stroked his other hand down her back, pressing her closer to him.

They became aware of each other at the same moment. He was totally naked. She was clad only in a thin white shirt. She needed comfort. He needed more.

Drake found Alex's mouth with his own, tasting the salt of her tears. He gave her no time to think or to pull away, for his arms wrapped around her like steel bands, lifting her slight frame off the floor, forcing her against his unclothed, thoroughly aroused body. Alex whimpered again, this time not in pain but in a combination of fear and awakening desire. Drake's kiss was shattering, weaving dark magic around her stunned senses, paralyzing her resistance. He took her mouth hungrily again and again, each time deepening the kiss, urging her to open to his initial penetration.

And Alex, who had fought him every moment of the day, surrendered, parting her lips to his insistent command. A jolt of pleasure shot through her at the unfamiliar erotic sensation of his tongue stroking hers. This could not be happening, her dizzied mind protested. She did not even know this man, and yet here she was in his arms, his mouth intimately invading hers in a way she had never imagined. And she was lost . . . lost.

She could feel the enormous power of his body, the

strong, taut muscles of his upper arms as they flexed beneath her tentative touch. Her hands, trapped between their bodies, grew restless. She eased them free, touched the soft dark hair that covered his chest, then slid up to his broad shoulders. The inky blackness of the room could not conceal his harsh gasp of pleasure, the urgent shudder of his body, the shallowness of his breathing, the wild pounding of his heart against hers. His mouth moved more feverishly on hers, taking, giving, promising more.

Drake's mind had long since given up its battle to retain control. From the moment he felt Alex's soft, trembling mouth beneath his, the hot need inside him had erupted, overruling all else. Blood surged through his veins, drummed in his temples, throbbed at his loins. And when he felt her hesitant surrender as she parted her sweet lips to his demanding ones, he went wild, devouring her mouth with endless, drugging kisses of fire.

He tore his mouth from hers, pressing urgent openmouthed kisses down her neck, her throat. Through the thin barrier of the shirt, he could feel her nipples contract with pleasure, their hardened peaks pressing against his burning skin. She tasted like the sea, wild and exciting, luring him closer, deeper into her spell.

Drake groaned, sliding his hands down to her legs, tugging the shirt up until he could feel her skin beneath his searching fingers. She was silken heaven, warm and shivery beneath his touch. His mouth moved hotly to her ear, nibbling lightly at the soft lobe as his hands slid up to cup her naked buttocks.

"I want you, Alexandria." His hoarse whisper penetrated her sensual haze. "God, I can't believe how much I want you."

Alex froze, the full realization of where this was leading sinking in. He was stark naked, darkness or not, and he wanted to take her to bed. Whatever that entailed exactly, it was something that should transpire exclusively between a husband and wife, and only after they were wed. And here she was behaving like a harlot, totally forgetting everything she had ever been taught to believe in, abandoning herself in the arms of a stranger.

She began to struggle, panic washing away the last filaments of desire.

"No . . . no, please. I cannot . . . You must stop!"

Drake paused, still lost to his raging passion, stunned by her rejection. "What is it?" His voice was harsh with unquenched desire.

Alex pressed her hands against the hard wall of his chest, desperately trying to break his iron hold. How could she explain her fear, her inexperience, her inability to discard everything she had ever been taught? He would mock her, call her a hypocrite, a product of the nobility. Well, maybe she was all those things, but she could not do this. She was too afraid.

"Please . . ." She wished she could see his expression. "I don't even know you. I'm afraid," she admitted in a tiny voice.

Drake lowered her to the floor, trying to control his ragged breathing. He was moved yet again by the genuine apprehension he heard in her voice. Yet he could think of no explanation for her sudden rejection. Unless . . . "Why?" he demanded. "Is it because of who you are . . . who I am?"

"No . . . no." Her voice shook from the intensity of the last moments' emotions. "I told you I cannot . . . I've never . . ." She trailed off weakly.

Damn her, why did he believe her? Why, despite his unyielding conviction that all women were treacherous, did his mind refuse to doubt this woman's sincerity? What was it about her that touched some unknown part of his heart that he had never known existed?

Damn her.

Drake released her so abruptly that she almost fell. Without a word he strode over to the desk, scooped up his clothes, and started dressing.

Alex was numb. She wrapped her arms around her shaking body and listened to him thrashing about. What was he thinking? What was he feeling? Suddenly it had become important to her to know.

"Drake?" His name fell naturally from her lips. She couldn't know the impact that single utterance had on his throbbing body, which still clamored for release.

"What?"

"What are you doing?"

Drake slammed into his boots, then stood and crossed the room.

"I'm leaving," he shot back. "You've gotten your wish, princess. The cabin is yours." He yanked open the door, allowing a weak shaft of light into the room.

To Alex he appeared furious, his jaw clenched, his eyes glittering as they studied her.

"I don't understand." She looked to him for clarification of his words. Even carelessly dressed, his black hair mussed, the shadow of a beard on his face, he was the most handsome and compelling man she had ever seen.

Drake took a deep, shuddering breath. In the dim light he could distinguish every one of Alex's desirable curves beneath his billowy shirt. Her tawny hair was wildly tousled, her lips swollen from his kisses. She was positively bewitching. If he did not leave this minute he would go to her, take her to bed, and love her as she had never been loved before. And damn her protests to hell.

"The cabin is yours. For the duration of the trip I will share Smitty's cabin." He paused, wanting her, hating himself for wanting her. "Good night, princess."

The door slammed and he was gone.

Alex stood where she was, feeling cold and alone. She had gotten her wish and her privacy—everything she had wanted.

She waited for relief to flood her senses, to ease her despair.

It did not surprise her that it was not forthcoming.

Chapter 6

The sails were being hoisted into a dawning sky as Alex poked her head topside. Clad in clean clothes, her stomach filled with the cook's delicious breakfast, she was ready to tackle *La Belle Illusion*.

She watched, fascinated, as one hundred feet above her, two men hoisted the royals. With grace and precision they moved quickly from one line to the next, their muscles bulging from the strain. Minutes later a whoop of success signaled the unfurling of the final sail. Ahead the horizon promised sunshine and smooth seas.

A new day. Filled with new hope.

"Good morning, my lady." Smitty came over to greet her.

A genuine smile of pleasure lit her face. "And a good morning to you, Smitty."

"How was your first night aboard *La Belle?*" he asked without thinking.

A crimson stain spread across Alex's face as she wondered how much Smitty knew of the previous night's events. Perhaps her brazen behavior was now common knowledge aboard *La Belle Illusion*. The thought made her ill.

The moment the words had left his mouth, Smitty wanted to kick himself. Whatever had transpired between his captain and Lady Alexandria was none of his business. But her reaction to his question told him that she thought otherwise. He cleared his throat uncomfortably. "The motion of the sea is not easy to become accustomed to," he qualified. "It is for this reason that I asked about your evening."

Alex instantly relaxed. Whether he knew of her scandalous actions or not, this kindly older man was making it clear that the others were not privy to the details of her sleeping arrangements. "My night was fine, Smitty. And thank you for the clean clothes and the food you left outside my door this morning."

"You are most welcome," Smitty chuckled. "But just how did you know that it was I who left those things for you?"

She shrugged. "Who else would see to my comfort?"

The unspoken name lay between them.

"Lady Alexandria," Smitty ventured, at last, "I don't mean to speak out of turn, but, in time, I think you will find *all* the crew to be loyal and caring men." He gave her a meaningful look. "I suggest you give them a chance."

Alex sighed. "I will certainly try, Smitty."

He nodded, content with her answer. "You seemed quite taken with *La Belle Illusion* last night," he continued, brushing a shock of white hair off of his forehead. "Your knowledge of sailing is admirable. If you have any questions, please feel free to ask them."

Realizing that he meant to leave her, Alex touched his arm in an unconscious appeal. "There is much that I want to learn, Smitty. Must you go?"

Smitty hesitated, glancing down at the small hand on his sleeve.

"Yes, my lady, he must." Drake's commanding voice pierced the silence. As his handsome, powerful figure strode toward them, Alex searched the brilliant green eyes for a hint of his mood. Would he be angry and manifest that anger in his treatment of her? She'd heard terrifying stories about the brutality of sea captains. And Drake certainly looked the part—so hard and formidable. Unconsciously Alex's eyes strayed to his full, sensual mouth. Memories of that mouth on hers swept, unbidden, through her mind and body. Her heartbeat accelerated, her palms grew damp.

Drake watched her reaction, the bright color that stained her cheeks, her reluctant concentration on his mouth. He swallowed, deeply.

"Much as I would like to oblige you, I am afraid it is impossible right now, my lady."

Her startled gaze met his. "Pardon me?" She was mortified that he could read her thoughts.

Drake treated her to a slow, devastating smile. "I would like to oblige you by providing Smitty as your guide, but I do require his skill at the helm."

"Oh, of course . . . I understand." Relief, overwhelming though it was, was short-lived, as Alex saw the triumphant gleam in Drake's eye. She held her breath, expecting more taunting, but when he spoke again, his tone was aloof, businesslike. "Make yourself at home, princess. If you require something of importance, we will be at the helm." Without waiting for a response, he turned to Smitty. "Is there anything I need to know?" At Smitty's negative shake of the head Drake looked upward, his sharp gaze taking in every detail of the ship's rigging and the clear skies around her. "Fine. I'm going to relieve Thomas."

"Captain?" Alex spoke without thinking.

He turned to face her. "Yes?"

"Since I am going to be a passenger on *La Belle Illusion*, is there nothing I can do to assist your crew?"

He walked over slowly, his expression impassive. "And what would you suggest, my lady?"

Alex stood tall, ignoring the sarcasm in his voice. "I am quite skilled, sir, and I hate to be idle. Merely tell me what you wish of me."

Drake folded his arms across his chest, tapping his chin thoughtfully with his forefinger. "Are you strong enough to lift cannonballs from the hold, should they be needed?" He shook his head in answer to his own question. "No, no, of course you're not. Hmmm . . . I know. You can load the powder and assist the gunners in case of an attack. No, that won't do. You've probably never even held a gun in your dainty hand. Any experience at swabbing a deck? No, of course not; you have servants to do your swabbing. Perhaps, with your vast knowledge of sailing, you could handle the rigging? No, I suppose a small skiff would not present a similar challenge. I know! You can assist the sailmaker. Surely you are a fine enough seamstress to mend canvas? No? Well, princess, I seem to be at a loss."

"You've made your point, Captain," she snapped. "I will not offend you with my offer again."

He shrugged. "Why don't you be a good girl and run off to your . . . *my* cabin. I have several good books that you might read."

"A grand idea, Captain. Of course, being so delicate, I will ignore any literature that might prove too taxing. Perhaps I'll find a sweet gothick romance? Surely that would not be too overwhelming for my inept female mind!" She turned on her heel and stalked off.

Smitty chuckled. "Rather bold-tongued, our Lady Alexandria is."

"She is not *our* Lady Alexandria," Drake growled. "She is a brazen little hellcat! Now let's get to work!"

Smitty trailed behind Drake, grinning broadly.

Alex fumed quietly on deck for a short while. But as her anger subsided, her boredom resurfaced. She had no intention of spending weeks in a dark cabin with only a book for company. She would simply find a way to be useful.

Drake was distinctly uneasy. The sun had slowly worked its way to the west and, having done its job, was gradually setting over the horizon. The day had been uneventful, the waters calm, the weather cooperative. It was a captain's dream—except for one thing: he had seen neither hide nor hair of Alexandria since she stormed off eight hours ago. In Drake's opinion, that could only mean trouble.

He sat down to his midday meal, served late. Thus far he had been too involved in maneuvering the ship to eat. And now that he found himself in his spacious cabin, utterly famished, studying what resembled a plate of wet meat, he had but one question.

"What the hell is this?"

Smitty looked up from his mug of rum, startled. "Why, I believe it is stew, Captain."

"Stew? Since when does Cook serve stew? I want to see him immediately!"

Moments later an ebullient, rotund Louis was ushered into the captain's cabin. "You wish t' see me, Cap'n?"

"I most assuredly do." Drake lifted a forkful of meat, sloshing the surrounding juices over the side of his plate. "What is the explanation for this?"

The cook beamed. "Ye noticed me stew! I'm so pleased, Cap'n! The 'hole crew has complimented me on it. Although, t' be sure, 'tweren't my idea but Lady Alexandria's. This way I was able t' use only 'alf the usual amount of meat and still serve the entire ship, with some left over for second 'elpings." He looked chagrined. "O' course, since most of the crew wanted second 'elpings, I 'aven't enough t' offer ye more. 'Ad I known that ye would enjoy it as much as t'others—"

"I hate stew." Drake interrupted the stunned cook, his anger intensifying at the mention of Alexandria's involvement. "And in the future make *no* changes in the menu without consulting me first."

"Yes, Cap'n." Poor Louis sheepishly inched his way toward the doorway.

Drake waved him away. "Now go!" He slammed his fork down on the table, raking his fingers through his hair. "First she tried to captain the ship; now she's invaded the galley. What next?" He shook his head in disbelief. "And to think I was under the misconception that it was Napoleon I had to fear."

Leaving Smitty below, Drake went topside to make his four o'clock check at the helm; the routine time when the afternoon crew was relieved by the first dogwatch. Fully expecting to see the rested men dutifully installed at their stations, Drake was astounded to find the same tired men he had left an hour earlier still on the starboard side.

"Cochran!" Drake's angry voice rang out. "Where is your relief?"

The lanky sailor looked distinctly uncomfortable. "On the way, I'm sure, sir," he said.

Drake was livid. He despised tardiness. He stormed below, heading for the crew's quarters.

Huddled at a large wooden table were the missing crewmen, their heads bent low.

Drake's first thought was that they were ill. "Jamison! Mannings! Warner! Parsons!" He strode forward to help.

At the sound of their names the men leapt to their feet. Handfuls of playing cards cascaded to the floor. "Yes, Cap'n!" They were, as one, at attention.

Drake stared from their guilty faces to the discarded cards at their feet. "What is the meaning of this? Eight bells were sounded ten minutes past!"

The men looked at one another blankly until finally Ezra Jamison replied, "We never 'eard them, Cap'n."

"Apparently not."

"We were just finishing our last 'and."

"Your last *what?*"

Realizing that nothing could make things worse, Jamison explained, "Lady Alexandria taught us t' play whist, Cap'n. It was a little difficult t' learn an' I guess we were concentratin' so 'ard that—"

"Never mind." Drake was beyond words. "I will deal with each of you later. Now get topside at once! Your fellow crewmen are exhausted!"

With a flurry of motion and dutiful salutes the four men fairly flew from their quarters.

Drake pressed his fingers against his pounding temples. He had a sudden throbbing headache, and he knew just what its name was.

In less than twenty-four hours she had wreaked havoc on his ship, and now she was nowhere to be found. But he would find her, oh, yes, he would. And when he did, she had better run for cover.

Shouts from above reached Drake's ears. *Now what?* He hurried to investigate. A perfectly pleasant day had deteriorated into a nightmare.

The nightmare continued. On the main deck five crewmen were engaged in a twilight scuffle, each pushing the other out of the way and attempting to lunge forward, only to be waylaid by the others in the group. Against the shadowy mainmast, young Thomas Greer stood, looking utterly miserable.

"Thomas! What is the meaning of this?" Drake demanded. The vein in his neck was pulsing wildly as he strode forward to break up the squabbling men.

Thomas looked relieved to see him. "It's Lady Alexandria, Cap'n."

"Of course it is. What has she done now?"

"Oh . . . nothin', sir. She just wanted t' know how we manage t' climb t' the royals and topgallants, an'—"

"And these fools are fighting over who will demonstrate this great skill to her?" Drake's tone was incredulous.

"Not exactly, sir. She didn't want a demonstration; thought she could do it 'erself."

"And did she?" Drake debated whether to choke her or beat her senseless.

"Well . . . yes, sir, she did."

"Then what the deuce are you men fighting over?" Drake raised his voice enough to be heard over the bickering. Aware that their captain had arrived on the scene, the crewmen ceased fighting.

"Over who will get her down, sir."

"Over who will . . ." Drake's voice trailed off as he followed Thomas's gaze up the length of the towering mast. Three-quarters of the way to the top platform, Alexandria clung to the windward rigging, looking down at the faraway deck with terrified eyes.

Drake's heart tightened with fear.

"Alexandria . . . don't panic!" he heard himself call in a hoarse voice. He moved directly below her, his arms extended. "Jump," he commanded.

"I can't," she whispered in a horrified voice.

"I'll catch you," he promised quietly.

"I . . . just . . . can't."

With a muttered oath he moved to the base of the rigging and, with lightning speed, shinned aloft until he reached her.

"Give me your hand." He reached out for her.

She wanted to, but she was frozen with fear, glued to the spot. She stared at him, wild-eyed.

"All right, sweetheart," he soothed. "Just hold on." Working his way over, he wrapped a strong arm around her waist. "Now just let go, Alexandria. I have you."

She hesitated, then slowly unwound her fingers from their death grip. Drake could see the deep gashes the rope had made on her delicate hands, so tightly had she clung. Gently he eased her against him, thankful for her slight weight. "Now wrap your arms around me," he told her, in that same soothing voice. "That's right . . . like that. Good girl. Just hold on, princess." Continuing to murmur words of encouragement, Drake moved cautiously, slowly, back down the rigging to the deck.

Alex kept her eyes closed throughout their descent and forced herself to concentrate on Drake's deep, caressing voice. This was the man she had glimpsed last night in the cabin during their moments alone together, this gentle, passionate man. She would be fine; he wouldn't let anything happen to her. Suddenly she heard the men cheer, felt Drake release his hold on the ropes. There was a brief rush of air, then the welcome sound of Drake's booted feet hitting the deck.

Alex slid weakly down his body. Her feet touched the deck, and she sagged against Drake, feeling his powerful arms holding her up. She wanted to thank him, to tell him she was sorry, to let him know how foolish she felt. The compassionate man who had just tenderly rescued her from certain death would understand. Of this she had no doubt.

Slowly Alex opened her eyes, simultaneously raising her face to look up at Drake.

He was shaking with fury, his jaw clenched so tightly he could barely speak.

"I am going to murder you."

It was one-thirty in the morning, and a still-seething Alexandria slammed her fist into the mattress. Murder her? If anyone deserved to be murdered it was he! How dare he humiliate her in front of the entire crew!

Alex buried her head in the pillow, trying yet again to soothe herself to sleep. Time and again the ship's bells had sounded, indicating the passage of night. And still she could not free her mind from its turbulent thoughts. Relentlessly it sought answers it could not find.

Why had Drake rescued her from the rigging, so warm and caring, only to lambaste her for her innocuous attempts to assist his men—attempts that he called her "list of sins"? The man was a monster!

Yet . . . even in anger, there was a spark between them, Alex mused. She was drawn to him like a small child to a forbidden sweet.

Sighing, Alexandria threw off the covers and rose from the bed. She crossed the room and turned up the wick of the oil lamp, instantly bathing the cabin in a soft glow. Slowly, and not for the first time, Alex brought her fingers to her lips, touching the place where, last night, Drake's mouth had been. The memory of his kiss still made her tingle—not only her mouth but her breasts, her stomach . . . and lower.

Alex knew she should not have such feelings. She should be repelled at the thought of his wanton advances, grateful for his decision to leave her alone.

And yet she was neither repelled nor grateful. Instead, she was restless, aching, and filled with unanswered questions.

Having always yearned for things that other women of her class seemed not to require, Alex was used to being unique. She had no doubt that one day, when she knew just what the craving in her soul was all about, she would find her heart's desire.

But her uniqueness had never taken such an unacceptable form. Reading, sailing, and longing to be valued by another human being were certainly unusual priorities for a noblewoman. Unusual, but not scandalous. Being unorthodox was one thing; being a trollop was entirely another.

Exasperated, Alex slid out of Drake's shirt and pulled on her discarded breeches and soiled shirt. If she could not rest, at least she could enjoy the night air.

The seas were calm, the undulations of the great brig

slow and steady. Gentle waves ebbed and flowed against the hull, making soft splashing sounds as they lapped up, then receded into the starless night. Alex slipped past the few sailors who were responsible for nighttime surveillance.

The forecastle was deserted. She walked to the railing and inhaled the cool air, allowing the sea to work its magic. Soon her melancholy was replaced by anticipation and hope for the future.

"Couldn't sleep, princess?"

Alex started, but didn't turn around; she could feel his presence without looking.

"No." Her voice sounded breathless, even to her ears.

Drake walked up beside her and stared into the hypnotic water. "I seem to be suffering from insomnia as well."

Alex allowed herself to glance up at him. He looked strained, tired, magnificent.

"You did not have to don the same clothing," he said without looking at her. "I can arrange for more of Thomas's clean clothes to be brought to my . . . your cabin."

"Thank you." She gave him an uncertain look. "It was very kind of you to forfeit your cabin . . ."

"Kindness had nothing to do with it."

Alex swallowed, falling silent.

"Tell me, princess," he resumed after a moment, "do you enjoy driving men to the brink of madness and then pulling away?"

He heard her gasp. He had hurt her with his ugly reference to last night, but damn it, he was hurting, too. The moment he had left her his body had been cast into hell. The dousing of cold water from Smitty's pitcher had not helped, nor had the hours of pacing the cabin.

Drake had spent countless hours thinking of Alexandria, cursing himself for all kinds a fool. Yet now, even after her unforgivable behavior today, seeing her standing small and alone on deck, garbed in men's clothes, he was drawn to her again like a moth to a flame. An irresistible, lethal attraction.

Alex recoiled from the anger in Drake's voice, but she also sensed his frustration. Before last night that emotion would have escaped her notice. But having experienced a newly awakened restlessness and an irrepressible longing, she was now able to understand some of what Drake was feeling. From his perspective, she must look not only like a trollop but like a tease as well.

"Captain—" she began.

He gave a harsh laugh. "Aren't we a little beyond the formalities, princess?"

Alex nodded. "Yes, Drake, I suppose we are." She ignored his surprised look. "I can neither explain nor excuse what happened last night. But I never meant for it to happen, nor did I mean to . . . hurt you in any way."

Hurt him? Did she have any idea how much, even now, he wanted her? How desperately he wanted to drag her to his cabin and bury himself inside her?

Drake turned to face her, ready to verbalize his anger. Until he looked into her eyes. Even in the blackness of night they shone, as clear and gray as polished jewels. Open, remorseful, waiting for his response.

His anger evaporated as if it had never been there.

Alex smiled. "Could we try to be friends?"

"Friends?" The dark brows went up.

She giggled. "All right, then. Not enemies, at least."

He smiled back, in spite of himself. "I suppose we could try that."

"And could we sit and talk for a while as well?" Her voice was so hopeful, her eyes so appealing. Drake's resolve slipped one notch further.

"Since we can't seem to sleep, why not?" He gestured toward a spot where they could sit and lean back against the foremast.

Without hesitation Alex sat, watching quietly as Drake lowered his tall frame beside her.

"When must you relieve your man at the helm?" she asked, attempting to fill the uncomfortable void of silence that hung between them.

"Not until the morning watch begins at eight bells." He saw her puzzled expression and explained, "Four o'clock in the morning."

"Oh." Alex waited patiently for him to continue talking. When he did not, she succumbed to her natural curiosity. "Do you have a family?" She could see that her question surprised him. He stiffened slightly.

"Doesn't everybody?"

Alex shrugged. "That depends on what one calls a family."

It was Drake's turn to be curious. "What does that mean?"

Alex rested her head against the solid mast. "Only that it must be lovely to be part of a real family, with sisters and brothers and a dog that sleeps by the fire."

He was struck by the wistfulness in her voice. "Is that so farfetched?"

She sighed. "For me it is impossible. I am an only child, and my parents forbid animals in our house. Do you have brothers and sisters?"

"Yes."

"Yes . . . what?"

"Yes, one of each."

"Really?" Her eyes lit up, gleaming silver in the darkness. "How old are they? What are their names? Are you very close to them?"

Drake chuckled. Her enthusiasm was endearing; her naïveté was hopeless. "My sister's name is Samantha. She is fifteen and a joy. She is rather like a frisky puppy, noisy and inquisitive and always following me about." He warmed to his subject. "She will grow to be quite lovely in a few years."

"Does she resemble you?"

He considered. "Yes, I suppose she does. She is tall with dark hair, several shades lighter than mine, and her eyes are as green as a meadow."

"She sounds wonderful. And your brother?"

Drake's smile vanished. "Sebastian is thirty years old, two years younger than I. We are nothing alike."

Alex could hear the hardness of his tone, but she wished she could see him better. All she could make out was the outline of his features.

"Does he captain a ship, as well?"

Drake laughed bitterly. "Hardly. Honest work has never been Sebastian's forte. He much prefers to play."

Knowing how devoted Drake was to *La Belle Illusion* and how proud he was to captain her, Alex understood his disgust for someone's idleness and lack of purpose. She thought of the frivolous members of the *ton* who constituted her acquaintanceship back at Sudsbury. Yes, she understood Drake's scorn, for she had felt it countless times herself.

She voiced her thoughts. "Your brother is but one of many who prefer to reap life's pleasures with no thought to the contrary, no need for something more."

Drake stared down at the shadow of her profile, hearing the derisive note in her tone.

"You sound as if you speak from experience."

She locked her arms around her knees, drawing them up to her body. "I do. In my world, all people are such as you describe. Our gowns, the balls we attend, the appropriate men we meet—such is our shallow existence."

"Shallow but entertaining, princess. Surely you are an avid participant in the festive life you have just depicted." She couldn't mean a word she had said. So why, then, was he awaiting her reply with bated breath and a pounding heart?

Alex settled her chin atop her raised knees. "As a sea captain you have never been part of my 'aristocratic upbringing,' as you call it. It is natural that in your mind my life is enviable. It is true that I have never had to concern myself with money; wealth has been mine since birth."

She paused. "But I have paid a high price for my affluence. I live within rigid constraints. There is judgment attached to everything I do. Noblewomen simply *do not* enjoy or long to do certain things. They meekly *do* and comply with other things. This is well and good if your nature enables you to be happy this way. But what if your life feels hollow? What if there is an ache inside you that you do not know how to fill . . . are not permitted to fill?"

Unbeknownst to Alex, her voice trembled. "In truth, I would gladly trade my gowns, my servants, and my cold, aloof suitors for a simpler life, a life with meaning, with a person who loves me and whom I love in return."

She turned to Drake. "I envy *you*, Drake. I know that you are not rich. But you go to bed each night feeling whole, knowing where you belong. You know what you need and have found it." She drew in an unsteady breath. "I long to find that same sense of purpose."

Drake had not spoken once during Alex's emotional talk. In truth he was moved. It was ironic. She thought he was poor and that his bitterness was based on envy when in fact he had been born into the very world of which she spoke, and he shared her scorn, for he knew only too well how vapid and restricted a life it was.

She was such a puzzling dichotomy. On the one hand she was haughty and arrogant. On the other hand she was a lonely and searching little girl, needing to love and to be loved. Which one was real? More important, which one did he *want* to be real?

Moving to safer ground, he asked gently, "Is your life really so dismal, Alexandria? What about your parents? I know that your father is the governor of York in Canada, but what of your mother?"

"She is beautiful, an excellent hostess, and a diligent mother. Of course I don't see her very often. She is terribly busy overseeing Sudsbury, not to mention the numerous balls in London during the Season. I was well educated as a child, taught all the social graces, and instilled with all the traditional values. My mother has done her job well." Alex fell silent.

Even as she defended her, Drake could hear the hurt in Alex's voice. He suddenly wanted to shake Lady Sudsbury for neglecting to see that Alexandria needed more than an overseer as a mother.

"She must enjoy her freedom while your father is away." Alex started at the grimness of his tone.

"I don't understand," she replied.

"Oh, I think you must. Surely it is far easier for her to,

shall we say, appease her restlessness without her husband there to curtail her liaisons?"

Alex felt shocked color rush to her cheeks. "Certainly not! How dare you even suggest such a thing!"

Drake gave a hollow laugh. "Surely you cannot be *that* naive, princess? People of your social class rarely keep only unto their spouses."

Alex winced. No, she was not that naive. She knew about the flagrant adultery that transpired in *ton* marriages. But not her mother. It was unthinkable.

She shook her head. "No," she insisted. "My mother would never deceive my father."

"Every woman is capable of deception, Alexandria. There are no exceptions."

"You are very bitter."

"I have reason to be."

"Perhaps, but I hope never to become that way. Hatred consumes too much energy."

Drake paused at her words, trying to ignore the truth behind them. "What *do* you hope to become?" he asked instead.

"Happy."

"Happy by whose standards, princess? The *ton* would define happiness as marriage to the right man."

"Happiness by *my* standards, Drake. And to me, marriage to the right man means marriage to someone I love. Otherwise, I want no part of it."

Her little chin was held high. Drake couldn't see it, but he knew it just the same. He grinned at the image.

"You're young, princess."

"I'm eighteen," she protested.

"*Very* young. You'll change." His words were bleak, even while his heart rebelled at the thought.

"I won't." Her tone dared him to challenge her.

Footsteps sounded nearby, and a moment later six bells sounded, reverberating across the forecastle.

Drake rose. "It is three o'clock. You had best get some sleep, princess. It will soon be daylight." He reached down to help her to her feet.

Alex took his hand and allowed him to pull her upright. For a time they stood, their hands joined, their expressions obscured by the darkness.

"Good night, Drake," she said at last.

He released her hand slowly, savoring the contact as long as he could.

"Good night, Alexandria."

He watched her slender outline as she crossed the deck, then disappeared below.

Drake shook his head in disbelief. Had it been but two days that he had known her? In that brief time she had succeeded in infuriating him, disrupting his ship, challenging his authority, displacing him, sexually arousing him beyond any shred of control . . . and touching something inside him that he had never known existed.

Somehow Drake knew his life would never be the same.

Chapter 7

A storm was brewing.

Alex could feel it the moment she emerged on deck. The winds were high, though not yet harsh. The sky was a moody gray, not quite threatening, but ominous nonetheless. And the waves were choppy, tossing *La Belle Illusion* none too gently to and fro. Alex's instincts told her a violent storm would be upon them by dusk.

"Mornin', Miss Alex!"

Alex turned toward the cheerful voice.

"Good morning!" She raised surprised brows toward Jeremy Cochran, who waved to her from his starboard watch. "I am surprised to see you up and about; I thought your neck was still causing you pain."

He grinned, shaking his head. "Not any more, thanks t' ye." He pointed to his neck, where a piece of material resembling a cravat was tied. "I took yer advice and 'ad our sailmaker cut me a strip o' canvas. Now I'm protected from the wind, and me neck is much better!" His eyes twinkled. "I don't suppose it's as fine a cravat as you're used to seein', but it works!"

Alex beamed. "It's every bit as elegant as the cravats worn by the *haut ton*," she teased back. "And I, too, am the beneficiary of our sailmaker's talent." She pointed to a thin band of canvas around her waist. "It's the sturdiest belt I've ever owned."

"Beggin' yer pardon, Miss Alex."

Alex turned to see stocky Ezra Jamison arrive beside her. "What is it, Ezra?"

"Cook be wantin' t' know what you added t' that stew t' get the Cap'n t' change 'is mind? We're 'aving it fer lunch today an'—"

"Shhh, keep your voice down, Ezra," Alex cautioned, looking around quickly. "We don't want Captain Barrett to know it was I who made that change, now, do we?"

"No, ma'am."

Alex smiled. "Tell Louis I'll be right there to locate the spice he needs. Also, remind him to serve less of the meat's juices to the Captain. The drier the stew, the less likely he will recognize it as the same meal that infuriated him weeks ago."

"Yes, ma'am. Oh, an', Miss Alex, will ye be joinin' us for the last 'and o' whist before lunch?"

"No, thank you, Ezra, not now." She had spied Smitty at the helm, and he looked peaked. She could be needed. "Perhaps later on today?"

"Yes, ma'am." Off he went.

Alex made her way to the quarterdeck. Irreverent, as always, she did not seek permission, but climbed gracefully up to stand beside Smitty.

He smiled. In the three weeks of their voyage he had become very fond of their unpredictable passenger. The entire crew had taken to her. And, despite his bellows to the contrary, so had their captain.

"Good morning, Smitty."

"And a good morning to you, my lady," he replied.

She had tried time and again to persuade him to call her Alex, as almost everyone who knew her did. Her governess had been the first to use the name, claiming that her young charge never stayed still long enough for anyone to utter her complete forename. However, even a fleet-footed four-year-old could not escape faster than it took to say Alex.

But no amount of persuasion had convinced Smitty to follow suit. The rest of the men were casual and friendly, but Smitty was always proper, ever formal. He had missed his calling, Alex decided. He would have made an excellent valet.

"A storm is brewing," Alex commented, looking out to the restless sea.

"Yes, my lady, it is."

"Why don't you rest for a while, Smitty? That way you will be refreshed when you are needed later today."

He gave her a warm smile. "I am fine, my lady."

"Where is Captain Barrett?" she asked.

"He is resting. He was at the helm most of the night."

No, he wasn't, Alex thought. He was on deck with me, talking. Their nightly talks had become almost a ritual, one that Alex had come to depend upon. Although by day a persistent tension still hung between them, by night they were able to share their thoughts openly and without anger. It made no sense at all, but Alex didn't want to question it. She enjoyed the easy closeness they shared under cover of darkness.

"Well, if you will not rest, Smitty, at least allow me to keep you company." She turned hopeful gray eyes to him.

He chuckled. She was an irresistible little thing. "My pleasure, my lady. You and I will steer the ship while Captain Barrett is resting."

Captain Barrett was not resting. In fact he had just about given up the idea of ever sleeping again. Every time he closed his eyes, he saw Alexandria's face.

He had never experienced such wildly careening emotions. One minute he was determined to throttle her; the next minute he was frantic to make love to her.

He did neither. But restraining himself was wreaking havoc on his body and on his mind.

And then there were the nights. It was then that he glimpsed another Alexandria. Someone alone and searching, who needed something but knew not what. Someone very much like himself.

With a groan Drake propelled himself from the bed and headed topside. The brisk morning air had picked up considerably since he had gone below three hours earlier. Now the waves were choppy, slapping against the hull with greater force. All the signs were present. A storm would be upon them by four bells.

Drake frowned. Preparations needed to be made and precautions taken. His ship had weathered many a storm; she would manage this one as well. It did not look too threatening—at least not yet—but Drake planned to keep a close watch on the storm's approach.

A sudden burst of musical laughter drew Drake's attention toward the quarterdeck. Smitty was at the helm with Alex close behind. Alexandria's eyes glowed with sparkling silver lights as she gazed up at Smitty's face. Throughout the voyage she had never bothered to bind her hair, and now it whipped wildly around her, a cloud of molten honey. Patiently she brushed strands off her delicate face, her features tanned and healthy from exposure to the sun. The familiar white shirt was belted at her narrow waist, her tiny feet were bare, the oversize breeches rolled up into generous cuffs at her calves. It mattered not that, by the *ton*'s standards, an indecent amount of leg was showing. She seemed to defy convention more and more as she left England farther behind.

Drake's breath caught in his throat. God, she was beautiful . . . so vibrant and alive.

"Based upon the stiff gale, I would suggest bringing *La Belle* farther alee, Smitty." Alexandria's advice threw a spray of cold water on Drake's tender observation. "Else we shall soon be all in the wind. Why, the sails are already protesting their battle with the elements!'' She smiled approvingly as Smitty veered farther alee, a course he had been intending long before he heard Alex's bright words of advice. "Excellent,'' Alex praised.

"Will you never cease ordering my men about, princess?'' Drake's furious voice boomed out, as he swung on the quarterdeck.

Alex jumped at the impact of his words and the fury in his glittering green eyes.

"Will *you* never cease attacking me for no purpose, Captain?'' she fired back. "I was merely helping poor Smitty out of a difficult situation.''

Drake saw Smitty bite his lip to keep back the laughter that threatened to erupt from his chest.

"You were *what?*'' Drake uttered in disbelief.

Alex sighed patiently. "Captain, even the best sailors need occasional assistance. Smitty has been laboring on deck for hours now, with no relief. He is exhausted. I had hoped—''

Smitty saw Drake's thunderous expression and hastily intervened. "It's quite all right, Captain,'' he assured him with a placating look. "Lady Alexandria made an astute observation.''

Drake looked incredulous. Smitty was giving credit for a standard maneuver, known by any adequate sailor, to an arrogant little twit. A twit who now stood before her captain, hands on hips, annoyed at his seemingly unwarranted outburst. From his peripheral vision, Drake saw Smitty take a protective step closer to Alex, intending to ward off Drake's forthcoming assault.

This was too ludicrous to be true.

Alex truly believed that Smitty needed her help, due to his fatigue. Actually, Drake noted, she wasn't entirely wrong. Smitty did look exhausted.

"Smitty, go get some sleep.'' Drake approached the helm. "I'll take over.''

Smitty frowned. "But you've gotten no sleep, Captain.''

Drake shrugged. "I'm becoming used to it. Now go." It was an order.

Smitty tried not to look relieved as he relinquished the helm to his captain. In truth his fatigue was caused not by his advancing years but by the sleepless hours he spent listening to Drake pace the floor of the cabin, cursing and muttering under his breath. It was almost a relief when he would finally storm out and, Smitty assumed, go to the helm.

Smitty made his way below, recalling Alex's belligerently beautiful face and Drake's steely stance. Pity that one acquired wisdom and insight only as one got older, he mused. Ah, well, they would soon discover for themselves what he already knew.

Left alone, Alex turned toward Drake's hard profile. "Do you feel the storm coming?"

"Yes, princess I feel it." He glanced up at the sky. "It will be several hours before it is upon us. After our midday meal we will batten down *La Belle*."

Alex nodded. "We've been very lucky with the weather until now. The winds have been strong, but the rains have spared us."

"Yes, well, we're not out of the woods yet, my lady," he reminded her. "We still have many weeks ahead."

"I know." Alex sounded delighted rather than upset by the prospect. She leaned back against the smooth wooden planks and looked up at Drake. "When will we near the Saint Lawrence?"

"Not for at least a fortnight," he replied. "Longer, if the weather does not cooperate."

Alex's eyes glowed. "I can hardly wait to see Canada!" She gave Drake a brilliant smile. "I have imagined it so many times—a great untamed wilderness with miles of untouched land and beautiful waters on which to sail."

Drake grinned. "Is that what you plan to do once we arrive in York? Sail?"

Alex nodded vigorously. "I plan to acquire another skiff as soon as possible. Then I can strike out on Lake Ontario on my own!"

Once again Alex's infectious enthusiasm warmed the coldness of Drake's heart. But the reality of her fate, while clear enough to Drake, seemed to escape her. "Don't you think your father might have other plans for you, princess?" he reminded her gently.

Alex shrugged. "At first, perhaps. But the novelty will wear off. He will be far too busy to be bothered with me."

"You're his daughter!"

"I know, but that is how it is between us. Perhaps if I had been the son he wanted things would have been different, but . . ." Alex gave a philosophical shrug. "Anyway, I have no fear that Father will monopolize my time. It will be far easier for him if I am not in the way."

Unbidden, a surge of protectiveness claimed Drake. Didn't Alex's parents recognize that she deserved better than two cold and self-centered providers who obviously had no time for their warm and headstrong daughter? Damn them!

The ship lurched unexpectedly, recapturing Drake's attention.

"Go below and eat," he ordered Alex quietly. "If you wait much longer your stomach may not cooperate."

Alex nodded, realizing the storm was moving toward them rapidly. "I'll finish my meal, then wake Smitty. By that time it will be necessary to ready the ship for its battle with nature."

Drake grinned at her choice of words. "Would it be foolish to ask if you were intimidated by the thought of the storm?"

"Yes."

"Yes, you are intimidated?" He raised questioning brows.

She walked past him, laughing and shaking her head. "No. I meant, yes, it would be a foolish question. I find the thought of a storm at sea fascinating."

Drake gave an exaggerated sigh. "I was afraid of that. I suppose that also means that I would be wasting my breath if I insisted that you stay below."

"Correct, Captain."

"All right, princess. You may remain topside—under two conditions," he added quickly, seeing her jubilant expression.

"Which are?"

"That you stay out of the men's way while they are working *and* that you obey me and go below *without question* if the storm is a bad one." Seeing her forthcoming protest, Drake shook his head emphatically. "I have made many concessions to you, Alexandria, but this is one I will not make. I expect my orders on this ship to be followed unconditionally, especially in times of danger. Do you understand?"

Alex recognized the unyielding glint in his emerald eyes. With a sigh of defeat, she agreed. "All right, Captain. You've made your point. I will bow to your command."

Drake smiled to himself as he watched her go below. Her sarcasm had not been lost on him. He would have to keep a sharp eye on her during the afternoon hours, for she was about as submissive as a wild stallion. In truth, however, he was not overly concerned, for he did not expect the storm to be severe.

By late afternoon the crew had readied the ship for its bout with the elements. The cargo had been secured, all hands were ready on deck, and still every sign indicated to Drake that the coming storm would be insignificant.

Before dusk he changed his mind.

All at once it was upon them. There was no time to react. Suddenly, without warning, the world erupted. The winds turned bitter cold and relentlessly fierce. Rain exploded from the sky, pouring down in icy sheets on the gleaming decks. The seas, taking their cue from the heavens, surged wildly upward from the blasting winds, rolling the helpless ship from side to side and flooding its decks with wave after turbulent wave.

The crew worked frantically to better secure the rigging, the lines biting into their flesh from the strain. No amount of forethought could prepare a ship for a storm of this magnitude, and the men had no choice but to bend to its command.

"Bloody 'ell, Cochran, restrain the mainsail!" Jamison demanded urgently, his voice muffled by the roar of the ocean.

"I can't," Cochran gasped back, tightening his grip. "The wind be too severe!" He shook his head, blinded by the rain, drenched from the downpour.

Thomas Greer clung to the lines beside the top platform of the mainmast. "The main topsail is set!" he called above the roar of the wind. He had reefed as much of the sail as he could to the boom, praying that it would catch the wind well above the waves, which were already breaking over the stern deck. The close-reefed main topsail might be their only chance to catch the wind and carry them out of the storm. He tried not to look down into the surging waves and imagine himself catapulting to his death. He had never weathered a storm of this severity. Terror gripped him.

Another huge wave swept over the stern, flooding the quarterdeck. Drake caught his breath, holding the wheel more tightly. The storm had a mind of its own and battled him for control of the helm. Thus far he was in command. But neither his strength nor his ship could hold out forever.

A huge crash resounded from the ship's hold.

"Damn it, Smitty, the cargo!" Drake yelled above the uproar. "Wasn't it secured?"

"It was, Captain!" Smitty called back from the main deck, having just assisted with the forward rigging. "But the ship is pitching too badly to keep it steady!"

"Well, send someone down to secure it again!" Drake shot back, bracing his feet wide apart in preparation for the sea's next onslaught.

"No one is free to go, Captain. Every man is working to keep *La Belle* from capsizing!"

Drake shook his drenched hair back from his face. "Then you do it."

Smitty looked stunned. "Captain, you can't manage the helm alone!"

"Smitty, I must deliver the cargo intact! Don't argue with me. Go!"

Smitty hesitated for a second longer, then hurried to

obey. He descended to the berth deck and moved toward the steps leading to the hold.

"Smitty?" Alex called to him.

He turned. "Yes, my lady?" For the first time he actually sounded impatient with her.

Alex could see his worry. "Can I do anything to help?"

Smitty shook his head. "Just remain in your cabin, my lady. I must check the hold. The cargo might be in jeopardy."

"But who is with Captain Barrett at the helm?" she asked in amazement.

"No one. Now excuse me, my lady. I must go." He disappeared down the steps.

Alex did not hesitate for an instant. In three seconds she had propelled herself up to the rolling main deck.

Drake was struggling; she could see it. His strong muscles were taut and straining, outlined through his drenched shirt. The cords in his neck stood out, his hands were white from wrestling the wheel against the violently raging sea.

Alex gripped the wooden railing and made her way to the quarterdeck. "Let me help," she gasped when she was beside him.

"What the hell are you doing up here?" Drake roared. "I told you to remain in the cabin. Damn it, Alexandria, go below!"

"No!" She was unmoved and unmoving. "You need help." She began to choke as a wave slapped against her, forcing her to swallow a mouthful of water. But valiantly she moved to stand beside Drake, determined to stay by his side.

Her loyalty staggered him. At the same time he wanted to beat her senseless. She was so slight that one overpowering wave could drag her to her death.

Fear gripped him.

"You stubborn chit, go to your cabin!"

Alex didn't answer. She couldn't speak. Beyond Drake had risen the most towering, fearsome wave she had ever seen. And it was bearing down on the stern of the ship at an alarming pace, rearing its angry head. She wanted to scream, but the sound was trapped in her throat. All she could do was stare, horror registering in her eyes. And then it was too late.

Drake saw the terror-stricken look freeze Alex's features. Abruptly he whirled around just as the wave hit.

An icy, suffocating blanket descended upon him, blasted his face with its frigid spray, and knocked the breath from his chest. He struggled to surface, but the wave was unrelenting and dragged him down with it, rendering him helpless under its forceful impact. He felt himself strike the deck, the water washing over him in torrents, forcing his head back. He felt the crash explode inside his skull, excruciating pain burst forth in bright lights.

And then . . . nothing.

Chapter 8

"Drake!" Alex screamed as his head struck the mainmast. Her cry was lost in the howl of the wind. Horrified, she watched his powerful form crumple, then go very still.

Fighting the force of the gale and the tossing of the ship, Alex made her way to Drake's side. Cautiously she lifted his head, searching for any sign of consciousness. There was none. She pressed her ear to his chest, but no sound was audible over the roar of the storm.

The ship rolled wildly to larboard, tossing Alex to the deck. Frantically she looked up, realizing that the unmanned wheel was spinning out of control, sacrificing the ship to the storm's destructive force.

"Drake," she whispered, half to herself. She lifted one hand from behind his head, ready to ease him back to the deck. Blood. Her hand was covered with blood.

Alex's heart contracted with fear. Drake was badly injured. He couldn't help her now. Her frightened gaze moved up and down the deserted decks. Every man was either securing the rigging or down below. It was up to her.

She laid Drake's head down gently, then struggled to her feet, pushing dripping strands of hair from her face. Slowly she made her way to the helm. Her hands closed over the spokes, desperately trying to still their motion. The wheel fought her, battling to be free. Alex yanked with all her strength. The ship lurched, attempting to right itself. Alex couldn't hold on; she hadn't the strength. With a whimper of pain she felt the wheel slip from her shaking hands, tossing the ship to starboard. The severe motion sent Alex sprawling to the deck again and at the same time shifted Drake's unconscious body toward the rail. Alex lunged for him and, with an unnatural strength born of fear, steadied his powerful body. She positioned herself behind him, her legs cradling his body on either side, and lifted his head, carefully laying it back against her chest. Then she braced herself and, using her legs for leverage, hauled him inch by inch across the quarterdeck. As soon as the mainmast was within reach, she grabbed hold of it and pulled herself and Drake to it, thus anchoring their bodies. Then she prayed.

Smitty knew something was amiss. In making his way back to the main deck he had been thrown against the bulkheads several times from the impact of the pitching ship. *La Belle Illusion* was out of control, which could only mean that the captain was in trouble.

He groped his way toward the stern, but could see nothing through the blinding rain. He cupped his free hand around his mouth. "Captain!" His voice echoed along the length of the ship.

Alex heard him. Instantly alert, she sat up as tall as she dared without releasing Drake's body. "Smitty! Help me!" she screamed at the top of her lungs.

My God, that was Lady Alexandria's voice! Frantic, the older man fought his way along the larboard side of the ship until he neared the quarterdeck. At this point he could make out the two forms sprawled against the mainmast.

Relief washed through Alex as she saw him. "Smitty, help me! Drake is hurt!"

Smitty asked no questions, but grabbed hold of the mast and lowered himself beside them. A small pool of blood had gathered beneath Drake's dark head.

"We must get him below, my lady," Smitty called over the wind. "I'll get help."

At Alex's nod, he stood and assessed the status of the surging ship. The helm could wait; his captain could not. He looked up from the base of the mast. Through the driving rain he could dimly make out the near-invisible form of Thomas Greer.

"Thomas!" he shouted. "Abandon the rigging and come topside at once!" He had to repeat the order three times, each time his voice growing more hoarse from the strain. At last he was rewarded by a faint shout from above, and moments later a soaked Thomas Greer dropped down beside them. Smitty gestured toward where Drake lay beside a white-faced Alexandria. Thomas needed no explanation. He moved with Smitty beside their captain. Slowly they lifted him, being careful not to touch his injured head.

Smitty turned to Alex. Left alone on deck, she was in danger, but there was nothing he could do. Thomas could not manage Drake's large body alone. And while the blow to Drake's head did not appear to be fatal, he had lost blood and the swelling was worsening. He needed the attention of the ship's surgeon.

"My lady," Smitty called to her, "I will send the men from below to assist you."

"No!" Alex shouted back. "I am going with you. I'll be fine, Smitty." Her frightened gaze returned to Drake. "He's lost so much blood."

Smitty saw no point in arguing with her, for he knew he would lose, and they had no time to waste. He merely nodded and returned his attention to the delicate process of getting Drake below.

Their progress was slow. As soon as the steps were in sight Smitty ordered Cochran, Jamison, and Mannings to go topside and man the helm. This done, he and Thomas half carried, half dragged Drake to the captain's cabin and eased him down on the bed.

Smitty turned to Alex. "My lady, can you locate the ship's surgeon?"

"Of course." She made her way to the officers' quarters, where she found John Billings preparing his medical supplies. When he heard that the captain required his attention, he immediately accompanied Alex to Drake's cabin.

Smitty and Thomas had stripped Drake of his sodden clothing and covered him with warm blankets. Billings set down his tools and performed a cursory examination. Moments later he turned to the room's occupants and frowned.

"It is most definitely a concussion," he determined, looking up at Smitty's anxious face. "The wound will need stitching, then cold compresses for the swelling." At his words Drake shifted slightly and moaned.

"I would prefer to stitch the wound before he is fully awake, to spare him the pain." Billings glanced over at Alex, who stood in the doorway, listening. "I would ask that all of you leave, except Smitty. I need Smitty to remain, should the captain awaken and need to be restrained."

Drake moaned again, tossing his head on the pillow, then groaning in agony at the pain that movement caused. His eyes opened, dazed and unfocused. Clearly he was not fully conscious. "Alexandria," he whispered, frowning as he said her name. "Alexandria."

The surgeon raised surprised brows and turned toward Alex.

"He is calling for you."

Alex went forward and leaned over Drake's supine form. "I'm here, Drake," she answered softly, stroking his face.

Her voice seemed to soothe him, for he immediately relaxed, the frown disappearing. Alex raised her face to meet Billings's curious gaze. She was beyond caring what people thought.

"Let me stay," she asked. "Please."

Billings glanced down at Drake and considered. Then he

shook his head. "The stitching of a wound is not easy to watch, my lady," he told her.

Alex stood, hands on her hips. "I am not squeamish, Doctor," she began. "Therefore . . ."

The decision was taken from them. The moment Alex lifted her hand from Drake's face he began to thrash about.

"Alexandria!" He called her name again in an anguished voice that tore at Alex's heart.

She did not wait for permission, but sank down on the floor beside the bed.

"I'm still here, Drake," she assured him, laying her hand against his cheek.

Instinctively, he turned his mouth against her palm, unconsciously seeking the comfort of her touch. Alex felt a lump in her throat.

Smitty watched the entire episode with great understanding in his eyes. Then he turned to Billings.

"The captain wants Lady Alexandria to remain, and so she shall," he stated simply.

Billings nodded. "Very well, Smitty. However, I still need you to hold him steady. Lady Alexandria might have the stomach, but she hasn't the strength."

"Fine," Smitty responded, gesturing for Thomas to leave the room.

Fortunately the worst of the storm had finally subsided, and the movements of the ship were less turbulent. Billings stitched quickly, to minimize Drake's discomfort. Every time he lurched with pain, Smitty would steady him while Alex spoke softly into his ear. The sound of her voice quieted him again and again.

Alex sighed with relief when at last Billings straightened from his task.

"It is done," he announced. "There will be considerable swelling and a good deal of discomfort when he awakens. He will need tending to." He gave Smitty a questioning look. "Will you remain with him?" It was common knowledge that the captain had gallantly relinquished his cabin to Lady Alexandria and was bunking with Smitty. Quite obviously, these arrangements would have to be altered until the captain was well.

Smitty nodded. "I'll not leave him alone, John."

"Good." Billings grinned. "I know our captain will not take kindly to his enforced bed rest or to his weakened condition. But it is necessary that he rest in order for the wound and the concussion to heal."

"I understand."

Alex listened to the men talk, staring down into Drake's face. His features were softer than when he was awake, giving him a vulnerable look that sparked a protective instinct in Alex. She stroked a lock of damp hair off of his forehead.

At her touch Drake opened his eyes. They were glazed with pain, but no longer unfocused. He blinked, turned his head slightly, and groaned.

"My head . . ."

"Shhh," Alex murmured. "Try not to talk or move."

"Alexandria?" He looked puzzled, trying to put the disoriented pieces together. "What happened?"

"You have a concussion, Captain," John Billings interjected. "Not a terribly severe one. It could have been worse, but thanks to Lady Alexandria's quick thinking, you were spared further injury."

"Thanks to . . ." Drake looked astonished. Then memory flooded his features. "The wave . . . I remember . . . I must have hit my head." He turned toward Alex. "The crew . . . Was anyone hurt? Was there any damage to my ship?"

Billings poured a healthy amount of brandy into a glass, then added several drops of laudanum to it. "Both the ship and the crew are fine, Captain. Here, drink this," he directed. "It will ease your pain."

Smitty helped raise Drake's shoulders, careful to anchor his injured head, so that his captain could drink. Drake swallowed the mixture in three gulps, then eased back shakily onto the pillows.

"Damn! I'm as feeble as a child," he muttered.

Billings nodded. "The weakness will last for several

days, but the pain should diminish by tomorrow. You must rest, Captain."

Drake scowled, but did not argue. "Has the storm subsided?" he asked.

"Yes, Captain," Smitty replied. "The worst is over and the ship is intact. You can rest easy."

Drake nodded. Once again his gaze sought Alex. "What am I going to do with you?" The question was asked half to her, half to himself. He gave her a rueful smile. "You're such a damned little hoyden, but how can I thrash you when you saved my life?" He seemed to contemplate his options, but before he could continue the thought, his eyes began to glaze over and his lids grew heavy. "Such a beautiful contradiction," he murmured, his voice slurred. "It's no wonder you drive me insane. . . ." His voice drifted off as his features relaxed in slumber.

Billings chuckled, gathering up his things. "He will probably sleep for some time now. He might run a fever, though I doubt it. I will leave another dose of laudanum, should he require it. In any case he will need compresses for the swelling. I trust you can manage, Smitty?" He turned questioning eyes to the first mate.

Smitty nodded. "Most certainly."

"Fine. Then I shall take my leave. I must see to the other injuries now." He went to the doorway, then turned to Alex. "Thank you, my lady. You made a very fine nurse."

Alex smiled. "Thank you for allowing me to stay, Doctor."

He glanced at the bed, then back at Alex. "The captain wished it," he replied. It was obvious to John Billings that the captain had feelings for Lady Alexandria. But those feelings were none of his business. He bade them good night, closing the door behind him.

"You are exhausted, my lady," Smitty said gently. "Why not go to my cabin and rest. I can arrange for a hot bath for you. I don't want you to become ill from staying in those wet clothes."

Alex looked down at herself in surprise. She had completely forgotten about her own condition. She was drenched, her breeches were torn, and her shirt was covered with Drake's blood.

"Oh . . ." she murmured, vaguely. "I am certainly disheveled, am I not?"

Smitty chuckled. "Go, my lady, before you catch a chill."

Alex was too drained to argue.

The hot bath felt wonderful, as did the change of clothes. But despite her exhaustion, sleep would not come. She tossed and turned for hours, until lying there became unbearable. Finally she rose and made her way back to Drake's cabin. Quietly she eased open the door so as not to disturb either man.

In the dim light she could see that Drake was tossing slightly in the bed, muttering unintelligible words. Beside the bed, Smitty dozed in a chair, unaware of his captain's restlessness. Poor Smitty. He was absolutely spent. Alex gently touched his shoulder. At the contact Smitty's eyes flew open.

"My lady? What is it?"

"Nothing, Smitty. All is well. I merely came to relieve you."

His eyes widened and he shook his head. "No, my lady, that is not necessary."

"I know it is not necessary, but you are positively exhausted. I am refreshed from my nap," she lied. "Now it is time for you to go to your cabin and sleep. I will watch over your captain."

Smitty glanced down at Drake, who was now perfectly still. Normally he would not have considered her suggestion, but every bone in his body was screaming for rest and the night was half over, without incident. Surely for a few hours he could leave his lordship in Lady Alexandria's capable hands?

He sighed. "If he should stir, you will awaken me? If there is any problem . . ."

"There won't be," she stated firmly, already nudging Smitty to his feet. "Now go. You won't be of any use to

Captain Barrett tomorrow if you are exhausted. You will no doubt need all of your wits to combat his foul mood.''

Smitty smiled in spite of his fatigue. "You are quite right, my lady. I will take your kind suggestion. Thank you.''

Alex grinned as she closed the door behind Smitty. He was one of the kindest and most loyal human beings she had ever known. *It must be wonderful to have someone in your life who cares so deeply for you,* she mused. *Drake is a lucky man.*

She walked back to the bed and placed her hand on Drake's forehead. It was cool to the touch; he had no fever. All was well. She sat down in the chair, staring off into space, daydreaming idly. The minutes ticked by and her eyelids became heavy. Her head drooped forward, the awkward movement causing her to come awake. Quickly she glanced down at the bed, but Drake had not moved. She stood, stretching from her cramped position. Her belt was beginning to cut into her flesh. It was certainly not meant to be slept in, nor were the oversize cuffed breeches. Longingly, she eyed Drake's huge white shirt, which had been serving as her nightrail and now lay neatly folded on the chest.

Why not? she wondered. No one else was present, and anyway the garment was so big on her that it reached below her knees. It was much less immodest than a sheer nightrail. With that thought she swiftly shed her constrictive clothing and donned the billowy shirt. Then she curled up in the broad chair, placing her head against its back.

I'll just rest, she assured herself. *That is all.*

Seconds later she was asleep.

Chapter 9

The moan awakened her. Blinking, she tried to get her bearings. She was in her cabin, but for some reason she was not in bed. Another moan sounded just in front of her.

Drake. She was on her feet in an instant, leaning over the bed. He was sweating profusely, thrashing about in discomfort. Alex hurried to the basin and rinsed a cloth in cool water. Returning to the bedside, she bathed his face, murmuring softly to him.

Drake's eyes opened, focused on her face. "Alexandria?"

"Yes, Drake, it's me."

"My head is throbbing." The words were unclear, but Alex understood them.

"I know it is," she soothed. "I'll put a compress on to ease the swelling." So saying, she gently pressed the damp cloth against his badly swollen head. Drake gritted his teeth but, after a moment, visibly relaxed.

She thought he had gone back to sleep when he suddenly said, "My mouth is so dry. Could you possibly . . ." He didn't finish the sentence, seeming to have forgotten what he'd asked for. But Alex was already filling his glass with water, making sure to add a few drops of laudanum.

"Here, drink this," she coaxed, holding the water to his lips. She hadn't the strength to raise him up, so she merely offered him a sip at a time. He seemed to understand, and after he had drunk his fill, he smiled.

"Thank you." His brilliant green eyes were slightly dulled from the drug, but his words were coherent. He watched her place the glass on the desk, then return to his bedside.

"Can I get you anything else?" she asked, seeing that he was still awake.

She looked so beautiful standing there, almost ethereal in her white shirt, with her delicate features framed by the cloud of tumbled, honey-colored hair. Perhaps the laudanum was making him silly. Still, the sudden surge of feeling was uncontrollable.

"Come here," he murmured, patting the side of the bed.

Alex hesitated, but then realized he was barely conscious. Soon the medicine would take effect, causing him to drift off again. There was no harm in sitting with him for a moment.

His gaze was intense as she lowered herself to the bed. Slowly he lifted his hand and wrapped a tendril of her hair around it. "Have I told you how beautiful your hair is?" he asked in a husky voice. "It generates its own sunlight, sometimes soft and glowing, other times blazing with fire." He reached up with his other hand to stroke her cheek. "When I opened my eyes and saw you here I wasn't certain if I was awake or dreaming. You've filled my dreams so many nights . . . and whether my eyes are open or closed, it seems you are always there. Can you tell me why that is, my lovely Alexandria?"

Alex could barely breathe. Reason told her the drug was making him behave so strangely, but her body was responding wildly to his caressing words. She stared at him with wide, apprehensive eyes.

Drake gave her a slow, melting smile. "Don't look so frightened, sweetheart. Surely by now you know I would never hurt you?" The hand that caressed her cheek slid around to stroke the nape of her neck. He was drowning in her eyes, which shone like flawless opals and spoke to him of need and want despite her mind's ambivalence.

Alex felt him tug her head down, and she placed her hands against his chest, holding herself back. But who was she afraid of, she thought wildly, Drake or herself? How many times had she relived those moments in his arms, longed to repeat them?

Drake glanced down at her restraining hands. "Don't,"

he whispered, meeting her confused gaze once more. "Don't stop me. God knows I fought it as hard as I could, but it's no use. I want you, Alexandria . . . God help me, I *need* you."

He drew her down to him, covering her trembling mouth with his.

The moment their lips touched, wild flames erupted, licked along their nerve endings, and ignited an explosion that shook them to the very core of their beings. Tightening his grip on her back, Drake parted her lips and thrust his tongue into her mouth in an act of undisputed possession.

There was never a question of denial. As much a prisoner of the overwhelming physical sensations as he, Alex capitulated completely to Drake's unspoken demand. Her hands slid to his bare shoulders; her mouth moved with his in a kiss that took and gave and still wasn't enough.

Drake tangled his hands in her hair, the pain in his skull minor compared to the unbearable ache in his groin. Nothing mattered now but putting out the fire that only this woman could ignite in him. Like a starving man, he kissed her eyelids, her cheeks, her nose. But always her mouth drew him back, and he drank from it. He wrapped his arms around her, flattening her against him, feeling her tense in his arms.

"No," he commanded softly. "Don't pull away." He couldn't let her go; he would explode with his need for her. He stroked her back through the barrier of the shirt, burying his lips in her hair. He wanted to tell her, to explain how badly he needed her. Determinedly he struggled to combat the inhibiting effects of the laudanum. "I need you," he repeated. "Alex . . . please."

He had never called her Alex before, and the name was like an endearment. She heard his plea, and it touched an answering voice inside of her. In a rush she melted against him, wanting to be absorbed into his power.

Drake felt her surrender and knew a sense of triumph that was staggering. Urgently, greedily, he took what was his. Her shirt had ridden up to her thighs, and he reached down to caress her bare legs. It still wasn't enough. He slid his hands beneath the shirt, exploring the contours of her naked body. Her skin was like hot silk, her body coming to life beneath his seeking hands. He stroked the slender lines of her back, then moved around to cup her breasts in his palms. Alex trembled, then moaned softly as Drake circled her hardened nipples with his thumbs.

Her reaction nearly drove him over the edge. Beneath the blankets his body throbbed painfully, and he knew that he couldn't wait much longer. It was a need like none he had ever known, defying description or reason. He slid his hands to her sides, then over her hips and down, defining the curves of her body with his fingertips. She whimpered, and he caught the sound with his mouth, savoring the taste of her as he urged her soft thighs apart.

"Alex, open to me," he gasped into her mouth. "Please, sweetheart, let me touch you."

Alex was dazed, drugged, submerged in her rampant newfound desire. Warring emotions tore at her mind and her heart—what she *should* do, what she *wanted* to do. . . . She tore her mouth from Drake's, panting, gazing down into his eyes. This was wrong, so wrong, but she wasn't sure she had the strength to deny him . . . to deny them.

Drake watched Alex's inward struggle, so clear to him despite his mind's fuzziness. She seemed terrified by her passion for him. But why? Had one of her previous lovers hurt her? Drake forced himself to stifle his own rampaging need, soberly watching her face.

"Alex?" he whispered, still caressing her exquisite body.

She closed her eyes tightly, her lips trembling with suppressed emotion.

A wave of tenderness swept over him. "Oh, Alex," he murmured. "Could you really be as innocent as you seem?"

Her eyes flew open, and he saw his answer. "My God," he breathed, relieved and thrilled in a way that unnerved him more than his passion did. Gently he smoothed the shirt down over her legs. "All right, princess," he soothed her, seeing the apology on her face. "It's all right." For a long moment he continued to stare up at her, his expression unreadable. His thoughts and emotions converged into a pleasant haze as the laudanum finally won its battle over him. With a bit of surprise he became aware of the dull throbbing in his head, a pain that only moments ago he hadn't even noticed.

Alex started to ease herself away from him, but Drake caught her wrists in his hands and frowned.

"Stay with me." It was a tender command.

"But you need to rest," she protested, her emotions still raw.

"And I will. But I want you with me. Please, princess. I promise not to touch you . . . at least not *that* way." He grinned, stifling a yawn. "Besides, I fear that I am not . . . at my best." His eyelids drooped. "So you're safe," he slurred, leaning back against the pillow.

Alex watched his handsome, chiseled features relax in sleep. His hands still held her wrists, but the grip was loose now, and she could easily withdraw if she wanted to. *If* she wanted to.

She paused for but a second. Then she cautiously lay down beside him, covering herself with the top blanket, careful to keep the other layers of bedcovers between their bodies. Her head was spinning from what had turned out to be the most turbulent day of her life.

The last thing Alex was aware of, before drifting off to sleep, was Drake's strong arm drawing her close to him and pressing her head to his chest. And then . . . blissful oblivion.

Smitty paused for a moment outside the captain's cabin. He could hear no sounds from within, and it occurred to him that the two occupants might be asleep. He hesitated, uncomfortable with the idea of disturbing them. On the one hand, Lady Alexandria needed her privacy, and Captain Barrett badly needed his rest. On the other hand, the captain's injury needed to be treated.

In the end concern won out over discretion. Quietly he let himself into the semidark cabin and closed the door behind him. He was totally unprepared for the sight that met his eyes.

Together in the narrow bed, wrapped around each other and peacefully asleep, were Captain Barrett and Lady Alexandria.

Smitty had no time to react, no time to reverse his decision and make a hasty departure. At the sound of the door, Alex's eyes flew open and she found herself staring into his stunned face.

At first she had no idea why Smitty was gaping at her in such a peculiar manner or what he was doing in her cabin, for that matter. Then she became aware of the heavy weight of Drake's arms around her, and the memories of the previous night came back in a rushing flood.

"Oh!" With a mortified gasp Alex snapped to a sitting position.

The sudden jolt startled Drake, and he stirred, blinking sleepily and looking around him. His head throbbed, and he wondered fleetingly if he had drunk too much brandy the night before. Then he dazedly focused on the disheveled beauty beside him and the highly embarrassed first mate in the doorway. And he, too, remembered.

He was still disoriented when Alex stepped from the bed, allowing the oversize shirt to billow out around her, and faced a speechless Smitty with as much dignity as she could muster.

"Smitty, could you check the hallway for me and make certain that it is deserted?" Her voice was high and shaky, but she kept her chin up and her gaze steady.

Smitty was thrilled to have a task that would divert his attention from the awkward situation.

"Of course, my lady." He inched the door open a crack, peeping out into the hallway. "It is clear," he confirmed. "The men are all working their morning shifts."

"Thank you, Smitty."

Without meeting Drake's concerned gaze, Alex yanked the top blanket from the bed and wrapped it around her. Fighting the urge to break down and sob with utter shame, she gathered her discarded breeches and shirt, walked past Smitty, and left the cabin.

"Alexandria . . . damn!" Drake's abrupt movement from

the bed caused a blinding flash of pain to explode in his skull. He staggered about, feeling a wave of sickness rise up in his throat. Clutching his head, he sank back down, muttering one oath after the next.

Smitty helped Drake resume his position beneath the bedcovers. "Another movement like that and you will reopen your wound," he cautioned him.

Through a haze of pain Drake glanced up at Smitty's impassive expression. He was not fooled. Smitty was furious; his icy tone told Drake so. And his anger had little to do with the injury.

"Nothing happened, Smitty," he heard himself say, with a wave of self-disgust. Why the hell was he explaining himself? What difference did it make what anyone thought? It never had before . . . but with Alex it was different.

Smitty gave him a cool, assessing look. "Apparently *something* happened, Captain. That child was visibly upset for *some* reason."

"Damn it, Smitty, stop calling her a child! She's a grown woman, for God's sake!"

"So it would seem."

Drake groaned at the censure in Smitty's voice. "I was in pain. She got me some water and more laudanum. I asked her to sit with me. We must have fallen asleep. Obviously she was embarrassed by your appearance in the cabin." He intentionally omitted the rest of the evening's happenings. Smitty did not look convinced, but the older man said nothing further on the subject.

"You should eat something, Captain," he suggested instead. "Food will help you regain your strength."

Drake watched as Smitty made to leave. "Where are you going?"

Smitty turned. "To have a breakfast tray sent to your cabin." Without hesitation he added, "And to check on Lady Alexandria. I want to see for myself that she is all right."

Drake was suddenly and inexplicably furious. "I told you nothing happened!" he snapped, tossing the bedcovers off his naked body. "Would it satisfy you to check the sheets for proof of that *child's* continued virginal state?"

Smitty was unmoved by the emerald fire blazing in Drake's eyes. "There are ways, other than physical ones, for one person to hurt or heal another. Perhaps it is time you remembered that, my lord." He gave Drake a measured look and was gone.

Drake leaned back and sighed. He didn't want to think about the meaning of Smitty's words or dwell on the intentional use of his title. The sort of healing Smitty referred to was impossible for Drake to contemplate. Too many years had passed; too much had happened to reinforce his cynicism and lack of faith.

He could see Alexandria in his mind's eye. Despite the dulling effects of the laudanum, the memory was clear—the feel of her skin beneath his hands, the taste of her mouth on his . . . but strangely, what he remembered most was the look of pain in her confused eyes. The pain . . . and the innocence.

There was no point in denying it any longer: Geoffrey Cassel's beautiful, headstrong daughter was a virgin.

That knowledge cast a whole new light on the situation, Drake mused. He might be a bastard, but even bastards had some honor. Lust or not, he would deliver Alexandria to her father intact. And that was that. Or was it?

It would be weeks before *La Belle Illusion* reached York. Weeks before he could safely hand Alexandria over to her father and never see her again. Weeks during which he would want her, during which he would deny himself what he wanted.

Mastering his driving urge for her would be difficult. Difficult, but surmountable. What truly unnerved him was the emptiness that stirred inside him at the thought of saying good-bye.

He had no choice. His only alternative was to keep his distance from her. That was the only way to survive.

In Allonshire's impressive library Sebastian Barrett read the unsettling headlines in the *Times*.

There was talk of another war with the colonies, this time involving Canada. Of course it was all speculation.

He folded the newspaper and glanced nonchalantly at the date atop page one: April 24, 1812. He tossed the newspaper onto the desk, folded his arms behind his head, and leaned back in the carved walnut chair.

Between the war with Napoleon and the threat of war with America, travel between England and the continents of Europe and North America would be terribly risky. There was no telling what disastrous fate might befall a merchant ship traversing the Atlantic Ocean.

A slow smile spread across Sebastian's lean features.

Fate was a funny thing. Sometimes it just needed a little assistance.

Chapter 10

"Smitty! There's land ahead of us!" Alex fairly flew onto the quarterdeck, breathless with newly awakened excitement.

He chuckled. "Yes, my lady, Canada looms in the distance. Without incident we are little more than a fortnight from your father." He saw the mixed emotions flash across her expressive face. "This has been an arduous journey for you, my lady," he said gently. "You must be glad to see it end."

Alex stared out to sea. "Yes, Smitty, I suppose."

The weeks since the night of Drake's injury had been strained and difficult ones for her. She had expected many things from him, but indifference had not been one of them. He no longer snapped at her or ordered her about, but he also no longer sat with her on deck at night, talking until dawn streaked the sky, nor did he look at her with that barely concealed desire that had once made her heart pound. He was polite, distant, self-absorbed . . . a stranger. And it hurt.

"It seems forever since we left London," she resumed. "The winds have been unusually strong, but that fierce storm we encountered in April blew us off course, and . . ." She raised her eyes to the clear May sky. "Smitty, I am afraid," she whispered in a small, shaken voice.

His expression was tender. "Of what, my lady?"

She waited a moment before answering. "I fear that I have deluded myself into thinking my father's reaction would be favorable. In truth he will be outraged by my arrival."

"Are you regretting your decision to come to York?"

She shook her head vehemently. "No. Despite my father's objections I am glad I came. It was something I had to do." She smiled up at him. "Besides, it gave me the opportunity to meet all of you. *La Belle*'s crew has become very important to me. Especially you."

Smitty gave her a knowing look. "And the captain as well?"

She shrugged. "Perhaps."

He chuckled. "Are you being entirely honest with yourself, my lady?"

"Does it matter, Smitty?" She met his gaze directly. "Regardless of any feelings I might or might not have for Captain Barrett, he must go his way and I must go mine."

"Are you so certain?"

She gave a brief nod. "Yes. There are some social boundaries that even I would not dare cross."

"What if you were to fall in love? Would that not influence your future?" he persisted.

She sighed deeply. "I cannot answer that. Perhaps I am a coward, after all, or perhaps I am just not strong enough to meet such a challenge. Let us hope that when I fall in love it will be with an acceptable man."

"Acceptable to your family?"

She nodded again. "I do not care what the *ton* thinks of

me, but the need for my family's acceptance, if not their approval, is too deeply ingrained for me to abandon."

"I suppose that the idea of a young lady spending her first Season running about a merchant ship clothed in a man's shirt and breeches is not their notion of how a noblewoman should spend her leisure time." His eyes twinkled.

Smitty's attempt at humor accomplished what he intended. His relief was evident when Alex giggled at the picture his words conveyed. "Definitely not," she agreed. "So the question is moot. Feelings or not, there can be no future for Drake and me." She turned her gaze back to the sea. "It is good that we have arrived. It is time for my new life to begin . . . and my old one to end."

He smiled wisely. "Only fate can show us what is ours to keep or ours to leave behind. Trust in her wisdom, my lady."

Alex looked back at him. "You are a wonderful man, Smitty. And you have been the very best of friends to me. I will miss you."

"And I you, my lady." He paused. "But it is not yet time for good-byes. Come and watch our approach to the Saint Lawrence. The view is spectacular."

Alex went to the railing, joy reflected in her face. She stared, transfixed, at her first view of Newfoundland's rocky cliffs. Flocks of birds circled the formidable rock formations, surveying the waters for fish, then diving after their prey. The waves broke fiercely against the towering stones, spraying glittering streams of water along their rough surfaces. It was glorious.

"What is it? I asked not to be disturbed!" Geoffrey Cassel, the Earl of Sudsbury and governor of Upper Canada, slammed his fist on the desk and glared at the nervous footman standing in the doorway.

"I am sorry, m'lord," the footman replied uneasily. "But this diplomatic pouch was just brought by military vessel, dispatched with great haste from England. I thought you would want to see it at once."

Geoffrey stalked over and snatched the pouch from the footman's hands, dismissing the servant with a cool nod. Impatiently he returned to his study, withdrew a key from the top drawer of his desk, and unlocked the pouch with combined anticipation and apprehension.

Expecting an important communication from the government, Geoffrey was startled to find a letter penned in his wife's hand. With a muttered oath, he scanned the contents of the frantic message. As he read, his lips thinned in anger.

The urgent missive from his countess was typically and glaringly devoid of details. But apparently his blasted, foolhardy chit of a daughter had run off at the very onset of her first Season, without a word to anyone and with only a short note in the way of explanation. According to his wife, Constance, Alexandria was supposedly on her way to Canada, of all places. Geoffrey scowled, shaking his head. Well, if she was coming, he would deal with her . . . oh, yes he would. This would be the last impertinent act his daughter would ever commit.

Drake stood quietly, unseen, watching Alex's radiant expression. She was glued to the railing, as she had been throughout the week since Canada had been sighted. Now she breathlessly watched the Long Sault Rapids rush past the narrow canal that carried *La Belle Illusion* along. Her reaction to the beauty around her was like a rebirth to him. To see each sight through her eyes was to see it for the first time, the only time.

He frowned. His exuberant passenger had a way of reawakening him to life's offerings . . . and awakening him to a vulnerability he never knew he possessed. There was a rare and beautiful innocence about her, a purity of both body and soul that had prompted Drake's emotional withdrawal. He told himself that he had kept his distance to preserve her honor. But in his heart he knew that avoidance was his only defense against his need for Alex. And the tactic had been unsuccessful, for despite his apparent indifference, he craved her body and her spirit far more than he dared admit, even to himself.

With a will of their own, Drake's legs carried him to Alex's side. He leaned against the railing, pointing into the distance. "Look," he said softly.

Alex was unprepared for the visual impact of the lush green velvet patches of land that greeted her eyes. Hundreds of them, all different in size and shape, were sprinkled throughout the Saint Lawrence as it approached Lake Ontario.

"Oh, Drake," Alex breathed in wonder. "What are those?"

"The Thousand Islands, princess. Lovely, aren't they?"

She stared. "There are hundreds of them!"

"Actually, there are close to two thousand of them in all, each one unique. There are many legends about their creation. Magical, romantic legends." He felt the islands' natural splendor pull at him more intensely, envelop his senses more fully than ever before, this time, with Alex beside him.

"Will you tell me the legends?" She looked up at him.

God, those eyes, those silver-gray, fathomless depths, clear as the sea, turbulent as a summer storm. He could drown in them.

Drake swallowed hard. If he wasn't careful the walls he had erected these weeks would topple all around him. He couldn't let that happen, not at this point. They were too close to their destination.

"Another time, princess." His voice was gruff as he struggled to control his emotions. "Right now I have to concentrate on steering the ship into Lake Ontario."

Alex studied Drake's handsome features, this time seeing through his intended brusqueness. The realization shouldn't have mattered to her . . . but it did. With a warm glow, she reveled in the intuitive knowledge that, despite his struggle to the contrary, Drake cared. Somehow she had reached the impenetrable Captain Barrett.

"All appears to be peaceful in Little York," Smitty observed.

"Yes" was the terse response from the helm.

Smitty studied Drake for a long moment. Despite the calm that prevailed as the brig moved through Lake Ontario toward the docks of York, Drake had been moody and silent since they sighted the modest buildings and sandy beaches that marked their destination.

His political concerns were not responsible for his foul temper. His impending separation from Lady Alexandria was.

Smitty frowned. He was torn between annoyance at Drake's damned stubbornness and hurt at the agony that tormented Drake's soul.

No father could love his son more than Smitty loved Drake, nor could anyone better understand the reasons for his protective walls. But everything had changed now. Smitty suspected that Drake knew that only too well, and he was fighting it.

It was time to break a cardinal rule. Drake's happiness was at stake.

"You don't have to let her go, you know."

The softly spoken words made Drake tense.

"Let it be, Smitty."

But Smitty could not. "Do not let your bitterness blind you to the truth."

"I'm too damned well aware of the truth."

Smitty suspected that they were speaking of two different truths. "She is not like other noblewomen," he persisted.

Drake gave a harsh laugh. "I know that, Smitty. And she is even more dangerous to me because she is different. For, in the end, she would be my downfall, and that is something I will never allow."

Smitty knew Drake was remembering another time, long ago, and a young boy's pain and disenchantment with the world. The damage would be near impossible to undo, but Smitty had to try. "She cares for you, Captain," he told Drake softly, knowing he was treading on thin ice. "And you for her."

"She doesn't even know me," Drake countered.

"Doesn't she, my lord? I believe she knows you quite well, indeed."

"But not *who* I am. To Alexandria it would make a world of difference."

"Then tell her and see."

Drake shook his head. "There is no need. In but a short time she will be with her father and we will be on our way back to England with our timber. It will be over."

"Will it?"

The astute question pierced Drake like a knife. No, it wouldn't be over. For even now, as he stared out at the approaching shoreline, all he could see was her laughing face, her small, utterly feminine body hidden beneath those ridiculous men's clothes. She had worked her way inside him; there was no denying it.

It was up to him to pry her out.

"Once we dock in York, I will need you to supervise the unloading of supplies." Drake's abrupt change of subject did not surprise Smitty. It was the captain's way any time their conversation became too personal. "I must deliver the missive to Brock. Then I will return and escort Alexandria to her father's home. That should be some reunion," Drake added with a scowl.

Smitty looked anxious. "Do you think Lord Sudsbury will be very angry with her?"

"Furious."

"Lady Alexandria is only now beginning to suspect the unpleasant reception that awaits her."

Drake's look became tender. "Alexandria is too naive for her own good. Disastrous outcomes never seem to occur to her. It's one of the things . . ." He caught himself before he had finished the thought. "Are the men prepared to dock?" he asked instead.

"Yes, Captain." Smitty knew that, for now, the subject of Drake's feelings for Lady Alexandria was closed. But Smitty had not had his final say, nor had he given up hope. He had never expected the resolution to be easy. If only there were more time . . .

For the first morning in weeks Alex had no desire to be topside. She sat on the berth in her cabin, rising only to give an occasional glance out the porthole. Within hours she would be in York with her father. Canada . . . freedom . . . a new life. At last she would be able to fulfill her dream.

Then why was she no longer sure she wanted it?

She curled up in a small ball on the bed, tucking her feet beneath her. Leaving the crew of *La Belle Illusion* would be more difficult than leaving her family had been. In truth they were more like a family to her than her own. Here among these rough-edged men she had found a warmth and companionship that she had never known existed. They were like brothers to her, and wise, compassionate Smitty was like a father.

And Drake.

She wrapped her arms around herself in an act of instinctive self-protection. So much remained unfinished between them; so much would be left unknown.

Perhaps it was better that way.

And perhaps not.

She heard the men call out to one another as the ship was maneuvered into port, heard the running footsteps, felt the gentle impact with the dock. She braced herself, waiting for Drake to come below and tell her it was time to go. Still, when the knock on the door did come, she jumped.

"Yes?"

Smitty opened the door. "Your pardon, my lady," he began, as Alex rose from the bed. "We have arrived in York. The captain had urgent business to see to, but he will return shortly to escort you to your father's residence. During his absence he thought you might enjoy a bath and a change of clothes."

"A change of . . ." For the first time in weeks Alex remembered her unorthodox state of dress. She looked panic-stricken. "Oh, Smitty, what will I do? My father would never accept this attire on a woman, especially his daughter."

Smitty had never seen her so distressed. Even the turbulent storm and the primitive conditions during the months at sea had not unnerved Lady Alexandria as did the thought of her father's reaction to her unseemly attire. The realization made Smitty dislike Lord Sudsbury immensely.

"Do not fret, my lady," he soothed. "If you will look in the trunk I believe you will find the solution to your problem."

Curious, Alex opened the trunk and gasped. There, atop the men's clothing, was her gown, freshly laundered and accompanied by all her undergarments.

"I don't understand," she murmured, fingering the dark muslin. "How did it get here?"

"I brought it down this morning while you were finishing your game of whist with the men."

"But Drake told me it was ruined!"

Smitty's eyes twinkled. "Yes, well, I suppose he was wrong. It was salvable, after all."

Alex's flashing eyes told him she did not believe a word of the ludicrous story. "I will have bathwater sent to you directly, my lady." He ducked quickly out the door to avoid any further confrontation. He did not envy Drake upon his return.

Drake was in a dark mood when he came back up on deck an hour later. His meeting with Brock had been most unsatisfactory. While the charismatic man had thanked him profusely for his services, he was not in the least inclined to discuss the contents of the message with Drake. Therefore, Drake now knew no more than he had in March when he left England.

Without pausing to discuss the meeting's outcome with Smitty, Drake scanned the bustling deck for Alexandria. She was nowhere in sight. Where the hell could she be? The sudden thought occurred to him that she might have gone in search of her father on her own. With Alexandria anything was possible.

He took the steps to the berth deck two at a time, marched to the captain's cabin, and flung open the door.

In the middle of the room, deeply immersed in a tub of warm water, was the object of his search. She started at his unexpected entrance, her half-closed eyes flying open in surprise.

"Drake! For goodness' sake, what is it?" She crossed

her arms modestly over her naked breasts, stunned by the look of intense concern on his face.

She was fine. The realization dissolved his worry instantly. She was also stark naked and more exquisite than his most erotic fantasy had allowed. Desire exploded like cannon fire through his bloodstream, nearly driving him to his knees.

"I didn't see you on deck. It made me uneasy. I . . ." He broke off, unable to continue. With one swift gesture he kicked the door closed behind him, then moved to the side of the tub.

Alex felt her face growing warm. "Well, I'm perfectly fine, as you can see," she answered in a soft, breathless voice. "So, if you will excuse me, I'll continue with my bath . . . Oh, Drake . . . don't."

He had dropped down beside the tub and was sliding his fingers through her thick, wet hair. "I have to," he whispered. "It may be the last time I get to hold you."

He covered her mouth with his. Her lips were warm, wet, trembling. He groaned, half lifting her from the water to pull her against him. The water sloshed all around them, drenching his white lawn shirt and trickling to the floor in thin streams.

Alex caught his arms for support. "I'm getting you wet," she whispered inanely, unable to catch her breath.

"I don't care."

"But Drake . . . your shirt . . ."

"Fine." He held her with one strong arm and reached around with the other to tear off his sodden shirt and drop it on the floor. "There. Now you need not be concerned about my ruined shirt." He didn't wait for her reply, but pressed her soft, pliant body against him.

It was a mistake. He knew it the moment he felt her soft breasts crushed against the hard wall of his chest. It was the first time their naked skin had touched. And he was unprepared for the impact.

Alex's soft moan intensified the violent shudder that seized Drake's body as wild, scorching flames leapt to life, igniting an inferno between them that could not be extinguished. He could feel her heart hammering against his, her hold on his forearms tightening, then sliding up to his shoulders.

"Oh, Drake," she whispered in a soft, husky voice that shattered his control.

Without a word he brought her face up to his, parting her lips and moving his mouth back and forth over hers in a kiss of savage need and possession. He took her tongue, her mouth, her breath, and made them his. Gently, almost reverently, he slid his hands up and down her back, stroking her, urging her closer, feeling her body shiver with each touch.

This time was different. This time Alex was responding to him with the same utter desperation, the same bottomless craving that gnawed at Drake's soul—because this would be the last time.

He tore his mouth from hers, gazing down into her smoky gray eyes. "Alex," he said in a hoarse voice, "I want you more than I have ever wanted anyone in my life. If I had my way, I would carry you to that bed right now and bury myself so deep inside you that you would know just *how* much." He shook his head, staring at her with a look of utter amazement. "God, how I want to be the one to unlock the passion that's inside you, to teach you what that beautiful body of yours is capable of feeling." He drew a deep, shuddering breath. "But that can't be. We both know that, don't we, love?"

Confusion warred with passion in her dazed expression. "Drake, I want—"

"I know what you want, princess—at least what you want right now. But in less than an hour I have to deliver you into your father's *very* proper hands. Can you go to him, begin your new life, knowing that you just came from my bed?" He shook his head again. "I don't think so, love. Nor could I look at myself with anything short of disdain if I were to take advantage of you right now." Absently he stroked a wet strand of her hair behind her ear. "I must be insane," he murmured softly, "but if I don't stop now I won't be able to stop at all. The feel of you in my arms . . ."

He paused again, this time lowering her back into the tub. "You'd better finish your bath." He smiled a little at her obvious disorientation. "I'll wait for you on deck."

"Drake." The softly spoken name made him pause, his hand on the door, his back to her.

"Yes?"

"I . . . thank you."

She couldn't see the pained expression on his face, the torment in his eyes. "I suppose even we lowly sea captains have a shred of decency in us," he managed.

Her next words made him stiffen. "My father is a very generous man. You won't be sorry."

He turned slowly, the eyes that had bathed her in warm green light now glittered with chips of emerald ice. "My beautiful, passionate princess, I already am."

He slammed the door behind him.

Chapter 11

Lady Alexandria Cassel was back.

The men stared open-mouthed as she glided toward them, draped in all the finery of a noblewoman. Those sailors who were wearing hats instantly removed them.

Alex waved away their formalities, then smiled fondly. "Please don't. Nothing has changed. You are still my friends, and I have enjoyed every minute of this voyage with you." She wrinkled her nose at some private memories of the crew's antics. "Well, *almost* every minute," she amended. She was rewarded with a few chuckles, though the men still seemed ill at ease.

"I want to thank all of you for making me feel like a part of *La Belle*. It was a privilege I shall never forget." She said good-bye to each man in turn, from the warm face of Jeremy Cochran to the worshipful expression of young Thomas Greer. Finally she met the tender, dark gaze of the first mate.

"Smitty, the only way I can bid farewell to you without disgracing myself shamefully is by telling myself that we will meet again," she whispered.

He squeezed her hands. "I don't doubt it, my lady. Not for a moment."

"Thank you for everything, Smitty." On an impulse she stood on tiptoe and kissed his weathered cheek. "I love you."

He looked as if he might cry. "Godspeed, my lady. Until we meet again."

She nodded, then turned to disembark.

The impeccably dressed, devastatingly handsome man who reached up to assist her could not have been Drake Barrett.

But it was.

His features carefully schooled, Drake drew Alex to the dock beside him, releasing her hand as soon as she was steady on her feet.

Alex was astonished. From the tips of his shiny boots to his perfectly tied snowy cravat to the superbly tailored coat and breeches, Drake looked every inch a gentleman.

"You can close your mouth now, princess," he drawled. "You look different, too."

And she did. How could he have forgotten the staggering effect of the breathtaking woman he had found in his cabin last March? Soon Alex would have more suitors than she knew what to do with.

Drake wanted to choke each and every one of them.

Then he reminded himself of her earlier behavior, not in his arms but afterward, and his resolve strengthened. He wanted no woman in his life—now or ever.

Alex sensed his anger, and she had a good idea of its source. The instant the patronizing words about her father's wealth had left her mouth she wanted to retract them. But she had felt so off balance, throbbing with some unfulfilled need that she did not understand. Yet he had been able to distance himself so easily, recover so completely. That reality had hurt.

She looked up at him now, wonder softening her gaze. Today he looked every bit the proper English gentleman . . . and still his blazing sexuality burned through.

"Welcome to York, princess," he continued, his expression carefully impassive. "You can finally cast your illusions aside and get a close look at your chosen home."

The town immediately captivated Alex's senses. The smell of fish permeated the air, the sounds of the farmers' market mingled with the shouts of the sailors unloading their cargo. Women with baskets moved about, purchasing fruits and vegetables from tables piled high with mouth-watering delicacies. In the distance Alex could see streets crowded with strolling townspeople.

She was enthralled.

Drake watched the exuberance of Alex's unguarded expression. He knew she had grown up in the lap of luxury, never mingling with commoners, and yet her reaction was anything but the one he had expected.

"I'll arrange for transportation to take us to your father at once," he began, only to be stopped by her small hand on his arm.

"Oh, Drake, don't. I want to see everything, learn everything about Upper Canada! Couldn't we walk?" She lifted her determined chin and he wondered briefly if that was a request or an order. "Also, I've just spent months on a rolling deck, and now it feels wonderful to have solid ground beneath my feet again. I realize riding would be faster, but . . . please?"

He gave her a grudging smile. "Why not? The streets are so clogged with carts that we will travel just as fast on foot."

Actually the idea of walking appealed to Drake. He told himself that he needed a change of scene, anyway. The pleasure he was feeling had nothing to do with the additional time he would be spending with Alexandria.

The little shops, the tradesmen, and the plainly clothed

women, their heads covered by large bonnets, seemed to fascinate Alex. Drake smiled in spite of himself as she began to fire questions at him.

"What was that great stone structure I saw in the distance?" she asked suddenly.

"That was Fort York."

She looked up at him as they strolled along a footpath, moving steadily away from the more congested streets.

"Is that where you went when we first docked?"

"Yes, princess, that's where I went."

"Then Major General Brock's offices are there?"

He nodded. "Why are you so interested in my meeting with Brock?"

"Because you were obviously disturbed when you returned. I merely wondered—"

"I had other reasons to be disturbed," he reminded her.

She blushed but refused to be put off. "You were in a dark mood before we . . . before you . . ."

"I know what we did, princess. And, yes, you're right. I was in a foul mood after my meeting with Brock."

"Is the situation worse, then?" she asked anxiously.

Drake shrugged. "I don't know. No information was imparted to me."

"You believe there will be war."

Drake started. He had forgotten how astute his little spitfire could be. Well, he wouldn't lie to her.

"Yes, I believe there will be war."

"Why?" She looked more curious than alarmed.

He should have known better than to worry about frightening her. "Because," he explained, "the Americans will not be content with their independence from England. Among their leaders are certain greedy expansionists who believe Canada will be an easy conquest because England is too preoccupied with Napoleon to intervene. But they are wrong. With our passage to Europe blocked, England needs Canada's vital resources more than ever. And Canada neither needs nor wants to belong to the States. The situation is highly volatile."

He stopped abruptly, watching Alex's face for a reaction.

"Perhaps you are judging the Americans too harshly," she returned.

"And how is that?" Drake's brows went up. How typical of Alex to defend the fledgling nation. She undoubtedly saw some parallel between the "oppressed" Americans and herself.

Her next words confirmed his opinion.

"Perhaps the Americans are guilty not of greed but merely of enjoying their newfound freedom, of reveling in their limitless opportunities. The British presence on their continent must unnerve them."

She had a way of making a power-hungry nation sound like an innocent colt that had just discovered his legs and learned to walk. Drake understood, better than Alex realized, her abhorrence of repression. She had suffered from it all her life . . . as had he.

Unfortunately this was different.

"I agree that the British presence in Canada must make the Americans uneasy," he countered. "But having fought for their own independence, they should respect the right of self-determination in another nation, not try to usurp that right, as I am convinced they intend to do."

"I hope you are wrong," Alex said sadly.

"So do I, princess."

They walked on in silence past a section of modest two-story homes. Then gradually the buildings grew more grand. Drake pointed to a huge frame structure at the end of the street. Its graceful balconies and ornate fence bespoke wealth and power.

Alex did not need to ask where they were. Grim anticipation seized her, and without realizing it, she reached for Drake's hand, seeking comfort and strength.

Immediately Drake's own larger hand closed around it, enfolding her trembling fingers in his warmth. "Your journey is over, Alexandria," he said softly.

Alex had a sudden overwhelming urge to run—anywhere—and hide. The security of *La Belle Illusion* felt far away, as did England. In mere moments Drake would be gone as well, and she would be alone with her father's coldness and disapproval. This was the part of the journey she had refused to think about. But it could be avoided no longer.

She turned to Drake. "I know you are eager to return to your ship and prepare for your journey back to England." She paused. "I am not sure how to express my gratitude for everything you've done for me."

"Everything?" He cupped her chin tenderly and was rewarded with a faint stain of color on her cheeks. "Save your good-byes, princess," he continued. "You will continue to be my responsibility until I place you safely in your father's hands." He didn't add that seeing her free spirit so tightly reined both pained and angered him. There was not a chance that he would allow her to face Geoffrey Cassel alone. The reasons did not matter; he would be there for her.

Alex smiled, seeing the reasons very clearly. "Thank you, Drake."

"Don't thank me until we've spoken to your father," he warned. "I do not anticipate a warm welcome."

She looked startled. "You know my father?"

"We've met." He gave her a mocking smile. "Why the surprise, princess? I do make frequent trips to Upper Canada. It is only natural that I should know its governor. Or did you think I mingled only with commoners?"

"No," came the rebellious reply. "I am only surprised that you hadn't mentioned it before."

Drake shrugged. "The subject never came up." He nudged her forward. "Come, my lady. It is time to pay the piper."

She gave him a scathing look, a direct contrast to the way she clung to his hand as they walked through the formidable gates that protected the governor's mansion.

A pinch-faced butler answered their summons, then calmly advised them to wait in the library while he informed Lord Sudsbury of their arrival.

Drake leaned against the heavy oak bookcases and watched Alex pace back and forth. He was more than a little curious to see how she would react when she confronted her father, who possessed about as much warmth as a Greenland iceberg. Yet, surely with his daughter . . .

Drake had no time to finish his thought. The library door was flung open so forcefully that vibrations of the impact resounded throughout the room.

The man who strode in was of average height and lean build. His hair was several shades darker than Alex's, his eyes the same unusual hue as his daughter's, but while Alex's eyes were warm with sunlight, bright with spirit, Geoffrey's were wintry cold, devoid of tenderness. And at the moment there were thunderclouds in their slate gray depths.

"When your mother's message arrived by England's fastest military vessel, I assumed it was an hysterical reaction on her part," he fumed, walking toward her with slow, menacing steps. "I *hoped* it was all a mistake. But I should have known better, shouldn't I, Alexandria? After eighteen years of blatant disobedience I should have expected no better from you!"

Alex flinched. "Father, this has nothing to do with disobedience. I begged you to bring me to York with you; you know I did. But you and Mother refused, over and over."

"Yet you came anyway. If that is not disobedience, what would you call it?" he roared.

Drake was amazed. He had expected to see annoyance, possibly anger, but not this callous chastisement prior even to listening to the facts surrounding Alex's behavior.

Such treatment, however, was not unfamiliar to Alex. She was well aware that in her father's eyes she was one colossal disappointment. But it didn't matter. Ultimately she would make her way without his support. She always had.

"I wanted to begin a new life, Father," she answered, straightening her spine and meeting his livid gaze. "And since you would not assist me, I found my own way of getting to Canada."

"You are insolent, impulsive, and headstrong, but you are also resourceful, Alexandria. 'Tis a pity you were not born a man. Then—"

"*Then* you would have the son you always wanted and Mother never provided," she concluded in a weary voice. "No, I am not a man, Father. But I *am* resourceful, as you pointed out. Captain Barrett was kind enough to provide me with passage"—she gestured toward Drake, who brazenly stared at Geoffrey, waiting for his reaction—"and I was able to achieve my goal without mishap. I am sorry my appearance here displeases you."

Geoffrey's startled eyes flew to Drake, seeing him for the first time. His shock escalated into fury. Then storm gray fused with ice green.

"Lord Sudsbury," Drake acknowledged Geoffrey's presence with stiff formality.

"Barrett, what sort of nonsense is my daughter spouting?"

Drake inclined his head slightly. "Alexandria is making herself quite clear."

Alex winced at her father's murderous expression. "Father," she hastily intervened, "please don't be rude. The men aboard *La Belle Illusion* were extremely kind and respectful, as was Captain Barrett."

Geoffrey's jaw was clenched so tightly that Alex feared it might snap. "So, kind and respectful *Captain* Barrett accompanied you to York, did he?"

Alex looked stunned by her father's scathing tone. Drake did not.

"Yes, father, he did."

"How gallant of him! And just what sort of payment did you offer him?"

"I thought I would leave that up to you," she replied, totally oblivious to the meaning of his words.

Drake's eyes were now blazing with a rage that equaled Geoffrey's. "No payment will be necessary, Lord Sudsbury."

"I see. Does that mean my daughter has already settled her debt?"

Alex felt totally bewildered. Seemingly, Drake was offended by her father's offer of money, and her father was enraged because he thought Drake was an accomplice in Alex's plan to escape. She frowned.

"Father, Drake had no idea that I was aboard his ship until after we had left London. I offered to pay my way, but he refused."

" 'Drake', is it?" Geoffrey paid no attention to the remainder of Alex's statement, but latched on to the casual use of Drake's given name. "Apparently it was a most interesting voyage."

"Father—" Alex began.

"Enough! I have heard quite enough!" Geoffrey exploded. "Now that you are here, daughter, you will have to face the consequences of your foolhardy actions."

Drake heard the implicit threat immediately. Alex heard only that her arrival had been accepted at last, and that the worst of her ordeal was over. She brightened instantly.

"Yes, of course, Father."

Geoffrey's smoldering gaze swept over Alex, then dropped to the floor beside her. "Where are your trunks?"

"I have none, Father," Alex declared cheerfully. "I came only with what I am wearing now."

Lord Sudsbury swallowed whatever he wanted to say, regaining his control with difficulty. "I see. Then we will arrange to have suitable clothing provided for you at once. In the interim one of the servants will show you to your room."

She beamed. "Oh, that would be wonderful, Father! I do want to rest, but only for a short while. There is so much I want to see, so much—"

"Alexandria, I have dismissed you," he cut off her enthusiastic discourse.

Alex flushed. "Yes, Father." Head held high, she crossed the room, pausing by the bookcase where Drake still stood. "Drake, I just want to thank—"

He shook his head, halting her words. "Do what your father says, princess," he told her in a quiet voice meant for her ears alone. "I will not be departing from York for several days. The supplies must be loaded and the men given a chance to rest before our return voyage. I will not leave without saying good-bye. However"—he raised his voice back to a normal tone—"I believe your father would like to speak to me alone right now." Over Alex's head, he calmly met Geoffrey's challenging stare.

"Indeed I would."

Alex looked uneasily from the hard, angry lines of Drake's handsome face to the restrained fury in her father's expression.

"It's all right, Alexandria," Drake told her in a low, soothing voice. "Go upstairs and rest."

With a resigned sigh, Alex left the room.

Geoffrey waited until the sound of her echoing footsteps had disappeared in the distance. Then he spoke.

"Suppose we dispense with the small talk, *Lord* Cairnham," he suggested in a scathing voice.

"All right," Drake agreed, steeling himself for an ugly confrontation.

"As I see it," Geoffrey said through clenched teeth, "we have two choices. Either I call you out and defend my daughter's honor . . ."

"Or?"

"Or before you leave for England Alexandria will become your wife."

A deadly silence filled the room. Moments passed.

At last Drake spoke. "Your ultimatum is absurd."

"You have compromised my daughter," was the terse reply.

Drake controlled his temper with a great effort. "Your daughter is untouched."

"Knowing your reputation, I sincerely doubt that."

"Knowing your daughter, you should not."

Geoffrey gave a harsh laugh. "My daughter is headstrong and opinionated and would dare anything to defy me."

Drake looked startled. "She wants only to please you."

"By stowing away aboard a merchant ship that is captained by a notoriously irreverent nobleman with the morals of a snake?"

Instead of being insulted, Drake looked amused by Geoffrey's accurate assessment of his character. "Alexandria has no idea of who I am."

"I surmised as much." Geoffrey studied Drake for a moment, then walked over to a table that held several crystal decanters and poured himself a healthy portion of brandy. He took a deep swallow before he spoke again. "Frankly I have no interest in knowing why you kept your true identity from Alexandria. The fact remains that you have spent numerous nights at sea with my unchaperoned daughter. Today is the twelfth of June. You left England on the . . ."

"Thirtieth of March," Drake supplied helpfully.

"Then you were alone with Alexandria for over two months. During which time—"

"Nothing happened." Drake had had enough. He faced Geoffrey directly, feeling as much disgust as he did anger. "I simply delivered your daughter to York. She was assigned her own quarters, and everything was quite proper. The subject of payment is absurd, since you and I both know that I have more money than I need or want. So, now that we've both had our say"—he turned and opened the library door—"I will take my leave."

"I will ruin your family name."

The cold, calmly spoken words halted Drake in his tracks. "What?" He turned, incredulous, toward Geoffrey, who was dispassionately sipping his brandy.

"I said I will ruin your family name," Geoffrey reiterated, slowly lowering his glass to the table. "Surely even a rebel like you must have some regard for honor?" Seeing the shocked expression on Drake's face, he nodded. "I can see that you do. Good, honor is a fine quality in a husband."

"Why would you want to do this?" Drake asked, his tone deceptively quiet. The anger he felt toward this overbearing man was extreme. It was true that Drake was irreverent about his future title and position, but he felt a great responsibility toward his family . . . or at least most of its members. Images of Samantha flashed through his head. She was young, but not too young to be affected by a scandal. And his father, though ailing, would be destroyed by a tarnishing of the family name. It was ironic, after all the decadent behavior in the family, that an act of total innocence had the potential to ruin the Barretts. But such were the rules of the *ton*—absurd, yet consistent.

Another, more surprising, realization overshadowed his train of thought, and that was that the idea of marriage to Alexandria neither repulsed nor upset him. She was so intelligent and spirited that he would never be bored by her. She was genuine in her likes and dislikes, never resorting to trickery to achieve her ends. She was as close to trustworthy as any woman could ever be.

And he wanted her.

The thought of finally possessing the beautiful body that haunted his dreams and fired his loins was quite an enticement to marriage. As for his inexplicable feelings of tenderness . . . those, he would simply control.

The comical thing was that Alexandria wouldn't want him. That thought almost made him laugh out loud. After being sought after by more females than he could count, for every type of liaison imaginable, he had met the one woman who would want neither his title nor his money. Oh, she wanted him sexually. That he knew, just as he knew that he could make her moan with passion, feel things she had never dreamed possible. The problem was that the one she wanted was a ship's captain. A simple man and a simple life.

He could give her neither.

Geoffrey was speaking, and Drake forced his mind back to the situation at hand.

"I am doing this, Lord Cairnham, to ensure a secure future for my only child. I take it from your silence that the idea of marriage to Alexandria does not offend your sensibilities?"

Drake walked back into the room, slamming the door behind him. "That is not the issue here," he shot back. "The issue is that your daughter has no desire whatsoever to be my wife."

"She should have considered that before she boarded your ship."

"So now she must pay for her folly by being forced to marry a man she hardly knows?" Drake was incredulous.

"Arranged marriages are hardly unusual in our circle, now, are they?"

"This is not arranged; it is forced."

"So be it." Geoffrey shrugged. "The fact remains that if word of Alexandria's escapade should become known back in England, she will no longer be considered a suitable wife for any of the eligible men I had in mind for her to meet during the Season. And even if the specifics are not uncovered by the gossips who populate the *ton*, my daughter disappeared at the height of her first London Season. Do you believe for one moment that this has gone unnoticed? My poor wife must have had quite a time explaining the situation without damaging our reputation. The only way for us to save face is for Alexandria to return to England a married woman." He smiled, refilling his glass. "And the future Duchess of Allonshire as well. Ample compensation for the damage that has been done, I should say."

Despite Drake's anger, he could not challenge the merit of Geoffrey's logic. Alexandria was, in many ways, ruined. Drake had not ruined her—she had, in fact, ruined herself—but apparently it was up to him to restore her respectability.

An interesting twist of fate.

"Her reaction will not be pleasant," he warned Geoffrey.

"Perhaps not. Ultimately, however, she will do as I tell her." Geoffrey poured a second glass of brandy and offered it to Drake. "I will not inform her of your real identity, Captain Barrett. *That* delightful task I will leave for you."

Drake accepted the glass, thinking of Alex's reaction to the news. Fireworks would ensue, a manifestation of her passionate nature.

He could hardly wait to take her to bed.

Geoffrey raised his glass. "To the future Duke and Duchess of Allonshire."

Drake raised his glass as well. "To Alexandria," he replied. "May she be up to the challenges that lie ahead."

Geoffrey studied Drake thoughtfully. "I believe, Lord Cairnham, that my untamable daughter has finally met her match."

A slow smile curved Drake's mouth. "Perhaps, Lord Sudsbury, we both have."

Chapter 12

Bright sunlight played insistently upon Alex's closed eyelids, demanding that she open them and greet the day. Gloriously aware of the absence of motion all around her, Alex resisted the relinquishing of sleep and snuggled back down into the warm blankets. Vaguely she wondered why *La Belle Illusion* was so still and why her berth suddenly seemed so luxurious. It was almost as if she were someplace else.

Her eyes flew open as memory reasserted itself. The dark, sparsely furnished room in which she found herself was her new home. She was in York.

After throwing back the covers impatiently, Alex scrambled out of bed. Apparently she had been more fatigued than she had imagined herself to be. It was obvious from the position of the sun, high in the sky, that it was almost noon.

Yesterday had been a most disconcerting day. She had been ushered into her chambers by a flustered servant and left there to rest. But Alex's excitement had not permitted sleep to come. After several unsuccessful attempts to drift off, she had given up and gone in search of her father. One glance had told her that the library was empty. That meant that whatever had transpired between her father and Drake had been settled. She only hoped that Drake had at last accepted her father's generous offer of compensation.

Upon questioning some of the servants she had discovered that her father had gone off to Fort York for an important meeting and was not expected back until late in the day. She had contented herself with exploring the mansion. Though it was modest compared to Sudsbury, Alex recognized that it was considered to be ever so grand a home in Upper Canada. She longed to return to the waterfront, to sail on Lake Ontario. But she didn't dare venture outside without her father's permission; she had no desire to further incite his wrath. And so she had waited, taking her evening meal alone and finally retiring to her room, restless and lonely.

But today was another day, she thought cheerfully, as she brushed her thick hair until it shone. She had no patience or desire to ring for a servant to arrange her hair or to help her don the lovely gown that had been hastily sewn and brought to her room the previous day. The months at sea had taught her to tend to her own needs. And really, if one thought about it, it was quite absurd for one perfectly able adult to be dressed by another.

She stood and surveyed her appearance in the gilt-framed oval mirror that stood in the corner of the room. The lemon yellow gown made her look soft and feminine. Well, that should please her father—perhaps enough to make him agree to provide a small skiff for her use? With a conspiratorial grin at her reflection, she left the room and headed down the winding staircase. Victory was but a moment away.

Lord Sudsbury looked up from his desk at the sound of Alex's knock.

"Come in, Alexandria."

She entered the room with a dazzling smile. "Good morning, Father. I hope I am not interrupting?"

Geoffrey Cassel shook his head, put down his work, and walked around the desk. "No, I am glad you've come. I need to speak with you. Unfortunately I was called away yesterday before I could do so. But that couldn't be helped."

Alex was itching to know if the meeting had anything to do with the message to Brock or with Drake's suspicions of war. But if there was anything Lord Sudsbury disliked more than Alex's independence it was her curiosity about things that "did not concern a woman"—of which politics was definitely one—so Alex held her tongue.

"I have resolved things with Lo . . . Captain Barrett," he announced.

Alex brightened. "I'm glad, Father. He is a trifle arrogant, but he really is a very good man." One whom I shall find hard to forget, she added to herself.

"I'm glad you feel that way, daughter."

"Oh, I do!" Alex praised. "He is a superb leader, somewhat stubborn and unyielding, but nonetheless respected by all those beneath him."

"Really."

"Yes." She nodded, warming to her subject. "He lends his strength to those who need it, is extremely kind and loyal to those who have earned the same from him, and is generous to those who are worthy of his generosity."

"He sounds like a most exemplary man."

Tenderness constricted Alex's throat. "He is."

"Then how fortunate you are."

"I?" She was puzzled. "Why am I fortunate?"

Geoffrey leaned back against his desk and smiled. "Because in precisely one fortnight you will become Captain Barrett's wife."

"His *what?*" Alex gasped.

"His wife." Lord Sudsbury regarded his stunned daughter impassively. "Oh, come now, Alexandria. Surely you are not that shocked by the consequence of your adventure."

"I certainly am." Twin spots of color burned in her cheeks, as fury and disbelief threatened to envelope her. "Father, I cannot . . . *will* not . . . marry Drake Barrett!"

"Oh, I assure you, my dear, you can and you will."

"But why? *Why?* I've done nothing to be ashamed of, nothing that could damage my reputation to such a degree

that it would drive you to take such a drastic measure."
There was pain in her broken question, pain and hurt.

Geoffrey was unmoved. "This measure is hardly drastic, Alexandria. Drastic is an impetuous young woman stealing away aboard a ship without the permission of her parents or the presence of a proper chaperon and expecting there to be no ramifications of her actions. *That* is drastic."

"And so I am to be punished by being married off to the first available man?"

"Not to just any man, Alexandria, to the man who has compromised you."

"But we've done nothing!"

Geoffrey shrugged. "That may or may not be so. Unfortunately, in the eyes of the world it matters not whether you are innocent or guilty. The fact that you were with Captain Barrett on his ship for all these weeks is damning enough. To anyone of significance you are indeed a fallen woman."

"And who is 'anyone of significance,' Father?" Alex's anger was back. "Your precious *ton?* Those immoral, judgmental, tongue-wagging gossips who have nothing better to do with their time than to discuss the lives of others and determine their acceptability or lack thereof even as they themselves are being similarly dissected by other upstanding members of our class?"

"Enough of your impudence, daughter!" Lord Sudsbury would be pushed just so far. "Despite your low opinion of our peers, they are in a position to destroy you and, ultimately, me. So cease your tirade at once! On the twenty-seventh of June in this very house you will take the vows that bind you to Drake Barrett for good or for ill!"

Both father and daughter had voiced their anger loud enough for anyone on the first floor of the manor to hear. Fortunately the argument was not overheard by the servants, as most of them were occupied elsewhere in the spacious home. Unfortunately, it *was* overheard by the dark-haired man who stood in the hallway just outside Geoffrey's study.

Drake had risen early after a fitful sleep and headed to the governor's home to see Alexandria. He had hoped to soften the blow and ease what he knew would be her furious, shocked reaction to the news of their betrothal. When he arrived, the same unfriendly butler informed him that Lord Sudsbury and Lady Alexandria were "unavailable" and that Drake would have to wait. Alone in the hallway, Drake heard Alex's angry voice, and frankly curious, he remained to listen.

Alex's mind was working frantically. She realized that there might be no way out, that she was trapped. Her father was unyielding in his decision, unaffected by her pleas or her anger. And all because the damned *beau monde* would blanch over her unseemly conduct. Well, what about their inevitable reaction when they learned that Lord Sudsbury's only daughter was married to a lowly sea captain?

Alex grasped wildly at her last hope.

"If the opinion of the *ton* is of such importance, then surely it is necessary for me to make what they consider a suitable match, Father. After all, it wouldn't do for the only daughter of the Earl of Sudsbury to marry just anybody, now, would it?" Her tone was challenging, her gaze triumphant.

For some reason Geoffrey seemed to find her statement amusing.

"That is quite true, daughter."

Alex played her trump card. "Then how can you possibly allow me to marry a man who is so far beneath us? A man who can offer me no family name, no great wealth, nothing but poverty and a transient life at sea? Surely a slightly soiled reputation is far better than a lifetime with such a man, is it not, Father?"

For one moment Geoffrey's eyes glittered with some emotion that Alex could not assess. Then he merely met her stare with his own. "The situation is of your own creation, daughter. And now you must pay the price of your indiscretion. I suggest you begin to make your wedding plans. I will have a dressmaker come to your room to fit you for a suitable gown. A fortnight from this day you will cease to be my responsibility and become your husband's." He paused. "I suggest that you attempt to curb your reckless impulsiveness once you are wed. Drake Barrett does not seem to be the sort of man who would tolerate such nonsense from his wife."

Drake Barrett. The reality of the situation struck her all at once: she was going to be married to Drake Barrett. The man who had unraveled all of her senses, left them raw and unsettled; the man who aroused her, thrilled her, infuriated her, patronized her, and reached deep inside her soul—that same man was going to be her husband.

She suddenly felt giddy.

"How did Captain Barrett take this unexpected piece of news?" she asked carefully.

"Why not ask him yourself, princess?" The familiar, resonant voice came from the doorway behind her, and Alex spun around in surprise. Drake's face was a mask of nonemotion, but Alex recognized the furious gleam in his eyes. Her heart sank. He was livid.

Geoffrey greeted Drake casually. "Well, good morning, Captain Barrett. Please join us. We were just discussing the plans for your wedding."

"So I heard." He moved to where Alex was standing, but did not meet her questioning eyes. His features were carved in granite, his lips tightly set, and the muscle that worked in his jaw bespoke his anger. "Let us make the arrangements and be done with it." It was an order, coldly issued.

Alex wanted to sink through the floor and die. Not only was she being discarded by her father, she was being given to a man who resented the idea of marriage more than she did. Of course, there *was* one thing he definitely would *not* resent having—her body. Well, damn it, if he expected her to meekly submit to his demands without receiving any tenderness in return, he had a big surprise in store for him. Drake Barrett would whistle before she gave herself to him, marriage or not.

Drake noted Alex's rigid stance and wondered if she was reacting to the idea of becoming his wife or to his cold treatment. He couldn't forget the scathing words he had just overheard her speak of what marriage to him would mean, or could he overlook the pain that her comments had caused him. And lashing out was the only way he could master the inexplicable feelings she aroused in him, feelings that made him weak.

The pull between them was as strong as ever, regardless of the anger that now hung in the air. The decision had been made. He would marry her. He would claim her fiery spirit and her delectable body. And in return, despite her anticipated dismay, he would give her his name, his wealth, and someday his title.

But the one thing he would never give her was his heart. That, if it existed, belonged only to him.

The wharf was dark and deserted when Alex arrived. For a moment she stared longingly out over the crystal-clear waters of Lake Ontario, the waters that she had dreamed of sailing. Now, instead of the freedom she sought, she was moving from a life of shallow flirtations and empty experiences to a lifelong commitment with a man who cared nothing for her and resented both her affluence and her sex. Life had become very complicated, and she felt unable to cope with its complexities.

Sitting down on the lovely stretch of beach near the wharf, Alex tucked her gown beneath her, buried her face in her hands, and closed her eyes. She had barely heard the details of the wedding that were discussed between her father and Drake. She'd been numb inside, needing only solace for her thoughts. Now her numbness gave way to the pain of rejection. Drake might owe her nothing, but how could her own father, a man who was supposed to love her, cast her aside so cruelly?

Despair washed over her as she huddled alone on the sand. She knew that she shouldn't be out by herself at night, but she, quite frankly, didn't care. What more could her father do to her that he had not already done? She swallowed, fighting back the tears. She felt so alone.

"Are you all right, my lady?" The dear familiar voice caressed her senses like a warm blanket.

"Smitty!" Alex sat upright, greeting the older man whose

face was nearly hidden in the shadows of night. At her eager smile he sat down beside her.

"I thought I saw you running about on the beach," he admonished gently, tender concern underlying his words. "Don't you know that it is not safe for you to be here alone?"

"I was hoping to be brutally murdered and left as food for the gulls."

He chuckled. "Now, now. It isn't as bad as all that, my lady."

Alex responded with a dejected look and a deep sigh.

"You know, my lady, ofttimes what appears to be a tragedy turns out to be a blessing. Many of life's most sacred offerings are not recognized as such."

"You know."

He nodded. "Yes, Captain Barrett told me."

"And what sort of humor is Captain Barrett in?"

Smitty grinned. "He is as cantankerous as an injured bear."

"He doesn't want to marry me."

Smitty shook his head. "Correction. He doesn't want to *want* to marry you. Therein lies the problem."

Alex looked skeptical. "Do you really believe he cares for me?"

"Without a doubt, my lady," was the firm reply. "Just as you care for him."

Alex did not argue the point. "It frightens me, Smitty. Marriage is a serious lifetime commitment, a commitment to one person."

"Not everyone views it as such." Smitty watched her reaction carefully and was rewarded with her almost violent shake of the head.

"To me marriage means lifelong respect, consideration, and caring."

"And fidelity?"

Alex nodded. "And fidelity."

Smitty stared out to sea. "There are those who would disagree, those who would agree, and those who would like to agree but are afraid to for fear of being hurt. The people who fall into this last category need our compassion and our understanding. They do not need to be taught to love, only to believe. For with belief comes trust. And once they trust, they will become capable of a love so profound that it will transform their lives and fill their souls with joy."

"Why do I feel that we are no longer talking in generalizations?" Alex asked.

Smitty merely stood, drawing her to her feet beside him. "Trust in your instincts, my lady. They will not fail you."

Alex remained silent for a moment, digesting his words. Then she said, "Will you come to the wedding?"

"I wouldn't miss it."

"Then at least I will feel as if my family is there," she replied softly, looking up into his kind face. Perhaps Smitty was right. Perhaps Drake really did care. Perhaps . . .

"Smitty! Where the hell are you?" Drake's drunken shout from *La Belle Illusion* shattered the silence around them. "We have a lot to do—load the timber, drink ourselves into oblivion. After all, it's not every day a man gets married, you know." A pause, during which Alex could picture him gulping down another drink. "Well, Smitty, what do you say?" the uneven raving continued. "Can you just picture my family's reaction when I arrive home with *Lady* Alexandria Cassel as my wife? *That* should certainly cause an uproar, now shouldn't it?"

Smitty winced, reaching a protective hand out to Alex. But she shrugged it away, stepping back, her chin held high.

"So much for your theory on Captain Barrett's loving nature, Smitty," she said in a shaky voice. "Well, you can give him a message from me. He may put a ring on my finger, but I will never, *never* go back to England with him as his wife. I'll see him in hell first!" With that, she lifted her skirts and ran from the beach.

Smitty stared after her, his expression sad. "He is already in hell, my lady," he murmured to himself. "Now it is up to you to lead him out."

Chapter 13

Dawn arrived. Rain exploded from the heavens in hard, battering pelts, that drenched the streets of York with merciless intensity. Then, suddenly, just after ten o'clock, the storm ceased, making way for a soft June breeze, trilling birds, and a warm afterglow of sunshine. Sparkling rain droplets shimmered on the trees, and a spectacularly vivid, multihued rainbow arched gracefully in the deepening blue sky.

It was Alex's wedding day.

Her moods were as changeable as the weather. One moment she was filled with impotent anger, trapped like a bird in a cage. The next moment she was overcome with tingly anticipation, wondering what it would be like to be Drake's wife. Most of all, she was terrified, for despite her bravado with Smitty, Alex was well aware of a husband's rights. What if Drake forced her to return to England as his wife and to perform *all* her duties as Mrs. Drake Barrett?

She was more terrified that he would leave her behind.

Since a fortnight ago in her father's study, Alex had barely seen Drake. Her days were filled with dress fittings, her nights with doubts and worries. And now that the day was here, apprehension and confusion seemed to converge, inundating her with a fear that was suffocating.

Wrapping her robe more tightly around her, she went to the bedchamber window and pressed her face to the glass, trying to calm her frazzled nerves. Before she could make any progress, there was a firm knock on her bedchamber door.

She jumped. "Come in."

Geoffrey Cassel opened the door and walked in, immaculately dressed and dreadfully ill at ease. His tone, however, was customarily brusque.

"I see you are awake, Alexandria."

"I haven't slept," was the pointed response.

He ignored the meaning behind her words and crossed the room to the small settee beside the window where Alex stood. "Sit down, Alexandria." It was an order. "Today you are to be married, and it is time for us to talk."

Alex suspected that his talk would not be the soothing, caring chat she needed but rather another issuance of rules and expectations for her to live up to. So be it. She sat and waited.

Satisfied with her action, Geoffrey continued. "If your mother were here right now she would be having this talk with you. Since you have made that an impossibility"—he scowled briefly, letting Alex see his disapproval once more—"the task has fallen to me. I want to assure myself that you are prepared for your duties and obligations as a wife."

Alex gave him an incredulous look. She hadn't the faintest notion why her father was so concerned. After all, the numerous rules that applied to being the most gracious of hostesses, the most versatile of conversationalists, the very paragon of London society, would hardly be put to the test in a cramped cabin of a merchant ship. Fascinated, she waited for him to continue.

"I recognize only too clearly that the words 'obey' and 'submit to' are not as yet in your vocabulary. You have precisely two hours to change that. Defiance and rebelliousness are not desirable traits in a wife." He took a deep breath. "Especially to a man like Drake Barrett, who is used to others doing his bidding. He will expect certain things of you as his wife, some of which may seem rather . . . distasteful." He cleared his throat, unable to meet her wide-eyed stare. "Do you understand what I am telling you?"

"You're telling me that I must relinquish every independent thought and opinion that I possess," she summed up.

Geoffrey did not smile. "Not only your thoughts. You must relinquish everything, Alexandria. *Now* do I make myself clear?"

Alex was torn between laughter and tears. "Are we discussing my wedding night now, Father?" she asked boldly.

He was taken aback by her forthright question. At last he nodded. "I presume you know what to expect?"

She had a very good idea, but there were so many questions she wanted answered, so much reassurance that she needed. Looking at her father's granite-set face, she knew that none of it would be forthcoming. "Yes, Father, I have been told what to expect."

His relief was evident. "Good. Bear in mind that your submission is necessary in order to produce an heir for your husband."

An heir. The one thing that her poor mother had never been able to provide Geoffrey, despite her repeated "submissions." Well, in this case, it didn't matter. There was no title or land to pass on. The only thing Drake's child would inherit was *La Belle Illusion*. Hardly a sizable fortune worth losing sleep over.

Submission. Alex allowed herself a brief reflection on her limited physical intimacies with Drake. The memories were vivid and bone-melting. Instinct told her that Drake would be bored to tears with the sort of wife Geoffrey was describing—the sort of wife she could never be. She understood enough about the chemistry that existed between herself and her husband-to-be to recognize that she could either violently resist him or go up in smoke with him. But submit to him? Never.

She stood up. "I understand what you've told me, Father. Now I need to bathe and dress. I wouldn't want to anger my *betrothed* by being late on my wedding day."

Geoffrey ignored her sarcasm. "Of course not. I will see you downstairs in two hours."

Alex closed the door behind him, feeling more alone than ever. It suddenly occurred to her that she wasn't sure exactly what Drake's plans were after the wedding. Since, during their few terse exchanges over the last few days, he had made no mention of the need for her to pack or ready herself in any way, it was possible that he meant to leave her behind here in York when he returned to England.

Well, that suited her just fine, the independent streak in her cried out. To hell with being a dutiful wife. She would remain in York, unavailable to men and therefore unencumbered by the demands society made on unmarried women. She would be free to sail her skiff, to make her own rules, to live her own life.

To be alone.

An undefinable ache filled her heart at the finality of the thought. Always she had dreamed, planned, anticipated the very life that now awaited her. So why did she feel so empty as the time to realize her dream drew near?

She pressed her fingers to her closed eyelids, sat down at the edge of her bed. Today, just after noon, in a quiet ceremony at the governor's mansion, she would become Drake's wife.

What was he thinking now? Was he angry, resentful? Did he loathe her for what had been forced upon him? Or was he, like her, confused and uncertain, wondering what fate had in store for them?

A soft knock at the door of her bedchamber announced the arrival of Alex's bath. In a few short hours she would have her answers.

Drake stood unmoving as Smitty tied the silk cravat about his neck. The stark whiteness of the material richly complemented the dark elegance of Drake's formal waistcoat and pantaloons and perfectly matched the crisp frilled shirt.

Once through, Smitty stepped back to admire his handiwork.

"Flawless, if I must say so myself, Captain," he declared, with a flourish.

Drake gave him a searching look. "The attire or the bridegroom, Smitty?"

"Both." Smitty was not put off by his captain's foul mood, for he knew what caused it, and it was time that the problem was addressed. Pausing only to firmly close the cabin door, he turned back to Drake's scowl.

"Why do I get the distinct feeling that a lecture is about to be delivered, Smitty?"

Smitty shook his head. "No lecture, my lord. Just a talk between old friends."

"I'm not sure I want to hear what you have to say."

Smitty smiled. "You are angry that today is your wedding day."

Drake gave a disgusted snort. "A brilliant deduction, my friend. You need not have closed the door for such a grand proclamation."

"Did you expect never to marry?"

"Of course I expected to marry. Someday."

"So you are angry that you are being forced to marry now, against your will?"

"I am not being forced to do anything," Drake shot back.

"Ah, that's right. You are doing this for your family."

"Yes, that's right." Drake gave Smitty a suspicious look, wondering where all this was leading.

"Then you should be proud—unless, of course, Lady Alexandria possesses some horrid quirk that I know nothing about and that would make her an unsuitable wife?" He waited.

"You know damn well that there is nothing unsuitable about Alexandria."

Smitty nodded. "So you are marrying a perfectly acceptable young woman for only the most admirable reasons and of your own free will." He paused, considering. "Actually there is no earthly reason for your foul humor, is there?" When Drake did not answer, he continued. "Unless you have some strong feelings for your wife-to-be. Now, based on your experience and your opinion of women, *that* would be a problem. To give this woman your name is most magnanimous of you, but to give her your heart . . . that would be an entirely different matter."

"Shut up, Smitty." Drake had heard enough.

Smitty regarded Drake soberly. His reaction had been as expected—angry, defensive, stubborn.

Afraid.

"Your heart may be hardened, but your instincts tell you that she is different," he observed wisely.

Drake stiffened. "She's a woman."

"She cares a great deal for you."

"Some of the time," Drake conceded, thinking of the way Alex responded in his arms.

"Be gentle with her, my lord," Smitty told him softly. "She does not understand the bitterness that drives you to her and then away."

Drake closed his eyes for a moment, and Smitty saw the struggle that raged inside him. "I will try not to hurt her, Smitty. It was never my intent."

"I know, my lord. I, better than anyone, know the kind of man you are."

Drake gave him a tortured look. "And what kind of man is that, Smitty?"

Smitty smiled. "I will let the future answer that question for you, Captain." He moved toward the door, gesturing for Drake to follow. "Come. It is late. We wouldn't want to delay your wedding, now, would we?"

Drake looked around the cabin, a new reality causing anticipation to replace his pain, heightening his senses. Tonight he would bring Alexandria here as his wife.

He glanced at the bed, imagining the long hours he would spend awakening her to her passion before he finally made her his wife in every way. Tonight, at long last, Lady Alexandria Cassel would be his.

No, he wouldn't want to delay the wedding. Or the wedding night.

Lord Sudsbury had done his work well. The special license had been obtained, the minister was already present to conduct the brief ceremony, and a small afternoon buffet awaited the wedding participants. The blue salon had been transformed, its elegant yet dignified furnishings enhanced with sprays of pastel flowers, the fire that burned in the wide stone fireplace stoked just high enough to suffuse the room in low, filtered light.

126

Geoffrey surveyed the room with a self-satisfied smile. Because of her reckless and impulsive nature, Alexandria had stumbled unknowingly into the most enviable match of the Season. She would wed one of the wealthiest, most sought-after men of the *ton*, a man whose fortune and family name were among the most prestigious in all of England.

A notorious rake whose reputation with women should have horrified his future bride's father.

It did not. As far as Geoffrey was concerned, Drake's lack of reverence for women was a small price to pay for restoring Alexandria's reputation and, in fact, raising her to the very pinnacle of society. No father could have asked for more.

A noise from the doorway made Geoffrey glance up. Drake stood with Smitty just inside the room. The bridegroom's splendidly tailored evening clothes outlined his powerful body; the expression on his handsome face was unreadable.

"Lord Cairnham," Geoffrey acknowledged with a nod.

Drake strode into the room, giving a cursory glance at his surroundings.

"Lord Sudsbury," he returned. "I am ready to begin. Smitty will act as my groomsman." He gestured toward the older man. "Also, I would ask that you cease to refer to me as Lord Cairnham. Alexandria will soon be my wife, and I shall decide upon the proper time to inform her of my identity."

Geoffrey shrugged indifferently. "As you wish, *Captain* Barrett," he replied, then lowered his voice. "As I told you when you first arrived, I have no interest in the details of your relationship with my daughter. The other guests are unaware of your rank among the peerage, so your secret is safe. How you handle Alexandria in the future is your responsibility, not mine."

Drake gave him a dark look. "Yes, I know. You made your parental interest in Alexandria's life quite clear to me. And to her as well." He looked back over his shoulder, not waiting for an answer. The more he spoke to Geoffrey Cassel the more certain he was that this marriage was the right thing for Alexandria. Her father's lack of regard for her happiness angered Drake to an irrational level. All he wanted right now was to take Alex as far from here as possible. As soon as possible.

Drake turned back to the earl. "Is Alexandria ready to begin?" he asked impatiently.

Geoffrey nodded. "She should be downstairs at any moment now."

"I am here, Father."

Alex's soft voice came from the open doorway. Both Geoffrey and Drake turned at the sound. Only Smitty waited long enough to catch the unguarded look of raw emotion that registered in Drake's eyes, then disappeared at the first sight of his bride.

Alex had stubbornly refused to wear a traditional bridal gown of white and silver, insisting that it would be absurd to do so at such an unconventional wedding as this. Instead, she wore a simple high-waisted gown of delicate blush-colored silk, trimmed at the bodice and hem with white lace. Its long, full sleeves flowed to her wrists, where they were tied with pink silk ribbons. She wore a wreath of pale pink roses on the crown of her shining golden brown hair, which hung in soft curls down her back.

She was the most exquisite bride Drake had ever seen.

Along with awed admiration and aching desire, Drake felt profound pride in the heart-stoppingly beautiful young woman who was soon to be his wife. She walked into the room, her head held high, proud and composed, ready to accept her fate.

Their eyes met. Everything she was feeling was reflected in the clear gray eyes that regarded him from beneath the long fringe of her gold-tipped lashes—all her vulnerability, her hurt, and her fear. Drake felt a surge of protectiveness so strong that it left him shaken. And in that moment he made a decision: no matter what lay ahead for them, no matter how little of himself he could offer her, no one, including him, would ever hurt Alex again. He would make sure of it . . . as her husband.

Alex was so deeply aware of Drake that it made her

tremble. His strength, his very presence, made her feel weak and afraid, protected and whole. Standing by his side, hearing his deep baritone voice speaking his vows, gave her the courage to speak her own.

It felt like a dream, and she was the omniscient observer watching it unfold. She stared at her own hand, fascinated, as Drake slid a simple gold band on her fourth finger, sealing their union. She raised her gaze to his face, and he smiled, leaning down to brush a soft, chaste kiss across her lips.

"Hang on, princess," he murmured softly, for her ears alone. "The ordeal is almost over."

She wondered vaguely if he meant her ordeal or his own. Either way, she nodded, managing to give him a small smile.

The dreamlike feeling prevailed even after the ceremony ended. The midday buffet was a quiet affair, hardly the elaborate celebration that usually followed the joining of two noble families. It mattered not to Alex, who wouldn't have been able to force down a bite if her very life had depended on it.

"Are you all right, my lady?" Smitty's compassionate voice penetrated her mental haze.

"Yes, Smitty, I am fine." She fingered the folds of her gown thoughtfully, considering whether or not to broach the subject of Drake's plans for her.

"You are the most beautiful of brides," Smitty told her with a warm smile.

Alex returned his smile halfheartedly. "Thank you for being here. Whether it was only for Drake's sake or for my own as well, I am grateful to you for coming."

"I am very fond of you, my lady," was the instantaneous reply. "Your happiness and well-being are as much my concern as your husband's."

"My husband." Alex repeated the words, looking across the room at the man they designated. Her husband. Tall and commanding. Bitter and angry. Gentle and passionate.

As if he felt her gaze upon him, Drake looked up from his conversation with Lord Sudsbury and met Alex's eyes.

A slow, appreciative smile spread across his handsome face, and at that moment Alex felt like the most beautiful woman in the world. And the most unsure.

"I must be getting back to the ship," Smitty was saying to her. "There is much work to be done before we depart for England at week's end."

"At week's end?" Alex asked. "Is that when you plan to leave?"

Smitty looked surprised. "Hasn't Captain Barrett told you of his plans?"

His plans. Alex's heart sank.

"No, Smitty, he has not." Out of the corner of her eye Alex saw the butler hurry into the room and speak quietly and rapidly to her father. A moment later Geoffrey excused himself and disappeared from the room. Well, now was Alex's chance to discuss the future with her new husband.

Smitty was frowning. "I thought for certain . . ."

He never completed what he had been about to say, for Drake's appearance at their side interrupted the conversation.

"Is *La Belle Illusion* going to be ready to sail on schedule?" he asked Smitty.

Smitty nodded. "Of course, Captain. The timber is nearly all loaded; the men are settling down." He grinned.

Drake grinned back. "Good." For the first time he looked down at Alex. "Smitty, I would like a few minutes to speak with my wife."

"Certainly, Captain." Smitty looked from Drake to Alex, his eyes shining with love and pride. "I want to congratulate both of you again. May the future bring you only happiness."

Smitty was gone before Alex could say good-bye. Well, she would just have to find him before the ship sailed. She needed to make him understand just how important his friendship was to her.

"Princess?" For the first time the word sounded like an endearment and not a mockery. "Are you all right? You look as white as a sheet."

Alex swallowed. "Yes, Drake, I'm fine. I promise not to embarrass you by fainting."

He chuckled, glad to see that her spirit was still intact. "Let's take a walk. I need to talk to you about the plans I've made."

At last. The moment of truth.

Alex allowed him to take her arm and lead her onto the wide balcony overlooking the front gardens of the estate.

"I have to get back to England." Drake did not mince his words. "I've already been away too long. Because of the winds and the storm, we lost a great deal of time. I must take the timber home as soon as possible."

"I know." Alex's voice was devoid of emotion.

Drake stared down into her pale face, trying to assess her reaction. "I'm sorry that things cannot be the way you want them to be. If it were at all possible I would make it so."

I will not cry, Alex told herself, fighting back the tears of humiliation that threatened to erupt.

She lifted her small chin and met his gaze. "You don't have to apologize, Drake. I had no illusions about this marriage."

He looked puzzled. "What are you talking about?"

"About your plans to return to England at week's end."

"What the hell does that have to do with your expectations of our marriage?" he asked in an incredulous tone. "Did you think I could remain in Canada forever? You know I have a job to do, Alexandria."

Her hands made tight fists of control at her sides. "Yes, I know you do."

"Have I not given you enough time? Is that it?"

"You have *given* me your name and respectability," she shot back. "I suppose that is more than any woman should ask."

"Apparently you're not any woman."

"No, I suppose I'm not. So perhaps this is for the best. You can live your life, and I can live mine."

"That's going to be rather difficult in such cramped quarters," he told her in a cold voice.

"Half a world away is not far enough for you, Captain Barrett?" she demanded.

"Half a world . . ." Drake broke off as the truth of the situation struck him. "You were planning to stay here in York?" There was such anger and accusation in his voice that Alex flinched.

"Evidently we agree it would be for the best." She would hold on to her pride if it was the last thing she ever did.

"The best for whom?" he spat out. "Damn it, Alexandria, you are my wife. Like it or not, you belong to me now."

The joy accompanying the realization that Drake intended to take her with him was obliterated by his dictatorial words.

"I belong to no one," she returned, her eyes blazing with anger.

"Funny, I remember the vows you took saying otherwise." His pain and hurt manifested themselves in rage. "The fact is that you are now my possession. You relinquished your rights as an individual the moment you became Mrs. Drake Barrett." He lowered his head until she could see the glitter of emerald steel in his eyes, feel his breath on her face. "You have three days to ready yourself, princess. And then we leave for England—*both* of us." He paused. "And don't plan on using your nights for packing. I plan to keep you thoroughly occupied at night. *All* night. Understood?"

Color flooded Alex's face. "You coldhearted bastard, I wouldn't submit to your lust if . . ."

"Submit?" he growled. "Is that what you planned to do, princess? Submit to me? Well, I assure you, you *will* come to my bed, and it *will not* be submission you feel when you do."

Alex raised her hand and slapped him hard. The sound echoed in the quiet afternoon. For a moment they both stood, stunned at her action. Then she backed away, her expression a mixture of fear and fury.

"We will never know, will we?" she spat out. "For I have no intention of ever seeing you again."

He caught her arms and lifted her easily off the balcony floor, raising her face to his. "This conversation is far from over, princess," he said in a deadly whisper. "For once in your life you are not going to do exactly what you want to do—"

"Drake." Geoffrey's voice came from the open doors to the balcony. He was totally oblivious of the violent argument he had interrupted, his usually composed face flushed, his hands shaking. "I need to see you at once."

Slowly Drake lowered Alex to the balcony, taking in Lord Sudsbury's overwrought appearance. "What is it?"

"It is urgent. I must see you alone."

Drake nodded, then gave Alex a withering look. "Wait here for me."

It was an order. How she would have loved to disobey him, to show him how little his authority meant to her. But her curiosity as to the cause of her father's distress won out. She nodded. "I will wait."

Satisfied that she would do as she said, Drake went inside to speak with Geoffrey.

Alex paced back and forth on the balcony. It seemed forever until Drake returned. When he did, his expression was dark.

"Drake? What is it?" Instinctively she knew that the news was bad.

"Go and get your things, Alexandria. Our plans have changed. We sail for England at once."

Alex's eyes opened wide with disbelief. "Now? Today?"

"Yes. Immediately." He turned to go inside.

"Drake." Her voice stopped him. "Please. Tell me what has happened."

He turned back, knowing he could not lie to her, knowing he had no choice but to tell her.

"An invasion of Upper Canada is imminent," he said in a somber tone. "Word just reached us that on the eighteenth of June, America declared war on England."

Chapter 14

Alex was still shaking. If the first half of the day had been a dream, the remainder had been a nightmare.

Precisely three hours after Drake told her of the war's onset, *La Belle Illusion* had set sail for England. Alex's new husband had left the mansion immediately following his announcement to assist with the preparations. The crew's festivities had ceased at once, every man returning to the ship.

Alex had quickly assembled several of her new gowns, all of her undergarments, and a few sundry items from her dressing table. At the last moment she had decided to pack the delicate ivory silk nightgown that had been laid out for her wedding night. It was certainly a luxury, but having spent countless nights at sea clad in a man's shirt, she felt entirely justified in packing it.

Her father had barely said good-bye. Moments after Drake's departure he had left to see Major General Brock. "Be well and safe, Alexandria," he had told her as he awaited his carriage.

"And you, Father," she had replied softly, praying that the war would end quickly and with minimal bloodshed.

Then he was gone.

Alex and her luggage had been delivered to the docks just after two o'clock. She barely recognized the crew of Drake's brig, so intent were they on their jobs. Gone were the jovial men who had laughed and teased their way to Canada with her. Now the air about them crackled with tension; their taut muscles were strained and sweating as they silently prepared for the treacherous voyage home. But Alex had expected no less. England was again at war.

Thomas Greer had been squatting at the opening to the hold when Alex climbed aboard. Peering down into the square pit, he wiped sweat from his brow with a tanned forearm and stood.

"That was the last of it, Cochran," he called down. "Time to ready the sails."

Cochran's affirmative answer echoed onto the main deck, and for the first time in hours, Thomas stretched, ready to begin his next task. He started when he saw Alex.

"Miss Alex . . . I mean, my lady . . . Mrs. Barrett . . ." The poor boy was at a total loss.

In spite of her depleted emotional state Alex smiled. "It's good to see you, too, Thomas. And nothing has changed. Miss Alex will do fine."

He looked relieved. "I'm real glad yer back with us, ma'am." He scanned the deck, his mind already on the work ahead of him. "I 'ope you understand . . . there's a lot t' do and—"

Alex waved away his apology. "I'll be fine, Thomas. Do what you must."

"Would you like me t' carry yer bags t' your cabin?" he offered.

"That would be wonderful, thank you." She wondered briefly where Drake was and then decided against asking. The last thing he would be concerned about right now was his bride and her fears.

"The cap'n is determined t' leave port within the hour," Thomas informed her, as if reading her mind.

Alex frowned. It wasn't like Drake to panic. "Is time *that* precious?"

He looked grim. "There's no telling what'll happen once word gets out that the Americans 'ave declared war," he answered. "And frankly, Miss Alex, Cap'n Barrett is really worried about ye. He wants t' make sure he gets ye home t' England quick and safe."

"Oh." Alex wasn't quite sure what to say. A warm feeling melted some of her earlier anger. While she realized that Drake simply felt responsible for her, still . . . it made her feel a little more secure, a little less desolate. "Thank you for telling me, Thomas."

"Yes, ma'am." He glanced down at her luggage. "Is that all you brought with you?"

"That's all."

"I'll take it down t' the cap'n's . . . t' yer cabin right away," he corrected himself. "Then, I'll go tell Cap'n Barrett that you've arrived and are safe below." He scampered off like a rabbit.

From the time the merchant brig left York and began its journey through Lake Ontario toward the great Saint Lawrence until bedtime Alex did not see Drake. Knowing him as she did, she was certain that he had remained at the helm to assist his men. She understood. First and foremost came his ship and his crew.

At dinnertime Smitty brought her a tray of food and asked that she remain in her quarters in case of any danger. Alex did not need to ask whose orders those were, nor did she question them. Now was not the time.

It was after midnight when Smitty finally persuaded a tight-lipped Drake to go below.

"Captain, there has been no incident as yet and no sign of an American ship. You will need all of your resources over the next few days to guide us through the Saint Lawrence. Please try to get some sleep."

Drake ran his fingers through his windblown hair and nodded. "All right, Smitty. But I insist that you wake me if there is the slightest hint of trouble."

"Of course, Captain."

Drake made his way to the lower deck, knowing he should be exhausted. Instead, his body was taut with the stress of the day, the blood pulsing through his veins, energy tingling through every pore of his body, making him wide awake. Only his eyes burned from the strain of scanning the horizon for hostile ships.

Drake opened his cabin door, then kicked it closed behind him.

How could he have forgotten? The beautiful vision who

stood at the porthole, who turned suddenly amid a rustle of silk at his entrance, who stared at him through wide gray eyes . . . that vision was his wife.

For a long moment he remained motionless, drinking in the sight of her. After nearly twelve hours of hell, she looked like an angel ready to guide him to heaven. The oil lamp was dimly lit, casting golden shadows that lingered on her tousled honey-colored hair, the delicate features of her face, the bare expanse of her shoulders and arms. The ivory of her night rail, shimmering and soft, clung to every perfect curve of her small, lush body.

His wife.

The realization struck him like a lightning bolt, igniting his every nerve and pushing his already overcharged senses beyond rational thought. Suddenly Drake could feel his entire body shaking, and his burning gaze locked with Alex's startled one. He watched her expression change from surprise to awareness to apprehension and realization. This was their wedding night. And despite the war, despite all that had transpired before this day, this moment, nothing and no one could stop what was going to happen between them.

He spoke at last. "Alex. Come here."

It was an order. She had sworn never to obey an order from Drake.

She walked across the room to him.

He made no move to touch her at first, just stared down into her face, reveling in the fact that she was his. His.

"Is it safe?" she whispered at last.

"The ship is. You're not." His eyes burned with a green fire that seemed to singe her skin. His words made her shiver.

"Drake . . ."

He seemed not to hear her, but brought his hand up to stroke her cheek, down her neck to her shoulder, then along the length of her arm. He grasped her hand and raised it to his mouth.

"Forever," he murmured. "I've waited forever for you. But no longer, my beautiful wife. Tonight I am going to possess you, body and soul, to savor every inch of you, to take and take until there is nothing left for you to give. And in return I am going to bring your body to life, to set fire to every part of you, to make you twist and cry out and finally beg until you come apart in my arms again and again, until you have no doubt that you are mine." He drew her fingers into his mouth, licking each one lightly.

Alex closed her eyes as waves of pleasure swept over her, dizzying her senses. As if from a distance she heard herself moan.

"Look at me, Alexandria," he commanded.

Her eyes flew open.

Drake smiled, a slow, sensual smile that wrapped itself about her like a heady spell. He guided her hand around his neck, reaching for her other hand to do the same. "Now kiss me." He saw the uncertainty in her eyes. "You've done it before," he reminded her in a husky, teasing voice. "Remember?"

"I remember," she whispered.

"So do I." He didn't wait, but lowered his mouth to hers slowly, an inch at a time, until he brushed her lips in the lightest of caresses.

Alex tightened her hold on him, pressing her palms into the corded muscles at the nape of his neck.

Drake chuckled. "Want something, princess?" he murmured against her soft mouth.

Alex stood on tiptoe, sliding her fingers into Drake's thick hair, anchoring his head more firmly, tugging him down to her. She opened her mouth the way he had taught her and traced a slow path across his bottom lip with her tongue.

Drake tensed. All playfulness having vanished, he lifted Alex off the floor and crushed her against his chest, opening his mouth and possessing hers with an urgency like none he had ever known. Again and again he kissed her, bruising her mouth with his rapacious need, which flamed higher with each blazing contact.

He carried her to the bed, never breaking the kiss, and lowered himself on top of her on the rumpled sheets. He had planned to go slowly, to tease her to the very limits of her control, to wait until she begged before he took her.

He had to have her now.

The wildness inside him grew steadily, destroying his reason. He had always known that she affected him as no other woman ever had, but this desperate, violent need was more than he could bear. She was soft and clinging beneath him, unaware of the torture she inflicted on him with each sensual twist of her body. Blindly Drake tugged at the straps of her nightgown, urging them down. At the same time he realized the impossibility of removing it when their bodies were wedged so tightly together. He couldn't wait, and he couldn't let her go—not an inch, not for a moment.

He slid his arms beneath her and with one violent tug ripped the gown in two and dropped the shreds to the floor.

Alex gasped. The shock of his action and the realization of her own nudity were too much for her. Instantly Drake began to caress her back in slow, soothing motions, softening his devouring kiss to a gentle seduction of her mouth.

"I'm sorry, princess," he rasped, struggling, yet unable to slow down. "I . . . lose all control . . . around you." His hands did not remain still. The moment he felt her relax he began to explore her body, touching, stroking, shaking with hunger.

Alex closed her eyes, melting into the bed. He had touched her before, but never like this. Never without a shred of clothing to protect her. Never without the realization that they would have to stop. Never as her husband.

Her body took over. With feline grace she arched against his touch, moving sensually as his hands roamed the length of her. Their tongues warred, mated, retreated, then mated again. And suddenly Alex wanted more.

"I want to touch you, too," she murmured into his open mouth. She slid her hands around to the front of his shirt. "Drake?"

With a raw sound of animal need Drake propelled himself from the bed. Never taking his eyes off her, he tore the clothes from his sweat-drenched body, flinging them to the floor. He paused for a mere second before he lowered himself back down over her trembling body.

"You are so beautiful," he ground out, barely able to speak. "I want to look at you . . . all of you . . . but I can't. Not this time. Oh, God, you feel so good. If I don't fill you soon I'm going to explode."

Alex was reeling. The sight of him, huge and aroused, had made her breath catch and her heart pound. The thought of him driving himself into her scared her to death. She was about to tell him so, to pull away, when he lowered his weight upon her. She whimpered at the sensation of their naked, melding skin. And all thoughts of denial were lost.

"Drake . . . oh, Drake." She wrapped her arms around him, gliding her hands down the rippling muscles of his back to his taut buttocks.

He groaned as if in pain. Raising himself on his elbows, he stared down at her with eyes that were almost black with passion. "What are you doing to me?" he rasped.

She paused. "Should I not touch you like this?"

"You should touch me everywhere, princess. And not only like that." He gave a husky laugh. "There are so many ways . . ."

"Teach me."

Ablaze with desire, he stared into her passion-flushed face. "Later. Not now. I'd never last." He lowered his head to her throat, lightly licking the sensitive hollow until she moaned with pleasure. "Oh, Alex, Alex, I'm on fire for you." His mouth moved down from her throat until it reached her breast. He brought his hand up to cup it, circling with his tongue over and over.

Bursts of heat flowed through Alex's body as she arched up to Drake's teasing mouth. When he knew she was desperate, he took the throbbing nipple between his lips and lightly tugged. She cried out, tossing her head from side to side on the pillow.

Her reaction was nearly his undoing. He repeated his action with her other breast, struggling for a control that seemed out of his grasp.

"I can't wait." The words were wrenched from inside him, an admission of weakness that he could no longer deny. Even as he fought against it, he was pressing her thighs apart with his knees, reaching down to touch her where he so desperately needed to be. She was warm and wet and soft. And he was frantic.

"Alex," he murmured her name, sliding his fingers up and down, stroking gently, feeling her tense at the unexpected caress. "It's all right, sweetheart. I won't hurt you. Let me touch you." He shuddered. "God, you are so wet, so warm." He slid his fingers inside her. "So tight." When he heard her ragged moan of pleasure, felt her open to his penetration, something inside him snapped. "Now, love." He withdrew his fingers and positioned himself at the entrance to her body. He slid his hands under her, lifting her to meet him. "Take me inside you. Wrap yourself around me . . . Alex, love me."

With those words he surged forward, tearing the thin membrane that guarded her womanhood, making her his wife.

The pain was a sharp stab within her, suspending the intense pleasure and making her cry out. She tensed her legs, and her hands, which had been clinging to Drake's back, moved around to his chest, trying to push him off her.

Drake was aware of Alex's pain, her bewilderment. But he was more aware of the incredible, euphoric feeling of being inside her at last. She was so very small and tight; he could feel her stretching to hold him, feel her body struggling to accept his intrusion. He gritted his teeth at the intense pleasure that coursed through his body. He knew he had to reassure her, to comfort her, but he could not speak, was afraid to move.

It took every fiber of his self-control not to spill himself at that moment. But he wanted more . . . he wanted it all. And he wanted it with his wife.

It was her soft shudder of pain that gave him the strength he needed. He pressed his lips into her hair, his thumbs making lazy circles on her hips.

"Don't leave me now, love," he whispered. "I promise you, the best is yet to be." He inhaled the scent of her hair and felt his body throb helplessly inside hers. "I'll wait," he managed, "until you get used to the feel of me." He rocked his hips gently against hers, giving her a small taste of what it would be like for them.

Slowly, slowly, he felt her begin to relax beneath him, felt her thighs unclench and ease. Without moving his body he slid his hand between them, finding and caressing her where their bodies were joined, immersing himself in her dewy wetness.

The pain receded. The passion was reignited at a fever pitch. Alex whimpered, arching helplessly against Drake's fingers, tightening all around him, but this time not in pain.

The final barrier was swept away, annihilated in a tidal wave of desire. Madness took over, invading them, possessing them. Drenched in sweat, Drake devoured Alex's mouth, her throat, her neck, her breasts, crushing her against his pounding body, desperate to be deeper inside her, lifting her legs higher around him.

Alex called her husband's name over and over, wrapping her legs around his waist and meeting his frenzied thrusts with her own. She threw back her head, panting, wanting, needing, and, at last, begging Drake to end the torture, to relieve the taut knot of escalating pressure that coiled tighter and tighter inside her, threatening to devour her very soul.

Her soft, desperate pleas took Drake's last shred of sanity. He plunged wildly inside her, grinding his body against hers, withdrawing only to bury himself inside her again and again.

"Alex . . ." Her name was torn from his chest. "Come with me. Now, love, it has to be now."

She opened her eyes at his broken command, and in that frozen moment in time just before the spasms claimed her, she knew that she was in love with her husband. She closed her eyes against the intensity of the emotion, then cried out as bursts of nearly painful pleasure convulsed her body.

She buried her mouth against Drake's shoulder, tasting the salt of his sweat and dying in his arms.

Drake felt the wild pulsations of Alex's climax all around him. He tensed above her, every muscle taut and straining, as his own climax built higher and higher, beyond bearing, until it exploded, tearing him apart, flooding from his body into hers in powerful spurts of completion that seemed endless.

And Drake knew beyond the shadow of a doubt that despite his reputation as an accomplished, controlled lover, he was utterly, entirely lost. For the first time he was unable to think, unable to breathe, incapable of holding back or remaining untouched. All he could do was to surrender himself body and soul to the only woman who had penetrated his walls of self-protection.

To his wife.

Chapter 15

"It seems almost too quiet, Captain."

Smitty leaned his chin on his folded arms and gazed out over the lake, worry evident on his weathered face. "Rather like the calm before the storm."

It was true. They were well into their second day of travel, and there had been no sign of American military ships on Lake Ontario. To the contrary, all was peaceful, with little traffic about them.

"I'm not terribly concerned, Smitty," Drake replied from his position at the helm. "Initially this war appears to be on paper only, a formal declaration of hostilities without any bloodshed. Remember, it took nine days for news of the war to reach York. Many Canadians are still unaware of its onset. That is why I wanted to leave York as soon as possible, before panic had set in and before the battles had begun.''

Smitty nodded. The weather was their ally, the skies a brilliant shade of blue and the crystal waters of Lake Ontario glistening beneath them. The favorable westerly winds blew fiercely, propelling them toward the point where the lake narrowed into the Saint Lawrence River.

Smitty relaxed a bit. ''With any luck we will be within sight of Kingston by daybreak.''

''Yes, that is exactly what I am hoping. The sooner we clear American waters, the easier I will rest.''

Smitty turned and glanced at Drake. ''We have some distance to cover before that will occur,'' he reminded him. ''These will be dangerous weeks, Captain. I pray we can reach London safely.''

''We will.'' It was a statement of fact. ''I presume our men and our guns are prepared, should they be needed?''

''Of course, Captain.''

Drake tightened his hands on the wheel. ''Then nothing can stand in our way.''

Smitty smiled. ''You are determined to protect her.''

Drake looked surprised. ''I have always protected *La Belle Illusion*.''

''I was speaking of your wife, not your ship.''

The slight softening of Drake's hard features was subtle, but Smitty saw it.

''Yes, Smitty, I will protect Alexandria. It is my duty, after all.''

''Of course, Captain,'' was Smitty's bland reply.

Drake knew his friend was not fooled by the casual mention of Alexandria, but he was not ready to discuss his wife with anyone. Hell, he was having enough trouble dealing with his feelings for her on his own.

Before last night Drake had possessed *some* control. No longer. Instead of extinguishing the blazing fire that burned within him, last night had only served to feed the flames, to make them lick higher and higher, spreading throughout his body and, far worse, igniting something fundamental, yet unwilling, within his soul. An internal voice of self-protection cried out with fear, warning him that he was exposed, vulnerable in a way that he had sworn never to be.

Alex had held back nothing of herself. Despite her fear and inexperience, she had budded and then blossomed like a beautiful flower in his arms, offering him her innocence and her newly awakened passion. And he had hurt her. No matter how many times he told himself that it was inevitable, he still could not forget her sharp, anguished whimpers as her virginal flesh tore with his frantic entry. Long after she had fallen asleep, he had stared down into her face, trying to comprehend the intensity of their passion. Her long lashes, lying on her cheeks like golden wisps of sunlight, were moist with tears. He had fought an overwhelming urge to awaken her, to promise her that he would never hurt her again. But he knew damned well that, if he did, he would only end up making love to her again. And he could not give in to that impulse, for her body and his emotions were still too raw and tender for that to occur.

After a few hours of sleep, Drake had reluctantly detached himself from her soft warm body, dressed, and gone on deck. He was still here, and no nearer to understanding his feelings than he had been last night.

He *did* know that, with Alex, once was not enough. Drake had the maddening, drowning fear that he would never have enough.

"Smitty, have you seen Alexandria yet today?" he asked abruptly.

"No, Captain. When I left the berth deck, Lady Alexandria was still abed."

Drake frowned. "But it is almost noon."

"You left instructions for her to remain below until we are safely down the Saint Lawrence," Smitty reminded him.

"Since when has my wife followed any of my instructions?"

Smitty chuckled. "Perhaps now that you are wed she is attempting to turn over a new leaf."

Drake raised a disbelieving brow. "I don't think we should hold out too much hope of that." He was silent for a moment. "Smitty," he said at last, "perhaps you should go below and assure us both that she is well."

Smitty studied Drake for a long while, then nodded, choosing not to ask any questions. "Very well, Captain. I will go at once." He stepped down from the quarterdeck and walked toward the stairs. "Have you any message for her?" he called back over his shoulder.

Drake shook his head. "Just remind her not to make any unexpected appearances topside, since no doubt she is contemplating doing just that."

This time Drake was wrong.

Alex had awakened several hours earlier, emotionally shaken and physically sore. And she needed time alone to think.

She had known Drake was gone before she even opened her eyes. The realization had left her both relieved and terribly disappointed. She wanted him with her, and yet she was unsure of the status of their relationship.

Once during the night she had drifted awake, acutely aware of Drake's strong body wrapped around hers. She had pressed closer, content to feel the power and security of his presence, the knowledge of their intimacy, the reality of her love for him. In his sleep Drake had tightened his embrace, and Alex had nestled against his solid strength . . . where she belonged.

Alex had never made love before, but she knew that what had transpired between them was a rarity. That knowledge filled her with a strange peace. Drake might not love her, but he most definitely wanted her, and that intense desire manifested itself in a passion that had stunned even him. And the *way* he had made love to her had told her more than he could ever guess. He had tempered his burning urgency with caring words and gentleness. He had wanted—no, *needed*—her pleasure as much as his own. And after their passion was spent, he had held her tenderly, limiting himself to soft kisses and soothing caresses.

Alex had known he wanted her again, and yet he hadn't

taken her. Her intuition had told her that Drake's self-discipline was based on his concern for her inexperience and her discomfort.

Now she sat up in bed, clutching the thin sheet against her. It was time to consider some of the colder realities. She raised her knees and rested her chin on them. She was Drake's wife now in every way. However, she reminded herself, making love with him was one thing; living with him was something else. He was domineering, didactic, embittered, and angry.

And he did not love her.

Because Alex was proud, that knowledge hurt her. She did not delude herself into thinking that it was her fault; she had seen and talked with Drake enough to know that something, or someone, had formed his opinion of women and relationships long before he met her.

Because she was stubborn, she had every intention of changing that opinion.

This could very well be the biggest challenge of her life. The thought amused her and encouraged her to rise and face the day. She hesitated. Face the day, perhaps, but not Drake. She still felt too close to the emotions of last night. Well, he had ordered her to stay below. For once she would obey him.

She climbed out of bed with a grin on her face. It appeared that her father had been wrong, after all. Within a few short hours she had acquired the ability both to submit *and* to obey. Apparently marriage was reforming her.

The smile left her face abruptly as her gaze fell upon a small stain of blood on the stark white sheets, a vivid symbol of last night's passion. Alex closed her eyes, feeling a bit ill. She remembered the girls at boarding school whispering about blood being part of the "first time", but idle gossip and blatant reality were far removed from each other. Alex ached for a woman to talk to, someone who understood.

It seemed that no matter where she was or how far she ran, she was alone.

Hurriedly she washed herself as best she could with

water from the pitcher and a soft cloth. What she really wanted was a bath, but she was far too embarrassed to ask for one, especially now. The whole crew would be aware of why she was making that request, and that would mortify her. So she shivered through her cold and thorough dousing, then dressed in one of the simple gowns she had acquired in York. She dragged the soiled sheets from the bed and was frantically searching the room for clean bedding when a knock sounded at the door.

"Who is it?" she called, desperately seeking a hiding place for the soiled sheet.

"It is me, my lady," Smitty called back.

Without thinking Alex hid the sheet behind her back, clasping it tightly in both hands. "Come in, Smitty."

He opened the door, his kind face filled with concern for her. "Are you all right, my lady?"

Alex gave him a bright smile. "Just fine, Smitty."

His curious gaze darted to the stripped berth, then back to Alex. "Captain Barrett asked me to check and see that you are well and comfortable."

"Oh, yes, very," she assured him, wondering why she hadn't had the sense to cram the sheet beneath the bed. Now she was forced to stand like a ninny in order to spare her maidenly sensibilities.

It took Smitty a minute or two to comprehend what was amiss. Then, suddenly, awareness struck him like a great untamed wave.

Carefully schooling his features so as to appear ignorant of Alex's dire predicament, Smitty continued.

"The captain also asked me to reiterate his desire for you to remain below during this part of our journey." At her typically rebellious look he added, "It is for your safety, you know." At her nod he turned back toward the door. "I will see that some food is brought to you at once."

"*No!*"

Smitty stopped in his tracks at Alex's vehement refusal. "My lady?"

Alex moistened her lips. "I mean . . . no, thank you,

Smitty. I will be ready in a short while and will go out and eat with the men."

"If you are certain . . . ?"

She nodded emphatically, praying for him to leave. Her arms were aching from their cramped position behind her back. "I am certain."

"Then I will go topside and allow you your privacy."

"Smitty?" Despite her discomfort, she had to know of their plight. "Has there been any incident with the Americans?"

Smitty shook his head. "No, my lady. All has been quiet thus far."

She gave a sigh of relief. "Thank goodness. Where are we located now?"

"We have traveled much of Lake Ontario. Thanks to the winds, we should be nearing Kingston by morning." He saw her shift uncomfortably and took pity on her. "I must return to the quarterdeck, my lady. If you will excuse me?"

Alex tried hard not to show her relief. "Oh, of course, Smitty, I understand."

Smitty laughed all the way up to the main deck.

Nighttime arrived and with it came a startling realization: Alex wanted her husband.

She had spent most of her daylight hours in thoughtful solitude, alone in her cabin. When she became restless, she passed the time talking with the men and cleverly beating them at whist. But in the back of her mind she kept wondering where Drake was and whether it was merely a coincidence that they hadn't seen each other all day.

Darkness had been a welcome reprieve. Never before in her life had Alex so eagerly readied herself for bed. And fatigue had nothing to do with it.

She giggled as she donned one of Drake's shirts. So much for her exotic night rail. Drake had destroyed it last night. Giddy with anticipation, she slid into bed. And waited.

Drake paused outside the cabin door. He had successfully avoided her all day. But after a full day at the helm, he needed his rest. He needed his bed.

He needed his wife.

The room was dark and quiet, with no movement from the bed. Drake's heart pounded as he undressed, his anticipation growing with each passing moment. Naked, he paused beside the berth. Her back was to him, and she appeared to be asleep. Slowly he slid in beside her, until he could feel the warmth of her body against his.

He wrapped his arms around her from behind. "Princess?" he murmured, nuzzling her hair.

She gave a soft sigh.

He grinned, recognizing the familiar texture of her nightwear. "My shirt, I presume?" he teased in a husky voice.

She smiled. "After you destroyed my night rail I had no other choice."

"Oh, I can think of a much more suitable alternative," he assured her, nibbling lightly on her ear, then outlining the sensitive lobe with his tongue.

She heard herself moan, whisper his name.

He rolled her onto her back, pulled her into his arms.

"I've thought of nothing but this all day," he growled, his mouth coming down on hers.

She wrapped her arms around his neck, reveling in his kiss. "I missed you, too," she breathed against his lips.

Drake lifted his head and looked down into her wide gray eyes. "Did you?" he asked, rubbing her lower lip with his thumb.

Alex nodded, barely able to breathe. "Yes."

A slow smile spread across his handsome face, along with an expression that was a mixture of tenderness and relief. "Next time I won't stay away so long," he promised, lowering his head again. He stroked her lips softly with his—once, twice. She sighed with pleasure, opening her mouth to his tender exploration.

He accepted her unspoken invitation, deepening the kiss instantly, tightening his arms around her. She leaned back in his embrace, dizzy from the sensations of his plundering tongue. Slowly she touched her tongue to his, feeling the hard shudder that racked his body at the contact.

"God, how can it be like this?" he gasped. He rolled

onto his back, pulling her on top of him. He cupped her face in his shaking hands, stroking his thumbs over her cheekbones, staring into her flushed face. They had barely begun, and already he was out of control. He shook his head in wonder. "What is it that you do to me?" He closed his eyes, overwhelmed by feelings he had tried to master, but could not.

"Drake?"

At her tentative whisper he opened his eyes.

"I want you, Alex," he told her in a choked voice. "More than you can know, more than I can bear." He swallowed deeply, then shook his head in denial. "But I don't want it to be like last night. I want to take my time, to love you the way you were meant to be loved . . . slowly, lingeringly. I want to savor every moment, every inch of your body." He watched Alex's flush deepen at his words. Slowly he rolled over until she lay on her back. He raised himself up on his hands, his burning look raking her slender body, still concealed by the shirt.

"At the same time I want to take you now . . . this minute. I want to lift that damned shirt and drive myself into you until neither of us can breathe or think or move."

In a slow, exaggerated gesture that contradicted the savagery of his words, Drake lifted his hand to the top button of Alex's shirt. "But I'm not going to lose control—not this time."

Drake held her gaze as, one by one, the buttons came undone until the shirt was entirely unbuttoned and slightly open, revealing a tantalizing amount of Alex's soft, full breasts, rising and falling with each shallow breath she took. His own breathing harsh, Drake dropped his eyes, simultaneously tugging the shirt open, exposing Alex's naked beauty to his hot gaze.

For a long moment there was silence as Drake stared, mesmerized by her beauty. Then he tugged the shirt off one arm, then the other, finally dropping the garment to the floor. Alex lay, quiescent, her arms at her sides, staring up at him. The predatory look on his face made her heart pound, made liquid heat gather in her body and pool between her thighs. She trembled, waiting.

"Exquisite," he breathed, lowering his mouth to the hollow between her breasts. He inhaled her fragrance, felt the wild fluttering of her heart. "I want to touch . . . to taste . . . all of you. Tonight," he promised darkly, "I will."

"Drake?" Her voice was so soft she wondered if he could have heard.

Drake raised his head. "What, love?"

"I bled."

He froze, startled, trying to see her expression in the dim light. He wondered if her words were meant to be an accusation, an expression of anger. Unsure, he waited.

She turned her face up to his, uncertainty in her eyes. "That's normal, is it not?"

Drake could feel the knot of tension inside him melt away in a flood of tenderness. Obviously no one had prepared her for last night. "Very normal, sweetheart." He kissed her eyelids softly, then her cheeks. "It happens only the first time, never again." He felt her relax beneath him. "I'm sorry I hurt you," he whispered.

She slid her hands up the strong muscles of his forearms, his shoulders. "I'm not sorry," she answered honestly. "The pain wasn't that severe and it didn't last long." Her own curious gaze dropped to the dark hair that covered his broad chest and tapered down to the flat, taut planes of his abdomen. He was magnificent.

Drake watched her, forcing himself to lie still and endure her scrutiny. Lord, she hadn't even touched him and he was on the brink of insanity. "Like what you see, princess?" he managed with a tight smile.

She raised her enchanted eyes to his face. "Yes, very much."

He groaned. "You are destroying me."

For the first time Alex knew the full power of her own sexuality. She gave Drake a worldly smile. "I hope so."

The combination of her alluring sensuality and her breathtaking innocence was going to be the death of him.

Unable to hold back, he lowered the full weight of his body onto hers, tangling his hands in her silky hair. They kissed, open-mouthed and unashamedly hungry for each other. Alex explored the hard contours of his back, the rippling muscles beneath the smooth skin. She could feel his maleness, hard and throbbing, against the soft skin of her thighs, and she arched slightly to increase the exciting friction it generated.

Drake gave a hoarse cry of need, tore his mouth from hers, pressed urgent, burning kisses down her throat and shoulders until he reached her breasts. He paused, his chest heaving, and stared down at her, watching her nipples tighten even before he touched them.

"Drake . . . please . . ." Alex couldn't bear the tension. She needed his touch desperately.

"Yes, princess," he breathed, lowering his open mouth to her yearning breasts.

The taste of her skin, the sweet intensity of her desire, was almost more than he could take. He circled each breast with his tongue, then drew the taut nipples into his mouth, using his lips and his teeth to drive her wild. He felt her writhing beneath him, heard her calling his name.

He needed more. When her nipples were wet and swollen from his mouth, Drake moved down, gliding his tongue along the slender curves of her body. He paused at her navel, dipping his tongue inside, circling slowly, then going lower still, kissing her legs, her thighs, urging them apart with his hands and settling himself between them.

Alex whimpered, torn between frantic need and embarrassed resistance. She felt his breath there, between her legs, and her whole body begged her to give in, to let him do this wonderful thing to her.

She felt his lips, his seeking tongue, and knowing that she would soon be unable to do so, voiced a weak token protest. "No . . ."

"Yes." With that one word she was his. He tasted her sweetness, the nectar of her passion, and the world went up in flames.

The pleasure was beyond endurance and growing stronger,

higher, consuming her in an agony of wanting. She clutched at his shoulders, arched wildly against his mouth, seeking more, all sensation centered beneath his stroking tongue.

Drake stoked the fire inside her again and again until he was shuddering, so close to eruption that he could wait no longer. He raised his mouth from her moist sweetness, panting, and leaned back until he was kneeling between her spread legs.

Alex's eyes flew open in protest. She was at the very edge of sensation, desperate for release. Her storm gray eyes met his blazing emerald ones.

"Drake . . . please . . . don't leave me . . . not yet," she pleaded, her voice shaking with passion.

He groaned, closing his eyes, fighting for the control he needed to take her gently, to merge their sweat-drenched, craving bodies without causing her pain.

Unsure of his actions, knowing only her own desperate need for fulfillment, Alex wrapped her small hand around his huge, rigid arousal. He flinched at her touch, his face contorted with pain. She stroked him gently, coaxingly. "Drake?"

It was no use.

With an anguished cry he entered her, taking her with all the violent need of his body and soul. He heard her cry out, but it was too late; he couldn't have stopped or slowed down if his very life had depended on it.

"Alex . . . Alex . . ." He called her name over and over, pounding into her welcome softness with all of his strength and passion, demanding all that she could give.

She sobbed his name, contracting around him with wild, utter abandon, feeling the warm flood of his seed as it poured into her body.

And then the room was silent, but for their ragged breathing.

Still shuddering with the force of his climax, Drake rolled to one side, his arms wrapped tightly around his wife, his body still deep inside hers.

"Are you all right?" he gasped, feeling her tremble in his arms. "Did I hurt you, love?"

She didn't answer for so long that Drake's fear escalated. At last he felt her breath against his chest, heard her ragged whisper. "Yes. And no."

He smiled, cradling her against him. Last night he had let her sleep. He had no intention of making the same mistake tonight.

Dawn cast its first golden glow on the waters of Lake Ontario. Kingston lay alongside them, signifying the end of the first leg of their journey, the beginning of another. Just ahead, the mighty Saint Lawrence beckoned, and *La Belle Illusion* surged forward eagerly, ready to accept the challenge.

The seamen moved about the ship, performing their jobs while keeping a constant eye out for danger. It was unprecedented for Captain Barrett to be conspicuously absent from the quarterdeck for more than three hours at a time. But if anyone noticed, no one made mention of the fact.

Below, in the captain's cabin, Drake gently kissed his wife awake. "Princess," he murmured between kisses, "I have to go topside. It's been hours."

Alex gave a sleepy sigh and opened her eyes. "We just went to sleep," she protested.

He grinned. "That may be, love, but that doesn't change the fact that I haven't been at the helm since sometime after midnight."

She stretched gracefully, feeling the physical tenderness that resulted from a night of lovemaking. The ache felt wonderful.

He stared down at her, seeing the effect of last night's passion. Her cheeks were still flushed, her hair wildly tousled, her softly parted lips still swollen from his bruising kisses. He felt the familiar surge of desire rise up inside him, coupled with a less familiar and most unwelcome tightening in his chest.

"Drake?" Her voice was questioning.

He shook his head, denying the feelings. He lowered his mouth to hers again, deepening the kiss until they both felt the magic of the previous night spinning its web about their senses.

The shrill sound of the officers' whistle pierced the air, shattering the fantasy into bitter shards of reality. Seconds later there were running footsteps and calls of "Captain! Captain!"

"Damn!" Drake tore himself from Alex's arms and hurried across the room, pulling on his shirt and breeches.

"Drake . . . what is it?" Alex sat up, alarmed.

He paused at the door only to give her a hard look. "No venturing from this cabin, Alexandria. I mean it," he warned.

She rose from the bed, the sheet draped around her. "Tell me what is happening," she demanded.

He had already flung open the door as he spoke. "*La Belle Illusion* is in trouble. God help us if it is an American attack."

Chapter 16

"It's a military ship comin' up behind us, Cap'n! An' she's flyin' the American flag!" Cochran stood at the top of the stairs, calling out to Drake as he reached the main deck.

Drake's head jerked around, his expertly trained eye instantly assessing the situation. The oncoming ship was a 160-foot military brig of over four hundred tons, with two towering masts and sixteen guns. She dwarfed *La Belle Illusion* in firepower, speed, and crew. The situation was grim.

All around Drake his men were following Smitty's orders, dragging the cannons into position and hoisting the gunpowder and cannonballs up through the hatch to the main deck. Everything would be ready should it be needed.

"Captain! They are definitely in pursuit!" Smitty shouted, as Drake leapt onto the quarterdeck.

Drake nodded. "We'll try to outmaneuver them." He took the wheel from Smitty in an iron grip. The Saint Lawrence was narrowing; the Thousand Islands lay ahead. It would be nearly impossible to escape. But with Drake at the helm, anything was possible.

"We'll not make this easy for them, Smitty," he vowed, steering *La Belle Illusion* windward.

Despite Drake's superb skill, the attempt to escape was futile. Not only was the enemy ship larger, with more expansive rigging, but the weight of the timber in *La Belle Illusion*'s hold made her slow and difficult to steer among the myriad small islands.

Minutes later Drake made his decision.

"Man the guns, men," he commanded. "We are in for a fight." His calm tone did not fool anyone. This was going to be a battle to the death.

The men hauled the cannons inboard and opened the gunports, then stacked the cartridges alongside the guns as they waited tensely for Drake's next order.

Alex stood, horrified, on the main deck, witnessing the scene around her. "Oh, my God," she whispered, pressing her hand to her mouth.

Thomas Greer spun about. "Miss Alex! You should not be up here! We're about t' do battle!"

"Yes, Thomas, I can see that." She was overcome by fear and by frustration. She might be a woman, but surely there was something she could do to help.

She hurried to the quarterdeck where Drake was maneuvering the ship rapidly downriver.

"Drake!" She flew up beside him. "What can I do?"

"Damn you!" He spat out the words, determined to avert the danger that loomed behind them. "I told you to stay below! Do I have to beat you into obedience?"

Alex looked stunned, then defensive. "We are about to be attacked! I thought . . ."

"You thought? No, damn it, Alexandria, you didn't think! You just acted, as always!" A muscle worked in his jaw, which was clenched in fury. He wiped the spray from his face impatiently. "Now get off my quarterdeck before you get yourself killed!" When she hesitated, he barked, *"Now,* wife!"

She had never felt more like chattel. Turning around, she retreated to the main deck without another word.

Drake gritted his teeth. He knew he had hurt her. But at least his harsh words had forced her below to safety.

Alex had no intention of going anywhere.

She made her way along the main deck, watching as the small crew worked frantically to ready the cannons. She bit her lip, cursing her lack of knowledge and experience, as the straining, sweating men prepared to fight for their lives.

The ominous white sails of the enemy ship loomed closer. Alex could make out the American crew as they manned their guns. The futility of the situation struck her like a violent blow as she counted the men and gunports of the vessel that would soon be upon them. How could Drake ever hope to emerge victorious?

"Cochran! Where the 'ell are the rest of those cartridges?" Jamison demanded, searching the deck.

"Mannings is below, filling 'em with powder." Cochran glanced toward the open hatch at the top of the hold. "He should be passin' 'em up any second."

Jamison swore under his breath. "Who the 'ell is goin' t' get 'em? We've got t' reload within a hairbreadth! There's no time for us t' run back t' fetch 'em!"

Before Cochran could respond, thunder exploded through the air, followed by huge sprays of water that swept the decks as the ship rolled wildly.

"They've missed us!" Thomas Greer shouted.

Alex looked up and fought back a scream, realizing that the Americans were now directly parallel to *La Belle Illusion* and that the tremendous explosion of a moment ago had been cannon fire.

"Ready the larboard guns!" Drake's voice boomed out.

Instantly the men loaded their cannons. First, a cartridge of powder was rammed down the barrel. Three good strokes of the rammer put home a wad of rope yarn. Next, the lethal ball itself was snugged up against the wad by the rammer. Finally, another wad was put home, leaving no space between the powder cartridge and the last wad. The touchhole was filled with powder and the guns aimed at their target.

"Larboard guns, ready, Cap'n!" Cochran called out.

Less than a minute had passed since the command had been given. Poised, the crew waited, knowing what came next.

"Larboard guns, fire!"

Alex said a silent prayer as the men blew upon their linstocks and ignited the cartridges through the touchholes of their guns.

The impact sent Alex sprawling to the deck. The mighty cannons boomed out, rolling backward from the force of their fire, yet held fast by the breeching rope that tied them securely to the ship. Alex recovered in time to see the balls fall into the water, far short of their target.

"God damn it!" Drake roared from the helm. "How many chances do you think we're going to get? Your range is short! Increase the elevation of those blasted guns!" He grimly noted that the Americans were preparing to fire again. "I'll dodge their fire and get in closer. And this time, don't miss!"

The men were already finished reloading, and Alex heard them muttering among themselves.

"I dunno what the 'ell 'appened," Cochran said, shaking his head. "That shot should 'ave 'it 'em."

"Mine, too," Jamison agreed, realigning the muzzle of his gun. He drew in a deep, nervous breath. "We've got to get 'em next time."

But they didn't. Not the next time or the next. The two ships moved in a zigzag pattern down the narrow river, their paths at times seeming to intersect, then move apart, giving each vessel ample opportunity to attack. Despite Drake's success at moving closer just prior to firing, the crew's volleys landed time and again far short of their mark, while the Americans had already destroyed *La Belle*'s jib and fore-royal sails.

Alex swallowed and eyed the shattered sails. Thank God they were small, inconsequential ones. But how much longer could Drake's clever handling at the helm hold up against the warship's tremendous power?

Thomas Greer gasped, raw fear in his eyes. "That was me last cartridge." He stepped hesitantly away from his gun. "I'll 'ave to get more from the 'old."

"We 'aven't time," Jamison shot back.

"Well, what the 'ell are we goin' t' do without ammunition?"

"I'll get the cartridges."

The men spun about at Alex's firmly delivered words. She could see the indecision on their faces, but then it was too late. Cannon fire exploded again, a chain shot piercing the main topgallant, causing the ship to roll precariously. The men steadied themselves, turning back to their guns.

"Aim for their rigging and try to slow them down!" Drake commanded. He gripped the wheel tightly in frustration. Something was wrong. He knew it. "Fire, now!" he ordered.

The roar of cannon fire filled the sky, but when the air cleared, he saw that the other ship had remained unscathed.

The balls had once again fallen short of their mark. The men were frantic. Alex waited no longer, but ran over to the hold.

"Mannings!" she called down. "I need those cartridges, *now!*"

She saw his stunned face below her, as well as the pile of powder-filled cartridges beside him. He hesitated.

"*Now*, Mannings!" Was that authoritative voice really hers?

Apparently, it was, for Mannings immediately began to pass the packets up to her.

She ran back and forth, piling them up beside the desperate men. On the quarterdeck Smitty turned, then paled as he saw what Alex was doing.

Drake heard Smitty's low, inadvertent gasp and turned his head, following Smitty's gaze. He froze with an outrage born of stark terror.

"Dear God . . ." he breathed. "What the hell is she doing?"

"Captain, they're about to fire again!" Smitty interrupted, seeing the larger ship pulling along their larboard side.

As he spoke, the balls were released, flying purposely toward *La Belle Illusion*. Water erupted all around them, and with a surge of panic Drake saw one ball fly just beyond where Alex stood, striking the fore-topsail and shattering it.

Alex screamed, clutching a wooden beam for support, realizing how close she had come to dying.

"That sail 'as to be changed or we've 'ad it," Jamison groaned.

"I'll change the sails," Thomas called out.

He was never given the chance. Another explosion of cannon fire rang out, and seconds later the sickening sound of splintering wood pierced the air as *La Belle Illusion*'s mainmast disintegrated all around them. Drake shielded his eyes from the slivers of wood cascading into the water.

Smitty gave Drake a grim look. "We're in trouble, Captain. We're not going anywhere without that mast."

The Americans seemed to know that, too, for seconds later another round of fire, aimed much lower, was released. The crash was deafening, and *La Belle* pitched violently, propelling all those on deck against the rail.

"Cap'n! We've been 'it!" Mannings's frightened voice came from below. "We're takin' on water!"

Drake had known immediately that the hull had been hit, but Mannings's words still caused a sharp pain in his gut.

"Can it be plugged?" he shouted.

"No way, Cap'n. They've ripped out our 'ole larboard side!"

Drake closed his eyes for a split second, calling up his strength for what was to follow.

There was never a question of whether to fight. His crew

was badly outnumbered. They would be slaughtered in hand-to-hand combat. And their lives were more important than anything else. Theirs and his wife's.

The Canadian shore lay just ahead. The currents were strong, but they could make it in the lifeboats. They had to make it.

He turned toward the tense faces of his men. "Abandon ship, men," he ordered, his own expression tormented. "We can make it to the Canadian shore in the boats before they board us." He drew in a shaken breath. "Now!"

The men took off to ready the boats. Drake turned to Smitty. "I want Alexandria off on the first longboat," he told him. "I don't care if she screams and kicks all the way down. Get her on that boat!"

"Yes, Captain."

"And I want you with her, Smitty, to keep her safe." He shook his head sharply at Smitty's protest. "I'll stay behind and evacuate the crew." He put his hand on his first mate's shoulder. "I would prefer it to be a personal favor . . . but if I need to, I will make it an order, my friend."

Smitty's eyes were suspiciously bright. "I will see to it, Captain."

"Thank you."

Without another word Drake turned to help the men ready the lifeboats. Alex worked her way along the lame ship until she reached his side.

"You are leaving on the first boat," he said without looking at her.

"Drake, no . . . I want to stay here with you."

"I don't give a damn what you want, Alexandria." He stood glaring at her, but she saw the agony in his eyes. All around them men called out to one another, their voices tense, their faces ashen, as the boats were lowered into the water.

"I am staying," she announced.

"Over my dead body." His tone was lethal. "You are going if I have to heave you over the side myself. This isn't a game, wife. Any minute the American crew is going to board this ship and try to kill us all." He cast a worried look at the enemy vessel beside them, wondering why they hadn't yet begun to throw their grapplings on board to lock the two ships together. They had certainly had ample time. Perhaps they didn't know how severe the damage was they had inflicted . . .

Drake had barely completed the thought, when a final explosion thundered through the heavens, destroying *La Belle*'s remaining rigging and striking the foremast.

The crippled foremast shuddered as the stays snapped, swinging its boom forward wildly. Drake saw it happen and let out a choked warning, but it was too late. Alex saw the terror in his eyes as he leapt toward her. Before she could turn around, she felt the impact of the boom as it grazed the back of her head, propelling her over the side of the ship. And then the waters closed over her, carrying her down to certain death.

Drake was at the railing before she hit the water.

"Smitty!" he screamed. "Get the men off the ship! I'm going after her!"

He didn't wait for Smitty's answer, but dived over the side of the ship, cutting cleanly into the river at the spot where he had seen his wife disappear. He scanned the river for Alex, fighting the swift currents that threatened to overtake him. How could his tiny wife hope to survive?

Alex was wondering that as well. Dazed by the blow to her head, she struggled to come to the surface. An excellent swimmer, she was nonetheless weighed down by her gown and petticoat. She kicked frantically, trying to counter their effect. Her lungs were bursting for air, her heart pounding from exertion. Just when she thought she had lost, she broke the surface of the water.

Gasping in air, she screamed Drake's name. She could see *La Belle Illusion*, now farther away, slowly sinking. Beside the mutilated ship, Alex could make out the lifeboats, as the men abandoned the doomed vessel. She called for Drake again, splashing wildly as she tried to save herself, hurting at the sight of the proud ship that was now nearly submerged in the Saint Lawrence.

Drake saw it, too. But the pain he felt at seeing his beloved ship go down was overshadowed by the joy that surged within him as he heard Alex call his name, saw the splash of color in the water that was his wife.

"Alex!" he screamed back, waving frantically at her. "Hold on, love. I'm coming!"

His words, his presence, made her heart soar.

Her elation was short-lived. The currents swept her up, dragging her downriver. Her head throbbed beyond endurance, and she searched frantically for something to cling to.

It found her.

A tiny island of rock jutted just out into the water. For the second time Alex felt the impact of something solid striking her head.

And then she felt nothing at all.

Chapter 17

He saw her go down.

Drake felt his heart lurch as Alex crashed into the sharp edge of rock and disappeared from view. He was but fifty feet away. With long, powerful strokes he reached the spot where she had been. He combatted the force of the river and dived beneath the surface.

Thank God for the bright color of her gown. With a strength born of fear Drake reached her side and pulled her limp form against him. It took three or four hard kicks until he had broken the surface. He gulped in air and forced Alex's head above water.

"Alex!" His voice shook. "Damn it, Alex, answer me!"

She did not.

But against his strong forearm Drake could feel the gentle rise and fall of her chest that told him she was breathing. She had been under water for only a few seconds, so she could not have taken in much water.

Satisfied that his wife was alive, Drake turned his attention toward reaching safety. A quick look told him that the lifeboats were no longer an option. They were too far off, close to the Canadian shore. The men would never hear his yell.

In the middle of the river *La Belle Illusion* was disappearing from view, as graceful in death as she had been in life. The American ship had deserted the scene, victoriously returning home. Apparently they were satisfied with the sinking of their English nemesis together with her valuable cargo. Possibly merchantmen were not nearly such sought-after prisoners as military men. Or perhaps the Americans believed the crew of *La Belle* to be dead, unable to survive the fatal onslaught. Whichever the case, the battle was over and *La Belle Illusion* was gone.

This was no time to dwell on what had been lost. Drake scanned their surroundings, holding Alex securely with one arm and struggling to stay afloat with the other. The Canadian shore was far off in the distance. Considering Alex's depleted condition and his own deteriorating strength, swimming there would be impossible. They were, in fact, too close to the American shore for Drake's peace of mind. There had to be another alternative.

He found it. Just behind them began a sprinkling of the small green dots of land that were scattered throughout the Saint Lawrence.

Those glorious islands that Drake had shown to Alex on their trip to York, the Thousand Islands, known for their lush foliage and exquisite greenery, beckoned to them. To Drake they meant salvation.

He wrapped his arm more tightly about Alex beneath her arms, forcing her head to remain above water. With one savage motion of his other hand he tore her petticoat and the skirt of her waterlogged gown from her body, eliminating the additional weight that hindered them. Then he assessed the islands within swimming distance, contemplating his options. Just off to the west was the answer to Drake's prayers. A tiny island tucked away in utter solitude. Determined, he set out for the haven it promised.

After what seemed like an eternity, Drake dragged himself and a still-unconscious Alexandria onto the golden shore of the island. He crawled onto the sand and collapsed, gasping, as he lay beside his oh-so-still wife. He felt the rough texture of the sand against his face, grateful to be alive. He was exhausted, utterly spent, but he would not succumb to the allure of sleep. Not until he knew Alex was all right.

Drake rolled over and propped himself up on his elbow, staring down anxiously into Alex's face. He had been watching her for hours. Evening had long since fallen, but the June night was still filled with lingering rays of sunlight, enabling him to see her clearly. She was so still, so frighteningly pale, with a huge gash on her forehead that would no doubt swell and bruise, and another swelling on the back of her head where the boom had grazed her. Just how serious the injuries were, Drake could not be certain. Nor would he be until she awakened.

Tenderly he smoothed the wet strands of hair from her delicate face. He stroked her cheek, which felt cold to his touch. To reassure himself he lifted her wrist and pressed his fingers to it. The pulse was there—faint, a little erratic, but there. He moved closer, pressing himself against her side and wrapping his arms tightly around her for warmth. He would hold her all night if need be, infuse her with his strength, but damn it, she would live. She had to live.

And then Drake did something he hadn't done since he was a boy.

He prayed.

It was after dawn before his prayers were answered.

Alex's first thought upon awakening was that she had died and gone to heaven. The sky above her was brightening to an intense shade of blue, and towering trees filled with plush green leaves rose all around her. The rhythmic sound of flapping wings heralded the appearance of graceful birds that soared about, and the smell of deep grasses and lush, aromatic flowers teased her nose.

She turned her head and abruptly decided that this could not be heaven, after all. Knives shot through her skull, making her moan and close her eyes to block out the pain. Her body felt weak, drained, her limbs too heavy to move. What was wrong with her and where was she?

"It's all right, sweetheart." Drake's voice seemed to come from a great distance. "Everything is fine now. Open your eyes, princess, please."

He sounded so worried. She forced her eyes open and met his deep green gaze, the dark brows knit with concern. He was drawn and haggard, his black hair disheveled, and a shadow of a beard covered his face. Actually, he looked for all the world like a pirate.

She giggled. The movement caused her to moan again with pain.

"And just what is so funny?"

She blinked, dazed. "Apparently I am dead. The scene looks much like what I had expected of heaven. But the pounding in my head and your strong resemblance to the devil himself leads me to believe that I fell short somehow and am, instead, banished to hell."

He grinned. "You look pretty dreadful yourself, wife." He pressed his lips to her forehead. "And I am sorry to disappoint you, but you are very much alive. Thanks, of course," he added modestly, "to my quick thinking and superb skill."

"Ever arrogant and cocky," she sighed. "Perhaps I do live after all."

"How do you feel?"

"Disoriented. And depleted as well." She looked up at him. "Where are we and what happened?"

His gaze fixed on the angry bruise that marred her forehead, and he frowned. "We were attacked by an American ship, and—"

"I remember," she cut in. Suddenly her eyes widened.

"Oh my God, Drake, I remember." She tried to sit up, but the effort cost her. Shards of pain pierced her skull, and her stomach lurched in protest. She swallowed, frightened by her pain and by her body's reaction to it. "Drake, I think I am going to be sick," she whispered.

"Fine, love." He kept his voice even and eased her over to her side, anchoring her head with one hand and stroking her back in soothing motions with the other. She retched helplessly, bringing up only water, since she had eaten nothing. But long after her stomach was empty she continued to heave with dry, shuddering spasms of her body. All the while Drake continued to comfort her with reassuring words and caresses. He was not overly alarmed. Since he was quite sure she had a concussion, it was not unusual for her to react this way. She was suffering from both pain and shock and, right now, fear at her body's lack of control.

When she was still, he rolled her gently back to the ground. Then he stood, shrugged out of his ruined shirt, and walked to the water's edge, dipping the material into the cold, clear water. Returning to her side, he squatted down and wiped her pale face with the makeshift cloth.

"Better?"

She nodded slowly, her eyes filled with questions.

"You were struck by the boom and knocked overboard," he answered, watching her expression. "Do you recall?"

"Yes," she whispered. "And I tried to save myself, but the currents were too strong and these damned clothes were too heavy." She paused, realizing as she spoke that not much remained of her formal attire. "You came after me," she went on. "I saw you."

He nodded. "But that tiny island of rock got to you first, unfortunately." He touched her forehead lightly, so as not to intensify her discomfort. "You have quite an impressive bruise, princess, and probably a concussion as well—not to mention an enormous bump on the back of your head from the boom." He gave a mock sigh, attempting to ease her stress. "As usual, princess, you got yourself into trouble, and I had to rescue you."

Alex didn't smile. "Oh, Drake," her voice trembled, *"La Belle . . ."*

". . . is gone," he finished.

Her pearl gray eyes softened with pain, his and hers. "I'm so sorry. I know how much you loved that ship. I grew to love her, as well."

"The important thing is that everyone got away safely—the entire crew and us." Drake kept his voice even. "Kingston is one of England's most important Canadian military posts. Once the crew arrives there, Smitty can arrange for safe passage home."

Alex could see the emotion Drake held in check. He was not yet ready to deal with the loss of his ship. When he was, she would be there to comfort him.

Her gaze darted about, though she was careful to keep her head still. "Where are we?"

"On our own island, princess." He grinned.

She looked startled. Drake proceeded to explain what had happened after she struck her head on the rock and how they came to be on the deserted island.

She listened carefully, then asked, "How bad is my concussion?"

"Now that I see how lucid you are, I feel relieved. I don't think it's too severe. However," he added, giving her a meaningful look, "you are going to have to remain quiet for several days. And that means that I am going to have my work cut out for me keeping you that way."

"How far are we from the Canadian shore?"

He considered. "Over a mile, I would say. We're far closer to the American shore, unfortunately. And if you have any ideas of going anywhere, you can forget them. You are in no condition to attempt another bout with the currents."

She gave a resigned sigh. "What will we do?"

He flashed her a devilish smile. "Why, survive in the wilderness, princess, of course. You did say that you were seeking adventure when first we met, did you not?"

"I'm not certain that this is what I had in mind."

He chuckled. "Well, we are going to find out." He stood, hands on hips, and looked behind them.

It was a paradise of nature. Magnificent birch, elm, and oak trees spread their densely covered limbs all around them, cloaking the thick grass in a velvet cascade of forest green. Brilliant wildflowers sprang up everywhere, along with bushes overflowing with berries. Overhead, in a sky as blue as the ocean, huge white gulls soared in exuberant abandon, the beating of their wings intermingling with the gentle lapping of the river upon the shore.

Perhaps Alex was right. Perhaps this was heaven, after all.

"We are very lucky, princess," he told her. "This region is brutally cold and frozen throughout the winter and far into the spring. We could not have survived long. But as it is, we will do just fine."

Alex shifted slightly, her eyes wide with interest. "What do you mean?"

"The Saint Lawrence is at our doorstep, providing us with water to drink and to bathe. It is also rich with more kinds of fish than you can imagine. That, combined with the native fruits and berries, will be more than sufficient to feed us." He held up the knife that he carried with him at all times, tucked in his breeches. "This and the dense cluster of trees on the island can provide us with more than suitable shelter for those times when we need it. Also—"

"You sound as if we will be staying forever!" she interrupted.

He shot her an impatient look. "I was about to say that the Indians used the boles of elm trees to make their canoes. During the time that you are recovering, I can begin to construct a raft of sorts to help us safely reach Canada."

"I want to help."

"You can help by getting well."

"I am not a good patient."

"Somehow that doesn't surprise me." He walked over and knelt down beside her. "Will you be all right if I leave you for a short while?"

Alex felt a surge of panic. "Where are you going?"

He ran his finger down the slender bridge of her nose. "Just to get us some food. We haven't eaten in over a day. You need to eat in order to get your strength back." His eyes twinkled. "And you need to get your strength back in order to make yourself useful."

"To help you?" she asked eagerly.

"Among other things." He gave her a suggestive look and chuckled at her blush. "I'll be within calling distance, should you need me." He stood. "I don't want to see you move," he warned, scowling. "As it is we have a few things to settle about your lack of ability to heed my instructions. Let us not add additional items to that ever-growing list, shall we?"

She gave him a weak smile. "I suppose I must obey?"

"Definitely."

Her look was innocent. "Must I also submit?"

"Over my dead body."

Alex smiled, listening to the sound of his footsteps move away toward the water. Above her, the sun was rising higher in the sky, drenching the island in brilliant rays of light. They were alone in this exquisite Eden, with none of the luxuries that Sudsbury provided, fewer even than those enjoyed aboard *La Belle Illusion*. They had no clothes, no servants, and only the most primitive means of survival. The real world seemed distant, insignificant. Far away were all their differences, all that had come between them in the past.

Alex closed her eyes, enjoying the feel of the sunlight warming her face. Who knew how long it would take to build a raft that could carry them back to civilization?

She hoped it would take an aeon.

Chapter 18

"There is absolutely no reason why I cannot provide dinner for us tonight!"

Alex stood before him, a diminutive waif clad only in a lacy chemise that was rather the worse for wear, her thick unruly waves of hair bleached more gold than brown by the sun. A delicate, desirable little flower that would have made any man want to shelter and protect her.

Except that her eyes were shooting silver daggers in his direction, her perfect, sensual mouth was set in familiar defiance, and her hands were planted on her slim hips in a bellicose stance.

Drake grinned, leaning against the heavy trunk of a tall oak and stroking the thickening beard that now covered his handsome face. "I appreciate the offer, princess, really I do. But I fear we would starve waiting for you to prepare a meal. Need I remind you that there is no servant to obtain the food from the market, nor is there a cook who is ready to demonstrate his fine culinary skill in a spacious kitchen?"

"Damn you, Drake Barrett, I am well aware of what has to be done!" she snapped back. Hadn't she already proved she could survive without the luxuries and pampering of her aristocratic upbringing? "I don't recall seeing any servants aboard *La Belle Illusion*, and yet somehow I managed alone. I am tired of your sarcastic comments and I am tired of being waited on! I feel fine and am no longer an invalid."

His grin widened. No, indeed, that she was not. In fact he knew exactly when she had begun to get better. Strange that there was a direct parallel between her improving health and her shrewish tongue. For the first few days she had been content to have him care for her, remaining docile as a kitten as he had fed and washed her and tended to her wounds. She had rested in the tall, cool grasses during the time it had taken him to build the lean-to that was now their home. Once it was completed, she had remained within its shelter, sleeping on and off throughout the day, weak as a baby. He had been scared to death.

And now, ten days later, she was bellowing like a fishmonger. He wondered how she would react if she knew what his thoughts really were. Looking at her now, her magnificent breasts heaving with indignation, Drake felt a surge of lust that shook his entire being. It had been too long since he had put her breathtaking passion to its best use.

There were definite advantages to having a fishmonger for a wife.

"Are you going to answer me?" she demanded, glaring up at him.

"Certainly," he replied good-naturedly. "What would you like me to say?"

"That you'll let me make dinner tonight."

"And just how will you do that, princess?" He folded his arms across his bare chest, trying desperately not to laugh. "Don't tell me . . . we're going to have blueberries and water for our evening meal!"

She was tempted to strike him. The damned man was arrogant beyond description, and his opinion of noblewomen was beginning to grate on her nerves. Well, blast it, she would make a superb meal if it killed her!

"No, Drake," she replied, her head held high. "I plan on catching a good-sized fish for dinner."

His lips twitched. "Forgive me, princess. I had no idea that you had such a feast in mind." He gestured grandly toward the water's edge. "Please, go right ahead. I will await my meal with the greatest of anticipation."

With that he walked off to the soft grass beneath their lean-to and lowered himself to the ground. Thanks to the strong trees and plentiful vines, he had been able to construct a more than ample shelter that shielded them from the sun and the rain. In truth, the two-acre island was a veritable paradise, providing everything one could require in order to survive. No, to do much more than survive. To be nurtured and to flourish.

Drake had never felt so at peace in all his life. The world, even the war, seemed part of some distant dream, unreal, existing only on the perimeter of his mind. Not even on *La Belle Illusion* had he felt such a sense of wholeness. He knew it was the island that was weaving its magic. The island and his wife.

The sound of splashing water followed by a very unladylike curse interrupted his thoughts. Rising up on his elbows, Drake watched Alex loping through the river along the shoreline, dipping her hands beneath the water and speaking in a soft, cajoling tone, presumably to the elusive fish. Apparently the fish were insensitive to her plight, for a moment later another muttered oath sprang from his wife's dainty lips and she shook her fist furiously at the retreating culprit. Undaunted, she tossed her damp hair from her face and began her search for another, more willing victim.

Rather than amusement or triumph, Drake was overcome by a feeling of poignant tenderness like none he had ever known. For the first time he did not attempt to fight or deny what he knew to be the truth. She had taken his heart, this willful, stubborn, impulsive, passionate, and seeking young woman he had married. And he had to believe that she would never betray this feeling that was between them.

God help her if she did.

He closed his eyes. God help them both.

"Drake! Drake! Come quickly!"

Her excited voice brought him to his feet, striding toward the spot where she stood. Clasped in her hands was a wiggling, thoroughly annoyed bass that would escape in precisely three seconds if it was not speared.

Drake pulled out his knife and did the honors as Alex looked away, unable to bear the sight.

"You did very well, princess," he praised soberly. "Now, will you prepare it or shall I?"

"Prepare it?" Alex's voice was weak.

"Yes, you know, scale it and cut off its—"

"I understand!" she interrupted, looking pale beneath her golden tan. She was torn between nausea and pride. She feared nausea would win.

Drake saw her dilemma and saved her. "I have a fine idea. I will clean and cook the fish while you gather some fruit to go with it."

Alex brightened immediately. "Wonderful!" She fairly flew from the water, spraying Drake's face in her haste to leave the scene of the fish's massacre.

Drake threw back his head and laughed, watching her sprint off into the trees. He adored both her spirit and her gentleness, the dazzling combination of contradictions that was Alex. He found himself most eager for dinner.

And even more eager for what he planned for after dinner.

It was that wondrous time of day when the sun was not quite ready to take its leave and the moon was impatient to makes its appearance, the result being a golden glow of twilight that bathed the island in a sheen of splendor.

Drake carefully carried the steaming skewered bass to the fire he had built just outside their lean-to. Off to one side of their sleeping quarters, hidden by a dense cluster of white birch trees, he and Alex had created their "dining room," which consisted of two smooth, flat stones, side by side, large enough to act as dinnerware. And of course their fingers made the perfect utensils. Barbaric by the *ton*'s standards, euphoric by the castaways'.

Drake made his way through the trees until he reached his goal. Then he stopped short, staring at the vision that greeted his eyes.

"Good evening, Captain Barrett." Alex smiled up at him, her wonderfully expressive eyes a deep, smoky gray. She was waiting for him, clad only in his familiar white shirt, her knees tucked beneath her, her hands behind her on the ground as she leaned back to give Drake a dazzling smile.

Before her was spread an array of freshly picked berries, surrounded by every type of exquisite flower imaginable—

violets, hepatica, trillium, even wild roses. Never had Drake seen a more elegantly prepared meal, or one he so badly wanted to savor.

Slowly he dropped down beside her and wordlessly deposited half the fish on her "plate," the other half on his own. The fresh scent of fruit and flowers rose up to tantalize his senses, and Drake fought the sudden compulsion to lay Alex down in their fragrant garden and forfeit the meal in favor of dessert.

"Everything looks lovely," he said at last in a husky voice that made her heart beat faster.

"I'm glad," she replied softly, then grinned. "We will have to imagine the crystal chandelier and the wine, however."

"The moonglow is magnificent, and I'm already intoxicated."

Something was different tonight, something that made Alex feel a wild sense of anticipation that transcended the mere physical. "It's this island," she murmured dreamily. "Its effect is devastating."

Drake nodded, helping himself to a ripe, sweet berry. "I know. I don't think I have ever been quite so content in all my life. It even makes losing my ship bearable."

Alex looked quickly at his face. It was the first time he had spoken of the loss of his ship, and she wanted to gauge his reaction. "I know what a blow that was to you," she said carefully. "She was a very special ship."

Drake gave her a small smile. "Especially to me. She was one of the few things I could rely upon in my life."

"Not your family?"

"No, not my family. With the exception of Smitty, who is ofttimes more a father to me than my own."

Alex looked surprised. "You have never spoken of your father before. What is he like?"

"Weak." Drake's voice and his face grew harder. "Very kind, but without backbone. He has always trusted too easily and too much. My sister is much like him in her nature."

"Your sister?"

176

He nodded. "Yes. She is warm and loving and too tender-hearted for her own good. I fear that one day someone will hurt her badly."

"Did someone do that to your father?"

Drake's jaw tightened. "How did we get onto this subject?"

"I just wanted to know more about you," Alex told him quietly.

Drake felt a stab of guilt at the reality that her words forced to mind. In truth, she knew nothing of him at all. And those things that he had never told her could change everything between them.

He pushed the unwelcome thought away. Now was not the time. "There is nothing more to know."

"Were there many women in your life?"

He looked stunned at the forthright question. "What?"

"Women. Have there been many women?"

"In my bed, yes. In my life, no."

She stared. "Why?"

"Because women are infinitely satisfying in the former and heartlessly treacherous in the latter."

His abrupt answer made her wince. He saw the movement and felt immediately contrite.

"I'm sorry, princess. It's just that no woman has ever been so bold as to inquire about my previous, er . . . entanglements."

"I'm not just *any* woman, Drake. I am your wife."

He smiled. "No, you are not just any woman, love. And *not* just because you are my wife. You are unique." He chuckled at her uncertain expression. "I mean that as the highest of compliments," he assured her.

She gave him a dazzling smile. "I'm glad. It is nice to be admired rather than frowned upon for being unique."

"Meaning?"

She sighed. "I have none of the appropriate skills of a noblewoman, which makes me a disappointment to my parents. They provided me with a string of ideal governesses, whose strict instructions were to educate me in all the social graces."

Drake smiled, picturing her as a rebellious child. "And did they?"

"Hardly," she admitted sadly. "All their diligent work was a dismal failure. I still cannot sew a stitch or draw a straight line. My French is fair, at best, and when I play the pianoforte all the hunting dogs my father keeps at Sudsbury howl in protest."

Drake grinned. "Your sailing is quite good."

"My father considers that a curse rather than a blessing," she replied in a defeated tone.

"You are very creative in the kitchen," he suggested, with a twinkle. "How many women, noble or otherwise, can boast of catching a fish with their bare hands? Not to mention your innovative approach to stew."

She looked crestfallen. "You knew?"

He chuckled. "Of course I knew, princess. Stew, no matter how elegantly prepared, is still stew. But I didn't want you to think me unappreciative of your efforts, so I said nothing."

She gave him a small smile. "Thank you. But somehow I do not think my parents would be impressed with my enthusiasm in the kitchen."

His brilliant eyes danced. Nor with her enthusiasm in the bedroom, he suspected. But he wisely refrained from pointing this out to her.

Instead, he said softly, "Surely they have gotten over their dismay. After all, you are no longer a child, but a very lovely grown woman."

Alex shook her head. "No. Actually, I believe they were looking forward to my first Season in the hope that it would reform me and transform my life. My father wanted to wash his hands of me and see me wed to an appropriate member of the peerage."

Silently Drake agreed. The earl was a cold, unfeeling shell of a man.

Alex was continuing. "My mother assumed that I would be ecstatic at the thought of meeting prospective husbands. She expected that I would immediately alter my personality and become the lady she always wanted me to be." She grimaced. "If I were home right now, I would be suffocated by visits from countless suitors—all wealthy, titled, proper, and horribly boring." She shuddered in distaste, remembering some of the men to whom her parents had been eager to introduce her. "John Hardsley, the Earl of Remdale, is dim-witted and balding. William Kendall, the Marquis of Darwell, is pompous and condescending. George Mackelroy, the Earl of Bladeston, is—"

"All of those things, not to mention obese, stingy, and quite a cheat when he plays chess," Drake finished in disgust.

"How on earth do you know so much about Lord Bladeston?" Alex's head shot up, and she stared at Drake in wonder.

Drake started. He had been so caught up in the conversation, so appalled at the choices Geoffrey Cassel had been entertaining for his beautiful daughter, that he had made a terrible *faux pas*. But, damn it, any one of those arrogant dandies would have broken Alex's spirit in no time.

He scowled. "It would surprise you just how widespread the gossip concerning the *ton* is, princess." He evaded the question as well as Alex's curious gaze. "Sometimes it even reaches the ears of a mere sea captain."

Alex fell silent then, sensing the beginning of the tension that always accompanied their talks of the upper crust. Desperate to reestablish the tender mood, she touched his arm gently.

"Drake, England is very far away from us right now. I don't want it to cast a shadow on the splendor of this island . . . please?"

He glanced down at the small hand on his arm, feeling a fresh surge of guilt. He would tell her, his conscience assured him. He would . . . but not tonight. No, tonight was theirs.

He lifted her hand, kissed her fingers. "Fine," he murmured. "We will enjoy the present while it belongs to us." He leaned over, picked up another berry and popped it into Alex's smiling mouth. "Let's eat our sumptuous dinner, love, before it becomes too dark."

They sat quietly for a while, eating and allowing the splendor of the evening to settle upon the island.

It was Alex who broke the silence. "It is difficult to decide which time of day here is my favorite," she murmured, staring up at the starlit sky. "The mornings are a slow rebirth that take one's breath away, the days are warm and vibrant, filled with sights and sounds that captivate every one of the senses, and the nights are deep and fragrant and filled with magic."

"Some things defy description," Drake answered softly.

"On our way to York you told me that there is a legend attached to these islands," she reminded him.

"I did, didn't I?" He smiled.

"Will you tell it to me now?" she asked.

"I couldn't think of a better time." He settled himself beside her, feeling the soft brush of her hair against his bare shoulder, and began.

"Actually, there are many legends, not just one. I know two of them." He gave her a meaningful sidelong glance. "Both are equally beautiful and appealing to those with a romantic nature."

Alex's eyes grew wide with interest. "I want to hear both of them," she urged.

He chuckled. "I rather thought you might." Always thirsty for knowledge of any kind was Lady Alexandria Cassel . . . Lady Alexandria Cairnham, he amended silently.

"The Indians believed that the Great Spirit, Manatoana, and the god of evil were at war. They stood on opposite banks of the river casting rocks at each other. Those stones that fell short of their target landed in the water and were transformed into the islands. Manatoana was, of course, victorious, after which the Thousand Islands came to be known as the Garden Place or the Happy Hunting Ground of the Great Spirit."

"How wonderful!" Alex's whole face was alight with pleasure.

"The second legend is even more poetic," Drake continued. "It is said that when white-robed angels carried Eden to heaven, one thousand flowers fell from the garden. These flowers lit upon the waters of the river and floated to the surface, thus becoming the Thousand Islands."

"That is an enchanting picture," Alex breathed. "And considering the euphoria that permeates our island, that legend is perfect . . . magical and mystical, as is our little paradise, don't you agree?"

He ruffled her hair gently. "Yes, princess, I do. Legends are people's ways of breathing life into their dreams."

Alex sighed. "Dreams are wondrous things. For in them anything you wish for can be yours."

Her words sounded so wistful. And suddenly all Drake wanted was to make her every wish come true.

"And what is your dream, princess?" he asked in the growing darkness. "Throughout your young and sheltered life, what has been your heart's desire?"

She stared up at the stars. "My answer will no doubt surprise you, for it is quite contrary to your opinion of my needs."

"Meaning?"

"Meaning that you are convinced that I delude myself into thinking that my happiness cannot be found within my aristocratic world. I have never denied being a product of my social class, for that is all I know. But we are speaking of dreams now, not realities." She continued to gaze up at the heavens, remembering all the lonely nights at Sudsbury when she had stared at those same stars, dreaming that same dream.

"Some women dream of princes, wonderful and powerful men who carry them off to their castles, where they will live happily ever after." Her voice had grown faint, and she was so far away, lost in her own thoughts and memories, that Drake wondered if she even remembered his presence. "I have lived in that castle and I know just how empty and lonely it can be. And princes are merely men who are consumed with themselves and their domains. There is no room in their hearts for love, true love that yearns for a partner to stand beside them rather than beneath them yet on a pedestal above all others." She shook her head. "I want no part of that dream. My dream?

A man who can take me from that castle to a simple cabin, where we can live as we will and love as we were born to do, side by side, with joy and with meaning. Sadly, I have yet to find that within the confines of my social circle."

"You are my wife now."

Alex turned, startled, at the ferocity of Drake's tone. In truth, she had been lost in her words, unthinking of how they would affect him.

"Yes, I am," she answered softly, looking up into his face.

Drake could barely understand his own reaction at her description of her dream. Everything inside him tightened with tenderness, with an almost violent determination to be everything she wanted and needed him to be. She thought he was that simple man of whom she spoke. Yet he was not, could never be, for he was as much a prisoner of his noble birth as she. She believed him to be a sea captain; that he was. And he was her husband, now and always. For now it would have to be enough.

"Drake?" She reached up to touch his cheek, stroked her hand over his beard. "I didn't mean . . ." She broke off. How could she tell him that he was everything she wanted, that she loved him so much it frightened her? He was none of the things she had been brought up to seek in a husband, and upon returning to England, she would suffer the *ton*'s scorn and ridicule . . . and yet, in spite of it all, she wanted him, needed him. Loved him.

She had no chance to speak. Wordlessly Drake pulled her to him, covering her mouth with his.

Alex required no urging, for she shared the same desperate feelings that shook his powerful frame. Drake made a sharp sound deep in his throat and pulled her onto his lap, crushing her against his bare chest and kissing her until she could hardly breathe.

She didn't care if she suffocated. It had been too long since she had been able to express through her body what she felt in her heart. She dug her fingers into the longer hair at the nape of his neck and held on, pressing herself as close to him as she could, wanting to be absorbed into his body.

Drake was already out of control. He stared down at her face, suffused by moonlight. "Your head?" he gasped.

"It doesn't hurt."

"Alex . . . are you sure?"

"Drake, please, please . . . I need you."

He was on his feet, lifting her into his arms and taking long strides toward their shelter. Alex buried her face against his chest, feeling the crisp hair tickle her nose, inhaling his wonderful masculine scent. She felt the warmth of the fire surround them as he lowered her to the soft grass that was their mattress, then dropped to his knees beside her.

Alex watched him gaze down at her with blazing desire and poignant tenderness that he made no attempt to hide. She reached for him; he covered her with himself. They wrapped their arms around each other, their mouths meeting in an endless kiss that said more than words ever could. Somewhere in the inferno that followed, Alex felt Drake unbutton her shirt, pull it from her body, then kick off his breeches, never ending the kiss. Their naked flesh met, pressed closer, ignited. Alex threw back her head, alive with sensation, as Drake buried his face against her throat, whispered her name, then licked a slow path around each swelling breast, reveling in her moans of pleasure, her pleas for more. He wet the tip of each nipple with his tongue, grazed it with his teeth, and finally drew it deep into his hungry mouth. Alex cried out his name, digging her hands into his shoulders, pulling him closer.

He was on fire, desperate to make her burn with the same intensity that throbbed through his loins. He needed her, all of her, this night. He trailed his open mouth across her shoulder and down her arm, kissing her palms, her fingers, moving then to the other arm to repeat the caress. He loved her slowly, fighting the rampaging desire that grew stronger, more insistent, each time his tongue laved her hot skin. His caress left no part of her untouched; he kissed her waist, her flat stomach, her thighs. She opened herself to him wordlessly, and he began to stroke his tongue again and again over the warm softness between her legs. He closed his eyes, inhaling her fragrance, drinking in her growing wetness. He listened to her cries of passion, felt the urgent arching of her body against his mouth. Cupping her soft bottom, he brought her closer to his seeking tongue until Alex began to cry out wildly, convulsing, shuddering against him. He felt every exquisite spasm of her body, not lifting his head until she went limp in his arms. Then he raised himself up, gazed down into her flushed, damp face. It still was not enough. With a ragged sound, Drake lowered himself to the grass beside her and pulled her over him, on top of him. He wrapped his arms around her with near-violent possession, crushing her breasts to his chest, feeling her silken limbs entwined with his strong, hair-roughened ones. He took her mouth with a hunger that transcended the mere physical, and she returned his unspoken words with her own.

Panting, Alex tore her mouth from his, pushing herself up and away from him. She saw the question in his darkened eyes and answered it.

"I want to love you, too," she whispered. Before he could answer, she lowered her mouth to the hollow at the base of his throat, tasting the salt of his sweat, then defined his magnificent body inch by inch with her seeking mouth. She lapped lightly at each male nipple and heard him gasp with pleasure. Slowly, gracefully, she moved down, nipping gently at the taut planes of his abdomen, the powerful muscles of his thighs. She raised her head.

Drake was watching her, his breathing suspended for the seconds that passed before she acted. Then, with a siren's smile she lowered her head and ran her tongue slowly, lingeringly, over his throbbing manhood. Drake called out her name, his whole body heightened to the very brink of sensation.

Alex was fascinated by his maleness, by his very size and potency. She wrapped her small hand around him, caressed him tenderly, then lowered her head again to explore the very essence of his masculinity. He was rock hard, yet satin smooth, and so very hot to the touch. Lightly she stroked her tongue up to the velvety tip, licking off the droplet of fluid that she found there. In one savage motion Drake reached down and pulled her off him, rolling her to her back.

Alex stared up at him, startled and unsure. "Drake?"

He parted her legs with his knees, desperately, frantically. "I've got to have you now," he gasped. "This minute . . . right now." He entered her in one violent thrust. Alex arched her hips, bringing him deeper, feeling the wildness take over as he filled her, stretched her delicate flesh to take all of him. Drake slid his hands beneath her, lifting her to meet the frenzied pounding of his body, claiming her enveloping softness again and again.

"Alex . . . oh, Alex." He couldn't seem to stop saying her name. He found her mouth with his, kissed her urgently, the primitive motions of his tongue matching those of his body. She met his tongue, his body, thrust for thrust, whimpering his name as he went even deeper, took her higher than she'd ever gone before. She lifted her legs, wrapped them around his waist, and clung to him as they moved toward the pulsing release that hovered just a split second away.

And then it was upon her, unbearable in its intensity. Alex tore her mouth from Drake's and cried out, skyrockets of sensation bursting through the very core of her being. And the words were torn from her, along with her heart and her soul, and she could no more have stopped them from being said than she could have stopped herself from feeling them.

"Drake . . . I love you!" she gasped. "I love you!"

She felt him reach a pinnacle of sensation. His body jolted as he poured himself into her in bursts of release that tore through him and flowed to her in a moment that seemed to hold them captive forever.

She never knew if he had heard her declaration of love, for that night there were no more words, only the union of husband and wife, as Drake conveyed to Alex again and again with his body what he felt in his heart.

Chapter 19

Alex stirred, the familiar sound of twittering birds rousing her from sleep. She was locked in Drake's arms, just the way she had fallen asleep.

How many times had he made love to her? She had lost count, but each time their bodies joined, the unnamed emotion that was between them seemed to grow more powerful, more meaningful.

He had never said he loved her. Somehow Alex had known not to expect the words. But she knew she had reached him, touched something inside him, despite whatever emotional scars he bore that kept him from her. It was a start . . . a fragile, wonderful beginning.

She squirmed out of his embrace and ran into the morning sunshine. Happily, she stretched her arms over her head and inhaled the sweet air. Another day in paradise.

First she would search for their breakfast. Then she would help Drake work on the raft until she became restless. By midday she would be off exploring the numerous gifts that nature offered on their island. In truth, she hoped it would take Drake years to complete the makeshift boat that would enable them to make their way to the Canadian shore. Civilization seemed less and less appealing as the days went on.

She donned her newly washed chemise and headed for the water. She approached cautiously after assuring herself that no American ships were in the vicinity. The river was quiet, with just a few small boats cruising past, and she sighed with relief. Ofttimes it was different. She and Drake would conceal themselves, holding their breath, as an American ship passed by. At times like this they were grateful

186

for their island's somewhat secluded location, which helped to ensure their safety.

Alex stepped gingerly into the river, finding the water frigid, yet somehow exhilarating. She waded in up to her thighs, then cupped her hands and splashed water on her face, as part of what had become her morning ritual since she had gotten well.

She was just about to return to the shore and begin berry-picking when she spied a sudden movement. Curious, she paused, shielding her eyes from the sun with one hand and searching for the source of the motion. In less than a minute she found it.

Clinging to a large piece of driftwood, looking soggy and pathetic and adorable, was a puppy. With a gasp of surprise, Alex waded farther out toward the log that served as the pup's lifeboat. He was just out of her reach, being carried further away by the current. Without thinking, Alex lunged forward, wrapping her hand around the shaking pup just as she lost her footing and plunged full-length into the icy depths of the river.

Drake had just awakened when he heard her scream. He was on his feet, pulling on his breeches, and heading toward the shore all at once.

"Alex!" he shouted, gripped with fear as he saw her thrashing about in the river. "I'm coming, love!"

He took off at a dead run, his heart pounding, and prepared to dive in after her. He came to a grinding halt as his dripping wife reached the sand, laughing and clutching a squirming brown object in her arms.

"Drake, look!" she laughed, oblivious to the stark terror on his face that was rapidly turning into blinding rage. "A puppy!"

"Do you have any idea how frightened I just was?" he thundered back at her. "I thought you were drowning *again!*"

Alex looked startled, then giggled. "Of course not! I really am quite a good swimmer when I'm not suffering from a concussion, you know."

Drake wanted to throttle her, but she looked so damned

appealing standing there like a wet sea nymph clutching the bewildered puppy, that he gave it up. He was just going to have to get used to living with an unpredictable tornado.

He grinned in spite of himself as he walked over to her, reaching out to scratch the dog's ears. "Rather sad looking, is he not?"

"*He* was close to drowning!" Alex defended. "I found him clinging to a piece of driftwood!"

"Yes, well, he probably survived a naval battle that resulted in the destruction of his captain's ship. Apparently you saved his scrawny life, princess."

Alex inspected the shivering pup and frowned. "He is thin. And cold. I have an idea!" She brightened. "You catch a fish for him to eat and I'll warm him in the sun!"

"I'll what?"

She gave him a beseeching look. "Please, Drake, he must be starving."

Drake shook his dark head and started toward the water. "Why do I know I am going to regret this?" He turned back, rather enjoying the protective way Alex cradled the puppy to her own wet body. "You are one lucky dog." He paused. "What are you going to call your new pet, wife?"

Alex chewed her lip thoughtfully, staring down into the warm brown eyes that now looked up at her adoringly. When he was dry, he would be quite the thing. He was lean and long-limbed, all golden brown but for a thatch of black fur beneath his chin. He looked like a handsome rogue. Just like . . .

"I have it!" she informed her husband. "I shall name him Blackbeard. He resembles you, Drake, a strong, gentle pirate." She gave a gaping Drake a dazzling smile. "Now I have two pirates on my island rather than one!"

Drake watched Alex scurry onto the sun-drenched beach, placing a willing and eager-to-please Blackbeard beside her on the sand. He smiled as the puppy snuggled against Alex and licked her face. Turning, Drake waded out to begin his quest for Blackbeard's meal.

*   *   *

"No, Blackbeard! Come back here with that blasted thing!"

Drake looked up from the tedium of his raft-building in time to see the frisky pup bound past him, Alex's chemise held fast between his teeth. Alex tore after him, lifting the bottom of Drake's shirt, which flapped about her knees and impeded her progress. Her golden hair flew out around her, her indecently exposed legs glowed with a newly acquired tan. Her concentration was fierce as she made her way through the trees and followed Blackbeard toward the water.

"You miserable wretch!" she shouted. "Give me back my clothing!"

Drake leaned back on his haunches and, seeing that no ships threatened nearby, grinned. Quite a sight indeed. Blackbeard, who in less than two weeks had become the apple of Alex's eye, had apparently fallen into disfavor with his benevolent mistress. Laughter rumbled deep in Drake's chest as he watched Alex catch up with her pet and begin a fervent tug-of-war to regain control of her undergarment.

In all his two and thirty years he had never felt as carefree as he had these past weeks. Alex filled his days with laughter, his heart with tenderness, his life with meaning, and his nights with passion. Unable to put words to the growing feeling inside him, Drake instead made love to her with an urgency that grew more and more frenzied as the days progressed. He couldn't seem to possess his wife totally or frequently enough to satisfy his bottomless craving for her. Some nights the first golden rays of dawn were already filtering down from the skies before he would let her sleep. And even then he would keep her to him, still deep inside her, joined to her even in slumber.

Each night she told him that she loved him. He had heard those words uttered countless times from women in the throes of passion and had dismissed them as meaningless. Until Alex. When she pressed her perfect body against him, shuddering with her climax, and whispered those words against his skin, he felt the queerest emotion surge in his chest. And he knew that, despite his past and the bitterness that it held, he wanted to believe she meant them.

A joyous bark broke into his thoughts. Alex and Blackbeard were now wrestling playfully in the shallow waves. Alex looked about her, then seized a long, thin stick and tossed it onto the shore.

"Fetch, Blackbeard!" she commanded.

Ever eager to please, the puppy dropped the wrinkled chemise and bolted, returning instantly, his tail waving with triumph, the stick between his teeth.

"I suppose you are waiting for praise!" Alex glared at him, trying, unsuccessfully to smooth out her undergarment.

The happy pup dropped his stick at her feet and gave her a hopeful look.

She melted, dropping onto her knees on the sand beside him. "Very well, I shall forgive you," she conceded, hugging his soft golden fur. "Although I don't know why. You are more trouble than any mongrel is worth."

Blackbeard yipped his protest at the slanderous remark.

"I am sorry if it offends you, but it happens to be the truth," she retorted. "I know you believe yourself to be a retriever of impeccable pedigree, and I do agree that there is much retriever blood in you, but your markings"—she stroked his soft black beard—"tell me that your parentage is questionable." She stroked his silky head. "But your heart is pure, and that is what matters, not your blood." With that she stood and released the pup, who took off eagerly into the woods.

Drake's breath caught in his throat as Alex, unaware that she was being observed, unbuttoned the shirt, which she rarely wore anymore, and tossed it onto the sand, then pulled the chemise over her head and let it flow along the contours of her body.

For a fleeting moment Drake contemplated shedding his breeches and actually taking Alex right there in the water. But another glance at the raft beside him brought him to his senses. As much as he wanted to give in to the excruciating pleasure of ravishing his wife's lush body, he could no longer put off this inevitable conversation.

He walked behind her, wrapping his arms about her waist. "Hello, wife," he whispered into her tangled hair. "Do you think you can part with that sorry excuse for a dog for just a moment? We need to talk."

Despite his teasing words, Alex heard the seriousness of his tone. She turned, met his gaze, and nodded. Hand in hand they walked away from the shore until they reached the spot where the raft lay, symbolizing their imminent departure.

"It is almost completed," Drake said quietly.

"I know." Alex's voice was devoid of emotion. "And my head is totally healed. After all, it has been nearly a month since my accident."

Drake caressed her with his eyes. "It seems, princess, that our time in paradise is coming to an end." His words hung heavily in the air. Finally, and with gentle understanding, he drew her fingers to his mouth and kissed them. "We should go back to the shelter," he suggested tenderly. "It is not wise to stay out in the open for this length of time."

Alex watched him stride back to the river's edge to collect the shirt she had discarded. He was the most magnificent of men; his taut, muscular body and strong, chiseled features never failed to make her pulse flutter. And, here, he was hers.

The future and all its uncertainties loomed ahead. Would they succeed in reaching Canada alive, and if they did, what fate awaited them? Their old lives had been snatched away from them. Yet here on their island they had been able to live as husband and wife, with all life's harsh realities held in abeyance. Would it be possible, in spite of their drastic differences, to build a new life together?

She honestly didn't know.

Drake lay awake far into the night, staring at the wooden roof of their lean-to. Beneath that crude and hastily constructed roof Drake had experienced a happiness and contentment that had been denied to him beneath the palatial, gilded ceilings of Allonshire. And now he would return to that austere world, to make a customary visit prior to another trip at sea.

If all went well, he and Alex would soon arrive safely in British territory. Then they would make their way to Kingston, where he could acquire another ship for their journey back to England . . . to Allonshire. The thought made him ill.

He sighed, shifting his weight on the soft grass. The movement disturbed Alex, and she mumbled something unintelligible in her sleep and snuggled closer against her husband's warmth, her hair draped across his chest. Drake smiled tenderly. Who would believe that this tiny, utterly innocent-looking angel had been an abandoned tigress beneath him less than an hour past? He had felt her urgency, understood it, and shared it. Their time alone together was growing short.

He had to tell her. He loathed the thought. He was a damned nobleman, heir to a dukedom, wealthier than hell— everything she had tried to escape. Perhaps she would understand that he, in his deception, was also trying to escape the rigid confines of the way of life they both abhorred.

But he had lied to her. And *that* she would never forgive.

He tightened his arms around her possessively. She was his. She would stay his, no matter what lay ahead. Alexandria Cassel Barrett was his wife.

It was the barking that awakened them.

"Drake?" Alex's voice was a sleepy question.

"Obviously Blackbeard has decided to begin his day at dawn," he grumbled back, drawing her against him. She felt so damned good—except that she was squirming to free herself.

"He never barks like that . . . so frantically," she said in a worried voice. "Perhaps I should see what the problem is." She paused. "Well?" she demanded. "Aren't you even a little curious?"

He groaned. "You wore me out last night, princess. I need to regain my strength."

Alex's eyes twinkled. "Very well. I shall investigate on my own." She shrugged into Drake's shirt and made her way through the trees toward the persistent sound of Blackbeard's bark. At the clearing she stopped short. "My God. A ship." Panic surged through her as she realized the danger they were in. She hurried forward before the ship was close enough to see her, snatched the long-limbed puppy in her arms, and raced back to their shelter.

"Drake!" Her voice was shaking.

He sat up immediately. "Love, what is it?"

"A ship. And it's very close to shore." She stared at him, terror in her eyes. "Do you think they've spotted us?"

"I don't know." He had already donned his breeches. "We must stay out of sight."

They both held their breath and waited. The ship was close, very close. They could actually hear the movement of the water beneath its hull. Blackbeard whined and struggled in Alex's arms.

"Stay still!" she ordered, holding him tighter.

The pup, who was accustomed to only the gentlest of treatment from his beloved mistress, gave a sharp bark of protest, then tore himself from her arms.

"Blackbeard, come back!" Alex was halfway out of the lean-to before Drake yanked her back in.

"Are you out of your mind?" he demanded. "You are not going out there!"

Alex looked up at him with frightened eyes. "But they'll see him. He could get hurt."

"That is still no reason to risk your life."

"But if the Americans see Blackbeard they'll suspect that there are people here as well," she protested weakly.

"That's a chance we will just have to take." He released her arm, convinced that she wouldn't dare defy him.

He should have known better.

The moment she was free, Alex sprinted out into the woods, calling Blackbeard's name frantically, pleading with him to return to safety.

"Damn you, Alexandria," Drake exploded, tearing through

the woods with the greatest of speed in the hope of overtaking his impulsive wife before she forfeited both their lives.

Blackbeard had reached the water's edge and was barking furiously at the approaching ship. Alex was close behind, terrified as she saw that the ample-sized schooner was almost upon them. And all at once she stopped dead in her tracks just as Drake grabbed her from behind.

"Drake," she breathed, "she's flying a British flag! How is that possible?"

Drake stared over Alex's head, and suddenly a huge smile broke out across his bearded face.

"There is only one person with enough nerve to fly the British flag this deep into American territory."

Simultaneously Smitty's voice reached them through his speaking trumpet. "Captain?" he politely inquired. "May I offer you a ride?"

Chapter 20

Blackbeard was hailed a hero.

As a result of his reckless behavior there was much cause for celebration among *La Belle Illusion*'s re-united crew as their newly-acquired schooner cruised down the Saint Lawrence. Fortunately the pup retained his humility and was satisfied with a hearty beef dinner and free rein on his new moving domicile. It was soon obvious that Blackbeard was indeed a sea dog who had probably spent his entire young life aboard a ship.

Having completed his exploration, he sprang unceremoniously upon the quarterdeck, curled up beside the helm at Drake's feet, and made himself at home.

Smitty began to laugh. "I see you have acquired a new admirer during your absence, Captain."

"He much resembles Drake, does he not, Smitty?" Alex asked from the main deck. "Especially their bearded faces?"

Drake looked down in amazement as Blackbeard contentedly sniffed the sea air, then began nibbling at Drake's boots. "His arrogance is staggering," he muttered.

"Another startling similarity," Alex agreed.

Drake shot her a dark look, and Smitty beamed.

"it is so good to have you both back again, alive and well," he told them.

There was a moment of hesitation. "It is good we are *all* safe, Smitty," Alex replied at last. "Thank God you and the crew were able to make your way to Kingston."

She was relieved when Smitty turned to Drake and plunged into a full accounting of the past month's events, for she needed a moment to herself. Walking over to the rail, she bade a silent farewell to the wondrous island that had been home for a brief, idyllic time. She had left a part of herself there, an innocence and joy that would remain forever amid the island's magic. She only prayed that a bit of the enchantment had remained inside her as well, to guide her through the weeks to come.

Drake glanced over at her. He knew what she was feeling, for he was experiencing mixed emotions as well—grateful to be alive, elated to be reunited with his crew and to know for certain that they had all survived, yet poignantly saddened at leaving their very own Eden.

Life had no easy answers, only very complex questions.

"Princess? Why don't you go below and get some rest?"

Alex turned to face him, nodding. "You and Smitty have much to discuss, no doubt. And I am already uncomfortable in Thomas's breeches. I had become so used to not needing . . ." She blushed scarlet, realizing what she had been about to say. "I'll go rest." She ducked below with great haste.

Drake chuckled. "That was the fastest I have ever seen Alexandria obey me. I dare not hope it will continue."

Smitty saw the softness in Drake's gaze, just as he had seen the glow on Alex's face. Perhaps, despite his own frantic worry about their well-being, the last month had served a good purpose.

"It feels wonderful to be back at the helm," Drake commented, gripping the wheel and looking about him. "I hope you did not mind relinquishing it to me?"

"It was my pleasure, Captain. I only wish it could have been *La Belle Illusion*."

Drake's jaw tightened. "There will be other ships, Smitty. The American ship was simply too powerful for *La Belle*. We did not stand a chance."

"No, we did not stand a chance," Smitty agreed quietly. "But I do not believe that it was because of the American ship's superiority."

Drake scowled. "What does that mean?"

"The men and I have had much time to talk, to reconstruct the events of that day. All of them swear that the guns were targeted perfectly, the elevations well suited to our distance from the military brig."

"Yet all our volleys fell short."

"Yes." Smitty was quiet for a moment, giving Drake time to absorb the information.

"You agree with their assessment?"

Smitty nodded. "I do."

"Perhaps the wrong amount of powder was placed in the cartridges," Drake suggested.

Smitty shook his head. "Mannings is skilled at filling the cartridges. It is possible that he could estimate incorrectly once, perhaps twice. But again and again? No, that I do not believe."

"Nor do I." Drake stared out to sea for a brief moment. "That leaves only one alternative. The gunpowder itself was not at full strength."

"I would have to agree with you, Captain."

"Do you suspect that it was tampered with?"

"I honestly do not know, Captain. It does seem to be a distinct possibility, although no one could have been certain that we would have need of our cannons."

Drake looked grim. "No, but there was every likelihood, in light of the impending war with America, that we would have to defend ourselves. The odds were good that cutting the potency of our powder would prove successful. And I intend to discover the truth." He paused. "Smitty, please do not mention this in front of Alexandria. I do not want to frighten her; she has endured a great deal these last months."

"Of course, Captain." Smitty studied Drake's face. "You haven't told her, have you?"

"No."

"Why not?"

"I believe that is obvious."

"Do you perceive your wife to be so shallow that she would think less of you for who you are?"

Drake met Smitty's gaze. "I think my wife would cheerfully murder me if she knew the truth."

"She will find out soon enough, Captain."

Drake nodded. "Yes. But I shall have weeks at sea to prepare her for the shock."

"Her reaction will be more severe the longer you wait."

"I do not need you to serve as my conscience, Smitty." Drake didn't know who he was angrier with, Smitty or himself. Suddenly all the doubts and the bitterness seemed to be resurfacing, reminding him of his vulnerability at Alex's hands.

"As you wish, Captain."

"Wishing is for romantics and fools." Drake's voice was hard.

"A man who chooses bitterness over joy could be considered a fool."

"Or merely a man who has learned that there is no joy that does not end in bitterness."

"Bitterness that was caused by another woman to another man; not your wife or yourself."

Drake shot Smitty a look of smoldering anger and raw pain. "My mother was hardly unique in her indiscretions. The majority of the *ton*'s simpering females are cuckolding their husbands and have been doing so for years. Both you and I know that."

"Lady Alexandria is different. You and I both know *that* as well."

Drake slammed his hand down on the wheel. "All right,

damn it, yes! Alexandria is different! She is beautiful and innocent and giving.''

''And?''

''And how long do you think she will remain that way once we return to Allonshire?''

''The world of the nobility is not new to her, Captain.''

''But deceit and the betrayal are. She has been sheltered, a child growing up on the fringes of reality. Hell, Smitty, she wants a loving home filled with warmth and caring.'' He raised a sardonic brow. ''Now, does that sound like Allonshire to you, my friend?''

''It sounds like something you could easily give to her, if you choose to, my lord.''

''I don't know what I choose anymore, Smitty. But I will not forfeit my life or my pride for any woman.''

''The giving of warmth and love does not require the relinquishing of self or pride.''

''Why are you intent on pursuing this distasteful, unresolvable topic?'' Drake demanded.

''Because you are behaving like a scoundrel,'' Smitty shot back, an uncharacteristic flush of anger reddening his weathered face. ''And because I care about you, Captain,'' he added softly, gently. ''Whether you know it or not, you are in love with your wife.''

Absolute silence followed Smitty's quietly spoken words. Then Drake drew a slow breath.

''I do not believe in love and therefore cannot respond to your statement.'' He stepped away from the wheel. ''I am going below to rest. I will return to relieve you when I awaken.'' He turned to go. ''We will not speak of this again, Smitty. Ever. Is that clear?''

''Perfectly clear, Captain.''

''Fine.''

He left Smitty, and the conversation, behind. But, all the way to his cabin Smitty's words kept resounding in his mind. And he was terrified that they were true.

The messenger paused at the foot of the steep stone steps to gape up at the immense Gothic mansion that sprawled endl≈ssly over acres of flawless land. It was not an unusual reaction from a first time visitor to Allonshire. Few country homes in England could boast its size or brilliant architectural design.

Minutes passed before the thoroughly intimidated messenger remembered his missive and hurried up the steps to deliver it. With great relief he left it in the hands of the stiff-faced butler who answered the door. His job was done.

Within the cavernous marble hallways of Allonshire the butler's footsteps echoed eerily as he marched to the dining room and approached one of the uniformed footmen who stood before it. Wordlessly he placed the message in his hands, then turned and disappeared.

The footman moved quickly through the arched doorway, past the antique statues, and over to the head of the intricately carved walnut table.

Sebastian Barrett looked up impatiently from his dinner. "Yes? What is it?"

"Excuse me, my lord. A message has arrived for you."

"Oh?" Calmly he lifted his napkin to his lips, then dropped it carelessly onto the table. He took the note, dismissing the servant with a curt nod of his head.

Sebastian read the contents three times. He was being regretfully informed that *La Belle Illusion* had been destroyed by an American military ship. There was no evidence of survivors.

Upstairs in his bed, Grayson Barrett lay ill, possibly dying. Sebastian was aware that he would have to tell his father of Drake's demise. A most unpleasant task.

Replacing his napkin on his lap, Sebastian continued with his quite delicious meal. The news could wait until after dinner.

Unlike Drake, Alex had no doubt as to what she was feeling. She was totally and irrevocably in love with her husband. Her fears lay elsewhere.

She tossed onto her back in the cabin's narrow berth, trying to come to grips with her trepidation. Drake had still not proclaimed his love for her, despite his tenderness and his passion, and that worried her. Now that he was back at sea where he belonged, Alex feared that the tenuous thread of their relationship would be broken.

And she had one other fear, one that she hated to admit, even to herself.

Was she strong enough to endure the censure she would receive when she returned to England married . . . to a sea captain? The gossip would be rampant, the snubs constant and cruel. She did not like those people, and yet they were all that she knew.

Alex felt like a hypocrite, denouncing the *ton* and their values, yet unable to withstand their scorn. And Drake was so proud, their relationship so fragile; she could never confide her fears to him. He already despised women, especially noblewomen. She had finally made some small progress in convincing him that she was different. She did not intend to undo all that she had done.

If only he loved her; if only he had said the words. That would have made all the difference in the world.

She closed her eyes, tired, drained, but not sleepy. Every roll of the ship bothered her; even the bed felt odd beneath her after weeks of sleeping on the ground. She felt so out of sorts.

The door swung open, and Drake entered the cabin, closing the door behind him. His thoughts were still in a turmoil from the conversation with Smitty. How he longed for the peace that had temporarily been his and now seemed lost and unattainable.

"Drake?" Alex met his troubled gaze.

Perhaps peace could be had . . . for a brief interval.

Drake tossed his clothing aside, climbed into bed, and seized his wife in his arms.

"Don't ask me any questions," he whispered. "For I have no answers to give." He stared into her concerned face and was gripped with a sudden irrational need to lose himself in her. "Don't talk at all," he growled, silencing her reply with his mouth. "No words, none. Just the feeling of your body next to mine, my body inside yours." He parted her lips with his, possessed the sweetness of her mouth with his tongue. "I need you. Alex . . ."

He never finished the thought. Nor was it necessary. For Alex, hearing the raw emotion in her husband's voice, wrapped her arms around him and helplessly gave him everything he wanted and needed from her. And he took it all, greedily, desperately, tearing the shirt from her body and plunging into her softness with every ounce of strength and passion he possessed. Alex cried out, but he didn't slow, couldn't stop. And it didn't matter. At this moment all that mattered to Alex was that she loved him and that he needed her.

The ache inside Drake built to excruciating proportions, and still he battered her with his frantic thrusts. The craving was bottomless, endless, consuming him in a white-hot blaze that raged on and on, built higher and higher. He was lost in a red haze of sensation, unaware of anything but his rampant need to find relief from the throbbing ache in his loins, in his heart. He caught his breath, poised on the edge of a feeling so stark, so intense, that it was unbearable. And then he erupted wildly inside her, calling out to her hoarsely again and again, burying himself so deep inside her that he could touch her soul.

Drake collapsed against Alex's small, soft body, reality filtering back to him in gradual stages of awareness. His first coherent thought was that he had all but raped his wife, and his heart contracted with fear.

"Alex?" He raised himself up on his elbows, searching her flushed, damp face. Her eyes were closed, her lips swollen from his brutal kisses, and scratches caused by his beard's abrasive contact stood out against the golden tan of her cheeks and her chin. His gaze dropped lower. Red marks of his passion marred the honeyed perfection of her shoulders and her throat.

He had never felt like such a bastard in all his life.

"Sweetheart . . ." His voice was hoarse, his hand shaking as he raised it to touch her face. "Alex?"

Alex opened her eyes slowly, barely able to focus. Her body was still awash with the wondrous aftershocks of her climax. She had never imagined such a fiercely tender union, never dreamed she could merge so completely with another person. Awed by what had transpired between them, she stared up at her husband's handsome face in wonder.

"Princess, are you all right?" As his words penetrated her sensual haze, Alex became aware of the concern in his voice, the harsh regret on his face. Why did he look so remorseful when she felt so utterly blissful?

"All right?" she repeated in a whisper, totally at sea.

"Did I hurt you?" He traced his fingers over the scratches on her face, then leaned down to kiss each one of them. "I didn't mean to. I would never . . ." His voice broke, and he rolled off her, because he knew if he stayed inside her he would make love to her again. Make love? Hah! He had brutalized her. And still she looked up at him with innocent adoration in her eyes.

For the first time Drake felt ashamed. Ashamed and unworthy.

"You didn't hurt me." Her soft voice interrupted his self-chastisement. "It was beautiful."

He turned toward her, seeking the truth in her eyes. She smiled, snuggled into his arms. "Actually, I feel wonderful. Quite a bit better than I was feeling before you arrived."

He cradled her against him, relief flooding through him like a great tide. "I never intended to take you so violently. I don't know what came over me."

She kissed one powerful bronzed bicep, wisely remaining silent.

He grinned, still heady with relief. "I must say that it was a welcome change to make love to you on a *real* bed, though."

"Oh, I don't know. I rather liked our crude bed of grass on the island." She laughed. "It made everything feel rather . . . primitive and exciting."

"Princess," he wound her hair around his fingers, "I don't think it can *get* more primitive than it just did."

He could actually feel her blush against his chest, and he chuckled, all the fear and confusion temporarily forgotten. But he knew that they remained, held at bay by emotions that superseded them.

He lifted her face, cupped it tenderly between his strong hands. There was so much he needed to tell her before they docked in London, so much she would have to absorb.

So much she would be unable to accept.

Gently he drew her mouth to his. "Let me love you again," he murmured, his voice husky, seductive. "Slowly this time, the way you were meant to be loved."

She paused, inches from his mouth. "Drake . . . we have much to discuss. You have to know what lies ahead of us when we arrive in England. We'll have to go to Sudsbury, and my mother—"

"Shhh," he whispered, enfolding her in his arms. "We have time . . . weeks before we reach England. Surely it can wait"—his eyes caressed her face—"an hour or two?"

Alex surrendered, letting him weave his magnetic sensual spell around her. And for the hours that followed the only words they exchanged were those of passion and of pleasure.

Much later, they talked.

"My mother is a snob." Alex said it without anger or censure, a mere statement of fact. "She is not going to be happy with my father's decision to see us wed. She had . . . different plans for my future."

To Alex's surprise, instead of becoming enraged, Drake seemed to be amused. "In other words I am not to expect her to welcome me into your family with open arms?"

Alex twisted around to look up at him. "Exactly. This was to be my first London Season, and I ran off with no warning and only a note in the way of explanation. She had arranged for me to meet countless eligible men."

"By 'eligible' I assume you mean titled and wealthy?"

"Yes." She waited for the explosion that did not come.

"Alex," he said softly, "all will be well; you'll see. I am certain that once your mother knows—"

She didn't let him finish. His tenderness caused her more pain than his anger. "Don't excuse her, Drake!" she said, her eyes flashing. "I do not. I only want you to know that, no matter what reaction we receive, I am delighted not to have married a nobleman! They are all shallow and cold like my father, acting only in their own interests." She grew calmer. "I say all this because I want you to know what to expect. In spite of all else, there has always been kindness and truth between us. That is more than many can boast, is it not?"

Alex's words cut through Drake like a knife. He would have given his soul right then to be merely the sea captain she believed him to be, to be worthy of the words she had spoken.

But he wasn't. And he knew he had to tell her the truth, to make her understand.

"Alex . . ." he began.

She laughed, tossing back the covers and stretching. "I know. You've been down here for hours, and you must go topside to relieve Smitty at the helm." She gave him a coy smile over her shoulder. "Very well, Captain, I give you leave to go to your post. But later tonight I shall again demand that you do your husbandly duty, and I warn you now that I intend to give you no quarter."

Drake was stunned, then delighted, thoughts of his confession disintegrating immediately. "I consider myself duly warned, wife. I shall expect to be completely at your mercy." He pushed his feeling of guilt aside. Later, he promised himself, he would tell her later.

But later never seemed to come.

Chapter 21

The docks were humming with activity as the schooner sailed up the Thames and into London. Alex gazed out the porthole, staring at the familiar scene with a peculiar sense of unreality.

She was home. It seemed an eternity since she had left this city, a mere child. She was returning now, a woman grown. A married woman.

She wished that she and Drake had talked more about what lay ahead. Where would they live? Would he captain another ship right away? Would they remain in England for a time or return at once to sea?

And there was her mother. It was September. Perhaps Constance Cassel was in London right now, having returned for the Little Season. If enough of her friends had come here directly from Brighton it was probable that she was here as well. Alex hoped not. She was not ready to face her mother's anger and disappointment. Perhaps in a day or two . . .

"Cap'n! 'ome at last!" Cochran's announcement rang out across the ship and was met with cheers of elation from the crew.

On the quarterdeck Drake smiled, though his eyes were troubled, and called back, "Tie down the ship, then away with all of you and enjoy yourselves! But don't be surprised when you miss the feel of a rolling deck beneath your feet."

A lot of good-natured teasing ensued, during which time Drake pulled Smitty aside.

"Go into town and see Madame DuPres, Samantha's *modiste*. She is talented and discreet. Tell her that we need a gown and accessories now, today. Explain that I will bring my new wife in to order a whole new wardrobe in the next week or two. That should ensure her instant cooperation."

Smitty flushed, unused to acquiring ladies' fashions. "And what will you do during my absence, Captain? Might I suggest mentioning your identity to your wife? That seems to have slipped your mind during the weeks of our voyage."

Drake scowled. "I intend to, Smitty. First I'm going to arrange for a bath for Alexandria. Then I'll walk over to the office of our shipping company to find out what has transpired since we left England. When I return to the ship, I will discuss the situation with my wife. Is that satisfactory?"

Smitty nodded, anticipating Lady Alexandria's reaction to the shocking revelation. "I do not relish the thought of sharing your carriage on the journey home."

"Then walk." Drake strode off, in no mood to be goaded. During the weeks at sea he had refused to think about the confrontation to come, but now he had run out of time.

He ordered a tub of hot water for Alex, then headed to their cabin to speak with her. Outside the closed door he paused, absently stroking his beard. He had to tell her.

At the sound of his entrance, she turned from the porthole and smiled her welcome. "We are here."

He noticed that she didn't use the word "home." Studying her face, he saw the strain there, knew that she was as uneasy about their arrival as he was. Well, by telling her the truth, he could eliminate many of her concerns. But he would also create many more serious ones.

"Yes, princess, we're here." He didn't smile. "I have arranged for your bath, and Smitty has gone into town to purchase some appropriate clothing for you."

"Thank you." Alex was touched. "That was very thoughtful." She hesitated. "Where are we going?"

He gave her a measured look. "To my family's home," he replied at last. "At least for now." Another pause. "Alexandria, I have a great deal to discuss with you. I am sure you have many questions as well." At her nod he continued. "I am going ashore to arrange for a carriage to take us home." The final word tasted bitter on his tongue. "After which I will return and we will talk." He opened the door again, without waiting for an answer. "I'll be back shortly."

Drake left the ship and made his way along the crowded docks to the warehouse labeled "Barrett Shipping." He walked through a narrow entranceway adjacent to the wide wooden cargo doors and went directly into the office.

A stout gray-haired man looked up from the desk and blinked. "Yes? May I help you?"

Drake broke into a broad grin. "Come now, John. I haven't been gone long enough for you to forget me."

John Rother, the overseer at the warehouse, bolted to his feet and gaped. "Lord Cairnham? Is that you?"

"Beard and all, John."

"Forgive me, my lord, but we all thought . . . that is, we received word that . . ."

"That I was dead?" Drake supplied calmly.

"Yes, my lord."

"Well, as you can see, I am very much alive."

"But your ship . . . ?"

Drake's jaw tightened. "Unfortunately, *La Belle Illusion* is lost to us. I will begin plans for her replacement immediately."

"Of course, my lord." Rother was still staring, stunned both by Drake's existence and by his disheveled appearance.

Drake chuckled at the disbelief clearly written on Rother's face. "I need a carriage to take us to Allonshire." He knew that by "us" Rother would assume he meant himself and Smitty. Which was fine. He had no intention of discussing his personal life with those in his employ. But Rother was shaking his head frantically.

"My lord, there is something that you do not know—" He broke off, wiping his damp forehead with the back of his hand.

Drake felt a twinge of fear. "What is it?"

"It is your father, my lord. He is quite ill."

"How ill?" Drake demanded.

Rother dropped his eyes. "We have been told that he is dying, my lord."

"Dying . . ." Drake repeated the word, denying it to himself even as he said it.

"He has been deteriorating rapidly," Rother rushed on, anxious to be done with it. "I have received no word for days now, so I don't know precisely what his condition—"

"Have that carriage brought around immediately," Drake broke in, heading for the door. Business could wait; he was needed at Allonshire.

"It shall be done at once, my lord," Rother assured him.

Drake and Smitty arrived back at the ship at the exact same moment. The worry in Smitty's eyes told Drake that he knew.

"Madame DuPres told me," Smitty answered his unasked question. He extended a package to Drake. "Under the circumstances she was very kind about hurriedly gathering together some necessary garments for Lady Alexandria. She told me to assure you that the wardrobe she designs for her ladyship will cause her to outshine all of London."

Drake took the carefully packaged articles of clothing. "The carriage should be here at any moment. I will get Alexandria."

"Very good, my lord."

Alex was drying her hair when Drake exploded into the cabin. She started.

"Drake? What is it?"

He tossed the parcel onto the bed. "Dress quickly. We must go."

Alex had never seen her husband so unsettled. He looked positively gray.

"Drake?" She dropped the towel, her damp tresses forgotten. "Please tell me."

His tormented gaze met her caring one.

"My father is dying. We must go to him at once."

"Oh, Drake." She walked over and placed her hand on his arm, feeling his fear and his pain. "I'm so sorry. Of course . . . I'll be dressed in a minute."

Her tenderness was like a soothing balm for his raw emotions. "Thank you." The words were said simply, humbly, but with a wealth of meaning that even he didn't fully comprehend. "I'll wait for you topside." He stood a moment longer, watching as his wife tore open the parcel and began to don the flowing gown. It was a willow green muslin of the latest style, but Alex wasn't even seeing it in her haste to get ready. She was nothing like any woman he had ever known, possessing none of their shallowness. And she was his. She would remain so.

He left, softly closing the door behind him. The future had lost no time in finding them.

The carriage ride was silent. Several times Alex glanced at Smitty, a thousand questions on the tip of her tongue. Apparently he was a close friend of the family's, for he was traveling with Drake to Mr. Barrett's side. That warmed her heart. It was just like Smitty to be there for Drake.

Drake was staring out the window with unseeing eyes. Alex sensed his distress, and yet she felt helpless to relieve it. She only prayed that the reports of Mr. Barrett's condition had been exaggerated and that they would arrive home to find him improved.

She knew their destination was Berkshire. She had learned that from Smitty at the onset of their ride, his information imparted in a clipped tone. She forgave him his shortness of temper and chose to remain silent for the duration of the ride. The trip was not a long one, as Berkshire was not far west of London, with the Thames forming much of its northern boundary.

In spite of herself Alex was curious. At last she would meet Drake's family.

The carriage veered sharply to the left and passed through formidable iron gates. Alex frowned. That was odd. She peered out the carriage window and saw acres of plush green grass, exquisite flower gardens, and endless rows of towering shade trees. She sat up taller, squinting into the distance, aware of Smitty's odd expression as he watched her reaction.

And suddenly it dawned on her. An estate of such grandeur would have any number of tenants who lived and worked here. Drake probably came from one of those families. She considered this new possibility. No doubt they lived in a small, cramped cottage devoid of luxuries. Her heart reached out to her proud husband. No wonder he was so uneasy about bringing her here. He thought she would scorn his way of life, look down upon his meager income. Well, she would show him otherwise. She would work right by his side, doing whatever a tenant's wife was supposed to do, and. . .

"Allonshire." It was the first word Drake had uttered since they left the docks. Alex looked over at him and followed his gaze.

"Oh, Lord . . ." she breathed, transfixed by what her unbelieving eyes were seeing.

Just ahead of them and to the right was the most awesome structure Alex had ever beheld. It was a Gothic mansion, each turret soaring higher and higher into the sky, a breathtaking fantasy of endless size.

The mansion sprawled as far as Alex could see, so she had no idea where the tenants' homes might be located. Far in the background rose the chapel's steeple, which marked the mansion's end. Alex could not begin to imagine how many hundreds of rooms Allonshire contained.

To her complete confusion the carriage pulled up directly in front of the wide stone steps leading to the front doors, then stopped. Bewildered, she looked from Smitty to Drake for an explanation.

Drake seemed to come back to the present with a start. Wasn't it ironic that everything was converging into one horrible moment of truth? He gave a humorless laugh and reached for Alex's hand.

"Come, wife," he told her. "The moment of realization has arrived."

Blindly she followed him up the steps, staring in astonishment as he flung open the front door and ushered her in. A flustered uniformed butler hurried toward the entranceway.

"I beg your pardon," he began, and Alex wanted to

weep with pity for her poor husband, "but all deliveries are to be made—"

"I'm flattered by your assessment of my appearance, Humphreys," Drake interrupted, eyeing the servant, who was now as white as a ghost.

"My God," he breathed, staring at Drake's bearded face.

"Not unless I've been granted a new title during my absence."

"My lord? Is it really you? We heard that—"

"Hello, Humphreys," Smitty interrupted, following Drake into the house.

"My lord?" Alex echoed slowly.

"How is my father?" Drake demanded, ignoring Alex's puzzlement.

Humphreys shook his head. "His grace is slipping away, my lord. You came home just in time . . ." His voice trailed off.

Drake headed for the curved marble stairway, dragging Alex along with him. "Where are Sebastian and Samantha?" he called back.

"Lord Sebastian is in London on business, and Lady Samantha is out riding, my lord. She hasn't been the same since we received word of your death."

"Find her. Tell her I'm here . . . with my wife."

"Wife, my lord?" For the first time Humphreys focused on the white-faced young woman who was being dragged along in Drake's wake.

"Yes, Humphreys, wife." They had reached the second-floor landing. "You will meet Lady Cairnham after I have seen my father. Smitty can tell you whatever you need to know." He and Alex disappeared from view.

Alex's feet were moving automatically, her gaze unfocused. Drake paused before a set of closed doors.

Alex stood, paralyzed, and stared up at Drake, her eyes, her voice, those of a stranger.

"My *lord?*"

Chapter 22

The room was cast in shadows, the drapes drawn. The only source of light was the fire that burned low in the stone fireplace.

Alex blinked, trying to accustom her eyes to the near-darkness. Her mind was numb, her body moving instinctively as her husband impatiently pulled her along. He stopped abruptly and released her hand. Alex could make out the curtained outline of a heavy wooden bed, but no movement came from within. Alex was beginning to believe the room to be unoccupied when a weak, gravelly voice reached her ears.

"Who is it?"

Alex could feel Drake tense, heard him swallow deeply before he spoke.

"Hello, Father."

There was a quick movement, a harsh intake of breath, and then a pained, "Drake?"

"Yes, Father, it's Drake."

"Come to me." Weak, but a command.

Drake obeyed. He pushed the curtain back and leaned over his father.

For a moment there was silence; then Alex heard Grayson whisper, "Am I dead, then?"

Drake stood up abruptly, strode across the room, and tore open the heavy draperies that kept out the September sun. Blazing light filled the room, illuminating everything with perfect clarity.

"No, Father, you are not dead, and neither am I. Look at me; I am very much alive, and I'm home."

Another silence. Then a very soft "My son . . ."

Alex looked at Grayson Barrett and smothered a gasp. The face of the man beneath the layers of bedcovers was chalk white, his skin drawn. He was obviously a big man, but he looked lifeless and frail, his pale blue eyes vague and unfocused.

She glanced over at her husband, who was apparently sharing her horrified reaction to his father's depleted condition. Drake looked ill.

"Closer." The quavering word sounded so pathetic that Alex wanted to weep.

Drake complied, returning to stand beside his father's deathbed.

Grayson stared at him for a long moment. "God has granted my last wish by sending you home safe." He struggled for breath, then continued, "I haven't much time or strength left. But before I go, I need to know that you will do what you must, what is your duty. You do understand?"

Drake nodded, his eyes burning with unshed tears. "Yes, Father, I understand."

Grayson closed his eyes and for one panic-stricken minute Alex thought he was gone. But then he continued, desperate to convey all he had to before it was too late. "Allonshire," he murmured. "You must . . ."

"I will."

"Samantha."

"I will always protect and care for Samantha; you know that. And when the time comes I will bring her out as you would want me to. I will see to her happiness, I swear."

Grayson nodded, relief settling upon his tortured features. "I had no doubt that you would see to her happiness. My only regret is that I could not see to yours."

Drake swallowed past the lump in his throat. "I am happy, Father. In fact I have some good news for you." He gestured for Alex to join him. Still in shock, she went to stand by his side. "Father, this is my wife, Alexandria."

The misty blue eyes looked startled as they turned to stare at Alex. "Your wife?"

"Yes, Father, my wife."

Something that resembled a smile touched the older man's lips. "Alexandria, did you say?"

"Yes, your grace," Alex answered softly.

"You are quite beautiful, but that doesn't surprise me, knowing my son," he managed. "But married, now that . . ." His voice trailed off. He continued to stare at her, his gaze unfocused. Suddenly he blinked and seemed to see her again. "Wife . . . Do I know your family?" At that moment he sounded more curious than demanding.

Did he know her family? His question triggered the first concrete thought in Alex's mind, and she almost laughed out loud. Of course he knew her family! How stupid she had been. No wonder her father had been so anxious to marry her off to Drake. She should have known better than to think he would dismiss his high hopes of her marriage to a titled man. A future duke, no less!

Reaction was beginning to take hold, competing with numbness for control of Alex's mind. She felt suddenly light-headed.

She looked down at the man before her. Despite all that had transpired, this poor man was dying. Now was not the time to focus on anything else.

Swallowing her rising hysteria, she gave Grayson a gentle smile. "I am quite certain that you must know them, your grace. My father is the Earl of Sudsbury and currently the governor of Upper Canada."

A flicker of interest registered in Grayson's dull gaze. "You are Geoffrey Cassel's daughter?"

"Yes I am, your grace."

"Then you . . . and my son . . ."

Alex saw what an effort it was for him to speak, so she quietly told him what he wanted to know. "Drake and I were married in Canada, your grace." She carefully omitted the colorful details of their first meeting. "We were on our way back to England when the ship . . . when your ship," she corrected, as that realization clicked into place, "was attacked by the Americans. We escaped, but *La Belle Illusion* did not. That is why you believed Drake dead." Her voice sounded wooden to her own ears.

Grayson turned slightly to Drake. "Smithers?"

"Smitty is fine and came home with us," Drake assured his father. After over thirty years of loyal service Smitty was respected by everyone at Allonshire.

Grayson nodded, continuing to gaze absently at his son. "Your wife . . . I want . . . to speak . . . with her . . . alone." Each word was a struggle.

Drake frowned. He was fairly certain of Alex's state of mind at the moment, and he had no intention of granting his father's request. The meeting could have catastrophic results.

"Father," he began, "I don't think—"

"It's all right, Drake," Alex said, her voice calm and even. But when she glanced at him her eyes were like a winter storm—cold, gray, dismal. He hesitated for a moment longer, then nodded, certain that Alex's inherent kindness would not permit her to hurt a dying man. Drake realized with a start that what he was feeling was trust. He trusted his wife. Quietly he left the room.

Grayson rested, his breathing shallow, then turned back to Alex. "Forgive me," he whispered, "but are you with child?" Seeing Alex's appalled expression, he added shakily, "I want to know, before I die, if there is another heir to Allonshire on the way."

She reminded herself that he was dying and forgave him his bold intrusion into her private life. He was waiting, clinging to a hope that meant so much to him. Alex made her decision.

"It is possible, your grace." As she uttered the words, she was stunned to realize that they were true. She hadn't bled since *La Belle Illusion*'s departure from York—since her marriage to Drake. She dismissed the thought as ludicrous. More than likely the irregularity was due to the stress of the past months.

Grayson was studying her face, his breathing growing more and more erratic. "My son is a difficult man . . . to understand."

At the moment Alex did not want to understand him. She wanted to kill him. "Yes, he is, your grace."

Despite Grayson's obvious pain, a smile tugged at his lips. "And are you . . . difficult . . . as well?"

She met his gaze. "Yes, I am, your grace."

Another smile. "Drake . . . has chosen . . . well." He shuddered as a flash of pain claimed him, but shook his head when she moved to help him. "There is . . . no time." He summoned all his strength, then looked at her calmly. "You . . . love my son . . . very much."

It was a statement of fact and therefore did not require a response.

Alex gave one anyway. "Yes, your grace, I do."

"Be . . . there . . . for . . . him."

Alex's eyes filled with tears. "I will."

He nodded, then closed his eyes.

"I will send Drake in now. He'll want to be with you," she murmured, knowing the end was near.

"Thank . . . you." It was a barely audible whisper, and Alex knew just what the words meant.

She went out into the hall and sought Drake out with her eyes. He was by her side instantly. "Is he . . . ?"

"He wants to see you," was all she said, standing aside to let him pass. Drake searched her face, finding no answers to his questions, questions that would have to wait. He entered the room, closing the door quietly behind him.

Alex leaned against the plastered wall, closing her eyes and wrapping her arms around herself, as she sought an inner strength that she was unsure she possessed. It all seemed a terrible nightmare; surely none of it true. She had to hang on just a little longer. Once she allowed herself to fall apart, her entire world would disintegrate into fragments around her.

"Are you all right, my lady?"

Alex's eyes flew open at the familiar voice. "Smitty." She stared at him blankly, thinking how out of context he looked in this palatial mansion.

"What can I do to make this easier for you, my lady?" he asked gently.

Alex would not give in to the urge to cry. "I thought you were my friend."

He winced at the coldness of her tone. "I am your friend, my lady."

"Friends do not lie to each other."

"Nor do they divulge another friend's secrets," he reminded her softly.

Alex gave a bitter laugh. "I always thought you far too cultured to belong at sea. I assume you work for Drake?"

He nodded.

She thought of the very capable way Smitty assisted Drake each day. "You are his valet, I presume?"

"Yes, my lady."

Alex covered her eyes with her hands. "I do not believe that any of this is happening." Hysteria bubbled up inside her again, refused to be silenced. "What am I going to do?" she whispered, half to herself. "Drake's father is dying. I cannot go to pieces . . . not yet."

Smitty ached for the broken, courageous girl who had been deceived in a most basic way and still placed her own grief second to that of others. She was every bit the unselfish, caring lady he had always known her to be.

At that moment the bedroom door opened slowly and Drake stepped out into the hall. He stared vacantly at Alex and Smitty, his emerald eyes damp.

"He is gone," he said simply.

Smitty went to his side. "Come," he murmured. "Let me get you a drink."

Drake nodded. "Yes. Let's go down to the library, Smitty. There are many things that need attending. And I must speak with Samantha and Sebastian as well." He stopped, meeting Alex's gaze.

"I'm very sorry about your father, Drake." The words were sincere, the tone forced and distant. "If you will show me which room is to be mine I will be out of your way."

Drake rubbed his eyes, feeling very weary and utterly alone. "Your bedchamber is at the end of the hall, opposite mine." He looked back toward the stairs at the sound of voices coming from the front hall, then turned to Alex. "Before you retire, would you mind very much meeting my sister? Under the circumstances, it would mean a great deal to her."

Alex nodded. "Of course."

As they reached the foot of the stairs, Humphreys was speaking with a lovely young girl with flowing sable hair and a haunted expression.

"Is there any change, Humphreys?" she was asking.

"I don't know, Lady Samantha. But your brother . . ."

She brushed tears from her pale cheeks. "My brother doesn't care whether Papa lives or dies, Humphreys. But once he is gone"—her lips quivered again—"I will have no one."

"That is what I am trying to tell you, my lady," Humphreys murmured. "When I said 'your brother,' I meant—"

"Hello, Sammy." Drake's deep baritone was filled with gentle emotion.

Samantha started. Only one person ever called her Sammy. He had given her the nickname when she was little more than a tot and was determined to be a boy rather than a girl.

She turned slowly, staring at the bearded man whose eyes lit with pleasure at the sight of her. "Drake?" Unlike the others, she had no trouble recognizing her beloved brother, beard and all. "Drake!"

The last was a shriek as she raced across the marble hall and flung herself into his arms. Drake caught her to him, smiling at her usual unruly behavior.

"What am I going to do with you, little one?" He rumpled her silky hair tenderly. "I thought I would return to find you a lady."

Samantha gazed up at him, adoration in her soft green eyes. "You're alive."

"I told you I would always come back, no matter how long I was away. Of course I'm alive."

She began to ask another question, then read the sadness in Drake's eyes. She stopped. "Papa . . . ?" she asked.

Drake cupped her face between his big hands. "I need you to be strong for me, Sammy."

Tears slid down her cheeks into her trembling mouth,

but she nodded. "I knew," she whispered. "I just knew. He has been so ill these past weeks."

Drake pressed her head against his chest and closed his eyes, holding her against him as she cried. He stroked her hair softly, soothing her until her sobs lessened and finally stopped.

Suddenly aware that they were not alone, Samantha stepped out of his comforting embrace and looked toward the steps.

"Smitty . . ." She smiled through her tears.

"Hello, Lady Samantha." His address, though formal, was uttered in the fondest of tones.

Samantha wiped her tear-streaked face with her hands. "Thank God you're both alive. When we received that message . . ." Her voice trailed off as she got her first look at the extraordinarily beautiful woman who stood beside Smitty, quietly watching the scene before her.

Drake caught Samantha's curious look and turned to gesture Alex forward. "Sammy, there's someone I'd like you to meet, someone very special to me."

Samantha raised her dark brows in surprise, her wet green eyes bright with curiosity.

"Alexandria, this is my sister, Samantha. Sammy, this is Alexandria . . . my wife."

"Your wife!" They didn't have long to wait for Samantha's reaction to the news. She looked stunned.

Alex walked over to her. "Hello, Samantha," she began, watching the younger girl's face to determine what lay beyond the initial surprise. "I'm so very sorry about your father, but I am also happy to meet you at last. Drake talks of you quite a bit."

Samantha smiled again, a smile that lit the whole room. At that moment she looked exactly like Drake.

"I can't believe it. Drake . . . married!" Her bright gaze surveyed Alex from head to toe. "You're beautiful," she said honestly and without guile. "And I'm happy to meet you, too."

The sound of an approaching carriage interrupted their conversation. Samantha looked quickly at Drake. "That must be Sebastian.'' Alex saw Drake's jaw tighten at his sister's words. "I'll have to tell him about Papa.'' Samantha turned and walked to the front door, which simultaneously opened, admitting a whistling Sebastian.

He nodded curtly at Humphreys, then stopped as his sister approached him. "Well, well, isn't this a surprise?'' he asked sarcastically. "To what do I owe the honor of being greeted by my often absent little sister?''

Samantha didn't react. She simply said, "Papa's dead, Sebastian.''

To Alex's amazement he barely shrugged.

"I was afraid of that,'' he said in a conversational tone. "He looked dreadfully peaked when I left for London.'' He gave a thoughtful frown. "I suppose arrangements will have to be made. Well, do not concern yourself, Samantha. From now on I will take care of everything.'' He sounded almost gleeful. Alex felt sick.

"That won't be necessary, Sebastian.'' Drake's tone was positively glacial. "I will oversee all the necessary arrangements.''

Sebastian gaped at Drake, the color draining from his face. "Drake? How . . . ? When . . . ?''

"Just today and by the grace of God. Any other questions?''

Sebastian shook his head, making an obvious attempt to regain control of himself. "It's a miracle that you've been restored to us,'' he said after a moment. Ignoring Drake's disgusted look, Sebastian moved his interested gaze to Alex. She returned it without flinching, feeling an immediate dislike for Drake's brother. If she hadn't known better she would have said he seemed *upset* by the discovery that Drake was alive. But that was impossible; no brother could be that cold.

Sebastian's light blue eyes roved appreciatively over Alex's very feminine curves, assessing her physical attributes. Alex could feel her cheeks burning with anger and humiliation at his blatant scrutiny.

"And who is this small and tempting morsel?'' he queried with a charming smile.

Drake struggled with his own urge to beat Sebastian senseless. He took a possessive step closer to Alex. "Your taste is superb, Sebastian. I hope you won't be too disappointed to learn that Alexandria happens to be my wife."

This time Sebastian could not disguise his astonishment, or his displeasure, at the news. "Your *wife?*"

Alex gave him a cool nod. "Hello, Sebastian."

"Your wife," he repeated again, shaking his head.

"Well, I think that it is wonderful," Samantha interrupted, giving Alex a small smile. "Perhaps the joy of having Drake returned to us and of welcoming Alexandria into the family will help to ease the pain of losing Papa." She swallowed, then lifted her chin. "You look exhausted, Alexandria. Let us leave my brothers to . . . do what they must." She shuddered at the reality of her father's death, but hung on to the fact that Drake was home. "Alexandria, I will show you to your room, if you like."

Alex looked gratefully at her. "Thank you, Samantha. I would like that very much." Without meeting Drake's eyes she raised her skirts and followed Samantha up the winding staircase. She was uncertain how much longer she could function without breaking down. Her entire life had blown up in her face. She desperately needed time alone to think.

"Your grace?"

Alex didn't turn.

"Your grace?" Humphreys's voice was tentative. "I shall arrange for a lady's maid to assist you at once."

Alex froze where she stood, realizing that Humphreys was addressing her. As of one hour past she was the Duchess of Allonshire.

She pivoted slowly on the stairway and looked down, her strained gaze locking with Drake's tortured stare. The words seemed to echo between them, within them, pulling taut the thin filament of their relationship, tighter and tighter, until it snapped.

Alex turned away first, walking gracefully up the curved staircase until she was gone.

Chapter 23

Dry-eyed, Alex stared up at the plush velvet canopy of the intricately carved mahogany bed. Her head ached painfully; her mind still raced with all it needed to absorb. Odd, she had been in her room for hours, yet she could not cry. Deep within her lay a core of grief so profound that it was not yet ready to be touched. She supposed that she was still in shock, would remain so for some time.

Shivering, Alex arose from the bed and moved toward the fire, drawing her wrapper more tightly around her. Shortly after she had taken dinner in her room, Molly, her lady's maid, had come to announce the arrival of some clothing for her grace. There had followed a procession of gowns, all the dark-colored crepes and bombazines that were necessary for mourning, and all of them fit Alex perfectly. As if to atone for the drabness of her initial wardrobe there were countless exquisite night rails and wrappers in soft colors and delicate silks. Alex had no idea how the *modiste* had managed all this without her measurements, but she assumed that Drake had something to do with it. It mattered not. Whatever was between her and her husband, she was his wife and he had just lost his father. Therefore, she would wear the gowns and show her respect to Grayson and to the *ton*.

The *ton*. The pompous, self-righteous group of aristocrats that Drake had mocked time and again, had bitterly resented for all they were. He had scorned her for being born into their world, had professed his loathing for the nobility and their values.

Lies. All of it, lies.

222

Alex turned, pressed her hands to her mouth and stared about the room with burning eyes.

Three of her rooms in Sudsbury could have easily fit into this elaborate bedchamber. The heavy furniture was hand-carved, and the upholstery was a rich pink velvet that matched the flocked wall covering and plush bedcover. The settee at the foot of the bed could easily have slept two, the ruffled dressing table contained every cosmetic a woman could desire, and the broad French windows led onto a large balcony that overlooked the grounds of the estate, giving her a breathtaking view of the endless gardens below.

Yet it all meant nothing.

Alex crossed the room to gaze out the window, searching the moonlit sky for answers. She had married a sea captain, a brave and dedicated man who led a simple life filled with purpose and commitment. A man she could respect . . . with whom she had fallen in love.

She had married a duke. A man who had lied to her time and again, whose very existence was a sham, who had accepted her love and her trust and then betrayed them.

And if Drake himself was a lie, then what of the feelings they had shared? She closed her eyes, unwanted images appearing before her. The heroic way he had rescued her from death, the tender way he had nursed her back to health on the island, the laughter they had shared, the words he had whispered, the look in his burning eyes when he'd made love to her—a look that had everything and nothing to do with passion.

Or so she had thought. She had deluded herself into think-ing—no, hoping—that he was falling in love with her, that all that was missing were the words he could not yet say. Perhaps that was what hurt the most. To admit the truth was to negate all that had passed between them these last months. And that truth her heart was not yet ready to accept. So the tears remained unshed.

She had to sleep. The next few days would be the most trying of her life. Her own grief and despair had no place in the day-to-day world of Allonshire. Alex's upbringing had prepared her to do her duty, regardless of her inner turmoil. But the overwhelming burden of being a duchess? For that, she was totally unprepared. Indeed, her mother had tried to teach her the skills required of a noblewoman, to ready her for the day when she would be the mistress of her own home. Alex had foolishly dismissed the attempts as inane. How she regretted that now! For now she faced the awesome responsibility of being the Duchess of Allonshire.

Then there was Drake's family.

Samantha was a softhearted girl with warmth and spirit. It was obvious that she adored Drake and that the feeling was mutual. Never having had a sister of her own, Alex wanted very badly to reach out and earn Samantha's friendship.

After showing Alex to her room Samantha had lingered, shy and eager all at once. And Alex's heart had ached for the younger girl's pain and loneliness. Yet her own emotional strength had been depleted by the events of the day. She had therefore asked Samantha if they might spend the next morning together, getting to know each other. Samantha's eyes had lit up, joy and anticipation making them glow. She had looked so much like Drake at that instant that Alex had almost wept.

Alex's tenderness vanished as her mind moved to Sebastian. There was a coldness about him that frightened her, and the hungry, lustful way he looked at her was unnerving and damned insulting. After all, she was wed to his brother.

Drake. Her mind returned to the complex man she had married. His father's death had obviously been a terrible blow to him and the weeks to come would mean a drastic change in his way of life. The adjustment would be tremendously difficult for Drake, she knew, for whatever else he had lied about, he had not lied about his love for the sea. And now that life would be over, lost beneath his staggering responsibility to Allonshire. The thought saddened her, but there was little she could do. She felt cold inside, cold and dead. She had little internal strength left for herself; she had none to offer Drake.

Alex slid into the bed, willing herself to go to sleep. Tomorrow would reveal itself in but a few short hours.

The door to her bedchamber opened. Alex started, sitting up in surprise. Silhouetted in the doorway was Drake, his powerful form revealed by the glow of the firelight, his face concealed by shadows. He walked slowly into the room, closing the door behind him and approaching the bed. He stopped just before he reached Alex's side, staring down at her, his expression enigmatic.

Alex returned his gaze without moving, noting that her sea captain was gone. Drake was clean-shaven, his hair cut shorter at the nape of his neck. His robe, made of dark green silk, was belted, but open enough for her to see the soft dark hair that covered his massive chest.

The man who gazed down at her was very much the Duke of Allonshire.

"What do you want, Drake?" Her voice was drained and devoid of emotion.

"I don't know what I want," he answered her quietly, searching for some softness in her eyes and finding none. "Nor can I answer any of the other questions you must have, for I myself don't know who I am anymore." He swallowed. "My father is dead. I feel so damned empty inside."

"So do I, Drake," Alex whispered truthfully. "And I need to be alone to think things through."

"I need you." He begged her with his eyes. "I'll go if you ask me to . . . but please don't ask me to." His jaw tightened, a muscle working furiously in his cheek. "I've never asked . . . begged . . . a woman in my life. Please, Alex, I need you to stop the pain. Just tonight. Please."

It wasn't fair of him to ask this of her. Alex knew it, and Drake knew it as well. She had yet to recover from shock and move on to acceptance. She could not begin to consider forgiveness. Not now; maybe never.

He needed her. She stared up at the green fire in his eyes, a fire born of pain and loss and desire. Yet he waited, and she knew he would leave her if she asked him to. She didn't ask. Perhaps this was all they could offer each other to fill the void inside them. Perhaps it was all they had left, possibly all they'd ever had. At that moment it didn't matter.

He saw his answer in her eyes, and she saw the flame of hope in his. He unbelted his robe, dropped it to the floor, and got into bed beside her.

"Alex, come to me," he whispered in a shaken voice. "I've never needed anything like I need you tonight."

They both moved at once, coming together in a desperate explosion of feeling, driven by the elemental need of one human being for another, the reaffirmation of life. Drake peeled the night rail from Alex's body, casting it to the floor beside his robe. A harsh cry was torn from his lips as he pressed her naked body against his, whether from desire or anguish, Alex wasn't sure. He held her for a long time, just feeling her heart pound against his, burying his face in her fragrant cloud of hair. His breathing was harsh, erratic, his body hot against hers.

Slowly Alex slid her arms around his back, pressed her face against the solid strength of his chest. She could feel the chill leave her as he enveloped her in the power of his embrace, molded each soft contour of her body to his hardened ones. Their legs intertwined, roughness and silk as one, their arms tightened about each other. For long moments neither of them spoke or moved, the only sound being the soft crackling of the fire. She could feel his arousal, hard and throbbing against her stomach, but he made no move to join their bodies. With a will of its own Alex could feel her body begin to respond to his nearness, pulsing slowly to life until her own breathing was irregular and her skin was covered with a fine sheen of perspiration.

Drake felt it, too, and a wave of relief swept through him. He could still make her feel something, be it only desire. He had been so afraid. And although he knew it was only a shell of what it had been before, he took what she offered him greedily and with a hunger that made him weak.

He lifted his head and, unwilling to see the bleakness in her eyes, lowered his mouth to hers, seeking another truth.

She tasted so sweet, so right. He parted her lips and drank more deeply of her intoxicating flavor, inhaled the wonderful floral scent that was Alex. His heart soared as she opened to him, meeting his tongue with her own, gliding her fingers through the short hair at the nape of his neck. All realities dissolved but this one, the reality that was in his arms.

Alex. His heart called out to her again and again, a silent message conveyed by his body. His lips left hers to brush butterfly kisses along her cheeks, nose, and chin, down the slender column of her neck, up to the delicate shell of her ear. His breath was hot and raspy as his tongue traced the soft lobe tenderly, with infinite gentleness. He felt her shudder in his arms.

"Ah, Alex," he murmured into her ear, "respond to me, love; just let your body take over. Give me your beauty, your passion. . . . God, Alex, breathe life back into my soul." He bit down lightly and she moaned.

"Drake . . ."

"I know, princess, I know."

She shook her head frantically at the painfully familiar endearment and tugged his head down to her breast. She didn't want to think, only to feel.

Drake responded to her gesture by running his tongue along the soft mounds of her breasts, drawing each nipple into his mouth, first lightly, then with such force that she cried out, arching her back.

He lifted his head, his face flushed with emotion and need. Her eyes were closed, her skin suffused with a rosy glow. She was so beautiful lying there bathed in firelight, her body telling him how much it wanted him.

Drake braced himself on one arm and slid his other arm beneath her, lifting her from the bed, burying his lips in hers for another shattering kiss. She clung to him, both arms around his neck, and he slid his hand down the smooth skin of her back, over the gently rounded curve of her hip and onto the silkiness of her inner thighs. She opened to him at once, parting her legs to his stroking fingers.

227

At his first touch she whimpered, and he groaned. She was hot and soft and satiny wet with her desire for him. The feel of her was enough to push him over the edge; he wanted to savor her and devour her all at once. His emotions were dangerously close to the surface, his body burning alive. But he wanted these moments to last; he needed to hold at bay what lay beyond tonight.

Softly, gently, he stroked his hand up and down her delicate flesh, until she was digging her nails into his back and begging him to end the torture. He worsened it instead. Gradually, maddeningly, he slid his fingers inside her, giving her a teasing penetration that brought her closer to the edge.

"Drake, don't do this," she pleaded, squirming helplessly against him.

"Let it last," he breathed back. "Let it go on forever."

"I can't. Nothing can . . ."

"You can. We will." His hoarse whisper was insistent, speaking of far more than their lovemaking.

"Drake! I need you!" she sobbed.

"And I need you." He pressed her legs farther apart with his knees, settling himself between them.

"Alex." He cupped her face, demanding with his hands and his tone that she look at him.

She opened her eyes, and their gazes locked for the first time since he had come to her bed.

"I'm your husband, Alex. Give yourself to me." And he drove into her with force and despair and an uncontrollable need to have her back.

They moved together in a rhythm that belonged to them. For the moments their bodies were joined nothing existed but the intensity of their union. There was no room for pain or fear or even doubt. There was only the power of his body moving inside hers, the softness of her body closing around his.

They reached the unbearable peak together. Alex tore her mouth from his, cried out in racking pleasure and welcome release. Drake lunged forward onto her and into her, calling her name again and again as he spilled himself deep inside her. Even as he helplessly surrendered to his own painful pleasure, he was acutely aware of his wife. He reveled in her cries of ecstasy, the hard contractions of her body gripping his, the stark beauty of her face in the throes of her release, even the tiny quiverings of her inner muscles in the glorious aftermath of their passion, when their bodies were still as one.

He held her while she slept, unwilling to let her go, his arms wrapped tightly around her, his chin atop her silky head. A cold dread grew inside him and settled tightly in his chest as he relived the past hour.

Their passion had burned as brightly as ever, yet even as Alex gave herself to him, she had held a part of herself back. Once her passion alone would have been enough for him. But no longer. Having tasted the rare gift of Alex's love, Drake wasn't satisfied with her body alone. He wanted it all—her heart, her soul, her trust.

He had had it once. Damn it, he would have it again. But before he could convince himself of that, another sinking realization about tonight's lovemaking asserted itself in his mind.

Alex hadn't said she loved him. For the first time in months she had not sobbed out her love for him at the moment of her climax.

He stared down into her face, soft and relaxed now in slumber.

"Please, princess," he whispered, "don't give up on me now. For my sake and for yours, not now." He kissed her forehead gently, praying that her feelings were strong enough to overcome all that stood between them.

Praying that his own newborn trust was strong enough to withstand the wait.

Chapter 24

"It's a glorious day for a walk." Alex glanced over at Samantha, who stood quietly beside her amid one of the sweeping clusters of oak trees that lined the grounds of Allonshire. Samantha had been silent during the onset of their stroll, but Alex did not fault her. Breakfast had been a somber event, filled with tense silence and the sad knowledge that there was to be a funeral. Alex had felt a protective urge to remove Samantha from the morbid atmosphere as soon as possible. It was painful enough that she had lost her father.

Alex herself had difficulty getting through the meal. She had been unable to meet Drake's gaze, uncertain of where things stood. And the speculative gleam in Sebastian's eye, as he looked from Alex to his brother, had only made things worse.

Now, overlooking the vast expanse of greenery stretched before her, Alex took a deep breath and turned to Samantha. "Would you prefer to be by yourself?" she asked, gently touching her arm.

Samantha shook her head. "No, not really. I am so eager to get to know you." She grinned. "It's not every day that my brother, the notorious rake, comes home married!" At the pained look on Alex's face she reached out hastily and touched the sleeve of Alex's black crepe walking gown. "Alexandria, I'm sorry. I didn't mean anything by that." She sighed deeply. "I have a dreadful tendency to say all the wrong things. Obviously Drake is very different now."

Different from what? Alex wanted to ask. But she didn't.

"I know my brother better than anyone," Samantha was

230

continuing. "And if he married you, you must be wonderful. It's just that I never thought he would marry."

Alex gave her a curious look. "Why not?"

Samantha shrugged. "He doesn't have a very high regard for women, that's all."

"Yes, I know." Alex bit her lip, willing Samantha to go on.

As if she sensed Alex's need, Samantha continued. "Women adore him; they always have. And why not? He is titled, he has wealth and power, he is breathtakingly handsome and devastatingly charming."

"When he wants to be," Alex modified.

"Yes," Samantha agreed. "But on the whole he believes women to be inherently faithless. I am the only exception . . . until now, of course," she hastened to add.

Alex took the plunge. "He even feels that way about your mother?"

For a long moment Samantha was silent, and then her words were so soft that they were barely audible. "Sometimes I think he feels that way *because* of our mother."

Alex's heart began to pound. "For what reason?"

Samantha gave Alex a thoughtful look. "I'm not entirely certain. It's just a feeling I've always had but never expressed. Besides, it doesn't make any difference. Mother has been dead for almost ten years."

Alex digested that information carefully. She had already surmised that Drake's mother was no longer alive, else she would have been with her husband at the end. And as far as Drake's bitterness being tied somehow to her . . . that came as no shock either. Alex had long suspected something of the sort.

She had thousands of questions that needed answers, but she would not take advantage of Samantha's need for company or her closeness to Drake.

Instead, she urged, "It's your turn, Samantha. You must have many things you want to ask me. I know I would if Drake were my brother." She waited.

Samantha hesitated, unused to such sensitivity from anyone other than Drake. Unable to resist the gesture of friendship, she gave Alex a grateful smile. "Alexandria, I will try not to pry. If I ask or say anything that offends you, please tell me."

Alex smiled back. "I doubt that anything you say would offend me, Samantha."

The younger girl giggled. "Don't be so certain." She pointed in the direction of a peaceful, rippling stream just beyond them. "Why don't we sit for a while?"

Alex nodded. More and more she liked this young girl whose honest, straightforward manner reminded Alex so much of Drake—the Drake she thought she knew.

They settled themselves on the ground, tucking their full, drab skirts beneath them.

"I hate wearing black," Samantha blurted out. "And I don't understand the point of it. True mourning takes place here"—she pressed her fingers to her heart—"not in a splendid cathedral for all the world to see." She turned tear-filled green eyes to Alex. "I told you I say outrageous things," she whispered.

Alex reached over and took her hand. "Samantha, I wish more people were as genuine as you. There is nothing outrageous about what you said. Quite the opposite, in fact."

Samantha brushed away her tears. "Then you don't think I'm awful?"

Alex smiled. "Actually, you sound very much like me."

"You? But you're so . . . ."

"So . . . what?"

Samantha looked at her shyly. "Oh . . . beautiful and feminine and accomplished at all the things that noblewomen are supposed to be. . . . Why are you laughing?"

"Samantha, if you only knew how wrong you are." Alex leaned closer. "I'll tell you a secret. Just this morning Mrs. Haversham, your housekeeper, very primly asked me how her grace would like things to proceed, and all I could do was assure her that things should proceed as they always have. Imagine her surprise if I had told her that her grace had no idea what changes should be made because, instead of observing her mother, the Countess of Sudsbury, all these years, her grace had been out sailing in her skiff!"

Alex nodded vigorously at Samantha's stunned expression. "Would you like to know how Drake and I met?" Alex asked.

"I assumed you met at some elegant ball in York," Samantha replied.

Alex raised her delicate brows. "Hardly." And she told Samantha the story of her daring escape to Canada. By the time she had finished describing her first days at sea Samantha was wiping tears of laughter from her eyes.

"I can just imagine Drake's reaction," she gasped between giggles. "Being undone by a female . . . and on his precious ship, no less!"

Alex chuckled. "We did not exactly have a conventional courtship."

"Then it's no wonder he fell in love with you. Drake is a very *un*conventional man."

Alex grew quiet.

"Alexandria? Is something wrong?"

Alex cursed herself for being so transparent. "The only thing wrong is the way you address me," she answered lightly. "Please call me Alex."

Samantha grinned. "Fine, Alex. Then you may call me Sammy. Drake has done so since I was small."

"Probably for the same reason I've always been called Alex." Alex gave a mock sigh. "By the *ton*'s standards I fear that we acted more like little boys than little girls."

"And still do," Samantha agreed.

The sound of joyful barking interrupted their conversation, and seconds later a very muddy Blackbeard exploded onto the scene and promptly threw himself upon his mistress with exuberant pleasure.

Alex tried unsuccessfully to dodge his onslaught. "Down boy, down!" She laughed in spite of herself. "Haven't you ever heard the word 'obey'?"

Samantha giggled delightedly. "And who is this?"

"*This* is Blackbeard. Drake and I adopted him during our travels. He was floating in the Saint Lawrence, the victim of a naval battle." She gathered the squirming puppy in her arms and kissed his damp head, heedless of the mud that was transferred from his filthy paws to her prim gown.

"I suppose he missed me and came to express his indignation!"

"He is adorable!" Samantha declared.

"And he is quite a sailor as well, aren't you, Blackbeard?" The dirty canine barked his assent.

"Alex . . ." Samantha hesitated. "Would you teach me how to sail?"

Alex's eyes sparkled. "Of course! Blackbeard and I will both teach you!"

Samantha sprang to her feet in joy. "Oh, thank you!" She pulled Alex up and hugged her, transferring the wet stains from Alex's dress onto her own. "I've always wanted to sail, but Drake is away so much. I know he wants to teach me, but it's not fair to expect him to spend all his time at home with me, and . . ." Samantha would probably have gone on for some time longer, had it not been for the questioning baritone voice that interrupted her.

"Are we celebrating something?"

Both women turned at the sound of Drake's voice. With sudden horror, Alex was aware of how they must look. Their dignified mourning clothes were soiled and disheveled, their joyful behavior was inappropriate.

Before Alex could explain, Samantha had released her and launched herself into Drake's arms.

"Oh, Drake, guess what? Alex says that she will teach me how to sail! I know we can't begin yet, but isn't that wonderful?"

Drake looked at Alex over his sister's bobbing head. "Yes, Sammy, that is wonderful." He set Samantha down and snapped his fingers. Instantly Blackbeard was by his side, quiet and composed. "I will contact Barrett Shipping tomorrow." His words were for Samantha, but his eyes never left Alex. "There is no reason for you to wait. I'll have a skiff brought to Allonshire at once so that your lessons can begin."

Samantha looked torn between joy and guilt. "But, Drake, is it right? With Papa . . ."

"Our father knew how much you loved him," Drake said softly. "It is not necessary to punish yourself with weeks of grief. We will do what we must and then go quietly on with our lives. He would want it that way."

She nodded, tears in her eyes. "I know."

"Sammy, why don't you take Blackbeard back to the stables? Six frantic grooms and stableboys are combing the grounds for him."

"I don't want him in the stables," Alex broke in quietly. "I want him with me."

Drake studied her earnest little face, stifling a grin. She looked like a belligerent child rather than a duchess, standing there in her bedraggled gown, with a brown smudge on one cheek. He wanted to lay her down in the scented grass and make love to her.

"Fine" was all he said. "Then he may go to your chambers . . . *after* he has been bathed."

Samantha watched the exchange with interest, feeling the electricity that flowed between her brother and his new wife. Then, tactfully and with as much grace as she could muster, she scooped up the wriggling pup and headed for the stables.

"I will see that he is bathed and brought to the house," she called back.

"Thank you, Sammy," Alex called after her.

Samantha turned and smiled, a smile of encouragement. "You're welcome, Alex."

Once Samantha had gone, Alex looked back at Drake. She knew that her behavior had been inexcusable and was prepared to apologize for it.

"Drake," she began, "I want you to know—"

"Where were you this morning?" he broke in.

She looked startled. "I told you I was going for a walk with Samantha after breakfast."

He frowned. "I meant earlier this morning."

She flushed. "I couldn't sleep. I—"

"Is it too much to ask that you awaken with me, or do you loathe me so much that you can no longer face me in the morning?"

"Drake . . . don't." She made a move to go past him, but he caught her arm, bringing her up against him. Alex could feel her heart begin to pound wildly, for what reason she did not allow herself to guess. Instead, she stared at his unadorned black mourning cloak.

He lifted her chin with firm fingers, forcing her to meet his gaze. "Thank you," he said tenderly.

Now she was completely at sea. "For what?"

"For what you are doing for Samantha. She needs some-one very badly."

"She is a very special person," Alex whispered.

"You never answered my question." His breath was warm against her lips.

"I don't know the answer to the question, Drake. I don't even know who my husband is."

"Don't you?" he murmured, then claimed her mouth in a kiss that made her knees buckle. He held her chin in place and fit their mouths together the same way he had fitted their bodies together last night. Alex moaned, closing her eyes. The kiss continued, on and on, until Alex thought she would faint.

When he drew back, she heard herself whimper a protest.

Drake chuckled. "That is the most delightful invitation I have ever received, princess. Unfortunately this is not the time."

Cold reality struck Alex in the face, and her eyes flew open in shock. Oh, what was it he did to her that only succeeded in confusing her more, making the important seem unimportant and bringing back the fantasy that she knew to be a lie? And how could she allow it when he had made a mockery of all they'd shared?

Damn him to hell, but she loved him.

"Forgive me, *your grace*." Ice dripped from her every word. "I realize that you have a great deal to do on your palatial estate. I won't keep you." She marched off.

He came up behind her, drew her back against his body.

"Feel what you do to me," he murmured in a husky voice. "Does that strike you as the reaction of a man who would prefer anything else to being with you?"

Alex felt her bones melt.

He pressed his lips into her hair. "I have a funeral to see

to. And while you and I might view the elaborate display as distasteful, it is my obligation to see that it is done. My father was a very successful and wealthy nobleman, and no doubt the church procession will be endless. No matter how much we rebel against protocol, you and I both know what our obligations are, don't we?''

Alex felt utterly ashamed.

"I'm sorry," she whispered. "I just have so much to sort out in my mind."

"I know." He held her to him for one more minute. "And we have to talk."

She shook her head. "I'm not ready, Drake. I need time."

Drake gave a deep sigh. "I know you do."

She drew herself up, out of the circle of his arms. "I'll be at the house," she told him without looking back.

He watched her go, a curious mixture of tenderness, pain, and hope stirring inside him. She had lashed out at him, shown him her anger. That was a good sign, a sign that she was recovering from the shock. Soon they would talk. But what could he tell her? He *had* deceived her, though not intentionally; he had kept the truth hidden from her. How could he convince her that nothing else had been a lie?

He rubbed his eyes, feeling weary. His tenuous relationship with Alexandria was but one part of his torment. Besides the dilemma with his wife, how the hell was he going to adjust to his new role, to cope with the awesome task of being the Duke of Allonshire, being tied to the land and the life?

How could he cope with anything, if he lost Alex?

Alex approached the Gothic mansion, her heart still pounding from the moments she had just spent with her enigmatic husband. Her head throbbed from too little sleep and too much tension. Her gown was filthy and needed to be changed . . . but not quite yet.

Just off the main hall was a large circular conservatory that seemed to beckon Alex. She went in, closing the door carefully behind her. Like all of Allonshire, it was unique, its high domed ceiling covered with branches of lavender blossoms, its graceful stone steps leading down into a veritable paradise of nature. Alex felt the room's peace stroke her raw senses, and she strolled contentedly about, deeply inhaling the wonderful floral fragrance.

"A lovely setting for a lovelier woman."

Alex started and turned to see Sebastian standing near the conservatory door. He smiled at her and strolled inside, his dark eyebrows raised questioningly.

"May I join you?"

A warning bell sounded immediately in Alex's head. "Actually I was about to return to my chambers. As you can see"—she pointed to her gown—"I am a bit of a mess right now."

Sebastian approached her, glanced at her gown, and shrugged indulgently. "It does nothing to detract from your beauty, I assure you."

"It is not my beauty I am considering," she responded quickly, feeling anger at his lavish compliment. Did he think her so shallow that she would blush and simper over such transparent nonsense? "I am hardly paying the appropriate respect due your father in soiled clothing."

Sebastian looked surprised by her sharp response. It occurred to him that he should not underestimate his brother's new wife. Drake would never have married a bland, empty-headed woman. All the more interesting.

"I apologize," he said smoothly. "It is just that I am accustomed to ladies who prefer flattery to substantial conversation."

"Then perhaps you associate with the wrong type of ladies," Alex suggested.

Sebastian gave a hearty laugh. "Perhaps I do."

Alex studied Drake's brother carefully. Yes, she could see a resemblance. Sebastian was not as tall or as broad-shouldered as Drake, but he had the same hard good looks. He was leaner than Drake, whose body was muscular and powerful, conditioned by months at sea. Also, their eyes were different. Not just the color, either. Sebastian had his father's blue eyes, but with none of the compassion and depth that Alex had seen in Grayson's eyes before he died. Sebastian's eyes were pale and cold, and despite his charming manner, Alex felt chilled and uneasy.

"Drake is a very lucky man," Sebastian said, watching her reaction.

"Yes, he is. Allonshire is a unique home."

"I wasn't speaking of Allonshire."

"He also has many people who care for him." Alex gave him a challenging look.

"And a breathtakingly beautiful, very loyal wife," Sebastian added lightly.

"We are both lucky." She'd be damned if she would give Sebastian the satisfaction of being privy to her torment.

"I agree. Especially since you came so close to death, but managed to escape it." He gave her a casual yet curious look. "I never did actually hear the details of your heroic survival. What did happen? We received word that *La Belle Illusion* had been attacked and destroyed, that there were no survivors."

Alex felt somewhat relieved that they were on a safer, less personal subject.

She nodded. "Your information was correct, for the most part. We were attacked, and *La Belle* was destroyed, just after we left Lake Ontario. Fortunately Drake's quick thinking resulted in a total evacuation of the ship without any loss of life."

"I see." Sebastian looked thoughtful. "Was the American ship that far superior to *La Belle Illusion*, then?"

"Yes . . . and no." Alex chewed her lip thoughtfully. "The enemy ship was much larger and with a good deal more firepower, but for some reason our cannons were unable to span the distance between us." She shrugged. "I suppose the wind was against us and we were unable to get close enough."

"Yes, I suppose."

"I feel dreadful about *La Belle Illusion*. I know how much Drake loved that ship."

"It was only a ship, Alexandria." Sebastian sounded amused. "And ships cannot keep you warm at night."

Again Alex was annoyed by the flippancy of his response. "I really do have to change."

He stopped her with his hand on her arm. "Does Drake?"

She stared up at him. "Does Drake . . . what?"

"Keep you warm at night."

Furious color stained Alex's cheeks. "Kindly take your hand off my arm and allow me to pass," she managed. "I have no intention of answering such a question!"

His gaze swept over her again before he released her. Her features were flawless, her body a man's dream. She was intelligent and witty, and she had fire, as well. He could just imagine her in bed . . . *his* bed.

"Because if he doesn't, or if you ever choose not to let him, I would like nothing better than—"

Alex jerked her arm away, lifted her skirts, and practically flew up the steps to the conservatory door. She faced him again, her hand on the door.

"Sebastian, you are my husband's brother. For that reason I am going to forget we had this conversation. But I suggest that you remember this. I am married to Drake, and I would do nothing to dishonor or hurt him in any way." She slammed the door behind her.

Sebastian grinned as the sound echoed throughout the cavernous room. She was even more passionate than he had dared to hope. Acquiring her would be a challenge worth savoring.

Well, Drake, he thought with a smug smile. *Father is gone. With better luck and more skillful planning, you will soon follow. And then, my dear brother, all of this will be mine.*

Your title. Your home.
Your wife.

Death pervaded the air.

The choir was still as the dignified bishop concluded the service. Alex shuddered, raising her head to look around. She had not been prepared for the swarms of nobility who had arrived at the majestic church, filling it to capacity.

Soon the mourning coaches would depart from the service, carrying Grayson Barrett to the family cemetery at Allonshire, where he would be laid to rest beside his wife. At that moment life felt very fragile and precious to Alex, her own mortality very real.

Drake had been strong throughout the ordeal of the day. Samantha leaned against his other side, clenching her handkerchief, fighting for the control that she had been taught to manifest to the world. Sebastian remained expressionless beside her, his pale eyes roving restlessly about the room, as though memorizing the list of those in attendance.

Alex saw the pain of loss reflected on Drake's face, and instinctively she stepped closer to him. In response, and to her surprise, she felt his fingers close around hers, squeezing gently. She realized that he was merely expressing his gratitude for her presence and her strength, and yet she was filled with such a sudden wealth of emotion that she had to blink back her tears. She felt a cold draft against the bare flesh of her palm as he gently disengaged his hand a moment later, when it was time to leave the church.

Holding Samantha's arm, he turned to Alex.

"Come, love," he said softly. "It is time to go."

Alex nodded, the ache inside her heart unbearable. She had a sudden, childish, desperate yearning to have things as they had been but a week ago, when Drake had been hers; to negate the past few days and be whole again.

She dropped her gaze to the floor. It was impossible.

Numbly she stood outside the church, watching the mourners depart, lost in thought.

"Alexandria." The voice was as familiar as it was startling.

"Mother?" Alex turned in amazement to stare at the dazzlingly beautiful golden-haired woman she had dreaded confronting and who now beamed down at Alex as though she were a small child that had done a most commendable deed.

Constance Cassel pressed her smooth cheek against Alex's, careful not to muss her own exquisitely arranged hair in the process.

"I'm so very happy for you," she murmured, as though they were close friends sharing a wonderful confidence.

"So very happy that a man is dead?" Alex was speechless with shock.

Constance raised her fair brows in amused reaction. "Of course not, love. Happy that you have found such a perfect husband."

Alex wondered if a scandal would result from the Duchess of Allonshire's sudden emptying of her stomach on the church steps.

Constance continued. "Of course I was a bit piqued when I discovered you had gone off to York, but when your father wrote and told me the circumstances—that you had wed Drake Barrett—well, that made things quite different." She beamed. "I suppose even your first London Season paled in comparison to marriage to the most sought-after man in the *ton*." She leaned forward conspiratorially. "I just wish you had confided in me. I, of all people, would have understood."

"Mother"—Alex had heard enough—"I don't know what Father told you, but—"

"Countess?" Drake's sudden appearance at Alex's side cut off her admonishment. He was all magnificent masculinity and charm as he kissed Alex's mother's hand. He was a damned duke.

"Hello, your grace," she addressed him in return. "I am so terribly sorry about your father," she crooned.

I'll just bet you are, Mother, Alex fumed inwardly, *I wonder how many of your friends you've already regaled with tales of your daughter, the duchess.*

"Thank you, Countess. And please call me Drake. After all, we are family now." His smile would have melted one of Greenland's icebergs.

Constance simpered prettily. "Thank you, Drake. And may I tell you how thrilled I am about you and Alexandria? I was just telling her how lucky she was that you found each other."

That did it. Alex was going to choke her.

"I am the lucky one." Drake's restraining hand stopped

Alex in her tracks. "Your daughter is a rare and precious gift. You should be very proud of her."

Alex looked up at him with startled surprise, realizing what he was doing. He hadn't forgotten their conversations about her mother, and he was reminding the older woman of Alex's virtues.

"Oh, I am," Lady Sudsbury assured him. "Terribly proud. I hope that all I have taught her over the years will contribute to her being a suitable wife to you and mistress of Allonshire."

"Oh, Alexandria's assets were obvious right from the start," he drawled back. "I never doubted that she would satisfy *all* of my requirements."

Constance beamed. "I am delighted to hear that." Remembering where she was, she lifted the edge of her black gown and dropped her eyes. "I will take my leave now, for this is not the time for joy. Please accept my condolences on the part of my husband and myself. Your father was a fine man."

"Yes, he was." Drake gave her a tight smile. "And I thank you for your understanding. Perhaps, when our mourning period is at an end, you will be our guest at Allonshire for a few days?"

"It will be my pleasure." Always aware of the right time to make her exit, Constance turned to embrace a rigid Alex again. "He is smitten," she whispered in Alex's ear. "Now all you need to do is provide him with a son and he will give you the world." She stepped back. "Good-bye, darling," she said with the right amount of emotion in her voice. After all, one never knew who was watching, now, did one?

And in a fragrant cloud of jasmine she was gone.

Alex turned slowly to her husband.

"Remember that we are being watched by countless eyes, my love," he reminded her softly.

She nodded. "I am uncertain whether to thank you or be ill."

"I would prefer the thanks."

Alex cocked her head. "You can be quite charming, your grace. I commend you on your performance."

Drake did not smile. "I only did for you what you have done for me all day. Support and loyalty are what a partnership is all about, are they not?"

He didn't wait for her reply.

"The coach is awaiting, Alexandria," he reminded her.

She nodded, emotion welling up inside her once more. Without a word she accompanied Drake to their mourning coach and to the burial that lay ahead.

Utterly spent, Alex leaned against the cool wall of the hallway for a moment's rest. Samantha had been put to bed, needing consolation and soothing words like a small child. Alex had sat with her until she drifted off, then made certain the manor was duly prepared for a lengthy mourning period.

Now she shook her head until the brief dizzy spell had passed, then walked down the hall, past the dining room and into the gallery where she knew she would find Drake.

He stood within the pillared walls, surrounded by rows of high-backed chairs, with a drink in his hand, staring up at the portraits of his ancestors.

Alex walked in quietly, coming to stand beside her husband.

"You are looking at all the previous Dukes and Duchesses of Allonshire," he told her, without taking his eyes from the portraits, "of which I am the eleventh." He took a deep swallow of whiskey. "Dignified-looking group, wouldn't you say, princess?"

Alex glanced up at him with concern. "Are you all right, Drake?"

He gave a harsh laugh. "Now, *that* is an excellent question, my love. Am I all right? I suppose I shall be. The will to survive is strong." He downed the rest of his drink in one gulp and placed the empty glass on the mantel over the fireplace. "Let me be honest with you." He raised a dark, sardonic brow in her direction. "You did want honesty, did you not?"

"Drake, you've had too much to drink."

He shook his head in denial. "Quite the contrary, my sweet. I have had but one drink. You are hearing the ramblings of a tortured mind." He stared up at the wall again, inhaled deeply. "It is not only the loss of my father we are discussing," he said in a defeated voice, "but the loss of my life as I have known it. I know what is expected of me. And in order to fulfill my obligations, I have to forfeit most of what I care for"—he glanced at Alex and amended softly, "possibly *all* of what I care for . . . most in the world."

"I understand," she whispered.

"Do you?" he demanded in a firm, quiet tone. "Do you understand that none of what has happened in the last few months has been a lie? That I am nothing more or less than you thought I was?"

His words echoed in her ears. Nothing more or less than she had thought he was? More in some ways, perhaps less in the ways that were more important. But what Alex really focused on was the first part of Drake's statement. He had said that nothing had been a lie. He was telling her that what they had felt between them, what she had felt for him, had not been a figment of her imagination. It had been real.

Perhaps, then, there *was* some hope for them. Alex was too tired to be certain. But she *was* certain that, despite all that had come between them, she loved him. Nothing could change that. Nothing.

Silence prevailed as Drake awaited her answer.

At last she replied, "Yes, I do understand exactly what you are, Drake, possibly even *why* you are that way. What I don't understand is why you didn't tell me."

"I was a fool."

"Yes, you were."

He chuckled, without humor. "Always forthright, my Alex." He studied her sad face. "And now that you believe me, where do we go from here?"

"I honestly do not know. I feel betrayed and humiliated. It seems the entire world knew who you were. Everyone but the one person who had the greatest right to know . . . your wife. I believed in you, in your honesty and your integrity." Her lips trembled. "I was willing to turn my back on my way of life and assume yours, to endure mockery and scorn from people I had decided were less worthy than you. And all at once I find that you are just as they are—if not in your heart, then in fact. I realize that Captain Drake Barrett is very much a part of the Duke of Allonshire. I realize . . . I comprehend . . . but I can't forgive you for lying to me. Not now, maybe never. I just don't know."

"Never is a long time to ask a man to wait." His voice was hoarse, strained.

She met his gaze. "I am not deserting you, nor will I. I am and will continue to be your wife, the mistress of your home."

"Publicly," he clarified.

"Of course."

"And in my bed?" His jaw was set, his eyes green jewels of fire.

Alex let out her breath, closed her eyes, then opened them again, meeting his waiting gaze. "There I cannot deny you."

"Because it is my right to have you?" he demanded.

She shook her head slowly, her eyes bright with unshed tears. "Because I am unable to turn you away," she said truthfully. "Because I need you." The admission took all of her courage, made a shambles of her pride. Yet she held her head high and waited for his reaction.

It was immediate.

Drake walked over to her, took her hand in his. "Come to bed with me, Alex," he said softly.

Chapter 25

"Most of the guests have arrived," Samantha whispered, peering over the staircase rail, her green morning dress brushing up against the polished banister. "I just saw Lord and Lady Kensgate make their entrance." She wrinkled her nose in distaste. "You cannot miss Lady Kensgate's perfume. She smells like a cinnamon bun."

Alex giggled, then, remembering her place, tugged Samantha back from her lookout point.

"Sammy," she scolded, her lips twitching, "I am having enough trouble calming my nerves without your colorful descriptions of our guests." She smoothed a shaky hand down the bodice of her soft blue muslin gown.

Samantha grinned. "You have nothing to be nervous about, Alex. All of the guests will love you. They won't be able to help themselves."

Alex sighed, wishing her queasiness would subside. But this was her first house party as the Duchess of Allonshire. If it had been up to her, they would have waited a bit longer. They had been mourning Grayson Barrett for only two months. But Drake had promised that the party would be small and intimate; just a few choice guests to meet the new Duchess of Allonshire, his new wife.

Six couples had been invited to Allonshire on this cool November morning. The party would last for several days. During the daytime the ladies would mingle and gossip while the men rode and talked business; the evenings would be filled with elegant dinners and dignified dancing.

Officially this was known as a country house party, but having quietly observed similar social events at Sudsbury,

Alex wasn't fooled for a minute. The truth was that six highly influential women of the *ton* were coming to viciously dissect her. All of them knew Drake; most of them had probably slept with him.

Her stomach turned over again.

"Alex"—Samantha chewed her lip, studying Alex's face—"you look so white. Are you all right?"

Alex managed a nod. "Yes, I'm fine. I shouldn't have eaten quite so much breakfast, though. My stomach is rebelling."

"You ate next to nothing."

Alex waved away Samantha's comment. "What made Drake think of this party, anyway?" she asked.

"That's the amazing part," Samantha told her with a twinkle. "Drake didn't think of it; Sebastian did."

"Sebastian?" Alex was stunned.

Samantha nodded. "I was surprised, too. But perhaps we have been too harsh in our judgment of him. Perhaps he really does care for the family."

The only thing Sebastian cared about, Alex thought in disgust, was coveting his brother's possessions—his land, his position, his title . . . and his wife.

Countless times over the past weeks she had dodged his less than subtle advances. If he kept it up she would be forced to tell Drake about it, though she hated to do so. Her husband was totally preoccupied with all the businesses he now had to manage and spent hours each day closeted in his study with George Bishop, his steward, wrestling with the complexities of running Allonshire.

The pressure was taking its toll. Drake had been drinking far too much and sleeping far too little. He could not seem to find any peace, except in Alex's arms. Night after night he buried his body inside hers with the desperation of a drowning man clinging to life. And, unknowingly, in the process, he penetrated her heart and her soul, brought to life all the feelings she was trying so hard to suppress.

She hurt for his pain. And more than ever, she loved him. Helplessly. Totally. Irrevocably.

"Alex? I can see that the idea of Sebastian suggesting

this party renders you speechless!" Samantha laughed. "But I was there when he announced he wanted to have a small gathering in your honor. His point was well taken. Papa has been gone since September, and we have to resume our lives. What better way than to welcome my new sister to the family?"

Alex gave Sammy a tender look. In the past weeks they had spent hours talking on Samantha's new skiff, which she could now proudly maneuver on her own. Alex could not have wished for a more loyal and loving sister.

She squeezed Sammy's hand. "Thank you for making this easier for me," she told her. "I could not have endured today without you."

Samantha threw her arms around Alex's neck. "I don't blame Drake for loving you," she whispered fiercely. "I love you, too."

Alex felt a slash of pain cut across her heart. Did Drake love her? It was hardly likely.

Samantha drew back, studied Alex's face with a wisdom beyond her years. "He does love you, Alex," she said softly. "He just cannot tell you so . . . not yet. He is still suffering from old wounds and coping with new ones. That is why he broods so much. Give him time, please. He needs you more than he knows . . . more than he wants to need you."

Alex's eyes grew damp. "Need and love are two different things, Sammy," she said in a voice that trembled. "I know he needs me, but love . . ."

"He feels both. You'll see that I am right." Samantha turned at the sound of laughter drifting up from the floor below. "We should see to our guests." She gave Alex an impish grin. "Now, remember what I told you. Lord and Lady Kensgate were close friends of my parents. All the other guests are acquaintances of Drake's. Lady Arabella Ravensley is a tall brunette who giggles too much and is married to Lord Eric Ravensley, a boyhood friend of Drake's. Lady Claudia Byrnewood is a plump redhead who bites her nails continuously. Her husband is Lord Roger Byrnewood . . . a bore. Lady Alicia Lyndale is sweet and blond with a beautiful smile, married to that delightful Lord Stephen Lyndale. Lady Lydia Scarborough, the wife of Lord Randall Scarborough, is tiny and treacherous, and Lady Elizabeth Dragmere, Lord Lawrence Dragmere's new bride, has a sumptuous body and huge blue eyes.'' She took a breath. ''Lydia and Elizabeth were involved with Drake in the past and would like to be in the future, Arabella and Claudia have had designs on him for years, but Alicia is happily married and devoted to her husband. Any questions?''

Alex frowned. ''How deeply involved was Drake with these women?''

Samantha gave a dismissive wave of her hand. ''They meant nothing to him. No woman ever has . . . except you. I didn't tell you those things to cause you needless worry. I told you so that you would be cautious about whom you trusted.'' She smiled, taking Alex's hand. ''There is no competition, Alex; remember that. Drake is in love with you; I know it. Now, let's go.'' She tugged a reluctant Alex down the wide marble steps to make her debut.

The men were already off to the stables, and only the chattering women were present in the drawing room. According to Drake's plan, Samantha would introduce Alex to the ladies now, and the meetings with the gentlemen would take place in the evening.

The buzz of conversation came to an abrupt halt as the women became aware of Alex's presence. Six pairs of curious eyes, ranging from interested to resentful, stared at the new mistress of Allonshire, the young woman who had managed to snare Drake Barrett. Alex, aware of how important this first impression would be, abruptly decided to make her own introductions. She held her head high and, calling upon eighteen years of rigid training, sailed gaily into the room.

''Good morning, ladies. Welcome to Allonshire.'' She walked up to the round redhead who sat primly on the ice blue settee nibbling on a pastry. ''You must be Claudia,'' she smiled, trying to control a peal of laughter from breaking loose as the plump woman nodded, licked the last flaky crumb off her finger, and began chewing on her thumbnail. "Samantha mentioned your lovely red hair. I am Alexandria. It's a pleasure to meet you."

She introduced herself to the other five women, making mental notes as to the reactions she received. Arabella Ravensley, buxom and tall, punctuated each sentence with a nervous giggle. Lydia Scarborough was petite and blond, like a tiny angel, but her eyes shot daggers at Alex and her tongue was acidic. Elizabeth Dragmere was breathtaking, with thick auburn hair, huge, melting blue eyes, and a provocative figure that would have aroused a dead man. Anne Kensgate was a regal silver-haired woman who greeted Alex pleasantly, yet studied her with cool, measured looks over her teacup. Only Alicia Lyndale, with her pale blond hair and warm brown eyes, greeted Alex with genuine warmth and proffered friendship.

Alex sought Samantha's gaze and raised her brows in a salute to the younger girl's superbly accurate descriptions of their houseguests. Samantha grinned back an I-told-you-so look, then seated herself in a high-backed chair, ready to watch Alex's performance at close range.

"Alexandria, please tell us—we're all dying to know—how did you and Drake meet? It was all rather sudden, was it not?" Lydia wasn't wasting any time with small talk. Despite her conversational tone, Alex recognized the brittleness of her smile and the sharp challenge in her dark eyes as she awaited Alex's answer.

Alex gave her a beatific smile. "Actually, yes, it was rather a whirlwind courtship," she confessed. "After all, this was my very first Season." Alex gave herself a silent round of applause as Lydia, older by at least five years, winced.

"Then you and Drake met in London?" Elizabeth's big blue eyes widened in surprise.

Alex was beginning to enjoy herself. "Why, yes," she answered truthfully, watching as the women exchanged surprised glances. They were obviously nonplussed at having no recollection of Alex attending any of the grand balls. "Unfortunately, the Season was a brief one for Drake and me. My father, the governor of Upper Canada, required my presence in York." A little white lie couldn't hurt. "Drake was gallant enough to offer me passage on his ship." Close enough to the truth.

"Drake took you on his ship to Canada?" Lydia's incredulous expression was mirrored on five other faces. For Drake to have allowed any female into that part of his life was unprecedented.

"Why, yes." Alex kept her expression innocent. "He was charming and so accommodating. Why, to spare my reputation he even forfeited his cabin to me for the entire duration of the trip."

"You were unchaperoned?" Anne Kensgate looked appalled.

Alex dropped her eyes. "Due to an unfortunate set of circumstances, my lady's maid was unable to accompany me." *Most probably because I never told her I was going.* "Of course, Drake's valet was ever so helpful, as was the rest of the crew. And, since we had planned on marrying once we reached York anyway, it was only a small impropriety."

Lady Kensgate gave a loud, indignant sniff as if to counter Alex's words.

"Well, I think that it is all wonderfully romantic," Alicia Lyndale put in with a warm smile. "Obviously it was love at first sight."

An image of Drake's blazing fury at finding her in his cabin rose before Alex's eyes, and she fought to control a giggle. She gave Alicia a grateful smile. "Yes, Drake and I had a rather powerful reaction to each other right from the start."

"Most women react powerfully when they meet Drake," Arabella jumped in, then giggled.

"They certainly do," Lydia agreed with a leer. "And the reaction only grows stronger as the involvement deepens." Her meaning was quite clear.

"True. But Drake rarely reacts the same way in return." Samantha's clear fifteen-year-old voice stunned all of them, and they turned to stare in surprise. They tolerated her presence because Drake insisted on it, but they were unused to being challenged by a mere chit.

Samantha met their stares calmly, looking much as Drake did when he was confronting an adversary. "My brother is usually unaffected by the attention bestowed upon him by eager women," she continued, smiling at Alex's startled, admiring expression. "Until Alex. I have never seen him so smitten. But then, I suppose he recognized the rare combination of good breeding, beauty, intelligence, humor, and charm in one woman. And he was wise enough, once he spotted it, to marry her." She smoothed a wrinkle from her gown and folded her hands demurely in her lap.

All of the women but Alicia gaped at Samantha's outspoken comments. Alicia gave a hearty laugh and nodded.

"You are quite right, Samantha. Drake has certainly had ample opportunity to select a wife. But a man of his great wealth and position must choose wisely." She gave Alex's arm a squeeze. "Apparently he did just that." She led Alex over to the tufted sofa. "Now, please come sit down and relax." She shot an annoyed look at the other occupants of the room. "Our intent is to welcome you, not to make you uncomfortable. Isn't that right, ladies?"

Five heads nodded reluctantly. After that, the conversation went on to the newest fashions, the latest gossip about who was involved with whom, and the upcoming Christmas parties they would be attending.

Alex wished fervently that she were back on her island with Drake.

"Your new stallion is a beauty, Drake." Eric Ravensley stroked the glossy neck of the proud black horse that stood in dignified silence, waiting to be mounted.

"So, I hear, is his new wife," Stephen Lyndale chimed in with a twinkle.

"You hear correctly, Stephen," Sebastian replied instantly. "Alexandria is an exquisite and noteworthy acquisition for my brother. She is a rare combination of grace and breeding."

"Alexandria is a woman, not a horse, Sebastian."

Drake's tone was cutting, his anger generated by the patronizing words and the damned intimate tone of his brother's voice.

Alex might think him unaware of Sebastian's ogling, but he was not. He was uncertain whether Sebastian's interest in Alex stemmed from jealousy or lust. Either way, Drake saw red whenever he caught his brother staring at her with that predatory gleam in his eye. If Sebastian ever so much as touched Alex, Drake would kill him.

He turned cold green eyes to where Sebastian stood, preparing to mount his mare for their morning ride. Sebastian felt Drake's stare, but chose to ignore it, swinging himself into the saddle.

Stephen cleared his throat, breaking the heavy silence. Drake's antipathy toward his brother was well known, and in truth no one blamed him for it. Sebastian was neither liked nor trusted by any of the men, but out of respect for Drake, he was not shunned.

"We are looking forward to meeting this mysterious lady who has finally put an end to your days as an eligible bachelor," Stephen teased, mounting his own chestnut mare.

Drake nodded his dismissal to the groom who had escorted the handsome thoroughbred out of the stables. With the easy grace that accompanied all of his movements Drake swung himself into the heavy leather saddle and absently stroked the horse's neck.

"You will have ample opportunity to meet Alexandria this evening," he told Stephen. He flashed him a quick smile. "I don't think you will be disappointed."

The men laughed, good humor restored, dissolving the tension of the last few minutes. The crisp fall day was perfect for riding, and Drake found himself anticipating the exercise with a great deal of enthusiasm. The vast grounds of Allonshire spread out before them, the immaculately trimmed hedges and numerous fences providing the perfect hurdles for jumping. Jupiter, his prize thoroughbred, had been well trained for such a romp, and the blood-horse now pranced with excitement as he awaited Drake's commands.

Drake's gentle slapping of the reins began the jaunt at a

relaxed pace, and soon all were riding in companionable silence.

Sebastian stared at his brother's broad-shouldered back with undisguised hatred. Even on a casual outing, the men automatically followed Drake's lead. There was something about him that commanded respect and spoke of leadership and power.

But not for long.

Sebastian walked his horse slowly, falling into step beside Lord Reginald Kensgate. The older, silver-haired man was not as quick as the younger men, and, had fallen some distance behind the other riders—a distance that Sebastian took good advantage of.

"Hello, Reginald. It's been a while," he greeted him cheerfully.

Lord Kensgate swallowed deeply, the familiar pain constricting his chest and making breathing difficult.

"I have nothing to say to you, Barrett. Nothing at all."

Sebastian raised his dark brows in mock surprise. "Now, is that any way to speak to a dear friend?"

Reginald's glance was withering. "We are anything but friends, Sebastian. It sickens me that I was weak enough to succumb to your vicious blackmail in the past. It will torture my conscience for the rest of my life."

"Such theatrics, Reginald." Sebastian shook his head. "It does not become you at all. And words like 'blackmail' are so ugly. I prefer to think of it as a shrewd business deal."

"A business deal?" Lord Kensgate looked ill. "You have a diseased mind. Thank God your father is not alive to see what you have become."

"You were willing to help me," Sebastian reminded him with a cold smile. "Remember that."

"I will never forget it," came the whispered reply. "And I thank the Lord that your plan failed." He urged his horse on. "We have nothing more to say to each other, Sebastian. If I were a stronger man, if I were not so afraid to leave Anne alone, I would confess my crime just to see you punished for your treachery."

"But you yourself admitted that you are weak." Sebastian laughed cruelly as he watched Reginald ride off to catch up with the others. "I don't need you any longer, old man," he muttered under his breath. "I am taking care of things on my own . . . as I should have done from the start."

Unaware of the angry exchange going on behind him, Drake let his rigid body relax in the saddle, allowing a small trace of the freedom he felt at sea to tantalize his senses. These past weeks had been laden with responsibility, and he had taken no time for recreation of any kind.

Almost any kind, he amended to himself, thinking of the nights he spent in his wife's arms. Making love to Alex was a balm to his tortured senses, the only time he could forget who and what he was. When they were together, nothing existed outside of their union. Time had not dimmed his insatiable passion for Alex, but rather increased his urgent need to possess her, body, heart, and soul.

Alex's adaptation had been incredible. While he was still reeling from his world's upheaval, she had slipped into her role as the Duchess of Allonshire with amazing ease and grace. Just as she had captivated the hearts of his crew on *La Belle Illusion*, Alex had done the same at Allonshire. The servants looked up to her, Samantha adored her, even Blackbeard guarded her with fierce protectiveness and slept nightly by her bedside. As always, Alex was blissfully unaware of her effect on people. Unconsciously she enchanted everyone, just by being herself.

He was far more than enchanted. Determinedly he refused to assign a name to what he felt for his intoxicating wife. But the depth of it staggered him. And though he told himself that it did not matter, he held his breath each night in bed, feeling her body contract with pleasure and listening for her involuntary declaration of love—a declaration that he had not heard in over two months.

Desperately trying to clear his mind, Drake broke into a gallop. The most challenging obstacles loomed just ahead, and a surge of anticipation rose up inside him as they drew nearer. Jupiter could make any jump with effortless skill;

Drake himself had painstakingly trained the stallion in hazardous jumps such as these.

The horse seemed to sense Drake's excitement. His ears went back, his nostrils flared, and he increased his speed, leaving the others far behind. Gusts of cold air blew past them as horse and rider moved as one, nearing the series of intricate jumps.

"Here we go, Jupiter!" Drake called out, nudging lightly with his feet. "Now!"

Then they were flying through the air, sailing with the wind. They had barely touched the ground when the next hurdle loomed before them. Again they went up and over, landing lightly on the other side, only to begin again. Each fence was higher than the one before it, posing increasing danger.

The final fence was before them. No one but Drake would dare to attempt this feat, and the men all paused to watch their friend's brilliant display of horsemanship.

Oblivious to all but the thrill of the sport, Drake urged Jupiter into a faster gallop and the bold horse responded instantly, gathering his legs under him and, in a flash of movement, springing up and over the fence.

Drake heard the snap when they were in midair. He had no time to think or react as the ground rushed up to meet him. And then a blinding flash of pain took his breath away.

"Would anyone care for more tea?" Alex asked, looking around the drawing room. Personally, if she had one more cup, she would explode.

There was a sudden din from the front door, and moments later Humphreys burst into the room, completely flustered. Alex had never seen the austere butler looking so harried, and she rose immediately to her feet.

"Humphreys, what is the commotion? Is something wrong?"

"Yes, your grace." He hesitated for a second, knowing that he should take the duchess aside to tell her, then decided that this was no time for protocol. "It is his grace," he told her. "He has taken a bad fall from his horse."

Alex was halfway to the door. "Is he badly injured, Humphreys?" she began, then stopped as she looked out into the hall.

Two footmen and a frantic Smitty were carrying a white-faced Drake into the house.

Chapter 26

"I tell you I am fine!"

Drake was sitting up, bare-chested, on the edge of the bed, running his fingers through his disheveled raven hair and addressing a doting Smitty, who was pacing back and forth across the bedchamber.

At Drake's words Smitty stopped, frowning. "You are not fine, your grace. You are badly bruised and cut, and your shoulder was dislocated."

"Which, thanks to you, it no longer is," Drake finished impatiently, gingerly moving his left arm, which still throbbed with a dull ache. It had been agony when Smitty snapped the shoulder back into place, but the worst of the pain had immediately subsided once the job was done. Now Drake was anxious to forget the whole incident. He glanced down at the raw skin and angry red gashes with a dismissive shrug of his uninjured right shoulder. "My bruises are minimal," he announced. "I am quite all right."

"Thanks to some very quick thinking and superb horsemanship, from what I hear." Alex stood in the doorway, a cool, damp cloth in her hand. She approached the bed, grateful that Drake was improving. She had been overcome with fear at the first sight of him, pale, groaning with pain, covered with blood. Now, an hour later, he looked almost normal, with only the nasty cuts and scratches a reminder of his ordeal. "Alicia said that, according to her husband, if you had fallen any other way, both you and Jupiter would have been badly hurt. As it is, only your arm and Jupiter's pride were injured." She applied the compress to his left arm, gently cleaning the wounds.

Drake grinned. "It was pure instinct, I assure you, princess," he said in a softer tone, enjoying the caressing motion of her hands on his arm. She bit her lip, concentrating on her healing ministrations, leaning over to examine the depth of the cuts. Drake relaxed, feeling soft tendrils of her golden brown hair tickle his bare skin. He breathed deeply, inhaling his wife's familiar floral scent, thinking how wonderful it was to see her in something other than drab mourning colors. Today she looked young and vibrant and very, very beautiful.

"Smitty, how is his shoulder?" Alex asked, dabbing at the wounds.

"It snapped right back into place, your grace," he replied. "But it is still quite tender."

Drake gave a disgusted snort. "Would the two of you stop discussing me as if I were not present?" he demanded.

"Stop moving," Alex ordered, unbothered by her husband's angry outburst. "I cannot cleanse these wounds if you don't sit still."

Instead of exploding, Drake surprised Smitty by chuckling. "You really are a tyrant, your grace," he teased, reaching up to wrap her hair around his hand. "You are never content unless you are ordering people about. First on my ship and now at Allonshire."

Alex's lips twitched despite her attempt to frown. "I order *you* about only because you are stubborn and unwilling to accept good advice."

"Mmm . . ." he answered thoughtfully. "Now that I think about it, there is but one place where you seem to have no complaints about my performance." His eyes twinkled as he awaited her blush.

It was Smitty who blushed.

Alex straightened, hands on hips, meeting Drake's challenging look. "That is because it is the only place where you are not in need of improvement."

Drake looked startled, then burst out laughing. "I will take that as the highest of compliments . . . since you are so very difficult to please."

"I do believe we are embarrassing Smitty," Alex informed him, looking sympathetically at the red-faced valet. "And I can see that you are quite well and have no further need of my attentions." She tossed the cloth onto the low table beside the bed. "So I will return to our guests."

Drake frowned. "I will join you shortly."

"You will not," she replied, pausing in the doorway. "You will stay here and rest."

"Don't push me, Alexandria," he warned, his expression darkening.

She gave him a bright smile. "But that is what we tyrants do best." She shut the door behind her.

Drake shook his head. "Why do I allow her to browbeat me, Smitty?"

Although the question was only half serious and was spoken more to himself than to Smitty, the older man answered it. "She is not browbeating you, your grace; she is caring for you. She does that because she loves you, just as you allow it because you lo—"

"Never mind," Drake hastily intervened. His emotions, when it came to Alex, were still too new and raw for him to discuss or analyze. But the thought that she might still love him caused a ray of hope to be born inside his heart.

He stood, wincing a bit at the pain in his shoulder. "I still cannot understand how it could have happened, Smitty."

"I suppose the saddle strap just wore through."

Drake shook his head. "That was a new saddle; I cannot believe the straps could wear so quickly."

"It is also not like Winthrop to overlook such an obvious flaw," Smitty mused, thinking of the efficient head groom. The elderly man had worked at Allonshire for twenty years and took great pride in running the enormous stables.

At that moment the very man they were discussing knocked lightly on the door.

"May I come'n, your grace?" he asked, when Smitty opened the door.

"Of course, Winthrop," Drake replied, sitting back down on the bed. He had planned on going back to his guests, but Drake's instincts told him that Winthrop's visit was more than just a token gesture to check on the state of his employer's health.

Winthrop stood just inside the doorway, obviously uncomfortable at being in the duke's bedchamber.

"I f-felt very bad about the accident, yer grace," he stammered.

"I know you did, Winthrop," Drake responded. "And I am certain that it was not your fault."

The groom looked relieved at Drake's words. "I appreciate yer faith in me. I was sure that saddle was new and in good condition. But it bothers me that the strap broke like that. It shouldn't 'ave 'appened. So I just checked on the saddle meself, t' make sure. . . ." He hesitated.

"Go ahead, Winthrop," Drake urged.

"Well . . . I wouldn't tell ye this unless I was certain, but the fact is that the strap did not wear out. It was cut."

Total silence filled the room.

"Cut?" Smitty echoed at last.

Winthrop turned his troubled gaze to Smitty. "Yes, cut."

"How can you be sure?" Drake demanded.

"There is no sign of wear, yer grace." He looked utterly miserable. "The slice is clean and so neat that only a knife could've made it. It looks like it was cut about 'alfway through, and the jumps ye took with Jupiter were strong enough t' sever the strap the rest of the way." His lips tightened. "There is no question in my mind . . . that strap was cut."

"Who knew that saddle was meant for Jupiter, your grace?" Smitty asked Drake quietly.

Drake raised his somber gaze to Smitty's. "Everyone. It was no secret. Anyone who had access to the stables would know I use that saddle for Jupiter." He swallowed deeply, then looked back at the groom. "Thank you for coming to me with this, Winthrop."

The groom nodded. "I'm sorry 'bout this, yer grace. I 'ave no idea who would do such a thing."

"Nor do I. But I intend to find out," Drake replied in a hard tone.

Smitty closed the door carefully behind the retreating head groom, then turned back to Drake.

"Do you know what this means?"

"It means that someone is trying to kill me."

They stared at each other as the full impact of Drake's words struck them.

Smitty walked toward Drake and sat down in a chair. "The question, your grace, is who?"

Alex was humming as she left the drawing room, and the chattering women, behind. She could not concentrate on their idle gossip, for her thoughts were still of the fall Drake had taken. Even though she had left him barely ten minutes past, she decided to check on him again, just to assure herself he was as well as he professed to be.

She walked lightly up the stairs, heard herself humming, and smiled. The fear she had felt earlier served only to remind her how very much Drake meant to her, how deeply she loved him. She grinned, thinking of their easy banter. It had been months since they had been able to tease each other so freely. She was healing, Alex realized. At last she was healing. Soon they would be able to talk. And then, perhaps, forgiveness would follow.

On the second-floor landing she passed Winthrop, who was on his way down. He was visibly upset.

"Hello, Winthrop," Alex greeted him. "Is everything all right?"

He jumped. "Oh . . . yer grace, forgive me. I didn't see ye." He managed a weak smile. " 'is grace is doing well. I just left 'im," he assured her, then bolted down the steps.

Alex looked after him in surprise, then shrugged. He was probably just shaken by Drake's close call. And he *had* said that Drake was all right. She continued on her way, her heart feeling lighter than it had in months as she neared Drake's bedchamber. She could hear the deep cadence of his voice, followed by Smitty's quiet replies. Her hand was on the door handle when Drake's next words made her freeze in her tracks.

"You know, of course, that this casts a whole new light on the destruction of *La Belle Illusion*," he said grimly. "Apparently you were correct in your assumption that the men were not to blame for missing their target."

"That does not surprise me, your grace," Smitty answered. "I suspected that the powder must have been tampered with. But it never occurred to me that it was an attempt to murder *you*. I suspected a traitor to Britain. But now . . ."

"Yes . . . now," Drake echoed thoughtfully. "Now it appears that someone would like to do away with me. Badly enough to murder a whole crew of men in order to accomplish it." He paused. "And badly enough to try again in my own home by cutting the strap of my saddle."

"Dear God . . ." Smitty whispered.

Alex repeated his words silently. She leaned against the wall outside the room, feeling the hallway spinning around her. Someone had tried to murder Drake—not once, but twice.

Memories of the fateful naval battle sprang to Alex's mind in vivid detail. She had been there, on the main deck, when the men had tried time and again to hit the American ship. She had heard their cries of surprise, of confusion, when their cannon volleys fell short each time. Unknowledgeable about sea battles, Alex had given it no further thought. But now she realized that Drake's crew was of the finest caliber. Their aim could not have been consistently poor. The only explanation was that the gun powder had been weak—too weak to propel the balls to their target.

And Drake's accident today. He and Smitty were saying that the strap of his saddle had been cut. That explained Winthrop's strange behavior on the stairs. He must have discovered the treachery. Someone had gotten into the stables and tampered with the strap in the hope that it would break, causing Drake to fall to his death.

Someone wanted Drake dead. And that someone was here at Allonshire.

Smitty heard a soft thud just outside the door. Hurriedly he opened it and gasped as he saw Alex's crumpled body on the polished floor of the hallway.

"Smitty? What is it?" Drake was standing, walking toward the doorway as Smitty stooped over Alex's body.

"It's the duchess. She has fainted."

Drake nearly knocked Smitty over in his haste to reach Alex's side. With his uninjured right arm he gathered her to him and, with Smitty's assistance, carried her into his room. By the time he had laid her on the bed her eyelashes were fluttering open.

"Drake?" She felt confused. Why was she lying on the bed when he was the one who was injured?

He smoothed her rumpled hair off of her face. "Are you all right, love?" His dark face was tight with concern.

"Yes . . . I'm fine. Why?" She wished she could get her bearings.

"Apparently, you fainted just outside my bedroom."

A cold wash of memory slapped her in the face, and she gasped.

"What is it, princess?" He was watching her face carefully, trying to assess how much she had overheard of his conversation.

In a fraction of a second Alex decided not to let him know that she had heard. He had enough to concern himself with, without worrying about her as well. She needed time to think, to plan her strategy. It never occurred to her not to get involved; this was Drake's life, and she would protect it with her own.

She smiled weakly. "I suppose it is the excitement of the day—first the party and now your accident." She took a deep breath and sat up. "I'm fine . . . really I am. I was just on my way to make sure you were all right."

He studied her face carefully. She was so pale. It worried him. He stroked his thumbs across her cheeks. "These have been difficult months for you, haven't they, princess?" The tenderness in his voice was so real that Alex found it hard to remember when he had called her by that name in mockery of her way of life.

"They've been difficult for all of us," she answered lightly, standing up. The room was still wobbling a bit, and she blinked to stabilize it.

Drake caught hold of her arms. "I think you should take your own advice, princess."

"What advice?"

"I want you to lie down and rest until dinner."

"But our guests . . ." she protested.

"You will have plenty of time to entertain our guests this evening." Alex knew that firm tone, just as she knew it would be useless to argue. Besides, she needed time alone to sort out everything she had just learned.

She nodded meekly. "Very well. I will go to my chambers."

"I will send Molly up at once," Smitty announced, hurrying out the door.

Drake wrapped his right arm around her waist and guided her to the door. "I'll take you to your room." He led her across the hall.

"It's really not necessary, Drake."

"Humor me," he answered, drawing Alex into her room. "I will feel better knowing you are safe in your bed."

He stayed with her until a clucking Molly scurried in to prepare her mistress for a nap. She gaped at the duke's half-naked state, turning several shades of pink and red.

"I'll let you rest now," Drake told Alex quietly, his eyes twinkling at Molly's predicament.

Alex nodded and yawned, suddenly overwhelmed by sleepiness.

Drake grinned. "Sweet dreams, princess." He walked toward the door.

Alex stared at his retreating back; the corded muscles that rippled across his broad bare shoulders, the powerful thighs that were emphasized by his buff riding breeches. A flood of feeling washed over her as she realized how close she had come to losing him.

How much she loved him.

"Drake . . . ?" She didn't realize she had said his name aloud until he turned to give her a questioning look. Without a word she went to him, wrapped her arms around his waist, and pressed her forehead against his strong chest.

"Princess?" He lifted his hand to stroke her hair. She knew she wasn't making any sense to him, but it didn't matter. She wanted to tell him how much she loved him, that she needed him, that they would resolve their problems. But Molly was standing just behind her, muttering disapprovingly under her breath. Now was not the time.

Alex raised her face to look up at him. "Are you certain you are not badly hurt?" she whispered.

He gave her a slow, devastating smile, then leaned over and touched his lips lightly to hers. "Get some rest, sweetheart," he murmured, for her ears alone. "Later tonight, when our guests are all asleep, I'll show you just how totally I've recovered."

She smiled back until the door closed behind him. Then she allowed her mind to begin working, trying to solve the terrifying puzzle of who wanted Drake dead.

When Molly had gone, Alex lay down, fighting the sudden need for sleep that tugged insistently at her body. She had to think this through . . . to determine who was behind the attempts on Drake's life.

Anyone could have tampered with the gunpowder. There was no way to narrow down the possibilities. She frowned, forcing her eyes to remain open. But the saddle . . . Very few people had access to the stables. She refused to consider the servants. Never had she seen a more loyal and dedicated group of employees, not even at Sudsbury. That left the guests . . . and the family. The family was more preposterous than the servants; so that left the guests.

What did any of the wealthy, influential people present at Allonshire have to gain by causing Drake's demise? It didn't make sense. Yet it had to be one of them. No one would suspect a member of the *ton* to be guilty of murder. She certainly couldn't accuse any of them.

But then, none of them knew they were suspected of anything. Drake would never tell them that his fall had not, in fact, been an accident, but an attempted murder. Therefore, the true culprit would not feel threatened. He might be caught off guard. Alex smiled slowly. It was time to utilize all the charm and feminine wiles that she had been taught but had disregarded all these eighteen years. What was it they said about catching more flies with honey?

She yawned again, rubbing her eyes in annoyance. Why did she suddenly require an afternoon nap? She had no patience with physical weakness. Yet, today alone, she had experienced several dizzy spells, been seized by acute nausea, and had fallen pray to the hateful female practice of swooning. She was not under *that* much stress.

It struck Alex suddenly, like a blow. Tossing the bedcovers aside, she rose and, in the same movement, tugged her chemise off and dropped it carelessly onto the floor.

The afternoon sun peeped through the draperies, casting more than enough light on Alex's naked body as she stood before the mirror. Slowly she ran her hands over the contours of her body, staring at her reflection as if seeing herself for the first time. Her breasts were heavier than normal, the nipples having darkened to a deep rose color. She continued her exploration, smoothing her palm over what had been the concave surface of her stomach. She felt the slight rounding with a sense of awe and amazement.

How could she have been so blind? She had been so preoccupied, so utterly consumed with her own emotional turmoil, that she had paid little attention to her physical self. And each night, when she and Drake came together, it was always in the dark, for neither of them was ready to read what was in the other's eyes. Now she frantically searched her mind, realizing that she had not bled in over four months . . . since her marriage to Drake.

Alex closed her eyes as the realization took hold, the absolute knowledge inserted itself in her shaken mind.

She was pregnant with Drake's baby.

Chapter 27

The ballroom was vibrantly aglow, the brilliant chandeliers scattering fragments of light, the highly polished floor reflecting the golden cast of the gilded ceiling. Liveried footmen scurried about, seeing to refreshments and pouring champagne into crystal glasses for Allonshire's guests.

Alex sipped at her champagne, watching the twelve people who laughed, talked, and danced in the elegant room. They had dined at seven o'clock; then everyone had gone on to the ballroom to continue the festive evening.

The men had been introduced to Alex at dinner, and despite Drake's disapproving frown, most of them still hadn't taken their eyes off her. In a flowing gown of rich red satin trimmed with delicate lace at the low-cut neckline and along the edges of the full skirt and sleeves, she looked like a radiant and majestic queen.

She felt, however, as if she might spill out of her bodice, and judging from the interested looks she was receiving from the gentlemen, she was not far from wrong.

Satisfied that she was unobserved, she gave a dainty squirm and a discreet tug at the uncooperative, square-cut neckline. It didn't budge. This particular gown had not been designed for a woman who was almost four months pregnant. She gave a resigned sigh just as a smooth masculine voice sounded from behind.

"Never have I seen a more beautiful woman."

Alex turned cool gray eyes to Sebastian's admiring face. "Never have I met a man more well versed in ineffective flattery," she responded pointedly. Her tone was light; her gaze was not.

Undaunted, he gave her a charming smile. "Not flattery, Alexandria, but fact. Surely you know how desirable you are to men?"

Alex considered tossing the contents of her glass into his arrogant, suggestive face, but she had no time to make a scene or to dodge Sebastian's amorous flirtations. Tonight she had a special mission.

"Sebastian," she asked softly, careful to retain her brightest smile, pretending to be enjoying a most delightful conversation, "have you not learned that desiring something and acquiring it are two very different things? Remember that even the loveliest of roses has thorns with which to protect itself."

He leaned closer. "And if the thorns are plucked?"

"Then the rose has no choice but to connect its knee to the appropriate part of the offending male's anatomy," she purred.

Sebastian gaped, then covered his shock with a hollow laugh. "You are by far the most outspoken female I have ever met."

"Now *that* I will accept as a true compliment, sir," she replied, prepared to end their conversation and resume mingling with her guests.

Sebastian caught her arm. "How is my brother feeling? Any ill effects from his accident?" The question was casual enough, but his gaze was oddly penetrating.

Alex glanced across the room to where Drake was chatting with Eric Ravensley. Her husband looked breathtakingly handsome tonight in a black dress coat that fit snugly across his broad shoulders and a contrasting white waistcoat. Above his frilled shirt was Smitty's handiwork—a perfectly tied white silk cravat that made Drake's tanned face and raven hair seem even darker in comparison. He laughed at something Eric was saying, exuding that inexplicable charisma that made Alex weak. Even from this distance, Alex could feel the unique magnetic allure that was Drake's alone and was responsible for devastating women's hearts effortlessly.

She realized that Sebastian was watching her expressions

with great interest. Schooling her features, she replied, "As you can see for yourself, Drake is unharmed. He did suffer a dislocated shoulder and some minor cuts, but that is all."

"He is quite lucky, then. He could have been killed."

Again, Alex added silently. There was something about Sebastian's tone, a certain sarcasm, that riled her. She drew herself up to her full height, prepared to defend her husband. "Luck had little to do with it, Sebastian. Drake is a splendid horseman. He made certain his fall caused minimal injury to himself and none to Jupiter."

Sebastian raised his glass in a mock toast. "Of course. Drake is superb at everything he does. There has yet to be invented a skill at which he does not excel, a feat that he cannot accomplish—not to mention a woman whom he cannot conquer. A most fortunate man, my brother." He sipped at his drink.

Alex had never witnessed such blatant envy within a family. There was no doubt in her mind that Sebastian wished nothing but ill for his brother. It angered and sickened her. She knew for certain that she could never confide in Sebastian her suspicions that someone was trying to kill Drake. He was no ally, but an adversary.

Sebastian interpreted Alex's dark silence to mean that his barb had hit its mark, that she was infuriated by the possibility that Drake might still have other women. Good. If his implication had made her doubt Drake's fidelity it would drive her to his own bed that much sooner.

Discreetly he brushed the bare skin atop her bodice with his fingers. "Do not look so mortified, my thorny little rose," he soothed. "As I have told you before, I will always welcome your attentions. It is charming and refreshing to see so lovely a woman champion Drake's cause. I much admire your display of loyalty."

Something inside Alex snapped. "Then perhaps you should acquire some yourself, you unprincipled snake!" She recoiled from his touch and walked off, not turning to see his reaction to her words.

Sebastian looked thoughtfully, expressionlessly, after

her. For now he would let her play her little game of indignant virtue. But in time she would be his.

Alex took deep breaths to control her temper. She would not allow Sebastian to deter her from her purpose. Come hell or high water she would uncover the identity of the person who had tried to kill Drake.

With a dazzling smile she approached Alicia and Stephen Lyndale, who were engaged in light, breathless chatter, having just finished a frolicking reel.

"Oh, Alexandria," Alicia said, still laughing. "This party is delightful! Stephen and I were just saying that it is a pleasure to enjoy a dance together without colliding with other couples. A small gathering like this one is a welcome change after the rapid pace of the Season and the cluttered house parties of the fall."

"I am pleased that you are enjoying yourselves," Alex said with sincerity. She truly liked Alicia, and had taken to Stephen immediately as well. He was the only man in the room, save the elderly Lord Kensgate, who looked at Alex without lust burning in his eyes. In fact, Stephen was totally absorbed in his wife. The tender glances he bestowed upon Alicia revealed his obvious and deep love for her. Seeing their closeness, Alex felt a momentary twinge of envy. How she wished Drake would gaze at her with such love.

"You are looking a bit pale, Alexandria." Stephen's voice held genuine concern. "Are you feeling well?"

Alex smiled up into his kind face. "Yes, of course, Stephen. I suppose I am still shaken by Drake's accident today."

He nodded sympathetically. "I understand. Thank heaven he seems to be none the worse for it, though."

Alex followed his gaze to where Drake remained in animated conversation with Eric Ravensley. Only now a flushed and simpering Arabella stood beside Eric, staring up at Drake as she hung on to his every word.

A surge of anger shot through Alex like a bolt of lightning. Was Eric blind? His wife was openly ogling his friend right beside him! As she watched and fumed, Alex saw

Arabella inch closer to Drake until her half-naked bosom was almost touching his arm. That did it. If Eric had no pride, Alex did.

She turned back to Stephen. "I agree. Drake seems to be quite himself tonight. Would the two of you excuse me, please?"

She didn't wait for an answer, but walked purposefully across the room as the musicians began the first notes of a waltz. Alex was certain that neither Stephen nor Alicia would harm anyone, least of all, Drake. It was time to investigate the Ravensleys . . . and to stake her claim on her husband at the same time.

She reached Drake in time to hear Arabella say, "Oh, how I love to waltz. But Eric does not succumb to decadence quite so readily as I." She licked her lower lip suggestively, then giggled. "So it seems I am in need of a partner for this dance."

"Then we will not hold you from your search, Arabella," Alex broke in, positioning herself possessively by Drake's side. "Since Drake has promised this waltz to me, we'll be out of your way at once." She smiled innocently at Drake's startled but amused expression. "Darling?"

He recovered immediately. "Of course, princess. I am all yours." He nodded their excuses, then smoothly guided Alex onto the dance floor, chuckling as he took his wife's hand. "Darling?" he teased, looking down into her flushed face. They both knew she had never used that particular endearment in the past. "Funny," he mused aloud, "I do not remember discussing this particular waltz, though it is a pleasure to dance with my wife," he assured her. In truth he was touched by her obvious display of jealousy, for it was a further indication that she cared.

Alex hastily changed the subject. "Is your arm causing you any pain?" The anger had waned, her real concern for Drake warming her eyes to a deep smoky gray.

"My arm is fine." His smile abruptly faded. When she looked up at him that way he felt everything inside him melt. Hell, she reduced him to a callow schoolboy, a burning mass of raw emotions. All evening he had struggled unsuccessfully to bring himself under control. Every time one of the men ogled her, Drake felt irrational and raging jealousy pump through his blood. He wanted to kill the offending bastard, to shout to the world that Alex was *his*. She looked so damned beautiful tonight, like an enchanted fairy-tale princess. His burning emerald gaze caressed her face and shoulders, then settled on the deeply cut neckline that seemed to expose far too much of her throat and breasts.

He frowned, desire warring with jealousy, pride, anger, tenderness—all heightened to a fever pitch. "Your gown is rather revealing, is it not?" he inquired in a tight voice.

Alex blushed at his meaning, then lifted her chin defiantly. "I happen to adore this gown," she retorted.

"So do I," he agreed, his jaw set. "What little of it there is."

Her eyes flashed, more so because he was right. "I am sorry that my attire displeases you, your grace."

He stroked her thumb with his, though his mood was as fiery as hers. "Careful, princess," he warned softly. "We are newly married and supposedly *very* happy. So smile and look totally besotted with me; hang on to my every word. All of our guests are watching us."

Alex controlled her fury with great effort, aware that he was goading her. Apparently he was angry about something, perhaps her gown. But whatever the reason, his earlier good humor had vanished. She forced a smile to her lips and endured the remainder of the dance in tense silence.

The waltz ended, and Alex stepped away from her brooding husband.

"I will mingle with our guests now, Drake," she told him, glancing about the room. Already her mind had returned to the problem at hand—uncovering the identity of the person who had attempted to take Drake's life. "There is no need for you to dance with me, since I have obviously annoyed you. I will find other partners." She lifted her skirts and moved off.

Drake caught her arm. "You will dance with me whenever I deem it necessary."

Alex looked up at him, startled at the bitterness of his tone and the blazing light in his eyes. "I am your wife, not your chattel," she answered softly. "Please refrain from treating me as such."

She shook her arm free and stalked off, then slowed her steps so as not to arouse curiosity among the guests. Her battles with Drake, his battles within himself, were no one's business but theirs.

"Alexandria?"

She turned to find Randall Scarborough by her side. He stared appreciatively at her bare shoulders, then continued downward as if he could see right through her clothes. Alex shivered in distaste.

Randall interpreted the shiver to be one of desire, and his smile deepened. "We have not had a chance to get to know each other," he informed her smoothly, taking her arm and leading her to a secluded corner of the ballroom. "And since my wife and your husband are old friends," he said with a meaningful emphasis, "I think we should become the same. Do you not agree?"

Alex bit back a scathing reply. If she was going to gain any information, she had to ingratiate herself, to play along with their sickening innuendos . . . to a point.

She gave Randall a winning smile, her expression friendly and innocent. "I would love to get to know you better, Randall. After all, I am still new to Allonshire, and I know very few of Drake's friends." She paused after the word "friends," allowing the implication to take hold. "Also, I did not get to enjoy my first Season, as I was compelled to travel to York in March. So," she concluded with a dainty shrug, "I really have had little opportunity to meet the right people."

Randall nodded sympathetically, still concentrating on Alex's breasts. "I certainly understand how difficult it must be for you. Anything I can do to help—"

"Oh, you are so kind," Alex broke in. "But then, I knew you would be." She leaned forward conspiratorially. "I must confess that tonight is not the first time I have seen you."

Her statement actually caused him enough surprise to make him return his attention to her face. "Really?" He sounded genuinely puzzled. "I cannot believe that we have met before now. I would never forget so exquisite a creature as you."

"Oh, we didn't actually meet," she assured him, studying his face for a reaction. "And it was just this morning. I was a trifle nervous waiting for the guests to appear, so I took a short walk about the grounds. I suppose you arrived early and had the same idea. When I saw you, you were strolling . . . let's see . . . I believe it was near the stables!" she lied.

Randall looked crestfallen. "Ah, your grace, I wish that it were so. How I would love to be the man you saw and admired earlier today. Unfortunately"—he cast an annoyed glance across the room to where his wife was chattering with a group of women—"we were delayed in our arrival due to a small family spat." He sighed deeply, dramatically. "Not all men are so fortunate as Drake in their spouses."

Alex feigned surprise. "I was so certain that it was you."

He shook his head regretfully. "No, we were quite late. Perhaps it was Lawrence Dragmere you spotted. He and Elizabeth reached Allonshire well ahead of the rest of us, and he does resemble me in height and build, although," he added, with a suggestive look, "our similarities end there. I am far more proficient than he in the proper way to treat a lady like you."

"Oh, of that I have no doubt," Alex assured him, already searching the room for Lawrence Dragmere. Her fishing had paid off handsomely. Perhaps she would soon have her answer.

Four hours later she knew otherwise.

Her feet ached from dancing, her head throbbed from idle conversation, and the lace on her bodice was shredded where she had been tugging at it all night. She was half convinced that she was lacking a head and neck, since all the men had seemed to be speaking directly to her bosom.

She was also no closer to the truth than she had been at the onset of the evening. Either she was a very poor investigator or none of their guests was guilty of anything other than flagrant adultery, shameless flirtation, falsely inflated feelings of self-worth, and shallow, boring conversation. She had batted her lashes, simpered and laughed, flattered and marveled, and endured countless scandalous offers until she could barely contain her disdain.

And what had she gained? Nothing, except that now four more men were sniffing at her skirts like ravenous hounds after a slab of meat. Only Stephen Lyndale and Reginald Kensgate had been polite and kind, rather than lecherous—although Lord Kensgate had seemed very uneasy throughout their conversation, mopping at his brow and giving terse, disjointed answers to her probing questions. But she attributed it to his age and his distress about Grayson's death. After all, they had been very close friends.

The ball was drawing to a close, and Alex felt only relief. She longed for her loose-fitting night rail and her comfortable bed. Politely she bade each of the guests good night, until at last all was quiet, and she could escape to her sanctuary.

It suddenly occurred to her that she had not spoken to Drake in hours. Out of the corner of her eye she had seen him chatting with their guests throughout the evening, and from time to time she had heard his deep baritone permeate the room. But now there was no sign of him in the still, empty ballroom.

Alex's footsteps echoed as she crossed the polished floor, nodding at the few servants who were hurriedly gathering glasses and straightening furniture. It was just as well that she and Drake had avoided being together, she mused, winding her way up the stairs. He was impossible when he was in one of his foul, dark moods, and she lacked the energy to cope with it tonight. She had too much on her mind, and her body was crying out for sleep.

Instinctively she placed a gentle hand on her abdomen

and smiled. There had been no time to revel in her discovery that she carried Drake's child. Tonight, alone in her bedchamber, she would savor the knowledge. And then perhaps Drake would come to her, in better spirits, and she could share the wondrous news with him.

Her smile grew soft. Perhaps this was just what they needed to solidify their bond—a baby. Despite her unresolved worry for Drake's safety, renewed hope stirred within Alex. She was suddenly most eager to see her husband.

Drake was totally, utterly foxed.

He stared broodingly down at the richly colored brandy in his glass, then flung himself into one of the high-backed chairs that stood against the wall of his bedchamber. He wondered fleetingly how many drinks he had had, then dismissed the concern. What difference did it make? Hell, he could order a dozen bottles to be brought to him, no matter how late the hour, and it would be done immediately. He *was* a damned duke, now, wasn't he?

He put the glass to his lips and swallowed deeply. He could drink until he passed out, but he wouldn't be able to erase her from his mind. The way she had looked tonight, an apparition of loveliness, a flowing-haired goddess of innocent, regal beauty.

A practiced courtesan who had all but seduced an entire houseful of men before his very eyes.

From the moment Alex had stormed from his side after their waltz, the evening had progressed from bad to worse. He had gone from unreasonable jealousy and possessiveness to infuriated amazement and painful shock to blind, trembling rage as his worst nightmare had unfolded before him.

Alex. His guileless, straightforward, unconventional Alex, scorner of the upper crust, had utilized every feminine wile and resorted to every flagrant flirtation of the most skilled adulteress. Flitting gaily from man to man, she had tantalized with her half-naked body and encouraged with her purring responses, until every male at the party was openly lusting after her.

For months his mind had warned him again and again that she was a woman, no more or less, and women were treacherous by nature. But his heart had refused to listen. He had steeled himself for this, frantically clung to his wall of self-protection, remained immune by holding part of himself back. And the damned thing was that it had done no good.

All his efforts had been for naught. He was in love with his wife.

A riot of feelings and emotions stormed Drake's senses, and he closed his eyes to the excruciating pain, which far surpassed the anger. He leaned back, drained the contents of his glass in one gulp, knowing that no amount of the burning liquid could dull the hurt and sense of betrayal.

So it was true. She was like all the others, only lacking the opportunity to show her true colors. Until now. Now, amid the glitter of the *ton*, she was everything he had feared she was, and prayed she was not.

And he was just as vulnerable as if he were a young boy all over again.

But he wasn't a young boy, damn it. He was a grown man. A duke, no less. And he would not allow his wife to make a spineless fool out of him.

He shot to his feet, his eyes blazing, and sent his glass crashing against the marble fireplace. She wanted a nobleman? He would give her one.

He collided with Smitty in the doorway of his room.

"Get out of my way, Smitty," he warned.

Smitty sized up Drake's drunken state immediately, then looked past him at the shattered glass against the wall.

"I think you should rest, your grace," he began.

"I don't give a damn what you think, Smitty, nor do I want any sage advice." He moved past him.

Smitty caught his arm. "You've had too much to drink," he said quietly. "Don't go to her like this."

Drake stared down at Smitty's restraining hand and gave a harsh laugh. "Do not *dare* to speak kindly of my wife to me tonight. Why, at this moment there is probably a line of eager men outside her door." He raised burning, pained eyes to Smitty's. "Don't interfere, Smitty. I mean it. Not this time." He shook his arm free.

"Do not do anything that you will regret, your grace," Smitty cautioned him softly.

Drake tightened the belt of his robe. "It's too late, my friend. Far too late to avoid regrets."

He crossed the hall to Alex's chambers and flung open the door.

Alex started. Having just dismissed Molly, she had been sitting at her dressing table, staring dreamily off into space. Her thoughts had been tender and happy, of Drake, of the baby. And into this peaceful haze came the crash of her door as it flew open.

She stood up hesitantly as he slammed the door closed behind him. "Drake?"

Why did she have to be so damned beautiful? The moonlight filtered in through the window, weaving golden highlights in her hair and making her ivory night rail seem transparent. He felt his loins tighten, and he despised himself for the weakness of his flesh. She was treacherous and hypocritical, everything he loathed.

And he wanted her so much that he throbbed with it.

"Hello, princess." His voice was slurred, but she heard the sarcasm immediately.

"You're foxed." An observation rather than an accusation.

His bitter laugh sent prickles of fear up her spine. Something was different this time, something that frightened her.

He approached her slowly, like a sleek wild animal stalking its prey.

"Yes, I am," he agreed, reaching for the belt of his robe. "I am also your husband, till death do us part, remember?" He didn't wait for her response. "I'll tell you who else I am, just to reassure you that your marriage to me is an advantageous one." He towered over her, his eyes blazing with green fire, his features taut with anger. "I am Drake Robert Barrett, the Duke of Allonshire, the Marquis of Cairnham, the Earl of Laneswood, Earl of Ravleton, Viscount Manvell, and Baron Winsborough. Surely that must be enough titles to satisfy you, your *grace*." He caught her trembling chin in his hand. "Enough to convince you to give to me what you've promised a roomful of men all night long."

"I d-don't know wh-what you mean." Alex was terrified. She had never seen Drake like this.

"No?" he asked softly. "Then I'll spell it out for you. I want my marital rights, princess. Right now. I want you to *submit* to me, to lie down on your beautiful little back and open your luscious thighs for me. I want to spend myself in your willing body, the body that you've flaunted so prettily before the world." He paused, lowering his mouth until his breath touched her lips. "The body that belongs to me. Only me. Do you understand? You are mine . . . *mine*. And I will never let you forget it."

Alex pressed her hands against his massive chest, frantically trying to make some sense out of his drunken ramblings. His arms were like steel manacles around her, not allowing her to escape. There was not a doubt in her mind that in his present condition he was capable of anything. Nor was there any doubt that she was the cause of his blind rage. Apparently he had interpreted her actions tonight as a betrayal of their vows. And he intended to punish her for it.

Alex shoved ineffectually at Drake's chest, twisting her head away from him, struggling to free herself from his relentless hold. He caught her face in his hand, forcing her lips to meet his seeking mouth. It was a brutal kiss, an assertion of power, and Alex whimpered softly in protest.

Drake lifted his mouth from hers only slightly, staring down into her frightened face. "You can skip the performance, princess. It won't work. I intend to have you. And there's not a damned thing you can do to stop me."

"Why are you acting like this?" Alex implored, their mouths so close that she could smell the brandy on his breath. Despite her trembling fear, she could sense a raw desperation at the core of Drake's violence. A desperation that she sought to understand.

"Because, despite your attempt to prove otherwise, I am the *only* man in your life and in your bed." His fingers tightened on her chin, and Alex winced with pain.

"You know I've never been with another man," she whispered in a small, shaken voice.

"There has never been an opportunity . . . until now."

She swallowed deeply. "It wouldn't matter. I don't want anyone but you."

"Stop lying to me!" he commanded in a hoarse voice.

"I'm not lying, Drake." Alex sensed that they had reached a precipice, that the solution to the problem lay just beyond her grasp. Instinctively she knew that she could heal him if she just reached far enough, was willing to take the enormous risk.

She reached up with a small, cold hand and stroked his taut jaw. Her fingers, her voice, trembled.

"I'm not like her."

Drake froze, staring down at her, a look of stark emotion on his face. "Like whom?"

It was time to risk it all. "Your mother."

He caught her by the shoulders, his fingers biting into her arms. "What the hell do you know of my mother?"

"I know she hurt you. I know you believe that all women are like her. We're not. *I'm* not."

He swore under his breath, pushing her away from him with a force so strong that she fell back onto the bed.

"Hurt me? No, she didn't hurt me, princess. I am far too strong to be hurt by anyone, least of all a common slut." At Alex's gasp, he laughed bitterly. "Oh, it was all *very* proper. She provided my father with an heir—two of them, in fact. And then she was free to play. And play she did, with anyone and everyone who had the anatomical requirement between his legs." He raked his fingers through his hair, sweat covering his forehead. "Oh, she was very discreet—so discreet, in fact, that no one knew about it, least of all my father. There was only one problem with all of this. He adored her, worshiped her, with his whole heart and soul. In his eyes my mother could do no wrong; she was just short of a saint. And she let him believe she felt the same way, gazing up at him so tenderly, making him think he was the only man on earth."

He turned away from Alex, his profile cast in shadows.

"I grew up believing my mother was the epitome of woman-hood, everything that was beautiful and soft and caring. And then I was out riding one day when I was fourteen, and I found her in a secluded spot far away from the house. She was beneath the Earl of Locksley, her skirts tossed up, moaning like a common whore.

"And that is not the worst of it. Later that night she asked to see me alone and calmly told me that she felt no guilt for what she had done, that my father was a fine man but just not enough for her, and that she would continue to live her life as she saw fit. There was not a drop of remorse in those cold green eyes. She *suggested* that I refrain from mentioning this to my father, for it would destroy him. Then she shrugged and said that, of course, it was my decision to make. She didn't even give a damn."

Drake faced Alex, angry and agonized and betrayed. "I never told him, because she was right; it would have killed him. I spent the next eight years of my life watching her deceive him again and again, unable to do a damned thing about it. No one else in the family ever knew. My father died without knowing what a bitch he had married.

"And I soon found, through my own experience, that my mother was far from unique. Every woman I encountered had the same shallow, destructive values. And I swore that no woman would ever do that to me." The memory of Alex's behavior tonight returned to claw at his soul. He took slow, menacing steps toward the bed, his words cold and deliberate. "You are never again going to humiliate me in public *or* in private. Ever." He towered over her, his body shaking with anger, past and present.

Tears streamed slowly down Alex's face as she realized the severity of Drake's wounds. "I would never do that to you, Drake," she whispered, then shook her head at the cynicism and hollow victory she saw on his face. *"Not* because I am afraid of what you would do to me, but because I love you."

He froze, his face set in rigid lines. Then he swooped down upon her, catching her hands in his and lowering the weight of his body on top of hers.

"Damn you . . . damn you! Don't you ever say those words to me again," he growled. "They are meaningless; there is no such thing as love."

"There is. I love you, Drake." She lifted her head to kiss the pulse that throbbed at his throat. "I would never hurt you, never betray your trust." She kissed his Adam's apple gently. "I love you," she whispered against his hot skin. "I love you," she repeated, rubbing her face softly against his chin. "I love you."

A deep groan rumbled from within Drake's chest as he capitulated to her words, her caresses. He lowered his face to hers, crushed her lips beneath his in a kiss of savage demand, tightened his fingers on hers as if to bind her to him against her will.

No coercion was necessary. Alex opened to his command, to his fiery tongue and burning kisses, arching herself against him and offering him everything she had, all that she was.

He released her hands to tangle his fingers in her hair, whispering incoherent words against her delicate skin. There was no escape from this madness, this insatiable need she aroused in him, and Drake wasn't certain he even wanted to try. He was on fire, lost in the flames of hell, desperately seeking the heaven she offered.

"Alex . . ." He buried his mouth in the scented hollow of her throat, as her hand moved between them and beneath his robe to find him, to stroke him in tender welcome.

"I love you," she breathed into his damp hair, feeling his hardness pulsing in her hand.

With a guttural sound he raised his hips, pulling up her night rail in one frantic motion and tearing open his own robe to free his rigid arousal. He separated her legs with his knees, slid his hands beneath her buttocks, and drove into her with a wild, powerful lunge that made them both cry out.

And then he was moving, his thrusts hard and fast and so deep that he swore he could touch her womb.

And Alex was with him, wrapping her arms around his back, bending her knees to hug his flanks, loving him to the very depths of her being. Her body was vitally alive, aware of the sensuous feel of his silk robe rubbing against her bare thighs, the crushing weight of his body on hers, each shudder he gave as he thrust into her wet warmth, the broken love words he could not contain.

She loved him. The Duke of Allonshire . . . Captain Drake Barrett; they were one and the same. And she loved him.

She sobbed out his name as her body contracted in unbearable pleasure.

Drake raised his head and stared down into her face to watch her as the spasms swept over her, his face contorted with pain.

"Damn you, Alex," he panted, closing his eyes as the explosion of his own release erupted within him. "Damn you for doing this to me." He gave an agonized groan, as waves of ecstasy crashed down upon him, submerging him.

He crushed her against him, molded her to him, and poured his entire being into hers, the tormented words torn from his heart and his soul.

"Damn you for making me love you."

Chapter 28

"Don't you think it is time we talked about it?"

Smitty stood beside Drake on the polished quarterdeck of the newly completed merchant ship. The vessel was larger than *La Belle Illusion,* more lavish in detail. She was also, as yet, nameless.

The two men had set sail on the Thames the morning after the ball. Yet, three days later, Drake had yet to discuss his turbulent encounter with Alexandria.

The men had spoken mostly of the unsolved mystery

behind the attempts on Drake's life. They had spent the remainder of the daylight hours acquainting themselves with their new ship, but there were frequent silences filled with unresolved tension.

Now Drake stared moodily out into the sunset, his features haggard with strain, dark circles beneath his hollow eyes. At Smitty's reminder of the night prior to their flight from Allonshire, Drake's hands tightened reflexively on the wheel.

"I have no desire to speak on that subject, Smitty. I am here to forget."

"And have you?"

A haunted look shadowed Drake's face. "No. I have forgotten nothing."

Smitty studied Drake's anguished expression and asked the question that had plagued him for days. "Did you hurt her, your grace?"

Drake closed his eyes at the accusation, seeing Alex as clearly as if she still lay before him. Her cheeks had been streaked with tears, her expression filled with pain, which she made no attempt to disguise, as she had silently watched him stagger toward the door, leaving her crumpled and alone on her bed. How many times had she told him that she loved him? Over and over, and yet he couldn't accept it, hadn't wanted to hear the words. Instead he had taken her in rage and in a frantic attempt to free himself from the emotional bond that she had forged between them. His only sane act had been to declare his love for her. But even that revelation had been disguised by anger and uttered at the very height of passion.

Had he hurt her? The answer to that was an unequivocal yes. He had hurt her . . . in more ways than one.

"How could you harm her?"

Drake's eyes snapped open at Smitty's angry tone.

"Because I am a bastard."

"Not a bastard, your grace, but a damned fool."

Drake nodded in agreement, the need to share his agony suddenly more than he could bear. "She told me she loved me. And I know it to be true. But damn it, Smitty, when

I saw her with all those men, flaunting herself, flirting openly with them, all I could think of was—"

"The worst," Smitty finished for him. "And without even speaking to the duchess first, you retaliated. Tell me, does your heart feel that your wife would openly seduce a roomful of men? Knowing her as you do, do you think she would show so little respect for your feelings as to acquire a string of paramours right before your eyes?"

Smitty didn't wait for Drake's response, but continued, determined to make his friend see the truth. "It is time to put the old scars behind you," he stated simply, placing his hand on Drake's shoulder, for despite Smitty's outrage at the thought of Drake causing Alex pain, long-standing loyalty and love made him sympathetic to his friend's internal torment.

"Hasn't your wife proved to you by now that she is unique? That she is interested in no man other than you? Try for once to think objectively, your grace, to see things as they really are, not as you imagine them to be. Lady Alexandria has forgiven you for your deceit, for the chaos you have made of her life, for the near-impossible adjustment she has had to make these last months. And why? Because she loves you, because she has always loved you. Now, are you going to nurture that feeling, revel in the beauty that it offers, or are you going to throw it all away because of the immoral women who have tarnished your past?

"I suggest you consider that question carefully, your grace, before you discard the only chance at happiness I believe you have."

Drake stared at Smitty, the final words piercing his soul. Smitty was presenting him with a choice, but in reality, no choice existed. To keep Alex's love he would have to risk everything, to offer her everything she deserved.

The choice had been made long ago.

Alex stared up at the portrait, seeing the coldly elegant beauty of the regal woman who returned her gaze through haughty, frigid green eyes.

Vanessa Barrett's exotic, brittle looks had tantalized, seduced, enchanted countless men, most of all Drake's father. She had used them all, taken what they had to offer, and given nothing in return. Even in a picture, Alex could sense her superficial beauty and her empty soul.

A sudden chill permeated the gallery, and Alex rubbed her arms with her hands, seeking warmth.

She stared defiantly at the portrait of Drake's mother. "You left your mark," she accused. "But I won't let you win. Drake needs me, I know he does . . . and he loves me as well." She placed her hand against her slightly rounded abdomen. "We are going to have a child, and we will raise it with love and commitment, neither of which you gave to your son. You hurt him, more than even he understands, but I won't let him remain a prisoner to your destruction. He is mine now, and no matter how long it takes, he will recognize it. He will."

The portrait did not answer, but continued to stare mockingly down at her. Nauseated, Alex turned away. Drake had been gone for three days—endless days of waiting and wondering. She knew he had been in torment; she had felt it throughout the storm of their physical union and afterward, when he had torn himself from her, as though he couldn't bear to be one with her any longer, and staggered from the room without a word, leaving her alone . . . so alone.

And so afraid. For three nights she had been unable to sleep, tormented by images of Drake being brutally murdered at sea. Whoever was trying to kill Drake was still out there, plotting and planning. The thought terrified her, for she loved him with all her heart.

He had said that he loved her.

Granted, it had been at the height of passion, words that were wrenched from within him. But he had meant them. Of that she was certain. It explained his almost desperate departure from her bedchamber and his subsequent flight to sea. She prayed that time spent alone, away from the pressures at Allonshire, would open his heart to the truth and bring him safely back to her.

She caressed the small mound that was their unborn child. They had so much to look forward to, so much to share. If only Drake would let them.

The door opened, allowing a shaft of light to catch Alex at her musing.

"Alex? Are you in here?"

Alex smiled, going toward the door. "Yes, Sammy, I'm here."

Samantha frowned. "I was worried when I couldn't find you. You haven't been yourself for days."

"I miss Drake," Alex replied, joining Samantha in the hallway.

Samantha sniffed in annoyance. "It was terribly impolite of him to go off like that without a word to anyone. Our guests were quite disgruntled, to say the least."

"It was something he had to do," was Alex's quiet reply.

Samantha turned back to Alex. "Still, I know that you have not been feeling well. I wish he would . . . Alex?" The last was said in panic, as Alex swayed on her feet, clutching the heavy wooden table in the hallway for support.

"I'm all right," she assured Samantha, blinking to clear her head.

"Let's go sit down." Samantha led Alex down the hall to the drawing room and closed the door behind them. Gently she eased Alex onto a settee, then sat beside her. "Shall I ring for something to eat?"

"No, please, nothing." Alex's stomach protested violently at the thought of food.

"Alex, what is it? And don't tell me you miss Drake. That is not enough to make you ill or to make you as tense as you have been, walking around like a drawn bowstring, quivering at every sound. Please talk to me."

Alex regarded Samantha's concerned little face and relented. She did need to talk, and while Samantha was young, she was old enough to understand and perhaps to help.

With a furtive glance at the closed door, Alex began. "Sammy, everything I am going to tell you must remain in confidence. Is that understood?"

"Of course."

Alex nodded, trusting Samantha implicitly. "There are two issues involved here, one very wonderful, the other very ugly. As far as my illness is concerned, there is a physical reason for it." She paused, savoring her news. "Drake and I are going to have a baby."

The words were barely out when Samantha flung her arms around Alex's neck. "Oh, Alex, that is so exciting! A baby! I cannot believe it; my brother . . . a father. He must be elated! Tell me, how did he take the news?"

Silence.

"Oh, Alex, don't tell me you haven't told him?" Her youthful voice was filled with dismay.

"No, I haven't," Alex admitted in a tiny voice. "There hasn't been a chance. I only just realized it myself. I was going to tell him the night of the ball, but . . ." Her voice trailed off.

Samantha knew something had happened the night of the ball to precipitate Drake's departure and Alex's melancholy, but she had made the firm resolution not to interfere.

"When will the baby be born?" she asked instead.

Alex smiled. "In mid-April, I think."

"I am so happy for you." Samantha took both of Alex's hands in hers. "Rest assured I will not divulge the news to anyone."

"I know." Alex paused, her lovely face clouding. "The second revelation is terrifying. I never wanted to involve you, but I know how much you love Drake, and I need your help."

"My goodness, this sounds so mysterious!"

"It is more than mysterious, Sammy. It's horrifying." She lowered her voice to a whisper. "Drake's riding accident was no coincidence. It was a deliberate attempt to harm him, just as the sinking of *La Belle Illusion* was no accident but a calculated plot to kill Drake."

Samantha's face drained of color, and she remained silent for a moment, digesting the information that Alex had just given her. "Are you saying that someone is trying to *murder* Drake?" she managed.

"Shhh." Alex put her finger to her lips. "Yes, that is exactly what I am saying. I have tried every way I know to figure out who it is, with no success."

"Did Drake tell you this?" Samantha demanded.

"I overheard him talking with Smitty. They have no idea that I heard them, nor do they have any intention of telling me. So I took matters into my own hands." Now that Alex had begun, the words tumbled over themselves in an effort to be said. "Drake's saddle strap was deliberately cut, and it occurred to me that a guest at the house party might have done it. I questioned every person at the ball . . . without their understanding why, of course."

"And?" Samantha asked eagerly.

Alex sagged back against the settee, looking bleak. "And . . . nothing. I gained no information as to who might be responsible."

"But, Alex, who would want Drake dead?" Samantha demanded in a fierce whisper.

"I honestly don't know. But perhaps between the two of us we can figure it out."

"My God," Samantha breathed, staring at Alex with awe and respect. "You have been shouldering all of this by yourself, dealing with it alone, these past days?"

"I didn't want to frighten you."

Samantha shook her head. "You will find that I am stronger than you think, Alex. I've had to be. And if it means protecting Drake, there is nothing I won't do."

Alex squeezed Samantha's hand, feeling relieved and proud. Sammy had all of Drake's strength of character and fierce loyalty to those she loved. Alex was honored that they were friends and sisters.

Sebastian paused outside the closed drawing room door, frowning. So this was where his sister and Drake's little wife were hiding. He had searched everywhere else, but to no avail. Having left Allonshire on the morning after the ball, Sebastian had expected to return from London to find a houseful of guests still enjoying the lazy days in the country. He had been surprised and a bit uneasy at Humphreys's explanation that the guests had all departed and his grace had left three days ago on a sea voyage of indeterminate length. Something was definitely amiss . . . and he intended to discover what it was.

He could hear Alex and Samantha whispering in the drawing room, but he could not make out the words. Whatever they were saying, it set off a warning bell in his head. Forcing himself to relax, he knocked.

For a moment there was silence, and then he heard Alex's voice call, "Yes?"

He opened the door, the usual charming smile pasted upon his face. "Hello, ladies, I suspected you were in here."

Samantha looked surprised. "Sebastian, I thought you were still in London."

"My plans changed," came the short reply. He leaned casually against the wall, his gaze, in contrast to his stance, as alert as a hawk's. "What is this I hear about Drake being away?" His eyes were on Alex.

"He is testing our new ship." It was Samantha who answered, regarding her brother coolly, with none of the tenderness or sparkle that lit her face when she looked at Drake. "He should be home any day now."

"And our guests?"

"They departed yesterday."

Sebastian's expression grew predatory. "Am I to understand that you ladies have been here unattended?"

Even Samantha could not miss the obvious gleam in her brother's eyes. She frowned. "We have a houseful of servants, Sebastian. We were hardly alone."

"Just the same, I am glad that my business concluded sooner than expected. This way I am here, should you need me."

Alex felt sickened by his innuendos. "What I need now is some warm food and a good night's sleep." She rose, averting her gaze. "If you will both excuse me, I will go to my chambers and dress for dinner."

Samantha watched Alex's pale face with concern. "Are you all right now?" she asked anxiously.

"Why? Were you ill, Alexandria?" Sebastian jumped on his sister's words.

"I am fine. Only a bit tired." Alex shot Samantha a warning look, which the younger girl understood immediately.

"Good." Samantha stood also, her tone cheery. "Then let us go and dress for dinner."

Any opportunity the women might have had to continue their talk was thwarted by Sebastian, who insisted on accompanying them to their rooms. He was undaunted by the clear message Alex conveyed by shutting her door firmly in his face, for he could sense victory . . . and it was close at hand.

Dinner was torture for Alex.

She wondered how long she could tolerate Sebastian's presence without Drake at her side to put a damper on his brother's lewd comments and suggestive leers. Even Samantha's chatter could not ease Alex's discomfort. She spent most of the meal staring indifferently at her food and pushing it around on her plate. Pregnancy had already diminished her usual hearty appetite, and Sebastian eliminated what little she had left. The evening could not end soon enough.

They were still savoring their apricot tarts when Alex pushed back her chair and stood.

"I hope you will both forgive me, but I am truly exhausted." The apology in her eyes was for Samantha, who nodded her understanding at once. "I am going to retire for the night." She gathered up her skirts and headed for the door.

"Sleep well, Alex," Samantha called after her. "Perhaps Drake will return with the new day."

Alex met her gaze with silent understanding. "I hope so," she replied in a wistful voice. She climbed the stairs to her room, praying that Samantha's words would become reality. Now that she carried Drake's child, Alex found that she needed her husband more than ever—needed him and wanted him by her side.

* * *

The night deepened. Gradually all activity at Allonshire ceased, and the lights were doused as the great house settled into slumber.

Alone in his chambers, Sebastian paced back and forth across the room, pausing only to take frequent gulps of brandy. He was frustrated and angry, for his plans had been thwarted at every turn. In truth, he had left for London on the morning after the ball because he had been unable to feign brotherly love for Drake any longer. The blasted man led a charmed life. Instead of being dead, he was very much alive . . . and being treated like an injured hero.

Sebastian lifted his glass and blazed a fiery trail of the dulling liquid down his throat. Things had been progressing so nicely; he had come so close to having it all. And then Drake had returned from the dead, just in time to assume his title—a title he had no use for and did not even want. Damn him to hell.

Sebastian raked his fingers through his hair, his mind searching for a new alternative. He sensed that Drake and Smitty already suspected something sinister. He could not afford to arouse their suspicions any further. But there had to be a way. A way to have Drake's title, Drake's power . . . Drake's wife.

Sebastian's head shot up as the reality of the situation struck him. Drake was away. It was very late at night, and the entire household was asleep. No one would hear him or try to stop him. A slow, satanic smile spread across his face. He might have to wait a bit longer for the title and the power, but tonight Drake's wife would be his. . . .

Alex welcomed her solitude with a great sense of relief. Anxious to be alone with her thoughts, she had dismissed Molly early, insisting that she could tend to herself this one night. She stood at her curtained window, staring out at the moonlit gardens below. Idly she drew her brush through her thick hair, which hung in loose waves down the back of her lemon yellow night rail. Her thoughts were of Drake and of their future together.

The sound of her bedroom door opening made Alex's heart leap with joy. She spun about, making no attempt to conceal her pleasure. "Drake?"

"No, Alexandria, not Drake."

A chill of dread replaced her joy. "What do you want, Sebastian?" Instinctively she backed against the wall.

"Need you ask?" He gave a harsh laugh and closed the door behind him, pausing to light a small lamp on the nightstand. He wanted there to be no chance of her escaping him.

Hands on hips, clad only in his breeches, Sebastian turned to face her . . . and waited.

Their gazes locked across the room—his, hungry; hers, alarmed.

Weaving slightly, he moved toward her. "There is no need to look like a frightened doe," he taunted. "I have no intention of harming you."

Alex swallowed. "Then what do you intend to do?"

He grinned, his eyes glassy. "Surely even you are not *that* naive, my dear. I intend to give you pleasure . . . and to pleasure myself in return."

Alex pressed herself more firmly against the wall, as if it could somehow protect her from Sebastian's onslaught. "You are foxed, Sebastian." She struggled to keep her voice from trembling. "And you are not thinking clearly. Go now, and I will say nothing of this incident to Drake."

He threw back his head and gave an eerie, hollow laugh. "Do you think I give a damn what you tell Drake?" he demanded, moving closer. "After the enticing spectacle you made of yourself on the evening of the ball, do you honestly think he will believe you did not invite me to your room tonight?" He loomed before her, fury and lust blazing in his drunken gaze. "In truth, your actions were a puzzle to me as well. My attentions are not good enough for you, but a roomful of strangers will suffice?" He placed his hands on the wall on either side of her head, his foul breath touching her lips.

In a flash Alex ducked beneath his arm and sprinted toward the door. She was two steps from her goal when

Sebastian's powerful arms closed about her waist, dragging her back into the room. She struggled, kicking and fighting frantically, but to no avail. With an unnatural strength born of hatred, Sebastian flung her onto the bed, his body shaking with rage.

"You defiant little bitch!" he ground out, pinning her down with his body. "So this is the way you want it? Fine. So be it."

In one quick motion he tore her night rail down the front, flinging the remnants of material to the floor. Waves of revulsion racked Alex's body as she found herself naked and helpless beneath Sebastian's bitter, hungry scrutiny, utterly exposed to his violent assault. Tears of rage and humiliation burned behind her eyes. Until now, her only experience of lying completely unclothed before a man had been with Drake in tenderness and mutual desire. Nothing had prepared her for the horror of this moment, the sense of despair at this ultimate violation of her self. Everything inside her turned cold.

Seeing the full force of Sebastian's hatred, Alex began to shake, sheer terror streaking through her blood. More determined than ever to fight him with every fiber of her being, she resumed her struggle, digging her nails into his flesh and kicking him.

"You really are a little hellcat, aren't you?" Sebastian growled. He caught her arms with his hands and held them over her head, triumph gleaming in his eyes. Then he lowered his head and took her mouth in a brutal, punishing kiss.

Instantly, and without thinking, Alex sank her teeth into his lower lip.

Sebastian tore his mouth away, cursing violently. While he licked the blood away, Alex made one last desperate attempt to escape. But Sebastian's grip was iron-hard. She was going nowhere.

"Try that again and I will make you sorry you were born," he ground out, tightening his hold until Alex thought her wrists would snap. She whimpered with pain, feeling Sebastian cruelly prying her legs apart with his knees. In a frantic effort to escape his final invasion, she brought her knee up, attempting to catch him off guard and make contact with his groin. But Sebastian anticipated the move and caught her leg, forcing it cruelly down, then out, opening her farther to him. Hysteria bubbled up inside her and she cried out in pain. Sebastian leaned forward, momentarily pressing his full weight against her.

"For that, you will pay," he snarled.

Alex winced, knowing that her action had cost her dearly. Now Sebastian meant not only to rape her but to hurt her as much as possible in the process. *The baby*, she thought to herself helplessly. *Please, God, don't let him hurt my baby*. She felt the pressure on her wrists ease slightly and opened her eyes to see Sebastian kneeling above her, his hot gaze raking her as he reached for the buttons on his breeches.

"I am going to enjoy every moment of this," he muttered, releasing one button at a time, his fingers unsteady from the large amount of alcohol he had consumed. "You have quite a body, my dear Alexandria."

There was no escape. Alex froze as Sebastian's swollen manhood sprang free, lurching toward her cringing flesh. The paralyzing realization of what was to come exploded through Alex like gunfire.

Sebastian was going to rape her . . . now.

The shrill, heartrending scream began deep inside her and split the eerie silence, vibrating through every corner of the room.

"Shut up," Sebastian hissed, crushing her face with his hand. Alex felt as if her jaw might snap.

"Drake will kill you for this, Sebastian," she choked out, fighting to keep back the tears.

He lowered himself to her, his words muffled by her hair. "You have that backwards, my fiery duchess. It is I who will kill—"

The end of Sebastian's sentence was lost in a crash that exploded through the room, followed by a bloodcurdling roar of anger.

"Sebastian, you filthy bastard, get the hell off my wife!"

Chapter 29

Drake crossed the room in three strides, tore Sebastian off Alex, and flung him against the wall. Sebastian crumpled and sank to the floor.

Alex cried out Drake's name, gathering herself into a small protective ball, her eyes wide with shock and horror.

Drake was shaking with the fierce primal rage of a wild animal, the sound of Alex's scream still echoing inside him. Every muscle in his body was taut, sweat gleaming on his face, as he crossed the room and yanked his unsteady brother to his feet.

"You miserable son of a bitch!" Drake slammed his fist into Sebastian's jaw, sending him back to the floor with the impact. It was still not enough. Drake fell upon Sebastian, blinded to anything but the explosive need to kill. His hands closed around Sebastian's throat.

But Sebastian had recovered sufficiently to defend himself. Using the full weight of his body, he rolled Drake off him, then sent his fist into his brother's stomach.

Drake groaned, doubling up in pain, but refused to release his death grip on Sebastian's throat. Panting, Drake rolled Sebastian beneath him and, holding him down with one hand, delivered blow after blow to Sebastian's face.

Blood spurted from Sebastian's lips and nose, but all Drake could see was the red haze of anger that clouded his vision—a vision of Sebastian raping Alexandria. He wanted his brother dead.

Alex's voice broke through his frenzy.

"Drake, that's enough! Don't kill him! He's not worth it!"

Still holding Sebastian by the throat, Drake turned his head slowly, really seeing Alex for the first time. She was naked, with only the sheet wrapped around her, her small body trembling, her eyes wide with terror. She swallowed convulsively, clutching the sheet that sheltered her from Sebastian's hateful touch.

"Please . . ." she begged in a pathetic voice.

Drake turned back to look at Sebastian. His brother's eyes were glazed from too much brandy, his entire face splattered with blood. He was a useless excuse for a human being, and his very presence sickened Drake.

"I want you out of my sight, you worthless bastard." Drake lifted his brother by the throat, crossed the room, and kicked open the door. With a feral growl he tossed Sebastian into the hall. Several frightened, gaping servants, awakened by Alex's scream, stood gathered in the hallway as Sebastian landed in a boneless heap.

"Take this slime away!" Drake ordered the stunned footmen, his emerald eyes ablaze. "I don't give a damn what you do with him; just remove him at once!" He looked down at Sebastian. "If you *ever* so much as *look* at my wife again I will kill you with no questions asked."

He strode back into the bedchamber, slammed the door, and turned to his wife.

Alex stared at Drake, white-faced, her body still shaking uncontrollably. She was at her breaking point, but at the same time, she was very much aware of the importance of this moment. Would Drake believe she was innocent or would he again believe the worst of her and assume that she had seduced Sebastian?

She waited.

Drake crossed the room and sat down on the bed, gathering Alex's quaking body in his strong arms.

"It's all right now, princess," he murmured softly, kissing her hair and tucking her head beneath his chin. "I'm with you, and I swear that he will never come near you again."

He paused, needing to ask . . . dreading the answer. "Did he hurt you, sweetheart?" he questioned at last, his voice raw. "Did he . . ." He couldn't bring himself to say the word.

Alex shook her head against his chest. "No," she whispered in a tiny voice. "You got here just in time."

"Thank God," Drake breathed. He rocked her gently in his arms, unwilling to think of what might have happened if he had arrived one moment later. The thought of Sebastian violating his beautiful, precious Alex made his guts twist.

Alex pressed her face against Drake's shirt. "Please hold me. Just hold me. Make his horrible touch go away. Please," she begged, burrowing deeper into Drake's embrace.

"I've got you, love." He tightened his arms fiercely around her, giving her his strength. "The only touch you will ever know will be mine." His hoarse, protective vow seeped into Alex's cold body.

And suddenly Drake's words, the joy of being safe in his arms, was more than Alex could bear. Succumbing at last to the tears that she had held in check until now, she gasped, "Drake, oh, Drake, thank God . . ." Her words were incoherent, her body racked with sobs that gave way to a torrent of tears, which spilled down her cheeks, drenching Drake's shirt.

Drake felt Alex's pain as his own, felt her tears wash the past away.

"Please, sweetheart," he implored her softly, "don't cry anymore. I can bear anything but your tears. Please, princess . . . no one, nothing, will ever hurt us again. I promise."

At Drake's fervent vow Alex leaned back to look up into his anguished face.

"I did not encourage Sebastian," she stated simply, watching Drake's reaction. "I fought him off as best I could."

Drake cupped her face in his hands, stroking the tears from her wet cheeks with his thumbs, his heart expanding with a feeling that he no longer wished to dispel. Smitty was wrong. He *had* been a bastard—a bastard *and* a damned fool.

He gazed tenderly down at his wife's beloved face, her

tear-filled eyes looking more than ever like the wondrous waves of the sea, her rare innocence shining so clearly that it could only escape a man who refused to see its splendor.

And she loved him. It was there in her eyes as they awaited his reply, in her lips as they trembled with hope, in her body as it melded to his in a need and an instinctive trust that told Drake all he needed to know.

Lord, how he loved her.

"You bore the brunt of my brother's sickness . . . and my own stupidity," he told her in a humble, reverent tone. "Can you ever forgive me?"

The tears flowed anew down Alex's cheeks, but this time they were tears of joy.

"Oh, Drake, don't you know that I forgave you long ago?" she whispered, reaching up to touch his lips. "I just need to know that you believe me . . . that you trust me—" Her voice broke.

Drake kissed her fingertips one by one, then pressed her palm to his mouth. "I believe you," he told her, his breathing ragged. He drew her into his arms, lowering them both to the bed. "I trust you," he whispered against her mouth. He gazed solemnly into her exquisite face. "I love you."

Alex blinked, afraid to believe her ears. "You love me . . . ?" she repeated, in a soft, hopeful voice.

"With all of my being," he answered, his own voice rough with emotion.

Alex sagged against his powerful body, feeling weak with joy and relief. But it was not over yet. Not until they had talked—about the misunderstandings of the past few days *and* of the past few months. "There is so much I need to tell you, so much you must understand."

"I know, princess, I know." He kissed her cheeks, her chin, her soft mouth. "And I will listen to everything you have to say, tell you all that you need to know . . . later tonight. Right now I need to hold you, to convince myself that you are really here, unharmed, in my arms. Can you understand that?"

Alex gazed up at him with all the love in her heart. "Yes," she breathed, sliding her fingers into his thick hair.

"Because I need that, too." She tugged his head down to hers. "I need you to take the ugliness of the night and make it disappear beneath your touch. I need you to tell me over and over that you love me. I need you to show me how much." She brushed her lips against his. "Will you do that . . . please, Drake?"

He enfolded her against his heart, covering her mouth with his in a tender, passionate kiss that claimed her totally, body and soul. "I love you," he murmured, sliding the sheet out from between them, shrugging out of his own clothes with determined, hurried movements. "I love you," he reiterated reverently, melding their naked bodies together. "I love you." He breathed the words, feeling the familiar sensual magic storm his senses. Familiar, yet so much stronger, so much richer because of the bond that had been forged between them.

Drake rolled Alex onto her back, gliding his hands up and down her bare arms, pausing to intertwine their fingers.

"You are mine," he told her in a husky whisper.

Alex felt treasured, warmed by the emerald fire that glowed in Drake's eyes. "And you are mine," she replied.

Soberly Drake nodded. "Gladly and forever." He bent his head to kiss her throat. "Tell me that you love me," he demanded against the scented hollow.

Alex smiled, giddy with pleasure. "I love you, Captain Drake Robert Barrett, the Duke of Allonshire, the Marquis of Cairnham, the Earl of Laneswood, Earl of Ravleton, Viscount Manvell, and Baron Winsborough. I love you."

Drake raised his head and, in the light cast by the bedside lamp, Alex saw the laughter on his face. "You are still the most outspoken of women, princess," he told her tenderly, nibbling on her chin.

"A tyrant, I believe you said," Alex reminded him, wrapping her arms around his broad back.

He kissed her again, a long, slow exploration of her mouth that left them both breathless, wanting more.

"There are compensations to being married to a tyrant," he managed, sliding his fingers through the tumbled waves of her hair.

"Mmm," she agreed, licking lightly at his mouth. "Just as there are compensations to being married to a man who is two different men."

Drake grew serious. "Just one man, sweetheart. One man who adores you and always will."

There were no more words as he covered her body with his, blanketed her in his love. He savored the taste of her, touching every inch of her skin with light caresses of his open mouth. Alex sighed, sensual pleasure coursing through her in great, surging waves. Every place Drake's mouth touched tingled with pleasure, ached for more.

He was more than happy to oblige the silent urgings of Alex's body. He ran his hands along the perfect contours of her hips and waist, finally cupping her full breasts in his trembling hands.

"Ah, Alex . . . what you do to me," he breathed against her mouth. Lightly he stroked her nipples with his thumbs, feeling the breath catch in her throat. He followed his hands with his mouth, circling, tasting, teasing the hardened peaks until Alex moaned, tossing her head from side to side. Drake slid down her body, defining it with his mouth, watching the flickering light cast its golden glow upon his naked goddess. It had been so long since he had made love to her in the light . . . so long, for until now, he had been afraid of what he would see in her eyes. But no longer.

Down, farther down the bed he moved, lost in the wonder that was Alex.

He reached the slight swell of her abdomen and froze, staring down at the obvious physical change in her body.

Alex felt Drake tense and raised her head to meet his stunned gaze.

"Alex?" He searched her face for the answer to his unspoken question.

Alex smiled, knowing that there could not be a more perfect time to tell him.

"I'm carrying our child," she whispered, her face radiant with joy.

For a moment Drake just stared at her in utter disbelief. Then, slowly, he lowered his gaze back down to the absolute proof of Alex's words. A baby. Alex was going to have his baby.

He rose to his knees at the foot of the bed, his gaze greedily raking her body for every telltale sign of pregnancy, signs that the darkness had obscured from his view. Transfixed, he stared from the swell of her stomach up to the ripe opulence of her breasts, the darkening color of the nipples that were still wet and taut from his mouth. Alex lay still, watching Drake learn of his child in the most beautiful way possible.

When he once again met Alex's gaze, Drake's eyes were damp with emotion. He lifted a shaking hand to stroke Alex's smooth cheek, lowering himself carefully beside her on the bed.

"When did it happen?" he asked in a raw voice.

Alex smiled, moving into his arms. "Probably on the island. In any case, not long after we were married."

"How long have you known?"

"Since the afternoon of the ball. I was going to tell you that night, but . . ." her voice trailed off.

Drake's features twisted in pain. "But I nearly raped you because of my stupid, destructive jealousy." He ran his hand caressingly over Alex's body, pausing where his child was nestled safely within her womb. "Love, I'm so sorry. The thought of hurting you or our baby . . ." He raised wondering eyes to hers. "Our baby," he repeated, cupping her belly possessively.

Alex moved closer, wrapped her arms around his neck. "Our baby," she murmured in agreement. "And you didn't hurt me, Drake. You've never hurt me . . . not physically, at least."

"I'll never hurt you, in *any* way, again," he vowed, sealing his promise with a tender kiss. He hesitated as Alex pressed her lush, desirable body against his. "Alex, is it all right?" he questioned her anxiously. "The baby—"

". . . will be delighted to learn how very much his parents love each other," Alex finished, running her hands along the muscled planes of Drake's back.

"His?" Drake barely got out the word, his body leaping to life beneath his wife's teasing caress.

"Or hers," Alex conceded, pausing in her exploration of Drake's body. "Do you have a preference?"

Drake ran his tongue over the delicate shell of Alex's ear, his hands sliding down to cup her silky bottom, pulling her against his throbbing erection. "Several preferences, princess. Shall I tell them to you?" He whispered a few choice, erotic phrases into her ear, and Alex melted against him with a soft moan of surrender.

"Your grace, your wish is my command," she replied in a sultry whisper, lifting her face for his kiss.

Drake's mouth opened over hers, his lips moved back and forth with barely leashed need. His tongue stroked hers slowly, with tender urgency, his hot breath filling her mouth. He loved her, and that knowledge made him want to give her everything, to shower her with every exquisite sensation a woman could know.

Alex arched slowly against Drake, making him wondrously and acutely aware of the presence of their unborn child. He had to be the luckiest man alive. For in his arms he held his life.

For a timeless moment they kissed. Long, deep, melting kisses broken only by Alex's soft sighs and Drake's husky words of love. When that alone was no longer enough, Drake began a slow exploration of Alex's body, worshiping her with every stroke of his fingertips, teasing her tingling flesh with soft touches and gentle caresses that brushed ever so lightly upon her sensitized skin.

By the time his seeking fingers found the dewy wetness between her thighs, Alex was trembling, her whole body ablaze with desire. She recognized Drake's need to be the aggressor, to have the opportunity to demonstrate his love for her. But waiting was rapidly becoming an impossibility.

She undulated her hips against his hand, trying desperately to deepen the contact, and was rewarded by Drake's husky chuckle.

"Still so impatient, princess?" he teased, nibbling at her

lower lip. He slid his fingers farther inside her . . . but only a bit.

Alex moaned. "I want you, Drake," she pleaded.

"Mmm, I can tell," he murmured, kissing the side of her neck, flexing his fingers slightly, feeling the inadvertent tightening of her inner muscles.

Duke, hell, he thought with a smile. The way she responded to him made him feel like a king.

His smile froze as Alex, relinquishing her passive role, began her own heavenly torture. Starting with the taut planes of his smooth back, she slid her hands over Drake's body, lingering on the solid muscles of his broad shoulders and the hard wall of his massive chest. When she lightly brushed his nipples with her thumbs, Drake let out his breath in a hiss.

"Is there some problem, your grace?" she purred. Before he could answer, she stroked one of her hands through the soft, dark hair on his chest, over his rigid abdomen, and paused deliberately over the throbbing symbol of his need.

"You are merciless . . ." Drake ground out, flames leaping through him.

She brushed her fingers ever so lightly against him, then lifted them, hovering. In response, Drake thrust his hips forward, seeking more of Alex's caress.

"Patience, Captain . . . remember?" she whispered against the vein that throbbed in his neck.

With a deep growl Drake seized her hand and brought it back to its original goal. "To hell with patience. Touch me, wife."

She closed her fingers around him, feeling his life, his power, the effect she had on both. He pulsed in her hand, hardening and lengthening until he had to grit his teeth to retain a shred of control. Deliberately, he kept his gaze locked with hers so that his beautiful wife could see what she was doing to him. And when he could bear the intensity no longer, when the need to be one was so powerful that it could not be denied or delayed, Drake drew Alex to him, looking deep into her eyes as he lifted her leg to rest over his and slid into her moist, welcoming warmth, pressing deeper and deeper until they were one.

He lay quietly for a moment, overcome with emotion, listening to Alex's uneven breathing and feeling the pounding of her heart as it beat against his. Then, slowly and with the need to give Alex more pleasure than she had ever known, Drake began to move inside her, lowering his head to find her lips with his. He made love to her with his mouth, his tongue, while he simultaneously drew her hips to his again and again, circling his body against hers until Alex was frantic, her body so tight around him that Drake knew it was time.

With one powerful thrust he gave her what she needed, at the same time pulling her to him, pressing her loins to his and holding them there to intensify the pleasure that exploded in wild, gripping spasms through Alex's body.

"Drake . . ." she cried out, digging her nails into his back.

Drake groaned as her contractions clasped him, pulling at his frantic, engorged manhood. But, unwilling to relinquish the moment and the sheer joy of watching his wife, he determinedly held himself back, forced himself to wait.

She was breathtaking in her utter, abandoned ecstasy, her face bathed with pleasure, her voice calling his name over and over in soft pants of release. And all Drake could think in that final moment of sanity was that this beautiful, sensual angel in his arms, this unspoiled and giving woman who had known no man but him, this gentle healer of his lifelong wounds, was his wife and would soon be the mother of his child.

Drake closed his eyes, his entire body tightening . . . waiting. He was dangling at the precipice of a peak that towered so high, fell so far, that it demanded all of him, left none of him untouched. And he gave himself to it willingly, gladly, for Alex was beside him, with him . . . always.

The eruptions began deep inside him, growing stronger and stronger until he helplessly surrendered to the wildness of his climax, shouting Alex's name, desperate, yet unable, to convey to her all that she made him feel.

And afterward, as he held his wife in his arms, he again whispered the words he had never said to another woman, the words that he hoped would begin to explain what was in his heart . . . the only words Alex ever needed to hear.

"Alex . . . I love you."

Chapter 30

"I never intentionally kept my identity from you. Circumstances thwarted every opportunity to tell you the truth."

Drake lay on his back, Alex cradled against his chest. Their bodies temporarily sated, the need to talk, to understand, and to be understood moved to the forefront.

Alex raised her head, giving Drake a slightly disgruntled look.

"You certainly did not try very hard," she reminded him, thinking of the months at sea when he had plagued her about her noble birth.

He grinned. "Not in the beginning, no. I was having far too much fun with our cat-and-mouse game."

"At my expense."

"At your expense," he agreed, tenderly stroking her back. "But remember, princess, that I was not in the habit of explaining myself to anyone, least of all a woman. Worse, a woman who touched my emotions, made me vulnerable."

"A woman who was everything you loathed," she added softly.

"Everything I needed," he corrected, wrapping his arms more tightly around her. "By the time I realized you had

307

the right to know, it was too late. You already thought of me as Drake Barrett, a simple sea captain. If I had told you the truth, that I was a member of the peerage, prisoner to the same hollow world as you, you would have hated me for lying to you. The ironic thing is that I never really lied, except about my titles. Everything else I told you, my whole jaded life, was true."

Alex rested her chin on his chest. "I cannot dispute your words. I'm sure I would have flown into a rage if you had told me who you were." She gave him a questioning look. "Why did it matter to you how I felt, whether I accepted you or not?"

Drake traced the line of her nose with a gentle finger. "Because, my beautiful, foolish princess, I was in love with you."

Alex's head came up. "Even then?"

He gave her a roguish grin. "Even then. Before then. From the moment I saw your impudent little self clad in a dusty muslin dress, glaring at me in my own cabin, I was lost."

"You despised me," Alex contradicted him, thinking back to that fateful meeting.

"I resented you like hell," he amended. "I thought you were the most arrogant, outspoken, patronizing chit I had ever met in my life." He paused, his eyes darkening to a deep, forest green. "I also never wanted anything in my life the way I wanted to be inside you. This"—he brought her hand down to the hard, hot arousal pulsing against his belly—"has been a permanent condition since last March."

"I'm flattered," she murmured, stroking softly, "and delighted that I render you so insatiable."

"Care to prove it?" He tangled his hands in her hair, drew her up to him for a bone-melting kiss.

"Gladly . . . *after* we finish our talk." Alex withdrew her mouth and her teasing hand, determined not to be side-tracked—at least not yet.

Drake settled himself back with a resigned sigh. "All right, princess. You win. But I have already told you everything."

"Not quite." Alex gave him an accusing look. "You over-looked one small detail."

"Which is?"

"That someone is trying to kill you."

Drake stared at her in stunned silence.

"How did you find out?" he managed at last.

"I overheard you and Smitty talking the day of your riding accident."

"Why didn't you tell me that you knew?" he demanded.

"For the same reason you didn't tell me. I did not want you to worry about me or my reaction to your suspicions. And I knew you would, especially once I had told you about the baby. Instead, I decided to do a bit of investigating on my own."

Drake scowled. "Why do I have the distinct feeling that I am not going to like this?"

"Because you never think I am capable of taking care of myself. Well, I am." She shot him a challenging look.

"Spoken by the woman who disrupted my ship and was unable to climb down the fifty feet of rigging she had managed to scale."

"Other than that time," she hastened to qualify.

Drake decided not to dispute the point by reminding her of the other occasions when he had rescued her from oncoming disasters. "Tell me about your investigation."

She nodded. "It seemed logical that only someone who was present at Allonshire could have cut that saddle. At the time the thought of any family member or servant doing such a heinous thing seemed impossible."

Alex's qualifying phrase, "at the time," was not lost on Drake. But right now he wanted the answer to a far different question.

"So you decided it was one of the guests?" The light was beginning to dawn in Drake's mind.

"Yes."

"So that night at the ball, when I assumed you were flaunting yourself to all those men . . ."

"I was hoping to learn something . . . anything."

Drake felt utterly disgusted with himself and, at the same

time, very proud of Alex, proud of her courage and humbled by the depth of her love for him. He had accused her of being unfaithful when, all the time, she had been protecting him.

"Drake?" Her soft voice interrupted his self-chastisement. He stared down at her, the moonlight making her eyes glow a silvery gray. "I don't blame you. Under the circumstances, I would have assumed the same thing you did." She grinned. "I acted a bit out of character that night."

"You have my word that I will never doubt you again," he told her in a solemn voice.

Alex's eyes twinkled. "I shall remember that promise when I next offer you advice at the helm, Captain."

Drake chuckled, contentedly anticipating the numerous turbulent quarrels that would accompany them to sea . . . and the equally turbulent reconciliations. With sudden clarity he knew that his restless journeys were ended. Any sailing from now on would be with his wife and children. It was time for Allonshire to become a home.

But first there was a mystery to solve.

Carefully he asked, "What did you learn from our guests?"

"That most noblemen are lechers and most noblewomen, whores."

"An accurate assessment," Drake retorted dryly. "But not terribly enlightening." He paused. "What did you mean when you said that 'at the time' the thought of a family member or a servant being guilty seemed impossible? Has something happened since to change your mind?"

Alex hesitated. "It seems too horrible even to consider," she said at last, "but tonight, just before you burst into my room, Sebastian mumbled the oddest thing to me."

At the mention of his brother's name Drake's mouth grew grim, his features tense with anger. "What did he say?"

"When I realized there was no escaping him, I told him that, if he did this unforgivable thing to me, you would kill him."

"And I would have." Drake's voice was steel.

Alex nodded. "I know. But he answered me by saying that I had it backwards, that it was he who would kill . . ." She swallowed nervously. "He never finished the sentence, because that was when you came to my rescue. I'm sure it didn't mean anything, Drake," she added quickly, seeing the flicker of suspicion in Drake's eyes. "He was foxed at the time."

Drake was not so sure. But, seeing the worry on Alex's face, he decided that enough was enough. She was exhausted; it had been an emotionally draining day, and she needed to sleep.

"It's time to rest, love." He drew the bedcovers up, tenderly tucking them around Alex's shoulders. "You look utterly spent."

"But, Drake," she protested, voicing the fear that gnawed at her nerves and crept, unbidden, into her mind like some horrid, poisonous insect, "what if *he* tries to . . . hurt you again." She could not even bring herself to say the word "murder."

Drake kissed her delicately arched eyebrows, smoothing away the worried pucker between them with his lips. "No one is going to harm me," he assured her, giving Alex the words she needed to hear. "I promise you that. I have far too much to live for to let anything happen." He saw her visibly relax, and he pressed her head gently to his chest. "The mystery will still be here for us to solve in the morning, sweetheart. But for now you and my child need to rest. So go to sleep."

Alex nodded, settling herself fully atop Drake, snuggling against him. He was here, he was safe, and he loved her. Alex was whole. "Stay with me," she whispered, unwilling to relinquish the security his nearness brought her.

Drake rested his chin on her head, lightly stroking her back in slow, soothing motions. "Always," he promised, wondering how he was going to endure lying beneath her all night without making love to her again. His mind knew that she needed to sleep, but his throbbing body was equally insistent about its own needs, and he didn't seem able to dissuade it.

Alex shifted slightly, trailing her silky hair across Drake's pounding chest and unknowingly rubbing her lower body against his rigid erection. She then settled herself against him with a sigh, the movement bringing his hardened manhood to rest between her soft, inner thighs.

A low moan escaped Drake's lips, as he instinctively sought the warm haven in which he longed to be. His mind warred with his body, insisting that only an unfeeling cad would attempt to seduce his half-sleeping, pregnant wife. But, God . . . she was so warm, so soft, her gently rounded body so lush. Drake gritted his teeth and strove for control.

Alex lifted her head, staring up at Drake with seductive, smoky eyes.

"You disappoint me, your grace," she said in a husky whisper. "And here I thought this was the one area in which you needed no instruction."

At her words a slow smile spread across Drake's handsome face. In one exquisite motion he raised Alex's hips and lowered her onto his seeking shaft, until he had impaled her completely and was buried deep inside her quivering softness.

"I humbly submit to your learned ministrations, princess," he managed, and then abandoned himself to his wife's magic.

Alex slept peacefully in Drake's arms, the soft rise and fall of her breathing a soothing caress against Drake's fevered skin. Tenderly he looked down at her, stroked the stray locks of hair from her face. Alex did not even stir. She was too deep in slumber to notice even an invasion of Napoleon's troops.

Drake's own body was possessed of a deep, ringing weariness, which tugged at him, insisting that he, too, sleep. But the events of the night weighed heavily upon him.

He and Sebastian were related by blood . . . but in all ways that mattered, they were neither brothers nor friends. Within Sebastian, Drake had always sensed an inner core of cruelty, of resentment, penetrating so deep that Drake had been unwilling to explore its magnitude. Until now. Now Drake was forced to consider the most abhorrent possibility of all. Was Sebastian's hatred so strong that he would actually kill his own brother?

There was no concrete evidence, but what alarmed and sickened Drake was that he could not, with certainty, dismiss the questions that bombarded his mind. A man who was capable of raping his brother's wife was capable of anything, even cold-blooded murder.

A dark feeling of foreboding drove the aftermath of warm lethargy from Drake's limbs. The questions would continue to plague him until they were answered. He had to know. Now.

Very gently, so as not to disturb her, Drake lifted Alex's arm from across his chest and disentangled her slender legs from his muscular ones. He rose from the bed and pulled on his breeches, shirt, and boots. Leaving the sole lamp burning in Alex's bedchamber, Drake left quietly, closing the door behind him. He glanced up and down the dark, deserted hallway, reluctant to leave Alex unattended without knowing Sebastian's whereabouts. The problem was solved when he spotted a nervous footman standing on the second-floor landing, peering down into the hallway below.

Drake strode toward him. At the echoing sound of Drake's booted footsteps on the polished floor, the footman jumped.

"Oh, yer grace, 'tis ye." He looked relieved, "I was wonderin' what ye'd be wantin' me t' do about dousin' the lights."

Drake frowned. "I don't understand the problem. There is no one about. Why would you need to leave the first floor lit?"

The footman shifted from one foot to the other. He was relatively new to Allonshire, and the last thing he wanted was to come between his grace and Lord Sebastian.

"I'm sorry, yer grace, but Lord Sebastian is . . . usin' the library." His pleading look and the accompanying crash from below told Drake that "using the library" in fact meant "destroying the library."

"Should I be waitin' fer 'im t' retire?" the footman continued.

Drake shook his head, feeling sympathy for the uncomfortable servant. "I don't think that will be necessary." He paused. "You are new here, are you not?"

Eyes filled with apprehension, the footman nodded. "My name's Richards, yer grace; I've been at Allonshire fer three months."

Drake studied the anxious little man. "And are you loyal to my family, Richards?"

"Oh, yes, yer grace, I am!" He winced at another crash from beneath them.

Drake nodded, satisfied that Richards would do nicely. "Good. I want you to do something very important for me, Richards."

The eager servant stood up straighter. "Anythin', yer grace."

Drake pointed in the direction of Alex's room. "At the end of the hall is her grace's bedchamber. The duchess is exhausted, and I want nothing and no one to disturb her sleep." He gritted his teeth as the sound of splintering glass pierced the quiet of the slumbering house. "I want you to stand guard outside her door, Richards. Under no circumstances are you to venture one step away. I will go down and see to the situation in the library." He almost smiled at the look of utter relief on Richards's face. "I repeat: do not budge from her grace's door until I return. Should there be any problem, you have my permission to shout for me at the top of your lungs. Is that understood?"

Richards nodded emphatically. "Yes, yer grace. I understand."

"Good. You may go now." Even as Drake's words left his mouth, the footman was hurrying down the hall, obviously proud of the responsibility entrusted to him by the duke himself.

Convinced of Alex's safety, Drake took the steps two at

a time, heading purposefully through the dimly lit lower level of the manor and flinging open the library door.

An utterly disoriented, thoroughly intoxicated Sebastian turned glazed eyes in Drake's direction. The blood had been washed from his face, but his lips and nose were swollen and limp strands of hair hung down over his flushed face. In his hand was an antique vase that he had been about to hurl against the bookshelves. A considerable amount of broken glass was already strewn across the exquisite Oriental carpet, and chairs had been heaved about and now lay on their sides.

Drake stepped into the room and slammed the door behind him. Scathing emerald eyes raked the pathetic human being who was his brother.

"Put it down, Sebastian."

Sebastian paused, lowering the vase to his side. "Why, your grace," he mocked, weaving unsteadily in his attempt to regain his balance. "What brings you down here?" He lifted his other hand, which clutched a bottle of claret, bringing it to his lips and swallowing. Pointedly he added, "I would've thought you'd be comforting your little wife. S'matter, brother? She tire you out already?"

Drake fought the violent surge that rose inside him at Sebastian's taunting, baiting words. "You sicken me."

"Perhaps, but I don't sicken your wife," he sneered back. "Does it bother you that your duchess wants me more than she wants you?"

Anger exploded in Drake's skull. He stalked across the room, tore the bottle out of Sebastian's hand, and slammed it down on the table.

"I want you away from Allonshire by dawn," he ground out between clenched teeth. "You are no longer welcome in my house, now or ever."

At Drake's words all the mocking amusement left Sebastian's face, replaced with a hatred as sinister as evil itself.

"*Your* house?" he snarled, his teeth barred with rage. "*Your* house? But for some cursed fate, this would have been *my* house." His unnaturally bright gaze moved restlessly about the massive room. "Allonshire and everything in it should have been mine. *You* never wanted it, never gave a damn about everything that would someday be yours." He stared back at Drake, but his glassy eyes were unseeing. "I was the one who wanted it . . . all of it. And I would have had it—the title, the land, the wealth, all of it—*if* you had died, as the missive reported. But, damn you, brother, you came back. After all that time, and when I was so close to having it all, you came back." Malice was etched in every line of his flushed face. "Why couldn't you be dead?" he spat out. "Why?"

Drake stared at Sebastian's wild, half-crazed expression and, in that moment, he had his answer. Sebastian's hatred was more than enough to provoke him to murder.

"You have a sick, diseased mind." With great effort, Drake kept himself from pounding Sebastian. "I want you out of my house and out of my sight."

"One day Allonshire will be mine," Sebastian shot back.

The ominous threat pushed Drake beyond any semblance of control. "That day will never come, brother. Never." Drake bit out each word. "Regardless of any ill fate that might befall me, you will never inherit my title or my land. Do you know why, you miserable bastard? Because the next heir to Allonshire is growing inside my wife's womb." Sebastian's head shot up, but Drake was beyond stopping, beyond rational thought. "That's right, Sebastian. Alexandria is with child. And, with the tendency toward producing male offspring in our family, I have no doubt that it will be a son. So hate me with all your heart, and wish me dead and in hell. No amount of hatred can change Allonshire's future!"

Sebastian just stared at him for a moment. Then an insane, primitive roar erupted from his chest. The delicate vase in his hand shattered from the force of his grasp, splintering into bits, spattering droplets of his blood on the carpet.

"No!" he screamed, shaking with the force of his rage. "It's impossible! You've always taken everything that should have been mine, but not this! Not this . . . not after all my planning!"

"Planning?" Drake's voice was suddenly deadly quiet. "What planning, Sebastian?"

His brother's expression was that of a madman. "I was so blasted close. Why did you live? It was so easy until then. He was weak and pathetic . . . always was. Even Mother was too much for him. He was so damned trusting. Never even suspected."

An icy wave of foreboding swept through Drake. "Never suspected what, Sebastian? What was it that Father never suspected?"

Sebastian gave a wild, crazed laugh. "All those men. You knew about them, didn't you? And he thought she was the epitome of virtue. What a fool! She laughed at him, you know. And I don't blame her! It was just as easy for me."

The surprising knowledge that Sebastian also had known about their mother's affairs was insignificant at the moment. Drake teetered on the bitter edge of discovery.

"Even the timing was perfect," Sebastian continued as if he were alone in the room. "The grieving father withering away over the death of his beloved elder son. Who would suspect he was being poisoned? And then it would have been mine. All of it." He turned his unfocused stare to his throbbing hand, watching small rivulets of blood trickle along his wrist.

"God . . ." Drake breathed, pain and rage uniting into a knot of explosive emotion in his chest. "You black-hearted bastard, you killed our father. You murdered him in cold blood . . . for a title?" He stared at the evil man before him, a man he had never really known at all.

A self-satisfied smirk played upon Sebastian's lips as he turned back to his brother. "Neither of you deserved the title. He was too weak; you have no use for it. Only I am worthy of being the Duke of Allonshire. Only I."

Drake walked over until he met Sebastian's drunken gaze.

"Tomorrow," he said in a lethal whisper. "At dawn. With pistols. To the death, brother."

Sebastian's watery eyes widened. "Are you calling me

out, your grace?" He laughed. "I accept. It will be my pleasure to see you dead at my feet, Drake. Then it will all be mine." He walked around Drake and staggered toward the door. When he reached it, he turned, a hateful gleam in his eyes. "Alexandria's luscious body can be no more than a few months along. After I kill you, I can easily *encourage* her to wed me and then claim the child as mine. I will greatly enjoy possessing everything that was yours, not only your worldly goods but your exquisite wife and your unborn heir as well."

Drake lunged at him with a wild growl, but Sebastian had anticipated the move and was gone long before his brother could reach him. Drake tore after him, murder in his heart. But, halfway down the hall, he got hold of himself. No, he thought, as the front door closed behind Sebastian's retreating figure. Not this way. Killing Sebastian now would be too easy, too painless for the miserable bastard who had killed their father and coveted Drake's wife and his world. Justice would be done, but in a most apt way.

Taking deep, calming breaths, Drake walked slowly up the steps and down the hall. They were all safe tonight. Sebastian would not return before dawn.

Richards saw Drake approaching and hurried to meet him.

"Yer grace? Are ye all right?"

Drake forced himself to focus on the concerned face of the footman. He nodded.

"Fine, Richards." He glanced at Alex's closed door. "Her grace?"

"The duchess 'as not been disturbed, yer grace."

"Thank you, Richards. I have one other favor to ask of you and then you may retire for the night."

"Anythin', yer grace," the proud servant replied.

"Awaken Smitty and inform him that I need to speak with him at once."

Richards blinked. "Now, yer grace?"

Drake nodded curtly, well aware of the lateness of the hour. "Yes, Richards. Now."

"Very good, yer grace." The firmness of the duke's tone

told Richards all he needed to know. In the blink of an eye he was gone.

Alex stirred as Drake slid back into bed beside her.

"Drake?" Her voice was sleepy, questioning.

"I'm here, love." He drew her against him, deriving an inordinate amount of comfort from the feel of her small, soft body against him. After the events of the last hour, she was his haven.

Alex sensed Drake's mood and rose up to look at him. "Where were you?"

He looked into her silvery eyes and knew he would never lie to her again.

"I had to see Sebastian."

Alex's face whitened. "And did you?"

"Yes."

His terse answer forewarned her of what was to come.

"Drake . . . what did he say?"

"He killed my father." Drake's expression never changed.

Alex stared. "Oh, my God," she breathed, at last. "He killed . . . How?"

"Poison."

"But why?" Even as she asked the question, Drake saw that she'd guessed the answer. "The title . . . Allonshire . . ."

Drake nodded. "With me presumably dead, only Father stood between Sebastian and his damned, wretched title." He felt ill all over again.

"Did he admit to the attempts on your life as well?" she demanded.

"He didn't have to. The hatred was there, in the way he looked at me. How could I have been so blind?" he asked, tormented. "There must have been something . . . some hint of his sickness."

"None of us saw it, Drake," she whispered back. "Tell me what else he said."

Drake related the details of the confrontation, omitting the gruesome threat that Sebastian had made regarding

Alex just before he disappeared. That would never come to pass. Not after tomorrow.

"I called him out," Drake told Alex softly, stroking her face.

She gasped. "Oh, Drake, no . . . please, no." Her eyes filled with tears at the thought of Sebastian killing her beloved husband.

"Sweetheart, I must."

"There must be another way . . . any other way." But she knew there was not. Drake's honor and integrity were at stake. And she could not blame him for wanting to avenge his father's death.

Drake cupped her face gently between his big hands. "Just trust me, love. All will be well. I swear."

Alex nodded, pressing her face against his chest.

Dawn was but a few hours away.

Chapter 31

"Drake, please . . . don't do this." Alex clutched his arm, tugging him to a stop in the sheltered cluster of trees that marked the most isolated section of Allonshire.

With the first rays of dawn all reason had fled, and she was left with only the stark terror of losing Drake to his brother's treachery. Now, standing at the edge of the clearing in which the duel would be fought, Alex was gripped by a bleak premonition that wrapped itself around her heart like a thick, suffocating blanket. She would do anything, resort to any measures, to persuade Drake to call off this insane duel.

Drake looked down into Alex's frightened face, and love

swelled inside him, softening the cold fury that had dominated his senses since last night.

"I must do this, sweetheart," he told her gently, taking her hand from his arm and pressing it to his lips. "Why don't you go back to the house and wait for me there?"

Alex looked at him as if he had lost his mind. "I am going nowhere," she informed him, raising her chin in the familiar defiant gesture that Drake had come to know. "If you insist on going through with this lunacy, I shall be here with you." Her brave facade slipped as she gazed up at Drake's strong features. "Think of our child," she whispered. "We need you."

"And you shall have me." He drew her against him, wrapping his arms around her and offering her his strength and his promise. "I swear to you, Alex, that our child will know his father."

She turned tear-filled trusting eyes up to him. "*His* father?" she asked in a trembling voice, striving for control.

Drake smiled, kissed her forehead tenderly. "Or hers," he murmured softly. "I shall be delighted to have a beautiful little tyrant who is just like her mother."

"How touching." Sebastian's cold voice washed over them like an icy spray. "Saying your good-byes, Alexandria?"

Alex turned rigidly to face Sebastian's mocking sneer.

"You are beneath contempt," she replied venomously, her expression filled with hatred.

His eyes glittered unnaturally. "Careful, little lady," he cautioned. "In but a few moments your fate will be in my hands. I would suggest you address me with the proper respect if you expect me to show you any mercy."

"I suggest you go straight to hell." Alex lunged forward, fully intending to claw him to death with her nails. Only Drake's restraining hand kept her from fulfilling her goal.

Sebastian swaggered over, confidence oozing from every pore of his body. He stopped ten feet from where they stood. "It is your esteemed husband who is destined to die." He tapped his chin thoughtfully. "But fear not. I am a generous man. I have every intention of taking excellent care of you . . . in every way."

"I would sooner be dead." Alex spat out, seeing the rage blaze on his face at her words. But when Sebastian took a menacing step closer, Drake acted instantly, pulling Alex behind him, shielding her from Sebastian's approach.

"Take one step closer to my wife and I will kill you with my bare hands," Drake warned him in a deadly tone.

Sebastian hesitated, then shrugged carelessly. "Fine. The point is a moot one. Alexandria will soon be at my mercy."

Drake merely smiled, unaffected by his brother's threats.

Soft footsteps approached, and a moment later Smitty appeared, carrying a flat black case, which Alex knew contained the dueling pistols. She felt ill.

Smitty threw a quick, scathing look in Sebastian's direction, then turned toward Drake. Their eyes met, and a quick current of communication passed between them, ending as quickly as it had begun.

"Do you have the weapons, Smitty?" Drake asked. A mere formality, since he knew what Smitty's answer would be.

"I do, your grace."

"Good. Who will be acting as your second, Sebastian?" Drake inquired stiffly.

Sebastian gave a disdainful laugh. "Second? I need no second!"

"Fine, then we can begin any time *my brother . . .*" Drake spat out the words contemptuously, ". . . is ready."

Sebastian gave an eerie laugh. "You should have thought more carefully before you chose pistols as our dueling weapons, Drake. You know what a superb marksman I am. I rarely miss my target."

Alex clutched Drake's arm again, Sebastian's words generating a fresh surge of fear in her heart. Silently she begged Drake to reconsider. But Drake seemed perfectly calm and unbothered by his brother's boasting. The look he gave Alex was a reiteration of his earlier promise.

"Trust me," he whispered again.

Alex nodded and stepped away from him, determined not

to create a scene. She went to stand beside Smitty, who was now opening the heavy, velvet-lined case.

Sebastian watched as the twin pistols were revealed.

"I do see one problem, Drake." He looked utterly triumphant, as though he had figured out some all-important secret.

Drake stared back, his face expressionless. "Which is?"

"Smithers here is unquestionably and eternally loyal to you." He raised a dark brow in Smitty's direction. "Since he is the one who loaded the pistols, how can I be assured that there are no . . . surprises in store for me? I would hate to fire my weapon only to find that it was without ammunition."

Drake and Smitty exchanged another glance, which did not go unnoticed by Sebastian. More certain than ever that he was correct, he waited with a victorious smirk.

"The problem is easily solved," Drake replied at last. With a quick movement of his head he gestured for Sebastian to approach the pistols. "You choose your weapon first."

Sebastian assessed the situation and then, with a brief nod, walked over to the open box in Smitty's hands. As he approached, Alex instinctively moved closer to Smitty. Sebastian's very presence offended her.

His cold gaze flicked briefly over Alex, but he did not address her. Instead, he studied the two pistols, realizing that his suspicions were unfounded. Drake would never risk his own life on a gamble. Obviously both pistols were loaded.

He selected one of the gleaming weapons and turned back to Drake. "Your turn, brother."

Drake walked over and lifted the other weapon from its velvet bed. He glanced briefly at Alex's pale face, then turned and walked back to where Sebastian stood.

Alex listened to Smitty's voice as he explained something about twenty paces being counted off. Her legs felt like water, and she wondered if they would continue to support her throughout this ordeal. Gritting her teeth, she prayed.

It all seemed like a dream—watching the brothers stand

back to back, then hearing Smitty calling out numbers while the two men took one long stride for each shout.

"Nine . . . ten . . ."

Alex grabbed Smitty's arm, afraid as she had never been in her life.

"Please, Smitty, stop them," she begged. "Please . . ."

"Eleven . . ." He never paused in his counting, but gently pressed her hand against his arm in a comforting gesture.

"Twelve . . . thirteen . . ."

Alex was about to repeat her plea when, from the corner of her eye, she saw Sebastian whirl about and aim his pistol.

"*Drake!*" She screamed his name, her piercing cry mingling with the sound of the pistol crack.

"*No!*" Alex sobbed, realizing that her warning had come too late. "Oh, God, Drake!"

Drake had stopped dead in his tracks as Sebastian prematurely fired at his back. Sebastian stood, a wildly triumphant madman, waiting for Drake to crumple and die.

Instead, Drake turned slowly and stared at the spot where Sebastian's bullet had fallen . . . far short of its mark. He raised glittering emerald eyes to his brother's shocked face.

"Surprised, Sebastian?" Drake took a step toward his brother, then another and another, raising his own weapon as he stalked the stunned man who stood before him, staring blankly at his own still-smoldering gun. "And I thought you were such an expert shot," Drake taunted, stopping when he was close enough to see the fear on Sebastian's face. "An expert on firearms in general, actually," he added. " 'Tis a pity that someone tampered with the gunpowder, is it not, Sebastian?" he continued, his voice growing hard, his pistol cocked and ready. "It becomes quite difficult to defend yourself when your ammunition is at only a fraction of its intended potency, does it not, Sebastian?" His eyes were blazing with rage and hatred, his voice hard and merciless as he continued his verbal assault on the cowering man before him. "*Does it not, Sebastian?*"

Sebastian emitted a sound like a whimper.

"Ah, I see you understand my point, you spineless coward." Drake placed his finger lightly against the trigger, seeing all the color drain from Sebastian's face. "You jeopardized twenty lives, you miserable bastard. Twenty men who are my friends. I should put one bullet in your head for each of them . . . and one more for putting your filthy hands on my wife. And then I should begin anew as punishment for our father's murder." He placed the barrel of the pistol between Sebastian's eyes. "And I assure you, you worthless snake, that, despite the diminished strength of my gunpowder, I shall not miss at point-blank range."

Time froze in a deathlike silence as Drake toyed with his terrified brother by tightening the pressure of his finger on the trigger, bit by bit.

Finally Sebastian sobbed out loud, "Kill me and be done with it! I cannot bear the torture any longer!"

Drake lowered the gun to his side. "Torture? You haven't begun to know the meaning of the word." He watched Sebastian collapse at his feet in a shuddering heap. "Death is too good for you, Sebastian . . . and far too compassionate. I would much prefer to see you rot in Newgate for the rest of your wretched life, along with the other rats and vermin! *That* is the fate you deserve!"

For the first time Drake turned toward where Alex stood, shaking violently, against Smitty. Wordlessly Drake extended his arm to her, and without hesitation, she went to him, pressing herself against his side . . . where she belonged and would always stay.

"I believe we are entitled to this extended and long-awaited wedding trip," Drake teased, drawing Alex toward the docks of London where their adventure together had begun.

She laughed. "We have spent most of our marriage on one journey or another," she reminded him.

He stopped before the gleaming masts of a waiting ship. "No longer, princess," he whispered, looking into her eyes. "I have found my journey's end." He kissed her softly on her mouth, tenderly cupping the gentle swell of her stomach. "You and our child are my life," he said simply. Without waiting for her response he turned, pointing to the shining hull of the exquisite vessel before them. "Behold your namesake, my love."

Alex felt a lump in her throat as she stared at the bold name, *La Belle Alexandria*, painted on the prow of the newly built ship.

"She's beautiful," she managed in a choked voice. "Thank you, Drake."

He understood. "Come." He led her onto the polished deck, then down to the magnificently crafted captain's cabin below.

"Let me see if I remember," he told her soberly, closing the door and leaning back against it. "A cabin, not a castle, where you have been taken by a man—merely a man, but one who loves you with all his heart." He walked toward her, drawing her into his strong, hungry embrace. "To live and love together with joy and meaning, as partners and equals . . . always." Drake kissed away the tears of joy that trickled slowly down Alex's cheeks. "I want to make all your dreams come true," he whispered against her parted lips, melding their bodies together. "But, Alex," he asked huskily, drawing her toward the bed, "in this one instance . . . would you mind very much being beneath me?"

She didn't answer. Not with words. Her body told him everything he needed to know.

Alex was free.

For, at last and forever, she had found her heart's desire.

Author's Note

The opening of the Saint Lawrence Seaway in 1959 was the culmination of almost four hundred years of planning, building, and rebuilding. As early as the first half of the sixteenth century, Jacques Cartier, in search of the Northwest Passage, was thwarted by the unconquerable currents of the Lachine Rapids near Montreal. Efforts officially began in 1680 to construct a canal system that would enable ships to navigate readily along the Saint Lawrence River connecting Montreal to Lake Ontario and Little York (now Toronto). The "Casson Canal," named after François Dollier de Casson, its creator, was a mere eighteen inches deep and less than a mile long at the time of Dollier de Casson's death in 1701. It was, however, not until the mid-nineteenth Century that a continuous water route was available to vessels of under eight feet draught and not until later in the century that the canals were deepened, a process that was completed at the turn of the century and that unified all canals to a depth of fourteen feet.

In truth, a merchant ship the size of *La Belle Illusion* would have had a draught of approximately twelve feet and would therefore have been unable to pass through the narrow, shallow canals that led from Montreal to Lake Ontario. But in order to tell Drake and Alex's story the way they demanded it be told—as you know, they are both impossibly strong-willed and unyielding—I took the liberty of allowing *La Belle* its passage into Lake Ontario and on to Little York.

Little York was much as I depicted it within these pages. I did take the following historical liberties. Fort York did exist in a far more basic form—a gun platform and a collection of log huts—in 1812. It was known as "the garrison on the lakefront" until 1816, when it was developed into Fort York. That name being rather cumbersome, I used "Fort York" four years prematurely. Also, the real governor's home, called the Government House, stood right beside the garrison in 1800 until it was destroyed by the Americans in 1813. Like most homes in York at the time, it was a simple one-story frame house, not a grand mansion like the one occupied by the fictitious Geoffrey Cassel.

Alex, Drake, and I thank you for your indulgence.

I also thank the Saint Lawrence Seaway Development Corporation for providing me with historical details on the Saint Lawrence River.